THE ANNIVERSARY

Roisin Meaney was born in Listowel, County Kerry. She has lived in the US, Canada, Africa and Europe but is now based in Limerick city. She is the author of numerous bestselling novels, including *The Reunion, Love in the Making, One Summer* and *Something in Common,* and has also written several children's books, two of which have been published so far. On the first Saturday of each month, she tells stories to toddlers and their teddies in her local library.

Her motto is 'Have laptop, will travel', and she regularly packs her bags and relocates somewhere new in search of writing inspiration. She is also a fan of the random acts of kindness movement: 'they make me feel as good as the person on the receiving end'.

www.roisinmeaney.com
@roisinmeaney
www.facebook.com/roisinmeaney

ALSO BY ROISIN MEANEY

The Street Where You Live
The Reunion
I'll Be Home for Christmas
Two Fridays in April
After the Wedding
Something in Common
One Summer
The Things We Do For Love
Love in the Making
Half Seven on a Thursday
The People Next Door
The Last Week of May
Putting Out the Stars
The Daisy Picker

CHILDREN'S BOOKS

Don't Even Think About It
See If I Care

Roisin MEANEY

The Anniversary

HACHETTE
BOOKS
IRELAND

First published in Ireland in 2018 by
HACHETTE BOOKS IRELAND

1

Cataloguing in Publication Data is available from the British Library

Trade paperback ISBN 9781473643024
Ebook ISBN 9781473643048

Typeset in Book Antiqua by Bookends Publishing Services, Dublin

Printed and bound in Great Britain by Clays Ltd, St Ives plc

Hachette Books Ireland policy is to use papers that are natural, renewable and recyclable products and made from wood grown in sustainable forests. The logging and manufacturing processes are expected to conform to the environmental regulations of the country of origin.

Hachette Books Ireland
8 Castlecourt Centre
Castleknock
Dublin 15, Ireland

A division of Hachette UK Ltd
Carmelite House, 50 Victoria Embankment, EC4Y 0DZ

www.hachettebooksireland.ie

For the people of Miltown Malbay,
for their warm welcome

WEDNESDAY, 26 APRIL

Lily

WHEN THE TELEPHONE RINGS SHE'S READING, OR trying to. Her eyes slither across the page, gathering up the words but not taking in the sense of them. She's doing her best to concentrate, but the department circular is as tedious and long-winded as official documents tend to be – is there a competition to see which of them can bore the fastest? – and her head anyway is in Land's End, where the rest of her will be in two days.

And then the telephone rings, its electronic burr jumping suddenly into her office, causing the document in her hand to give a little answering jump. She lifts the receiver, throwing a glance towards the window that looks out on the schoolyard and the back gate. A room with a view it is not – or rather, the view isn't exactly edifying.

'Yes.'

'It's Enid,' her secretary says. 'She wants to talk to you. She's insisting.'

Enid, for crying out loud. Her third call this week – or is it her fourth? Has the woman nothing better to do?

'Tell her I'm in the middle of something. Say I'll call her back tomorrow.'

'She says it's very important.'

Lily sighs. It's always very important with Enid. 'Take a message, Norah. Say I've just gone out.'

'I've already told her you're here, I'm afraid.'

And there it is again, the polite obstinacy, the almost-defiance that Norah usually manages to insert into every one of their exchanges, however brief. Norah hadn't appreciated having her inefficient filing system changed when Lily came to power seven years earlier: her manner since then has veered dangerously close to insolent. One of the days she'll cross the line, and Lily will seize her moment and send her packing, union or no union.

'Right. Put her through – but please hold any other calls until the afternoon. Say I'm in a meeting and can't be disturbed. No exceptions.'

There's a small click and Enid is on, breathing noisily into Lily's left ear. Big-chested, multi-chinned Enid, the current chairperson of the PTA. A mole to the left of her lower lip spouts a trio of long dark hairs that Lily's repulsed gaze is drawn to each time they meet. You'd think she'd bleach them at least, if she can't bring herself to yank them out.

Lily lets her wait, her eyes still on the yard, clocking the latecomers, the usual suspects who scurry in every morning. There go the two O'Neills, couldn't be on time if they tried – not that they try very hard. And here comes poor old Babs Harty, the last in a long line of Hartys, looking as patched-together as the siblings that preceded her. A miracle she makes it to school at all, given the chaotic home situation. Those seven unfortunates should have been taken into care years ago, with a mother who drinks like a fish and curses like a sailor, and a father in jail more often than he's out.

And now Ivy Lyons is pulling up to the gate in her BMW,

right on schedule at ten past starting time, looking brazenly across the yard to the office window as she drops off her two darlings. Lady captain in the golf club, her husband Victor's restaurant the only Michelin-starred place for miles around. The Ivys and Victors of the world make their own rules; a wasted exercise trying to challenge them, so Lily doesn't bother.

She swivels her chair from the window, regards instead the framed photo of Poll and Thomas on her desk. 'Enid – what can I do for you?'

'Oh, good morning, Mrs Murphy.'

Mrs, never Ms, despite it being employed on every written communication from Lily, despite *Ms L. Murphy, Principal* clearly displayed on Lily's office door. Women like Enid have no time for Ms.

'I'm sorry to bother you again' – she isn't: she loves bothering people, she lives for it – 'but I'm afraid there have been one or two complaints regarding the play the fifth years were taken to see last week.' Mannish voice thick with importance, stuffed full of it. Lily imagines the mole hairs bobbing along as she speaks. 'I felt I should pass them on to you, Mrs Murphy.'

You bet she did. The woman thrives on a bit of controversy. 'What exactly is the problem, Enid?' As if Lily doesn't know exactly what the problem is.

'I understand there were some – profanities.'

Ah, profanities. The terrible F-word, the same F-word Lily overhears in the school corridors multiple times every day. Throw it around like confetti, some of them. She turns a deaf ear, or she'd be forever pulling them up.

'I'm afraid, Enid, I have no control over that. As you know' – she probably doesn't, her darling Conrad not yet in fifth year – 'the play is on the Leaving Cert programme, and as such can hardly be avoided. I can only suggest that the parents take the matter up with the Department of Education and Skills. I can give you contact details if you want them.'

Silence. Not the correct answer. Lily tilts the photo a fraction to the right, noting how happy her children look in it. Poll is about three years old then, which would make Thomas five or six. The two of them on the beach at Land's End, wrapped in Kitty's towels. Wet hair, wide, wide smiles. Poll's adorable little teeth, her freckly face that American guests at the B&B always went mad for.

'I'll pass that information along then,' Enid says eventually, managing to drench the words in resentment, and off she goes to be important somewhere else. Roll on the AGM in September: with any luck someone new will step up for chairperson and push her off her perch.

For the rest of the morning Lily deals with letters and emails, and returns missed phone calls, and ploughs through the various circulars in her in-tray. When the bell rings for lunch she makes her way to the staffroom, conscious, as she pushes open the door, of the usual tiny adjustment among those already assembled. After seven years at the top she's well accustomed to the shift of gear her promotion caused. She's not one of them any more, and they're not about to let her forget it.

She's at a loss to understand it. She doesn't throw her weight around, she's fair in her dealings with them, she backs them up when there are problems with parents – even if she privately sides with the parents – but in spite of all this she's acutely aware that she's not popular. Respected, yes. Liked, not so much. The fact that she's the most efficient principal the school has had in a long time doesn't seem to matter.

She tells herself it's for the best. She's their boss, not their friend: trying to be both would never work. And she has plenty of friends outside school.

'Lily – coffee?'

She sees Yvette by the sink. Her deputy, and the closest thing she has to an ally here. 'Yes please.'

She takes a seat and peels the lid from her yogurt tub, recalling the murmurings among the staff when she and Charlie had broken up. Nothing said to her face – well, she'd never made a formal announcement, knowing they'd hear about it soon enough, and they had. She could tell in the more considered way they looked at her, in the low-voice conversations that tapered off whenever she appeared.

And when Chloë entered the equation, they heard that too. The news didn't take long to spread, some no doubt delighted to be passing it on. Lily ignored the pitying glances, pretended she didn't hear the occasional sniggers. She told herself it was the price she paid for having climbed to the top of her profession, for getting the more generous payslip each fortnight.

'Phew.' Yvette deposits two mugs on the table and lowers herself slowly into the chair beside Lily. 'Remind me how many more decades to the weekend.'

'That tough?'

The younger woman gives a smile that's more of a grimace. 'Counting the hours at this stage, if I'm honest.'

Eight months pregnant with her fourth child, going out on maternity leave in nine days. Her husband Eddie is a painter and decorator, in theory if not exactly in practice. Not a great name as a worker, and Lily has overheard staffroom whispers of him enjoying the drink a bit too much. She pays no heed to the whispers, never has.

'You all set for the weekend?' Yvette asks.

'As set as I'll ever be. I'm thinking of heading off a bit early on Friday, maybe around two – will you hold the fort?'

'I will, of course.'

She's blessed with Yvette, reliable and conscientious – but when she goes out Lily will be left with Marian, next in line and the obvious choice to step up. The only problem with this is that Marian and work have never been properly acquainted. Marian is the last to arrive each morning – *Traffic was dreadful again!* – and the first to vacate the car park after school, and Lily has been forced on more than one occasion to talk to her about parental complaints of uncorrected homework and erratic testing. Roll on Yvette's return, sadly not till January.

After lunch she meets with a couple whose son isn't doing as well as they'd hoped, and tries, without being too blunt, to make the point that it might have something to do with the fact that he's not as intelligent as they'd hoped. The mother becomes tight-lipped, the father huffs and puffs. None so blind as devoted parents with big ambitions for their rather dull offspring.

When she finally gets rid of them, fifteen minutes before the end of the school day, she checks her silenced mobile and sees a missed call from Agneta, who's left a voicemail. Of course she has.

Lil, I've found the most adorable florist – you'll have to meet her. She does amazing bouquets. Call me.

The trouble is, Lily couldn't give a damn about bouquets, amazing or otherwise. The difficulty here is that she wants a quiet wedding – her second, in her fifties: who makes a fuss about that? – whereas Agneta wants precisely the opposite. Lily is sorry she ever told her she was getting married again – but of course she had to be told, because Agneta will be the only non-family member there on the day. If she'd only stop trying to turn it into something Lily doesn't want it to be.

She'll return the call tonight, and she'll be persuaded to go and meet the adorable florist, and no doubt she'll end up ordering a horrendously expensive bouquet that'll be in the bin a few hours after she marries Joe – unless Agneta whisks it off to be frozen or dried or something. Yes, she can see *that* happening. How on earth did they ever become friends, let alone the very best of friends?

She tidies her desk and checks the time. Eight minutes before she needs to take up her position by the back door to monitor the going-home behaviour. Usually Yvette's job but Lily took over a couple of weeks ago, when standing for any length of time became an issue for her deputy. She sits back and closes her eyes and returns to the weekend ahead of her, and travels in her mind's eye to Land's End.

Six of them, two couples and two singles, to be divided between the five bedrooms. Thomas is easy: he'll take the small back twin. Charlie, she knows, will be hoping for the green room with its sea view, the one that was Lily's growing up, the one he and Lily were allotted after the children outgrew the summer holidays at Land's End, and Kitty reclaimed her family bedroom at the top of the stairs. The green room is pretty, the second best in the house. He'll want it, but he's not getting it.

She'll put him in the back double beside Thomas, nice quiet corner room with two windows, and let Poll and Aidan have the green room. If he complains she'll say she thought Aidan should have the sea view for his first stay at Land's End: nothing he can object to there.

Which leaves her and Joe in the main bedroom.

Of course it does. Where else would they go?

It's just.

Stop. Don't be ridiculous. It's a bedroom, that's all. It's a bed and a wardrobe and a chest of drawers and a wingback chair, all of which have seen better days, and a bedside rug that came from America nearly fifty years ago, and a beautiful bay window that looks out on the Atlantic.

It's the room her grandparents slept in, and after them her parents. And now it's Lily's turn, and Joe's. His first time to stay overnight at Land's End – and if her plans for the place work out, probably his last.

Her plans for the place – as if she was embarking on a big project, when nothing could be further from the truth. Her decision hasn't been arrived at lightly: plenty of soul searching and sleepless nights went into it. What she's planning will be no cause for celebration – on the contrary, she expects her news to be received with some dismay – but it does seem the only logical way forward.

She feels a tiny bit guilty, keeping Joe in the dark along with the others. They're getting married in a matter of months, pledging to spend the rest of their lives together. They're already sharing her house in the city – he moved in last December – so it's hardly fair not to let him in on this now. Then again, he has no ties to Land's End, no sentimental attachment at all to it. No, best to wait, and tell them all together. At dinner on Saturday maybe, when everyone's finally landed. Yes, that should work.

In the meantime, there's the main bedroom. There's her mental block with the main bedroom.

In twenty-six years of marriage, she and Charlie never slept there. With her mother still in residence, it simply wasn't an option – and by the time it became necessary to move her out, Lily and Charlie were well separated.

And now Mam is dead, gone from them six weeks ago, slipping away as they sat around her nursing home bed with its awful shiny blue coverlet. And even though it's been two years since she occupied the bedroom at Land's End, it will still feel like hers. It will still smell like hers. Everything in it will be a reminder of her.

Nonsense. It's just a room. Get over it.

At least Chloë isn't coming. Be grateful for small mercies. Although as mercies go, Chloë's absence from the weekend gathering is a pretty humungous one.

She opens her eyes and checks the time. She tidies her desk and leaves the office and makes her way to the back door.

Poll

SHE MOULDS A NOSE, EASING IT OUT CAREFULLY FROM the globe of the face, forming its curves and dips and little whorls. The clay is cool and wonderfully smooth. She inhales its wet, slightly metallic scent, feels it at the back of her throat, can almost taste it. A smell she's grown to love, a smell that never fails to lift her to a more contented place.

Not her favourite smell of all though. That has to be the sharp, almost antiseptic perfume of the sea that tumbles onto the pebble beach not a hundred yards from the front gate of Land's End, and the seaweed that washes up with it. The scent that inhabits the house too, lodging in every nook and cranny, so even lying in bed there she feels like she's floating on water.

Two years, more than two, since she set foot in the place, but not a single day has gone by since then when it hasn't wandered into her thoughts. She can still call it perfectly to mind when she closes her eyes, the big sprawling blue house by the sea. She can walk through it in her head, identifying every bump in the wall, every threadbare bit of carpet, every creaking floorboard - and now she craves to see it again in reality.

And she will see it again, the day after tomorrow. The thought prompts a great joyous leap in her chest. She's going back and she can't wait, even while the prospect of the visit has her completely torn, even if it will also be drenched in sadness. Land's End without Gran in it, without even the possibility of ever seeing Gran in it again, isn't something she can dwell on for long, but still she wants to go. Now, more than ever, she wants to walk through the rooms and remember all the good times.

'Tea?'

She turns. Emma is at the sink, filling the kettle. 'Go on.'

'Lemon and ginger?'

'Vanilla chai. Thanks.'

She dips her fingers into the bucket of water that sits at her feet. She rubs her palms together and turns her attention to the mouth. Today she's working on Felicity, a sixty-four-year-old matron in a busy maternity hospital who dreams of riding a camel across the Gobi desert. Felicity can be sharp-tongued, particularly with the younger nurses, but she'll stay past clocking-off time, long past, if anyone needs her.

When she was fifteen, Felicity fell in love with her Spanish teacher, who didn't reciprocate. She never found anyone else, unless you count Gregory. On her days off, Felicity dresses up and goes dancing in the afternoons with Gregory, who paved her driveway one sunny long-ago summer, and who's been trying to get her to marry him for the last twenty years.

Poll names every head, gives each of them a story. It makes them feel real to her as she forms their features, as she carves out ear lobes and decides on eyebrows and noses and cheekbones. The only problem with creating lives for them is that she misses them when they're complete, when she has to let them go and move on to the next.

Sometimes she finds herself thinking about them, wondering if they've ended up in good homes. Where is Belinda, the twelve-year-old asthmatic prodigy who speaks five languages and who's already read *Anna Karenina* in the original Russian? It wouldn't be everyone who could handle Belinda. And what about Thaddeus, at a hundred and thirteen the oldest man in Ireland, still swimming in the sea every day? Poor Thaddeus wouldn't be happy in the middle of a city, not at all.

They all take time, and lots of patience. This is her fifth attempt at Felicity. It's not always easy, getting the features to match the image in her head, the image that she can see so clearly in her mind's eye – but once she gets there, it's worth all the false starts. Once she gets there, they can almost talk to her. They can almost breathe.

The tea is made. She cradles her mug, inhaling cinnamon. 'Did I mention how much I can't wait for the weekend?'

'Once or twice.' Emma tucks dark brown hair behind an ear, leaving a turquoise streak on the lobe. 'Two sleeps to go. Family group though – you sure you can handle it?'

'I can handle it. We all get on fine.' More or less. More with Mum, less with Dad. Fine with Thomas.

'Remind me, has Aidan ever seen the house?'

The mention of his name brings a glad skip of her heart. 'No, this'll be his first time.' And maybe his last: the notion courses through her, like a shard of ice.

'It's by the sea, isn't it?'

'That's right. About half an hour west of Galway.'

'Nice. Bit chilly yet for a swim though.'

'I'll pack the togs, just in case.' Of course she'll swim. You can't go to Land's End and not swim. 'Your ear is blue, by the way.'

Emma blows on her tea. 'Duly noted, thanks.'

Her ears - and other exposed parts - are generally quite colourful by the time she finishes her day. Emma turns photos of people's houses, or their gardens, or their children, or their pets, into beautiful watercolour images. She has a waiting list, but takes her time with each commission. She can afford to: her husband, Tom, runs his own successful courier company. For the long weekend they're flying to New York and staying in an apartment overlooking Central Park, and turning the weekend into a week.

The studio belongs to Emma. She and Poll met in hospital five years earlier, when Emma underwent an emergency appendicectomy on the same day that Poll had her tonsils out. After their respective surgeries they ended up in neighbouring beds - and when Poll mentioned, somewhere along the way, that she'd recently graduated from art college and was looking for studio space, Emma offered to share.

I don't need rent, she said, *but someone to chat to over a cuppa when I take a break would be nice. The rest of the time I have to have complete silence. No talk, no music, no radio. You OK with that?*

Poll was OK with that, more than OK. She couldn't imagine conversing with anyone while she created her heads - it would be like inviting someone she hardly knew into the bathroom to watch her brush her teeth.

The arrangement suits them both perfectly. They work in the same space five days a week - and if asked, Poll would say they're friends, but neither of them has ever suggested going for a drink after they finish up, and no cards or gifts are exchanged at Christmas or for birthdays. Their relationship is primarily a business one, with two ten-minute chats thrown in each day, during which time details of their respective lives trickle out. It works for both.

They finish the tea and resume their silent labours. Poll works on Felicity's smile, pokes a dimple into a cheek, tweaks the eyes to give them a more melancholic quality. Maybe the matron is thinking of all the babies she's delivered down the years, or the ones she never had herself. Maybe she's pondering Gregory's latest gift, a diamanté brooch in the shape of a teddy bear that she'll definitely only be wearing on their dancing afternoons. Generous, clueless Gregory: if he'd only stop trying so hard she might say yes. He doesn't need to set her world on fire; she gave up hoping for that a long time ago.

This Felicity is working. This Felicity might be the one.

Pottery is Poll's salvation. Working with clay keeps her demons at a safe distance; at work she can believe herself happy. She *is* happy, or as happy as she can ever be.

Aidan makes her happy too, of course – or he used to, until the demons got wind of it and decided that enough was enough. She's fighting them like she always fights them, but she's never beaten them yet, and she isn't hopeful now.

As she refines Felicity's chin she scrolls back in her head and calls up her first encounter with Aidan. She can remember every word of their conversation. She was two years out of college, sharing a house with a couple of friends, and working three evenings a week and every weekend in the bar of a small hotel owned by acquaintances of her parents. The work was easy enough and the wages covered her bills, her clay and other knick-knacks required for the heads, but with weekdays spent in Emma's studio she was left with precious little free time.

She was also running out of space to store her heads. She made every effort to find customers for them. She took photos and posted them on social media, and asked everyone to share. She gave sample heads to friends, who promised to display them in their workplaces. She took a stall at any craft event that came up. She did what she could to spread the word, but sales remained sporadic, and brought in a pittance.

Whenever one of her parents - usually Mum - asked about finding an official outlet for her work, Poll would say she was still building up a collection, when in reality her collection was well and truly built.

You'll have to find a gallery to take them, Emma told her. *You're a hopeless businesswoman – you should be asking three times the price.*

What? But I can hardly sell them as it is.

That's because the right people aren't seeing them. You should call to that gallery on Portland Avenue – Tom and I have got some lovely stuff there.

Poll cringed at the thought of visiting a gallery, any gallery, but particularly the one on Portland Avenue. She admired it as she passed on her way to the studio each day. It looked classy and terribly expensive, with its pale grey façade and burgundy door, and its pieces of pottery and jewellery beautifully presented on glass shelving inside the window. She'd never ventured in. She'd have liked a browse, but she felt intimidated by its polished appearance.

I don't think my stuff would fit in there, she said. *It's not posh enough.*

Rubbish. No such thing as posh art: it's all in the eye of the beholder. Your heads are delightful – lots of people would adore them. Come on, you have nothing to lose by trying, and the owner's friendly. Imagine if you could earn enough from sales of your heads – you could give up the bar work and have a bit of a life outside here.

Making a living from her art: it was the dream, wasn't it? It was so wonderful it almost scared her. Wasn't it worth putting herself through a bit of mortification to pull her dream a little closer?

She deliberately made no contact with the gallery owner in

advance of her visit. *Just turn up,* Emma advised. *Easy to put you off in an email if he's busy. He'll be curious to see what you have to offer if you call there in person.*

She decided to bring along three of her favourite pieces. She had it all worked out, her script prepared in her head – and on the day, nothing went to plan.

As she approached the gallery, an emerging man pushed the door open with some force. Poll stepped back hastily to avoid a collision but the edge of the door struck the cardboard box she was carrying, knocking it out of her grasp, and her precious pieces – Hattie and Gordon and Chester, the three she was most proud of – were smashed to smithereens.

She subsequently disgraced herself by weeping without restraint in the middle of a rather chilly afternoon until the owner emerged with a paper cup of water and ushered her inside, waving off the still-apologising man who'd caused the catastrophe.

When she'd recovered her senses somewhat she saw a wide mouth, dark-rimmed glasses, a flop of sandy hair. He gave a tilt of his head towards the box, which she still clutched. *I'm guessing the contents were breakable.*

She nodded, not yet trusting herself to speak, blotting at her face with her sleeve. She could hardly look at him. Talk about making a fool of herself before they'd even met properly.

So what was it?

Pottery. I – make heads. From clay. God, even that sounded ridiculous. Her script had fled from her mind the minute the box crashed to the ground.

Clay heads, he repeated. *Human heads?*

Yes, but smaller. Caricatures, really.

Are they mounted?

Yes – at least, they have a wooden base, but they're on springs. They sort of – bob.

Bobbing heads. For the first time, he smiled, a sudden beam that softened his entire face. He no longer looked stern, he looked … lovely.

It gave her courage. *It makes them seem more alive. When they can move, I mean.*

I'm sure it does. Do you have any pictures on your phone?

Yes, she had plenty – but when she searched for her phone, it was to discover, to her horror, that she'd left it behind at the studio. Talk about seeming even more amateurish.

Still he didn't look put out. *I assume you have others though.*

She took him in properly for the first time. Greenish eyes, or between brown and green. Copper might be a better description, or bronze. The glasses looked expensive. All of him looked expensive.

And then, inevitably, the demons kicked in. Look around, they said. Couldn't she see his gallery was far too classy for her clownish heads? He must be accosted every other day by idiots like her, hoping to impress him with their pathetic endeavours. Get out, they urged her, before she completely humiliated herself.

He was waiting. She had to say something.

I'm sorry – I think I might have … got it wrong. Suddenly she wanted to get away, bury this awful episode and forget about it forever. The bar work wasn't that bad. Only a handful of artists made a living from their art – how conceited to imagine she might be one of them.

Why don't you let me be the judge of that? he asked. *Can you call by tomorrow with some more?*

He still wanted to see them. He wanted her to come back. The demons were momentarily silenced.

Yes, she said, trying not to let an idiot grin erupt on her face. Cordelia, she was thinking. And Jason, and maybe Heather. *When – what time would suit?*

Around now would be fine.

Thank you, she said. *For your help, I mean.*

No trouble.

And for agreeing to – look at my work.

It's what I do, he said. Another smile. He had a really good smile.

He hadn't asked her name. She didn't know his. *I'm Poll Cunningham*, she said, putting out a hand.

His grip was firm. *Aidan Grimes. Good to meet you, Poll. See you tomorrow.*

When she returned to the studio Emma was out. She salvaged what she could from the destroyed heads – two turquoise buttons, a pink feather, the gold wire she'd used for Hattie's hoop earrings, the strands of orange string that were Chester's hair – and binned the rest. She deliberated over the forty-seven remaining heads in her collection, choosing first one, then another, selecting and rejecting until she couldn't think straight.

Finally she went with her original choices: shy, blushing Cordelia, dog trainer, happier around animals than with humans; sixty-plus Jason, retired librarian, amateur detective, clandestine cross-dresser; and little freckly chuckling Heather, at two years old the youngest of her creations. She packed them up – more bubble wrap, a lot more bubble wrap – and presented them to Aidan Grimes the following day.

And in the time it took for him to enthuse over them, and to suggest that she bring three more so he could exhibit half a dozen for a six-week trial period, in the time it took him to suggest a selling price that was four times what she'd envisaged, and to make her an excellent coffee to seal the deal, she fell in love with him.

Love always took her by surprise, and happened fast. But love was her enemy as much as her friend. Countless times her heart has been broken; countless times she's vowed to avoid love for ever more, to run in the other direction whenever she senses its arrival.

But the stupid truth is that love isn't the enemy: she is. The stupid, senseless reality is that she's always the one to call time on the relationships. Over and over again she walks away, compelled by something, some inner voices – yes, some demons – that insist she put an end to things.

You don't deserve to be happy, the voices whisper. *You're not good enough for him. Walk away before he finishes with you* – and coward that she is, she *does* eventually walk away, because the voices, the demons, pester and torment her until she does.

But then Aidan happened to her. Love struck again, seven months after she'd said goodbye to John, her last boyfriend, leaving him mystified as to her reason, leaving her unable to explain why. A year after she fell for Aidan – a year of the heads beginning to sell, a year of them gaining steady sales, a year of her silently loving him – he asked her out; three months after that she spent her first night in his apartment. Now they've been together for over two years, longer than any of her previous relationships – and just when she thought they might have got fed up and moved on, the demons are beginning to whisper again.

And she's afraid. She's twenty-six and completely in love, and horribly afraid.

She doesn't want to end it. Everything in her rebels at the thought of ending it. How can she walk away from him, when everything he says, everything he does, makes her heart full?

How can she say goodbye when he's the other half of her, the half that makes sense of the rest? What is wrong with her that she can't allow herself to be happy? Is she destined to spend her life alone?

She's going to ask Gran, when she gets to Land's End. She's going to hunt down Gran's spirit, or essence, or whatever you want to call it, and she's going to ask her to help. She's not going to give up Aidan lightly, not without a real fight, but she does need help – and if anyone can help her it's Gran.

Her beloved gran, who called her Pollywoll when she was small, and taught her how to make omelettes when she was old enough to beat eggs and grate cheese. Gran, who braided Poll's impossible hair so it twined down behind her like a thick burnt-orange rope and ended in a beautiful sky-blue ribbon.

It was Gran who said that her eyes were the colour of the sea on a stormy day, which made grey sound so much less boring. It was Gran who said that her freckles were signs of beauty, and that her smile was magic. It was Gran who told her, when Poll sobbed on her shoulder after each teenage tragedy, that it was for the best.

You weren't right for each other. That's why it finished. Some day you'll find the right one. You'll find him, or he'll find you, and when that happens, you'll know. When I met your granddad, I knew.

But Gran didn't know about the demons: Poll was too embarrassed to tell her. She pretended after every break-up that the boy had finished it, not her. It didn't feel like a lie, because she felt exactly as sad as if he had. It was the only thing she hid from Gran. But she'll tell her everything now. She'll find a way to tell her about the voices, and Gran will know how to silence them.

For the rest of the day she refines Felicity's features – yes, this is the one – tweaking every line and curve. When she's satisfied with it she uses a darning needle to poke careful holes all over the scalp for the spirals of thin copper wire that will serve as hair once the drying and firing is over. Felicity, sadly, has hair like Poll's own, frizzy and infuriating. She fashions the hat, a green felt beret, to perch on top. She transfers the head carefully to the sheet of wire mesh that lies on the slatted table by the dehumidifier. She cleans up and says a whispered goodbye to Emma, who paints on. She walks home.

Just before six, in the kitchen of Aidan's apartment - *our apartment*, he insists, but she still calls it his in her head - she chops vegetables into matchsticks and takes two salmon darnes from the fridge. She brings a pan of water to the boil and slides in the fish. She adds a tablespoon of coconut oil to the wok, and while it pools into liquid, she phones Aidan.

'Dinner in ten.'

'Great. Starving.'

He disconnects with a click. He's not a phone-chatter. She adds vegetables to the wok, imagining him five streets away, gathering up keys, slinging on his navy linen jacket. She pictures him pressing numbers on the alarm pad and locking the door, hearing the many deadbolts click into place. She sees him pulling down the metal shutters, keeping all his beautiful precious things safe.

Now he's turning onto the street: there's the soft, hurried tap of his leather-soled shoes on the concrete as he passes the deli and the off-licence and the halal butcher's shop, whose scrubbed façade still shows echoes of the red paint that's thrown regularly at it. Now he walks past the children's boutique, with its tiny, ludicrously priced clothes, and the narrow little alterations shop run by two glamorous women from somewhere in Eastern Europe. Sisters they must be, with those identical noses, although one is tiny and the other is taller than Aidan.

In and out of light and shadow he passes, under the dapple of leaves on the laurel trees that line Portland Avenue. Now he turns the corner to pass the park on his left with its silver-painted railings, and the school on his right with its faded green and white bunting flying in the yard, and the church beside it, and the priest's house beside that, its garden full of rose bushes. The journey is so familiar to her she could do it blindfolded.

Gran never saw the gallery. Poll would have loved to bring her, would have loved to show her the walls of paintings, the shelves of delicate, fragile objects. Even if she didn't understand what she was looking at, mightn't she have appreciated the works of art on some level? Wasn't she entitled to a chance for them to gladden her poor befuddled heart?

And wouldn't she surely have recognised Poll's own creations nestling among the rest, a card attached to each that gave the character's story, with *Poll Cunningham, potter* on the reverse? Poll had given her one of her first heads, Josephine the sheep farmer, for Land's End; she had bobbed on Gran's bedroom windowsill for years before accompanying her to the nursing home.

But it had never happened. Gran had never got to see the gallery, and Poll knew it would never happen, however much she wanted it to.

She shakes the wok, making everything tumble. She arranges cutlery and condiments on the table. She lifts the fish pieces carefully from the water and plates them, and covers them with tinfoil.

She hears the sound of the front door, followed by his quick tread on the stairs. She smiles at the wok as she waits to see him, happiness fluttering like a caged butterfly inside her. She thinks about Saturday, when he closes the gallery for the long weekend and follows her to Land's End.

But he hadn't seemed all that enthused, had he, when she mooted the trip a couple of weeks ago? *I thought we might just do nothing*, he said. Didn't he say that?

Yes, but then he agreed.

Only to keep you quiet. He doesn't want to go – it's the last place he wants to be.

Stop it. *Stop* it. Shut up.

The door opens. 'Hello, beautiful,' he says.

She turns and gives him a bright, bright smile.

Thomas

'I WAS JUST WONDERING,' SHE SAYS, 'IF YOU'D BE interested in something. You mightn't be bothered, it mightn't be your cup of tea at all – but I won tickets, two tickets, on the radio, the night before last, or was it the one before that? Anyway, it doesn't matter and, well, I've already asked Michelle, and she *would* go, she'd really enjoy it, only Saturday is her book club night, and she was the one who chose the last book – they take it in turns – so she can't very well not show up, and I might have persuaded Mam to go, only she's not really that mobile at the moment after her hip, and anyway she's not a great fan of concerts, well, of any kind of show, really, so I just said I'd run it by you, and of course you mustn't feel at *all* obliged, it won't bother me a *bit* if you wouldn't fancy it, honestly. No pressure.'

And all the while she's scrubbing out one of the soup saucepans, digging in there with her brush as if her life depended on it, not once looking his way. He can get the gist of it – she won a pair of tickets to a concert, and she's looking for someone to use the second – but she's certainly taking her time getting to the point.

He lifts the last chair onto a table and begins to sweep the floor. 'What kind of show is it?'

She gives an odd kind of sound, halfway between a cough and a giggle. 'God, silly me, forgot the important bit.' Still splashing about in the saucepan, which must by now be the cleanest it's ever been. 'It's called a summer medley, three classical composers, Wagner and Bach, and someone else – who is it? Anyway, the pieces are being performed by a visiting orchestra from … Poland, I think – Liszt, that's the third. Like I say, it mightn't be your thing at all, and if it's not, don't give it another thought.'

Despite his father's attempts to interest them in classical music as kids, Thomas isn't a huge fan. He quite liked *Fantasia* when Dad put on the video, but more for the cartoons than the music. He's not a big concert-goer either – the last one he attended with Sam and Matt, a jazz-night fundraiser for a suicide prevention charity, must have been well over a year ago – but why not attend this one with Freda? A couple of hours won't kill him, and she's easy company.

He thrusts the brush under a table and brings out a fork, and bends to retrieve it. 'Sure, I'll go. That'd be nice.'

When he straightens up she's beaming at him. 'Oh, would you, Thomas? Really? Are you positive?'

'Absolutely.'

'You're not just coming to please me? Because I really don't—'

'No, I'd like it.' He might like it. He won't rule out the possibility.

'Well, that would be great, thanks a million.' She sets the saucepan on the draining board and reaches for the next, the smile still wide on her face. 'It's actually my birthday that day, total coincidence!'

'Is it really?'

He couldn't have said when her birthday was - although she knows his is in November. Every year for the past four, ever since he started working in the café, he's got a card from her. She must have asked him when it was sometime, and filed the information away. He feels ashamed now that he didn't know hers. Why did he never make it his business to find out?

She gives another little laugh, darts him another glance. 'I'll be the big three oh - imagine!'

Thirty, a few months older than him. He would have thought younger. There's something childlike in the way she looks at the world, a lack of cynicism, a genuine belief in the innate goodness of others. Open to abuse, of course - she's had her trust shaken by customers who occasionally duck out without paying, by a man who grabbed her bag on the street once, by bogus gutter-cleaners who took money in advance of the job and disappeared - but it doesn't alter her innate faith in her fellow humans. Such an outlook would probably be scoffed at by many, but Thomas finds it appealing.

'So where's the concert on?'

'In the arts centre. Really looking forward to it, actually - I *love* classical music.'

Another thing he didn't know about her. The music she plays in the café is generally a safe mix of the likes of Ed Sheeran and Michael Bublé, Imelda May and Harry Styles.

'And when is it on?'

'This Saturday. I know it's short notice, but I hope that's OK.'

This Saturday?

He stops sweeping. 'I'm so sorry, Freda,' he says. 'I won't be here. I'm going away for the weekend, remember? The family thing. I'm sure I mentioned it.'

Her smile stays in place, but all the light ebbs from it. 'Oh, yes,' she says. 'You did mention it. I'd completely forgotten.' It's painful to watch the disintegration of her happiness. He feels terrible. 'Don't give it another thought,' she says, running fresh water into the second saucepan, taking up the pot scrub. 'It makes no odds - it's not as if I paid for them.' Scrub, scrub.

'I'm sorry to let you down. If it was any other—'

'Honestly, it doesn't bother me at all, Thomas. Don't worry a bit about it.'

Of course it bothers her. It's plain to see how much it bothers her.

'Is there no one else who's free?' Doesn't she have other friends? Michelle is the only one he's met. She worked - still works - in the hospital canteen where Freda started out, but Michelle talks, whenever Thomas encounters her, about quitting. Not exactly full of the joys. 'There must be someone else you could ask.'

'Not really, nobody I can think of - but I'll go on my own, I don't mind.'

He watches as she hoicks up a slipping-down sleeve and runs a forearm across her forehead, water dripping from the tips of her blue rubber gloves. He doubts she'll go to the concert: despite her cheery demeanour in the café he senses that, like him, she lacks the kind of courage, the confidence, that would allow her to attend a social event without a companion.

He feels a stab of real pity for her. So big-hearted, so eager to make someone else happy - and here he is, disappointing her. But what can he do? It's not as if he can switch the Land's End trip to another weekend.

She rinses the saucepan and sets it on the draining board beside the other. She fixes him with a wide, empty smile. 'Do you want to take Saturday off? I know Arthur isn't going anywhere - he could fill in.'

For a second he's tempted. More time at Land's End would be good. He could take it out of his holidays: he has plenty left. And her cousin Arthur has stepped in before for Thomas: it wouldn't be a big deal.

But Saturday is her thirtieth birthday. And she won tickets to a concert, like a birthday present from the universe, and she can't use them. The least Thomas can do is be around during the day, try to make it special if he can.

'I'm happy to work on Saturday, thanks. There's only so much family time I can take.'

She laughs, or tries to. 'I know what you mean.'

He'll make it up to her. He'll say nothing on Saturday morning, let on he's forgotten it's her birthday. He'll wait until the café is full at lunchtime and then he'll surprise her. He'll raid the little box of pastel-coloured birthday candles that she keeps in a drawer, just in case she ever overhears a customer being wished a happy birthday.

To date the candles have lain undisturbed in the drawer – Glorious Food isn't the kind of place you'd come to for a birthday celebration: it's more an everyday breakfast or lunch spot – but Thomas will finally put some of them to use on Saturday.

He'll stick it into a muffin. He'll do what she would, if ever the opportunity arose – or he might buy her a cake, yes, that would be better. He'll get her a lemon drizzle, her favourite – he can nip out mid-morning and cut across to the bakery on the next street. He'll stick three candles into it, one for each decade, and he'll ask one of the regulars to start a chorus of 'Happy Birthday'. He can give her that much.

She lays the saucepan on the draining board and peels off the rubber gloves. 'It's your mother's home place, isn't it, where you're going?'

'Yeah.'

She pats the saucepan dry with a tea towel. 'I presume this'll be her first time back there since your gran's funeral.'

'It will, yes.'

'It'll be tough for her. Well, for all of you, but for her especially.'

Thomas thinks about that. Mum has never been one to show much emotion, never one for the heart-to-heart conversations. When he and Poll were growing up, Dad had been the one for the bedtime stories, the one who gave treats after good report cards, the one who brought them from door to door on Halloween nights, and helped them eat the treats afterwards.

It wasn't that Mum didn't care; it wasn't that at all. She was just the more practical parent. She was the organiser of days out, the lunchbox packer, the holiday planner, the one who sewed name tags onto school uniforms, and made sure they wore PE gear on the right day, and took time off school to bring them to their dental appointments.

She didn't cry when Gran died, or at least not when they were all there, when the four of them were gathered around the nursing home bed and Gran took a few rattly breaths and then went quiet. None of them cried much, apart from Poll, who can generally be relied on to cry at any remotely emotional occasion.

But this trip to Land's End was Mum's idea, so she must be feeling loss of some kind, mustn't she? She must be looking for consolation, or closure or something.

'We used to go there as kids on holidays,' he tells Freda, wanting to share with her, wanting to make amends for letting her down. 'It's lovely, right by the sea. My great-grandfather built it. It's big – he wanted loads of kids, and he had them, but they all emigrated to the States except for one daughter, and that was Gran.'

'And she inherited the house.'

'Yeah. She never left it. My grandfather moved in there when they got married. Gran turned the place into a B&B after he died, and she ran it for years. It wouldn't be very classy by today's standards, none of the bedrooms had en-suite bathrooms – still don't – but we loved it, and she was always full in the summer. Americans especially went mad for it.'

He wonders suddenly if Mum and Dad had paid Gran anything to stay at Land's End. Five or six weeks they'd spent there each summer, taking over her family room, denying her that income. He and Poll had slept in bunks, Mum and Dad in the double bed across the floor. Such a tight unit they were then, the four of them.

The break-up of his parents' marriage had come as a complete surprise to Thomas. He'd accepted their coupledom as a given, as much a fixture as the house they'd lived in for most of their married life, the home that he and Poll had grown up in. He'd never questioned their relationship – why would he? They'd always seemed content with one another; he'd seen no indication that either of them wanted out.

And then, abruptly, it was gone. Over dinner in a local restaurant his parents broke it to him and Poll that it was to be no more, that *they* were to be no more. That was a shock, no use saying otherwise. It had taken some digesting. It had caused a shift in his mindset, an unsettling realisation that even the most apparently solid edifices could crumble and collapse without warning.

But time had passed and he'd got used to the new way of things. Not long before the split he'd moved in with his friend Sam, and Sam's partner Matt, and he'd just started working with Freda in the café. Life was busy. Whole days could go by without the changed situation crossing his mind – and then Poll would ring, crying down the phone to him, needing to pull it all apart again, and he'd feel newly astonished that it could even have happened.

And the way Mum and Dad seemed to take it in their stride, as if long-married couples separated every day. A number of them did, of course: more than a few of his classmates at school had had divorced parents. He'd always assumed extenuating circumstances, drink or unfaithfulness or other unhappy situations. His own parents' lives were so ordinary – but maybe that was where the problem had lain. Maybe one or both of them had needed more than ordinary.

And then, six months later, his father invited him and Poll to drinks at the apartment and introduced them, half proudly, half warily, to Chloë – and Thomas's world had shifted on its axis again.

He regards Freda, scrubbing now at the counter top where they prep the food. There is a slight inward cast to one of her pale blue eyes that lends, he always thinks, an air of faint bewilderment to her demeanour. Her nose is a fraction too large, with a small bump across its bridge. Her smile, often seen, pokes a dimple into a rosy cheek. If not classically beautiful, hers is a face with a pleasing openness and warmth.

In physique she's as different from Thomas as it's possible to be. Where he's long and gangly she's short and round of shoulder and solidly built, with a broad back and wide hips, and calves that protrude stoutly from the longish skirts she favours.

In every way, she is the polar opposite to Chloë.

Porcelain-skinned, elfin, poised, stylish Chloë, who touches a violin and breathes magic into it. Even Thomas, with his limited musical ear, can appreciate the depth of her skill.

Chloë who smells of roses, whose small nose tips up adorably, whose teeth are creamy white and perfect. Chloë who clothes her slender frame in layered tunics and wraps made of a fabric so gossamer-fine that they billow out gently behind as she moves, and trousers that taper to a stop at her dainty ankles, and soft-looking pixie boots with buttons and bows.

Chloë the nymph, whose face has taken up residence in his head. Chloë, the perfect creature who floats into his dreams at night, tantalising him. Chloë, who is never far from his thoughts.

Chloë, who lives with his father.

Chloë, who has replaced his mother in his father's affections.

He is in love with his father's partner. It's like something you'd see on *Jerry Springer*. It would be laughable if it wasn't chipping away at his heart. It would be funny if it wasn't tearing him to pieces.

They finish cleaning up. They remove their aprons - bottle green, with *Glorious Food* embroidered in gold on one pocket - and get their things. Outside the café Thomas pulls down the shutters while Freda stands by. Before he started working with her she had to bring out a chair each evening to reach them.

He locks up and hands her the keys. He looks down at her, a head and a half below him.

'Bye, Freda. See you in the morning.'

'Goodbye, Thomas,' she says brightly, her smile still a faint echo of what it was when she'd thought he was going to the concert with her. 'Thanks for today. Have a good night.' The same thing she says to him every time they part.

She slips the shop keys into her bulging canvas bag and makes for the lane where she parks her battered Ford van. Her rear view looks defeated - yellow raincoat, belt trailing, inch of purple skirt below it, flat black sandals. Again, he feels a stab of pity. Again he resolves to make a fuss of her in the café on Saturday.

On the way home he thinks ahead to the weekend. Wash

clothes this evening. Get his hair cut, late opening tomorrow. Remember to bring his bedding and a towel. He wonders what room Mum will put him in. Plenty of choice, with five to pick from. One bathroom between them all is a bit of a bummer, but they'll manage for the few days. They managed during the summer holidays, when the house would often have ten sleeping in it. You adapted to what you had at your disposal.

He'll pick up a couple of six-packs of beer; Joe and Aidan drink it too. And food – Mum didn't ask, but he'd like to contribute something. Sausages and rashers maybe, a few tubs of yogurt. With six to be fed, whatever he brings won't go to waste.

Chloë isn't joining them. He'd been secretly hoping she would, ever since Poll told him that she'd been invited – *I don't know what Mum is thinking, asking her along: I'm not going if she is* – but Chloë said no, she had other plans for the weekend. Probably just as well: his heart might not survive two nights under the same roof.

He reaches the traffic lights and turns left. He passes a hotel, a bus stop, a library. So familiar, all of them, that he hardly sees them any more. As he walks, he considers the meandering path his life has taken. Working in a café had never been part of the plan – but in truth he never really had a plan, not a proper one.

Growing up, he'd had the usual childish dreams. Airline pilot, astronaut, Olympic swimmer, circus acrobat. After seeing the film with Robert Redford, a career as a horse whisperer took over the top slot for about a month – but nothing stayed with him for long enough to turn into a real ambition. He sleepwalked from school into college, hopping from Film Studies to Arts to Commerce over the course of two fraught years, much to his parents' dismay.

You need to settle on something, his mother said. *You're not giving any of them a chance* – but eventually Thomas realised that it wasn't the courses that were the problem, it was college itself.

He wasn't built for it. He wasn't the right fit to be a student. The fault didn't lie with the study, he didn't mind that – it was the various deadlines that undid him. They'd loom in his head, muddying his thinking, pushing known facts out of reach, preventing sleep at night. The more he tried to ignore them, the more they prodded and poked at him, making it more and more difficult to complete each assignment.

The other side of college, the social side, wasn't for him either. He'd never been good in crowds, never comfortable mixing with more than one or two at a time. In primary school he'd been virtually friendless, his quiet demeanour singling him out for attention from the bullies, which only caused him to withdraw further into himself, shutting out even the boys who meant him no harm, who might have become his friends if he'd allowed them to.

Secondary school had been better when Sam materialised, their shared passion for chess drawing them into a friendship – but separated from Sam in college, he felt again like the solitary young boy of his childhood, surrounded by laughing, chattering others and lacking the wherewithal to join them.

In the two years he'd spent trying to be a student, he hadn't made a single real friend. He'd avoided the discos and pubs his fellow students frequented, opting instead for long walks or solitary movies after he closed his books each day. Sometimes an entire week of lectures would go by without anyone at all interacting with him.

He told himself he was happier left alone – and on one level he was – but with nothing much to distract him from his studies, the days dragged by, and his future, when he dared to consider it, seemed bleak. Commerce, his third course option, was rapidly becoming as uninviting as his previous choices – no third time lucky for him – and nothing else on the syllabus appealed.

Finally he confided in Sam, who'd moved straight from school into a management position in his uncle's car dealership, where he'd been working part-time since the age of sixteen. *Leave*, Sam said immediately. *If it's making you miserable, stop doing it. Figure out what you really want, and go for it.*

Easier said than done. Easy for Sam, who'd come out at eighteen to his family – he'd confided in Thomas before that, and sworn him to secrecy. Easy for Sam, who'd sold a used Porsche to Matt when he was nineteen, and moved in with him a few weeks after their first encounter. Easy for Sam, for whom doors seemed to open without him having to knock on them. It had taken Thomas a few more years, and many more wrong turns – bicycle courier, theatre front of house, call-centre operator, hospital porter – before he figured out what he really wanted.

Then again, it wasn't so much him figuring it out as Freda paving the way for him, while he was wondering how much longer he could stick the porter job at the hospital. He has a lot to thank Freda for.

When he gets home he lets himself in with the key that's attached to the little *Titanic* keyring that Freda brought him back from a trip to Belfast last year. He gets a memento from everywhere she goes: last month it was a bar of handmade chocolate from some factory in Kerry; when she went to Cork after Christmas to visit some cousins he got a Beamish stout bottle-opener.

The house smells faintly of the previous night's curry. Sam

and Thomas are big Thai curry fans; Matt is more a vindaloo man. In the hall he picks his way around the usual scatter of Rasputin's toys – a little rattan mouse with a feather for a tail, a grinning rubbery chicken that clucks when it's prodded, a well-chewed gingham square filled with catnip – and climbs the stairs to his room. It's small but he likes it, with its view of their neighbour's magnificent magnolia, and the rockery at the end of their own garden that Matt has filled with various rambling colourful plants.

Rasputin is curled in the centre of Thomas's bed. He lifts his grey head a fraction and gives a sleepy, guttural mew. 'Hello,' Thomas says, dropping his satchel to scratch behind the cat's ears. Rasputin is Matt's pet but he gravitates towards Thomas, who has no objection. Growing up he would have loved a cat, but with Poll allergic to animal hair it was never an option. She still can't get within three feet of a cat or dog without sneezing.

He sits on the bed, his thigh pressed against the warm heft of Rasputin. He slides his laptop from beneath the pillow and flips it open. He finds the YouTube clip among his bookmarks and watches Chloë in a sea-green dress playing a piece by Massenet on the stage of the music college. He'd never heard of Massenet before Chloë.

She was twenty-one when this video was made, in her second year of college. Slightly older than her fellow students, having taken two gap years after school to travel the world with her mother. Twenty-one, studying music with Dad as her tutor, but not destined to embark on a relationship with him until she'd completed her college course and left.

What if Thomas had met her before that happened? He often imagines the scenario: the day after the concert she's injured and taken to the hospital where he works as a porter. (Never mind that the porter job didn't materialise until a year after the concert: timeframes don't matter in his fantasies.) They get to know one another while she recuperates; a friendship develops that deepens into love. His father meets an older woman and falls for her, or his parents are reunited (this even after Mum takes up with Joe, which is unfortunate for Joe, but necessary for Thomas's plot). Everyone lives happily ever after.

Chloë is twenty-seven now, two years younger than Thomas. Chloë will never look at Thomas the way she looks at him in his imaginings, will never lean in to drop a soft kiss on his mouth, never lie next to him, never put her head against his chest to feel the fervent hopeless beating of his heart.

When the piece finishes he folds the laptop shut and finds his phone and presses his father's name in his contact list.

'Hi, Thomas.'

Her voice, so unexpected, causes a great leap in his chest. He visualises her, pulling at a stray curl with her free hand. 'Um – is my, er, father there?' Reduced to a stammering fool, as he always is when he encounters her – even if it's only on the phone.

'He's taking a shower. Can I help at all?' The words light and musical. 'Or did you want a man-to-man talk?' A gurgle of delicious throaty laughter.

'No – I was just going to ask if he wants a book, the new one from, um –' In his flap, the author's name completely escapes him. 'Listen, I'll – I'll call him tomorrow. I haven't got it to hand. It's just that I've finished it and I could bring it to Land's End if he wanted it.'

'OK, I'll pass that on. Are you all set for the weekend?'

'Yeah.' Silence, stretching. He must speak. 'Are you?' Moron. Such scintillating conversation he comes up with. He has no idea what she's doing for the weekend.

'Absolutely. I'm sorry I won't see the famous Land's End though. Charlie has told me all about it.'

Charlie has told me. He swallows the stab of jealousy.

'You'll have to come to dinner after the weekend,' she goes on. 'It's ages since you've been.'

It's three weeks since he's been. Dinner with them is torture, but he can't keep away. He always says yes when Dad invites him. Poll never goes, she finds excuses every time, but Dad continues to issue invitations to both of them. *How can you go?* Poll demands, and he tells her he does it for Dad's sake, he does it to keep the peace, and she doesn't seem to hear the lies.

'Are you still there? Did I scare you off with my dinner invitation?'

He can hear the smile in her voice. 'No, yeah, that'd be good. Thanks.'

'Great – I'll get Charlie to set it up. I don't see you half often enough. Take care, Thomas.'

His name on her lips sounds like a caress. He keeps the phone pressed to his ear until she disconnects. His palms are damp: he wipes them on his jeans and regards the cat, asleep and impervious.

I don't see you half often enough.

I, not we.

He buries his face in his hands. What is he to do with her? Is he to be tormented for the rest of his days, doomed to love her silently and uselessly?

If Poll knew. If Poll had the slightest inkling, she'd kill him.

Isn't it obscene? she'd raged, that first night. The night Dad had invited them to drinks at the apartment, saying there was someone he wanted them to meet. *She was a year ahead of me in school – how creepy is that? How could he do it to Mum? Jesus, he's as bad as Humbert Humbert!*

Thomas, having no clue who Humbert Humbert was, could only remember the perfect creamy ovals of Chloë's nails as she'd placed dishes of nuts and olives on the coffee table. While Poll continued to fume, wondering aloud how long the liaison would last – *I give them three weeks* – Thomas recalled how soft Chloë's hand had felt when he clasped it briefly on meeting her. *Thomas,* she'd said, a smile nudging up one side of her mouth. *You have your father's height.*

A joke: he towers above his father's five foot ten frame. At six four, he towers above most people. Next to him, Freda says she feels like a leprechaun. Next to Freda, Chloë is a pixie. Thomas could pick her up as easily as he might lift one of the café chairs. He could curl his body around hers, enfold her with his long limbs—

No.

God.

Stop.

He rises abruptly from the bed, the movement startling the cat into wakefulness. He leaves the room and goes downstairs to reheat the shepherd's pie leftovers that Freda sent him home with.

Charlie

'WHO WAS THAT?'

She places his phone on the dressing table, checks her reflection in the mirror, adjusts her neckline. 'Thomas. Something about a book. He'll call you tomorrow. I asked him to dinner next week – you can organise a date when you see him.'

'Fine.' Charlie rubs his hair with a towel. 'What time is it?'

'Quarter to.'

'Sweetie, do I honestly have to go? I'd really rather a night in.'

'Oh come on, old man. It'll be fun.'

It won't be fun, not for him. He's tired, not in the mood for her theatre crowd. Nobody but himself over thirty-five, everyone addressing him in the careful, polite tone he knows they reserve for old folk. He keeps waiting for someone to call him sir, or to say something extra loud for his benefit. The last time they were out together someone said 'fuck', and at least two heads swung in his direction. Don't swear in front of the grown-ups.

They're launching a play tonight. Chloë's told him which one, but he let the information slide into one ear and dribble out the other. She works four days a week in the theatre's box office: when she's not doing that she's playing at weddings and the like in a silly little string quintet that would be nothing without her.

You could be first violin in any orchestra you wanted, Charlie has told her more than once. *You could do solo world tours with the right manager. You could earn far more than me: they'd pay whatever you asked* – but she prefers to let her talent go to waste, saying she's not dedicated enough to be that serious a musician.

I like the mix of music and theatre, she says. *I like working in the theatre. Don't you want me to be happy?*

She's hopeless. He's learnt to hold his tongue on the subject, although the thought of her playing violin for drunken wedding guests who wouldn't be able to tell the difference between a Bach fugue and some third-rate music piped into a lift kills him.

As a music tutor of thirty-odd years' experience, as head teacher in the city's prestigious music college for the last decade, Charlie has encountered few truly gifted students. That magical combination of passion and skill, that ability not only to interpret a piece of music in precisely the way the composer intended, but also to breathe fresh life and emotion and *soul* into the notes, to lift it beyond the sum of its parts, is rarely found.

Chloë has it. Her playing regularly reduces him to tears. Listening to her, he is swept away. He is transfixed, enslaved.

Take me, she murmured, seeing the effect of her music on him. *You can have me.* Laying aside her violin to curl into his lap, to press her palm to his chest as her mouth found his for the first time – and he obeyed, there in his office in the middle of the afternoon. Unable, or unwilling, to resist her. His wife, his family forgotten in the rush of emotion the girl-child's playing had induced, the final perfect notes of her Beethoven sonata playing and replaying in his head as he had unbuttoned and unzipped, as he had done what she wanted.

And there's the thing. There's the bit nobody would believe, if they knew it. *She* had seduced *him*. She was the one who had instigated the affair that ultimately led to the break-up of his marriage.

'Sit,' she orders now, indicating the bed. She tosses his towel into the laundry hamper and starts easing out the damp tangles with her fingers. 'Tell me more about Land's End,' she says. 'Paint me a picture of the house.'

How well she knows him. Switch his attention to the upcoming trip, take his mind off the evening ahead.

'I've told you all about it.'

'Tell me again.'

'It's blue. It's always been blue. Two storeys, five bedrooms. Kitchen, bathroom, two sitting rooms. A dining room that's not used any more – everyone eats in the kitchen since the B&B closed. A scullery off the kitchen.'

'What's that?'

'Little store room, like a larder.'

It used to disconcert him, having to explain things he'd grown up with but she'd never encountered. A roll of camera film, a cassette tape, a fax. A VCR machine, for God's sake. He's trained himself to let it go.

'Are there shutters on the windows?' Her fingers kneading his scalp now: if he was a cat he'd purr.

'No shutters. Two bay windows, front sitting room and main bedroom. Glass fanlight over the door.'

'What colour's the door?'

'White, and the window frames too. A veranda in front, running the width of the house, wooden railing around it. Three steps down to the drive, which is gravelled.'

'Go on.'

'Trees on one side of the drive, ash and poplar. Hydrangea bushes on the other.'

'And the beach?'

She knows all this. She's humouring him. He doesn't care. 'The beach is just down from the house, beyond a low dry-stone wall. It's pebbly, and about half a mile long. It curves like a wide horseshoe.'

His description brings him there. He feels the smooth, rounded stones beneath his bare feet, breathes in the ammoniac tang of the seaweed, hears the soft plash of the little waves as they come running up onto the pebbles. He turns, and there is the house to his rear, blue and white, curtains billowing behind the open windows.

He can hardly believe he's going back in two days. He was convinced he'd never see it again.

From the very first time Lily brought him there, over thirty years ago, he was drawn to Land's End. *Here we are,* she'd said as he steered his Austin Mini through the gates, *home sweet home* – and Charlie regarded the sky blue façade and felt something, a sort of primal response he'd never before experienced. For whatever reason it *did* feel like home to him, before he'd even stepped across its threshold.

And if everything had gone according to plan, if Charlie and Lily had remained together, they'd have retired there. He can't remember when they made the decision, it was so long ago: all he knows for sure is that once the possibility was put out there, it became a given. It was what they both wanted, what they both regarded as inevitable. They'd see out their lives at Land's End, or as much of them as they could.

Over the years – in the idle spaces between classes, standing in a queue, waiting for sleep to claim him at night – Charlie would leap ahead and envisage living there full time. They'd close off the rooms they didn't need, the extra bedrooms, the back sitting room and the formal dining room where Kitty's guests had had breakfast.

He planned to read his way through the wonderful old books in the little front sitting room, bound sets of Dickens and Hugo, the Brontës and Chaucer and Charles Lamb. He'd swim all year round, regardless of the weather. He'd go fishing as often as he could with whatever local boatman would oblige – or he might even splash out and get his own humble craft. In the evenings he and Lily would walk the half-mile to Sully's for a couple of small gins and bitter lemon before dinner. Or maybe a couple of large ones – why not?

And Thomas and Poll would turn up every so often with the grandchildren. They'd open up the spare rooms then, fling the windows wide, fill the place with sea air, dot tall vases of blazing montbretia about the place the way Kitty used to do.

Charlie would teach the kids to swim, just like he'd taught his own two. He'd gather shells with them, show them the best stones for skimming, push marshmallows onto sticks and toast them on a driftwood bonfire if they got a warm summer evening. He'd make memories with them, he'd ensure that they came to love the place like he did.

But of course none of that is to be now, because he and Lily are no more. In July their divorce will become final – and not long after that, Joe will sign a register in some office and become the husband of the woman who owns Land's End. Now it's affable Joe who'll get to spend holidays and weekends there, Joe who'll walk the pebble beach, Joe who'll skim the stones.

Joe will be the one who wakes to the sound of gulls, who tastes salt when he runs his tongue across his lips, who sits on the front veranda in the evenings to watch the sun slipping beneath the horizon. And in ten or fifteen years, it will be Lily and Joe settling there in retirement, Lily and Joe welcoming Charlie's grandchildren when they tumble from cars, all excited.

His grandchildren, not Joe's – but Joe will have full access to them. They might even call him Granddad. It's not something Charlie cares to contemplate.

'I wish you were coming,' he says. 'Why won't you come?'

Chloë is working on his head now with a comb. 'Charlie, we've been through this.'

They have. She wouldn't feel comfortable, surrounded by his family for an extended period of time. He understands – and he has to acknowledge that it will be easier all round without her. But still he wants her there. Lily will be with Joe: he should be with Chloë. She was invited, for God's sake – she's perfectly entitled to go. Without her he'll feel untethered, unbalanced, the spare wheel.

Thomas will be there on his own – but Thomas is always alone. His son has never, as far as Charlie is aware, been tethered to anyone. It's a constant simmering concern, but not one he feels he can do anything about. The subject of Thomas's lack of partners came up often between Charlie and Lily, but neither of them ever broached it with Thomas. What do you say that doesn't sound like a criticism? How do you ask why there's never been a romance?

'Ten minutes,' Chloë says, tossing the comb aside, abandoning him. He takes his suit from the wardrobe and gets dressed, willing the evening to pass quickly. He pulls on his navy trousers, drawing in his gut as he secures the waistband button, keeping it in as he eases up the fly. Tight, too tight for comfort. Not enough exercise, that's his problem. He should swim, but he isn't a big fan of pools. He hates the cloggy smell of the buildings that house them, the claustrophobic overheated feel of them.

He could walk in the local park – he could do a few laps on his way home from work. He could, but he doesn't. The spirit is willing, that's about it. Middle-age spread got something to do with it too, no doubt. Fifty-nine next birthday: at least he's still on the right side of sixty.

He won't think about sixty until it happens. He'll ignore it, like he's been ignoring anything to do with the future since he chose to share his home, and his life, with someone thirty-one years younger.

Thirty-one years. It can still stop him in his tracks when he allows himself to think of it. Chloë was just twenty-two when they began their affair, the same age Lily was when he married her more than a quarter of a century ago. Far more mature, it has to be said, than Lily had been at twenty-two – or Charlie, for that matter. Wise in the ways of the world, assured and unafraid, with none of her peers' insecurities. Her years of travel, no doubt, coupled with a formidable mother whose own strength of character must have filtered down to her daughter.

He puts on cufflinks – he likes to think of them as his only affectation. He ties his shoelaces, stows his wallet in its usual place. Nobody thought they'd last, of course. The wives who used to be his and Lily's friends were at pains to avoid him when the news broke, their husbands calling him a lucky bugger to his face and sniggering, he suspected, behind his back.

Charlie Cunningham and his newer model. Charlie Cunningham losing the run of himself. Male menopause mentioned more than once, he's quite sure. Everyone placing bets on how long it would last. Coming up for four years, boys, more than that if you count the time when nobody knew about us. Anyone bet on that?

The music college's directors weren't impressed when the news broke. Nothing was said, at least not to his face - there was no charge to answer, with him and Lily broken up, and Chloë graduated - but their cool glances said it all, the pressing engagements they suddenly had whenever he appeared said it all. He rode it out until it blew over, until the next bit of gossip caught their attention.

He gives a final glance in the mirror, ruffles the hair that Chloë flattened with her comb, tweaks his tie. He leaves the bedroom and finds her reading on the couch.

'Ready?'

She looks up with the dazed expression he's become familiar with. She loses herself in books, immerses herself completely. She slides in a bookmark and gets to her feet, and follows him silently to the car.

The thing about Chloë, the thing nobody understands, or believes, is that it's not just physical with them. She's been to every continent, thanks to her travel-hungry mother; she speaks four languages fluently, and has a fair understanding of several more. She's better informed than himself, reading across most genres, alternating between fact and fiction. Books piled by her side of the bed, more on her e-reader, still more stored audibly on her phone.

She's politically aware, and well able to argue with his often more right-wing stance. She beats him regularly at poker, challenges him at Sudoku, completes cryptic crosswords that defeat him. In and out of bed, she's more than a match for him.

And when they make music together, she on the violin, he on the cello, it is something close to perfection. They fit, they dovetail beautifully in every possible way.

Not surprisingly, Lily didn't take the news well. He and Chloë went public six months after the end of his marriage. If it had been up to him, he'd have waited longer, but Chloë was tired of sneaking around. Lily was the first person he told, not wanting her to hear it from anywhere else.

Chloë Richardson? Isn't she one of your students?

Not any more. She graduated last year. As if a year or two made a difference, with such a mammoth age gap – but it was a straw, and he duly clutched at it.

Last year, Lily repeated. *So she's Poll's age.*

She's older than Poll. She's almost a year older.

Almost a year older. Almost a whole year older than your daughter.

She must have wondered about them, must have wondered when they'd really started up, but she didn't ask. For this he was silently grateful. If she'd asked outright, he would have lied. He'd thought it would be kinder to lie.

And Poll, when it was her turn to hear the news, took it much harder. Barely able to look at Chloë when Charlie introduced them, the disbelief at his choice of partner all too evident in her face. She's still not at ease with the situation, enduring rather than enjoying their company whenever she can't avoid it. It pains Charlie to see it, but what can he do?

Thomas doesn't approve either. When he meets Charlie on his own, things are the way they've always been between them, but he's clearly uncomfortable in Chloë's company. Unlike Poll, he comes to dinner at the apartment whenever the invitation is issued, but Charlie suspects he'd rather be anywhere else. Despite Chloë's attempts to draw him out – and she can be very charming when she wants – he remains ill at ease under her scrutiny, and rarely makes eye contact with her. He may as well have *I don't like you* tattooed across his forehead. It's unfortunate that neither of his children has taken to her.

They arrive at the bar where the launch is to happen: there isn't a parking spot to be seen. 'Let me out here,' Chloë orders, already reaching for the door handle. Eager to connect with her buddies. Glad, no doubt, of the chance to warn them that the old man is on the way.

Charlie circles the block and finds a space eventually. He parks and sits, in no rush to make his way back. If Lily saw him now, psyching himself up for an evening of small talk with Chloë's twenty-something friends, she'd have a good laugh.

Would he and Lily have parted without Chloë? It's a question he's often asked himself. Their marriage had become such an insubstantial thing, such a one-dimensional entity. On the surface they were fine, they got along – but beneath, there was nothing. No passion, no fire, no delight in one another any more. They still occupied the same bed, still made love, albeit seldom, but the act had become more of a comfortable habit, more sleep-inducing than anything else.

But it has to be said that this state of affairs didn't unduly dismay him. The marriage had fallen into disrepair so gradually that it didn't seem like such a big deal. He and Lily had reached a plateau: that was how he looked at it, on the rare occasions that he did. He imagined most of their friends' marriages had taken a similar route to the same plateau. On the whole it didn't seem like a bad place to be. Yes, the fireworks had been wonderful, but fireworks by their nature didn't last.

And then Chloë had arrived on the scene, and he was reminded of what he had lost with Lily. Thankfully, when he finally mooted the idea of a split with her, again urged on by Chloë, Lily didn't put up any real objection. She was thrown, of course, caught unawares by the suddenness of it. She even suggested they attend counselling to heal whatever they'd broken – but she didn't come across as devastated, far from it.

In fact, it occurred to him, as they talked about it so civilly, that she might well have been thinking, even subconsciously, along the same lines. She might actually have been relieved when he requested a parting of the ways. Theirs must have been the most amicable split in history.

His big regret about the whole thing continues to be Poll, and what it has done to him and her. It pains him to see how damaged they've become – but short of giving up Chloë, what can he do?

He's tried talking to Poll, on the phone and in person – and invariably the shutters come down. She changes the subject, or finds a reason to end the conversation, or gives him a flippant response that tells him nothing. She won't allow him to reassure her that his feelings towards her are unchanged – but he might find a way to get through to her at Land's End. They both loved it there; maybe she'll lower the barricades long enough for them to reconnect. He'll live in hope.

Two young girls walk past the car. Can't be more than sixteen, skirts just about covering their backsides, long bare legs, heels like stilts on their shoes. Tottering along, arms linked, a bottle – vodka? – dangling from a hand. Three leather-jacketed lads, possibly a bit older, follow some distance behind. Admiring the view, no doubt.

When they've turned the corner he gets out. He locks the car and walks back to the pub, thinking of the large Glenfiddich he's planning to pour himself the minute they get home.

THURSDAY, 27 APRIL

Chloë

'BUT HOW DID IT HAPPEN? I MEAN, WERE YOU NOT ON the Pill?'

'Of course I was on the Pill.'

'Did you … forget to take it?'

'For God's sake – what does it matter how it happened?'

It comes out more sharply than she intends, and Abby's face washes from white to pink. Take it easy, keep her on your side. 'Sorry, I'm upset. I didn't forget, but the Pill isn't foolproof – none of that stuff is. I was unlucky, that's all. Some people are just unlucky.'

The shock of the two blue lines this morning, the last thing she wanted to see. Clear as anything, no possibility of a mistake. The warning signs had been there, of course – a lack of energy, a queasiness in the morning, tenderness in her breasts. They'd been there but she hadn't picked up on them, until she'd added up days and realised how late she was.

And now the blue lines have made it official, so she must fix it – and until the laws are changed she must travel to the UK to do that. The thought of it, all of it, horrifies her.

She summons up the pleading look – tremulous smile, wide eyes – that works every time on Charlie. 'Abby, I'd like – I mean,

I *need* someone I can rely on, someone I can trust. I thought you'd want to help, but if you'd rather not get involved ...'

'Of course I'll help.' Jumping into the pause. Flattered that she's been chosen, as Chloë knew she would be.

'Are you sure? This is really important.'

'Yes, absolutely, I'm sure. Tell me what you want me to do.'

Look at her basking in the attention, like the other grateful misfits Chloë has encountered over the years. Thrilled to be needed, delighted when someone like Chloë calls on them for help. You could almost say Chloë is doing her a favour, reaching out to her like this.

'Well, you know I don't drive –'

'Mm-hmm.' Nodding along eagerly, waiting to hear what part she'll play.

'– so I was hoping someone could bring me to Shannon airport and pick me up the following day. It will mean taking time off work.'

'That's no problem,' Abby says quickly. 'I've got plenty of holidays coming to me.'

'Great. I'll make an appointment then – hopefully I'll get some day next week.'

'OK. Let me know.'

Chloë reaches across the café table to squeeze her hand. 'Thanks so much, Abby. I knew I could count on you.'

'Of course you can.' The flush rises in Abby's face again. She lifts her chocolate éclair and takes another bite. An errant blob of cream lodges at the corner of her mouth: she nudges it in with the tip of her little finger, throwing Chloë an apologetic smile.

Easy to see where the double chin comes from.

They'd met through the theatre. One of Chloë's first duties when she'd begun working there was to organise the printing of a show programme. This necessitated an email correspondence with the secretary of a local printing company. As the show date approached, the secretary suggested that Chloë drop in and view a mock-up of the programme prior to final printing, *just to make sure you're completely happy with it* – and there Abby awaited her, bespeckled and fluffy-haired, timid and eager to please. The kind of person you knew would be there if she was ever needed.

And now she's needed, because public transport to and from the airport doesn't bear thinking about, and because telling her real friends about this – Charlene and Robin in the theatre, Dervla in the string quintet, Phil and Justine and Izzy from school – is out of the question.

She chose her friends with care. She chose people like herself, who monitor their weight, and their water and alcohol intake, and who are careful to get enough exercise and enough sleep. She chose people who know – who were born knowing – how to enter a room, and when to leave it. People who have no problem making chit-chat at gatherings, who recognise one another upon introduction, who need no special handshake to identify a kindred spirit.

People who wouldn't dream of getting pregnant by accident.

They'd look at Chloë differently if they found out: this she knows instinctively. They'd blame her, even though she's blameless – or pity her, which would be far worse. Nothing would ever be said aloud, but the knowledge would lessen her in their eyes, so telling them is out.

The only one who can help her now is Abby, who'll be too busy feeling important to look on Chloë any differently.

'Will you tell Charlie?'

She's never met him – and after this, she never will. Chloë will make quite sure of that.

'No, I won't. It would only upset him.'

She can't tell him: it would contradict what he already knows, or thinks he knows, about her. She'll make up a story to explain her overnight absence – she'll think of something.

'Chloë, are you … quite sure?' Abby asks then. 'That you don't want to … keep it, I mean?'

Abby would keep it: this Chloë knows instinctively. Single and mid-thirties, Abby might well harbour dreams of becoming a mother. Poor deluded Abby. Chloë must tread carefully.

'I can't,' she says softly, lowering her gaze. 'It's not something I can talk about, but keeping it is simply not an option.' Looking up again. 'I'm sorry I can't explain, but I hope you understand, Abby.'

'Of course I do.'

Of course she doesn't – but how can she argue? Chloë lifts her cup of green tea and casts about for a change of subject, unwilling to dwell on the other now that she's got what she came for. 'So what are your plans for the long weekend? Going anywhere nice?'

Abby, her mouth full with the last of the éclair, hastens her chewing, exaggerates her swallowing. 'No, I'm staying at home. I was thinking of painting the kitchen – it badly needs it. And I might do some gardening if the weather's OK.' A little laugh. 'Not a very exciting timetable, really.'

Not exciting at all. About as dull as it gets. Chloë has been told about the little bungalow that Abby bought a few years earlier. She imagines a magnolia-painted kitchen, a suite of leatherette that's too large for the sitting room. Monet prints on the walls, or maybe Van Gogh. Thin pastel towels in the bathroom. A scrap of lawn to the rear, edged with a bed of flowers that are spaced too far apart.

'What about you? Are you travelling anywhere?'

'Charlie's taking me to the coast,' Chloë replies, the decision made that instant.

She's going with him, because she has to go somewhere. She can't stay alone in the city, dreading what's ahead and unable to meet friends, who will see the fear in her face and ask the wrong questions. She will go to Charlie's holiday home, even though it's the last place she would choose, even though she's certain nobody will want her there - except, of course, Thomas, who will adore her quietly when he thinks she can't see him, and stutter and stumble at her the rest of the time.

She'll endure Lily's polite resentment, and Poll's rather more evident disapproval. She'll seek out the company of boring Joe, whose conversation she suspects might put her to sleep but who has no reason to dislike her - on the contrary, it was Chloë who freed up Lily for him - and Aidan, who appears to be a bit of a ponce but who might be alright: she hasn't met him often enough to find out.

'Oh, lucky you. That'll be lovely.'

It won't be lovely. It will be far from lovely. It's a necessary evil, that's what it is, to distract her from the other.

She'll endure it. She'll survive.

FRIDAY, 28 APRIL

Lily

ON HER WAY TO THE CAR SHE MEETS THE CARETAKER, wheeling in one of the school's giant bins from the path.

'You're off so, Ms Murphy.'

'I am, Simon. Have a good weekend.'

'And you.'

He's lived alone since the death of his wife from cancer, a year before Lily took over as principal. One son who lives in Australia – or is it South Africa? No other family that she's aware of. He's first to arrive each morning, last to leave. He's also unfailingly obliging, happy to undertake tasks that shouldn't fall under his remit.

Despite Lily's ongoing efforts, he consistently and politely turns down her invitations to their staff nights out, at Christmas and at the end of the school year. *I'm not much of a one for social occasions,* he tells her – so on the last day of each term she slips him an envelope of folded banknotes instead. She lives in fear that he'll decide to retire, or be killed or horribly injured in a sudden accident, leaving her searching for someone who'll do half as good a job.

Before she's pulled out of the schoolyard her phone rings. She sees Charlie's name and cuts the engine. 'Hi, there.'

'Lily – have you left yet?'

'I'm on my way to pick up Poll. Everything alright?'

'Fine. Just thinking I should have said I'll do dinner tomorrow night. It's not too late to offer, is it?'

'Not too late, thanks. It's fish tonight.'

'In that case I'll bring steaks, OK?'

'Lovely.' He doesn't stint on ingredients: the steaks will be fillet, and he'll cook them to perfection. And he'll bring wine to accompany them. Something French, it'll be: he has no time for the New World offerings.

'Looking forward to seeing the place again,' he says. 'Been a while.'

Been a while is right. 'See you soon,' she says. 'Drive carefully.'

'There's something else,' he says, as she's about to press disconnect. She waits.

'Chloë would like to come after all.'

Everything in her tightens. She feels the warmth leave her face. Poll, she thinks. 'Chloë is coming?'

'Would that be OK? I know it's short notice.'

'I thought she had something else planned.'

'… Seems it fell through.'

Nothing planned, then. A lie to get out of coming with them. Why the change of heart now though?

'Is it OK?'

She nods, even though he can't see her. She nods, even though she wants to say no, it's not OK, it's far from OK. 'Yes. I mean, of course it is. She was invited, wasn't she?'

Chloë is coming. Poll will hit the roof.

'Thanks. We'll see you later so.'

She hangs up, mind spinning. She'll wait until they're well on the way before breaking the news – otherwise Poll would surely refuse to come. Inviting Chloë had to be done – if Joe and

Aidan were invited, then she must be too – but Lily never for a second expected her invitation to be accepted. Damn the girl, foisting herself on them at the last minute.

Might have done it on purpose, just to annoy Lily. Wouldn't put it past her.

She would never have put him with Chloë, never in a million years. Hadn't taken them seriously for a second. Not an ounce of embarrassment evident in the girl when they came face to face that first time, holding Charlie's hand like it belonged in hers. *We met before*, she said, *at the college concert a couple of years ago*, and Lily recalled a green dress, yes, and everyone enthralled at the child's music. They'd met briefly after the concert, Charlie had introduced them and Chloë had admired something of Lily's. His student then, his partner now.

What should I call you? she asked, having commandeered Lily's husband, and Lily replied *Lily, of course*, and her voice sounded stiff and ridiculous as she took in the slim ankles, the smooth, unlined face, the little-girl breasts, clearly braless, beneath the flimsy top. Was that really what he wanted now?

This silliness wouldn't last, it couldn't. No doubt the child had been flattered by Charlie's interest in her – bit of a coup to have your old tutor making advances – but surely she'd set her sights higher than an ageing, second-hand mate. It wasn't as if he was filthy rich, for Heaven's sake. He was perfectly solvent, on a very decent salary from the music college, but hardly in the league of sugar-daddies.

No, the novelty would wear off, and whatever crush Chloë had would fade. She'd catch him favouring the hip that didn't ache – of course he refused to get it checked out – or she'd notice the sagging skin beneath his chin, or the emerging pale brown liver spots on the backs of his hands, or the deepening lines fanning out from his eyes. She'd find someone younger and cast him aside, and after another few weeks of adjustment – and a quiet satisfaction, let's face it, on Lily's part – normal service would resume.

But time passed, weeks and months passed, and it didn't happen. The girl stayed put in the rented apartment Charlie had found when he'd moved out of the family home. Against all the odds, the silliness had lasted – and now, for the sake of harmony, they all put up with the girl's continuing presence in their lives, because they had no choice.

Lily will wait till they're well on the road. She'll say she only just heard, which is true, but of course Poll will still take it out on her.

She hates him for putting her in this position. How could he? She should have insisted he ring Poll himself – but that would have driven an even wider wedge between father and daughter, and Lily doesn't want that, much as he might deserve it.

Traffic is light, no bank holiday rush in evidence as she makes her way to Aidan and Poll's apartment. Poll had fallen on her feet there, no shortage of money, and he's a nice man with it. A failed relationship behind him – people don't get to their thirties without some baggage – but according to Poll, the daughter is lovely. Probably best, all the same, that she lives with her mother in a different country: better for Poll and Aidan to concentrate on their own relationship, at least until he puts a ring on her finger.

If she lets him.

What is her daughter's problem? It's a question Lily has asked herself more than once, a question she and Charlie pondered when they were still together. Boyfriends would appear, boys who would come across as perfectly fine to Lily. Things would seem to be going well – and then it would suddenly be over, with no explanation from Poll other than *It wasn't working.*

Granted, every woman had to do her searching until she

found the right one, but the impression Lily got was that Poll had instigated every single break-up, with very little reason that her mother could fathom. It was as if she was afraid to commit, afraid to trust her heart to anyone.

Before Aidan there had been two long-term boyfriends. Poll met Keith while she was still in school; they went out for the best part of a year, as far as Lily can remember. Perfectly polite anytime Lily met him, arrived with flowers for her the first time Poll brought him home. Hair stiff with gel, shoes with pointed toes. Studying in Dublin to be a radio technician or something, only home at weekends.

Poll certainly seemed smitten, out with him every Friday and Saturday night, on the phone every other night. And then, out of the blue he was gone, with Poll leaving her parents mystified as to the cause, shying away if either of them attempted to broach the subject.

Her other serious boyfriend, John, lasted all of two years while she was in art college. Lily wasn't as taken with him, mainly because he drove a sports car, which she was convinced would careen into a wall some fine night with Poll in it – boy racer, with all its ominous connotations, came to mind whenever they met – but other than that admittedly groundless classification she couldn't really object to him. Brought Poll to Land's End whenever she wanted to visit her gran, took her out to dinner, treated her well as far as anyone could see.

And again the relationship came to an abrupt end, and Lily and Charlie weren't told why. Poll seemed upset by the break-up, as she had with the earlier one, and still Lily was convinced it had happened at her instigation. Call it mother's intuition, call it what you like – but if she was right, what would make Poll end a seemingly happy relationship, other than some kind of psychological block?

She's always been complicated. Never one for the books,

never shone academically, but from a young age her paintings had been startling in their maturity. Some of them very dark – alarmingly so, Lily thought – but showing great artistic promise nonetheless. Charlie's creativity coming out in her, art instead of music.

Never made friends easily, spent pretty much all of her first school year alone – but she's been utterly faithful to the few she eventually took up with, Pam and Colette and Bríd. Generous to a fault too, ready to drop everything if someone needed her, while preferring to keep her own problems bottled up – or away from her parents, at any rate.

There's a vulnerability to Poll, a lack of assurance. There's a darkness in her that she hides behind smiles. She pretends she's happy, and thinks she's fooling her mother. It saddens Lily to see it, but she's at a loss as to how to help. Anytime she attempts a cautious probe, anytime she tries to coax Poll to open up – to her or to anyone else – she gets nowhere.

And the curious little heads she makes. The jolly little faces, the rosy cheeks and perky hats and crooked little smiles. Giving them all names. Making up life stories for them, investing so much in each creation. Mounting them on springs so they can nod away perkily.

On one level, Lily can see their appeal. There's a charm to them, a quirkiness that some would find amusing – and, of course, it takes a level of artistic competency to produce them, she'll admit that. It's just that they're not very … sophisticated. Not what you'd call great art. And Lily is frankly astonished that people are happy to pay the laughably high prices that Aidan puts on them. Still, each to his own.

Poll and Aidan *must* work out, for practical as well as emotional reasons. He's Poll's biggest stockist – the only one, if you don't count the little place in West Cork that sells about two heads a year: imagine the double whammy a break-up would be for her.

It can't happen. Hopefully it won't. With any luck, this relationship will be the one that lasts.

The front door of the apartment block is ajar. As Lily pulls up Poll appears, pulling a small maroon case on wheels, and wearing a trouser suit that Lily remembers from the last gallery event. That shade of green doesn't flatter her, but at least the cut of the jacket is kind to her hips. A little more make-up wouldn't hurt either, a slick of mascara to bring out the pale lashes, a rosier, more flattering shade of lipstick than that awful brown.

Not that she'd dream of mentioning it – Poll is sensitive enough about her appearance. The lemon juice she slathered onto her face in her teens, in an effort to banish her freckles. The lotions and potions she put on her hair, trying to tame its unruliness. Nothing worked: the freckles stayed, the hair refused to conform.

How thoughtless of Charlie to choose a partner who showed up his daughter so cruelly, with her perfectly behaved curls and her blemish-free face. Not an ounce of spare flesh either: little wonder Poll, with her ample curves, resents her.

'Back seat for your stuff,' Lily tells her. 'Boot is full.'

Poll's luggage is stowed, along with a black plastic bag of bedding. They set off. Poll produces a pack of Silvermints from the small leather rucksack that serves as her handbag. 'I brought my togs,' she says, peeling away the foil.

Lily regards her in amazement. 'What? In this weather?' Sky the colour of sheet metal, a smell of rain in the breeze.

'I don't mind the weather. Mint?'

'But the water will be freezing, love.'

'Just at the start. It's fine once you're in.'

'Well, rather you than me. Don't go out of your depth.'

'*Mum*.'

'I'm serious, You're planning to swim alone, which you know isn't recommended. The least you can do is promise not to go deep.'

'OK.'

Lily isn't a swimmer. Well, technically she is – she can stay afloat with a lumbering breaststroke – but she's a complete novice compared to Poll and Thomas, who were taught by Charlie almost as soon as they could walk, and who are consequently as comfortable in the water as out of it.

She should be more proficient, given that she grew up literally within a stone's throw of the ocean – but neither of her parents swam, and she was never encouraged in that direction. Charlie offered more than once to coach her, but she lacked the enthusiasm to take him up on it. She's happier walking on a beach, has always preferred looking at the sea to immersing herself in it.

'Pity Joe couldn't come with us,' Poll remarks, as they make their way through the streets to the outskirts.

'He hopes to be on the road by four. We'll see.'

She's glad they get on, Joe and Poll. She was wary of introducing them, conscious of the trauma caused by Chloë's arrival, but she needn't have worried. Joe gets on with everyone – it didn't take him long to win Poll around – and of course it helped that he didn't come on the scene until Lily and Charlie had been separated for two years. Probably helped too that he was Lily's age, and not some toyboy who'd taken her fancy.

They approach the roundabout that will bring them onto the dual carriageway. Not yet three o'clock, and the traffic is beginning to thicken. Joe will be caught in it, and Charlie too.

Charlie and Chloë. She's dreading bringing it up.

'I prefer the old way,' Poll says.

Lily glances at her. 'Do you?'

Of course she does. So does Lily. In the days before the new road was built, it was their only option for getting to Land's End, a meandering country trail that took them through villages and past castle ruins and fields full of livestock or crops. Even after the advent of the dual carriageway, habit kept them on the old – so why does Lily automatically opt for the other today?

Because it's the way she travels to Land's End now. After she and Charlie split up she made what changes she could, needing to leave her old life behind and move on – and this was one easy way to achieve that. The new route has none of the charm of the traditional one, but it gets her to Land's End just the same – and today it suits them, cutting twenty minutes off the travel time.

She might revisit the old way sometime. She's survived; hurts have healed. It won't kill her like it once might have.

Because the truth, of course, is that Charlie Cunningham broke her heart. Contrary to what everyone believed, contrary to what they told everyone, even the children – that it was a mutual decision – Charlie was responsible for ending the marriage, he was the one who'd had enough. It had come out of the blue for Lily, had thrown her completely. The idea of them separating, of calling time on the life they'd built together, the home and the family they'd created over a quarter of a century, was incomprehensible to her.

But being Lily, being the capable, organised, proud woman she was, she kept her head. She didn't beg, she didn't cry. She *did* demand an explanation – and what she got felt wholly inadequate.

Our marriage has become stale, he said. *We've lost what we once had. We don't connect any more, not in any real way. I just can't see the point in continuing with it.*

They'd had good times, he said, plenty of them, but now they'd come to the end of the line, like many before them. Now it felt, he said, like they were sharing a house but not their lives, not in the way they used to. Why trundle on, just because it was comfortable and familiar?

Why not? she thought. What was so terrible about trundling? Granted, she didn't remember the last time they'd gone out to dinner, just the two of them, or the last time they'd done more than sleep in the double bed they still climbed into every night – but that didn't mean they should just end it all, did it? That didn't mean they should throw up their hands and walk away, did it?

She imagined life without him, imagined being single again – and the prospect filled her with dismay. She didn't want them to separate; she wanted to go on being married to him. She still loved him, even if it was in a gentler way than before.

Then again, what was the point of loving him if he no longer loved her back, which he clearly didn't? How could the marriage continue with only one of them invested in it? A quarter of a century of togetherness was all very well, two children, a nice home, yes, yes – but you wanted love to be part of it too, didn't you? You deserved that, didn't you?

Charlie was still fond of her; she knew that without having to be told. But fondness was what you might feel for a pair of well-worn slippers, or the cup you always filled with your morning tea, even after it had lost its handle from being dropped into the sink. Fond didn't make your blood race, didn't have you aching for the sound of a voice, the thrill of a kiss, the touch of skin on skin.

Get over it, she told herself. He's fallen out of love: it happens. You'll survive without him. Living alone again would certainly take some getting used to, but she'd handle it. She'd focus on the positive, would even try to relish the freedom her new status afforded her.

So she did what she could to help this process along – and one thing she could do was take the dual carriageway to Land's End.

'You can go home the old way with Aidan on Monday,' she tells Poll.

A beat passes. 'Yeah, maybe,' Poll replies, turning to look out her window so her mother can't see her face. Let them be alright, Lily prays again. Let them stay together.

'How's school?' Poll asks after a bit, and Lily tells her about the student who almost set the science lab on fire, and the other student who's been selected for the Irish Olympic swimming team, and the parents who donated a stone seat to the schoolyard when they had a modest Lotto win. She doesn't mention the student whose older brother has just been diagnosed with leukaemia, or the clash of personalities on the board of management that turns every meeting into a diplomatic challenge, or the accusation of assault that's been levelled quietly – for now – at one of the younger male teachers. Poll doesn't need bad news.

'Any more wedding plans?'

Lily smiles. 'Agneta is trying to fix me up with a florist. I'm not sure I'll be able to escape.'

'Mum, you're *so* uninterested – anyone would think you didn't want to get married.'

'I just don't want a fuss. I'm too old for a fuss.'

The wedding is scheduled for September, a few weeks after her divorce comes through in July. It'll be low key, just the kids and Aidan and Agneta, and Joe's father and stepsister, and a couple of his cousins. They'll exchange rings and vows in an office, and have drinks or a meal somewhere classy afterwards.

Charlie won't be there. *I won't invite you*, she said. *I hope you understand* – and he told her that of course he understood. It was one thing staying friends, one thing being able to get beyond their own changed situation for the sake of their children; it was quite another for Charlie to be there while Lily bound herself permanently to someone else. That would be weird, for everyone involved.

The honeymoon will come later. They're going to wait till the mid-term break for that, end of October – or maybe they'll put it off till the Christmas holidays. Plenty of time for arrangements, although Agneta keeps reminding her that they'll pay top dollar if they leave it till the last minute. They're thinking of a week in Vienna, or possibly Rome. Somewhere ancient and lovely, and not too far away: Lily has never been a fan of long-haul flying.

She reminds herself why she agreed to be his second wife. She lists the reasons in her head. He's a good man. He's kind and generous, and he loves her. He surprises her with gifts; he humours her moods. He's no comedian, but occasionally he can make her laugh. He's a considerate lover, if not the most thrilling.

She wouldn't mind a little more excitement in the bed department. She might work on him. They might download a few blue movies or something.

'And you haven't even looked for a dress yet.'

'Oh, a *dress*. I don't care what I wear.'

'Mum, this is what I mean. It's your *wedding* we're talking about.'

'I know, I know. I'll look soon, I promise. You can help me.'

At length they reach another roundabout, the one where they leave the dual carriageway behind. Half an hour more and they'll be landed. Lily thinks again about the news she's planning to break to them all at the weekend, and wonders how

Poll in particular will take it. Of the four of them, she suspects her daughter will be the most affected.

But before that there's the other news, the more immediate news. She opens her mouth, but Poll gets there first.

'Land's End is going to be weird without Gran there, isn't it?' Giving her mother a fleeting smile that has no happiness in it. She hasn't been near the place since her grandmother left it.

Since her grandmother was forced to leave.

Lily pushes the notion away. She had no choice; there was no other way. When it became obvious that her mother had gone beyond living alone, Lily had done her best to find a fulltime live-in minder without success, so her only option had been to take Mam out of Land's End and bring her to the city.

Not to Lily's home, not with her working fulltime. She was living alone at that stage, Charlie having flown the coop, Poll and Thomas both moved out, and Joe not yet moved in. There was nobody else to help look after Mam, even if Lily had been in a position to take on that responsibility.

She wasn't. Giving up her job was never in the running. She was a teacher, not a nurse – and, anyway, what would they live on if she resigned? The nursing home had a good reputation, everyone said so. The staff members were friendly, the rooms warm and comfortable, and it was close enough for the four of them to visit anytime they wanted. No, there had been no choice – and anyway, at that stage Mam hardly knew what was happening.

And still the guilt festers. Still Lily feels as if she betrayed the woman who brought her up, the woman whose only home, ever, was Land's End.

To give him his due, Charlie never lost contact with his one-time mother-in-law. Following his split with Lily there was an initial wobble – Mam was never afraid to speak her mind, and

Lily didn't doubt that Charlie had got an earful the first time he'd made contact with Mam afterwards – but they'd got over it, and Charlie continued to travel to Land's End to see her, liaising with Lily so there was someone calling most weekends.

Along with the rest of them, Charlie bore witness to Kitty's slow disintegration – and when Lily made the painful decision to remove her from Land's End, he was the one who accompanied her on the final difficult journey. Poll or Thomas would have done it if she'd asked, but she was reluctant to involve them in such a harrowing task – so she turned to Charlie, and he obliged.

Chloë, of course, was never brought to Land's End when Charlie visited, or to the nursing home afterwards. *I think it would be best not to say anything to Kitty, don't you?* he'd asked Lily. *She wouldn't like it.* Wouldn't like him, he meant. Wouldn't take too kindly to him replacing her daughter with a girl her granddaughter's age, so Chloë had remained his dirty little secret. But Lily was glad Mam never knew, never had to be disappointed again in Charlie, whom she'd always had such time for.

But now Chloë is coming to Land's End, for whatever reason, and Lily must put up with it, and be polite. Friendly might be beyond her, but she'll be civil – and maybe Poll will be able to set her feelings aside and do the same.

It's three nights. They'll survive.

Here goes. 'I have a bit of news,' Lily says lightly.

'What?'

'Chloë has decided to join us.'

Dead silence. She risks a glance: Poll is regarding her in disbelief, the colour rising in her face.

'You're not serious. Mum, you *said* she wasn't coming. You *promised.*'

'She wasn't, I was told she wasn't. But I got a call from your Dad, just as I was leaving the—'

'Mum, she *can't* come. Why is she coming? She'll ruin everything!'

'I don't know, love – he didn't say why the change of plan. Look, it's just three nights.'

'Three nights! Why didn't you tell me when you picked me up?'

'Because I thought,' Lily says carefully, 'that you might change your mind –'

'I would have! You *know* I would!'

'– and I really want you here. I need you here, love.' Emotional blackmail – but what else can she do?

'No, you don't – you have all the others!' Her voice rising, on the verge of tears. Again Lily silently curses Charlie.

'Darling, it's my first time home after Gran's … after she's gone. The others don't understand like you, they don't realise how tough it's going to be. I *do* need you, I just do, Poll.'

More silence. Lily risks another glance. Poll is chewing a nail. Lily resists the impulse to slap her hand down.

'Well, I won't be nice to her.'

'You don't have to be. Just promise me there'll be no weapons.'

No smile, no response.

'We can do it, Poll. I don't like it either, but we're not going to let her ruin our weekend, right?'

Silence.

'OK, love? Will you try, for my sake? If I can do it, you can.'

A heavy sigh. 'Yes, alright.'

It's enough. Lily reaches across and squeezes her arm. 'Thank you, love. Really, thank you.'

They drive in silence until they approach the village. There are the familiar shop fronts. McHugh's hardware, yellow bottles of gas lined up outside. The Jolly Fisherman chipper, the descendant of the one where Lily and her friends had got brown bags of chips every Friday with their pocket money. Fogarty's chemist, a barley sugar stick from Gus Fogarty, long dead, whenever Lily called in with Mam. Queally's pub, unchanged since the year dot, and a favourite of Charlie's: he always goes for the spit-and-sawdust places. Fox's shop next door to the church, a new lick of paint since Lily saw it at the end of February.

She throws another glance at Poll, who's taking it all in. 'Remember the ice-creams Gran got you and Thomas in Fox's after Mass every Sunday?'

'Mm.'

Poll swivels in her seat then to look directly at her mother. 'Mum, do you think Gran is still here – I mean, do you think she still exists, on some level?'

The question throws Lily. She searches for a response. 'God, I don't really know the answer to that, love.'

'But what do you *think*?'

'Well … I think, I hope, she's at peace now. I feel … she's in a better place, wherever that might be.'

Does she believe it though? She's a regular Sunday Mass-goer, always has been. She's organised a Mass for Mam this Sunday in the village church – but Mass these days is little more than a habit, something she does as unthinkingly as buying the Sunday paper afterwards. Full of rehashed nonsense – the paper; or maybe both of them – but part of the ritual. Privately she doubts the existence of an afterlife, and has no expectation of meeting either of her parents again.

What would that even be like, coming face to face with the father who would be younger than she is now? How would that even work? And would her mother's mind be magically restored, or would she still look at her daughter without recognition? So many unanswered questions, which of course is where faith comes in, but it's so hard to accept blindly, to believe without a single shred of evidence.

Poll lapses into silence again. They drive out of the village, past the rusting gates of Karina Clery's house, and the tiny old cemetery directly across the road. Five generations of Murphys buried there, ending with Lily's father. Her mother's parents there too, and their parents. Mam isn't among them: the cemetery was closed to new arrivals some years ago, so she's buried in the plot that Charlie and Lily bought in the city a dozen years earlier, when they still assumed they'd be together till death parted them.

What happens to all that now? Who goes where when they die? They'll have to sort that one out. Presumably Charlie will get a new one and leave the other for Lily and Joe, and his children.

His first children. He may well have more, with Chloë so young. He'll be the oldest dad in town if that happens, changing nappies in his sixties. Not that he changed too many nappies when Thomas and Poll were babies – men got away with it then – but Lily suspects he'd have little choice now.

The notion of a second family for him has crossed her mind before this; it occurred to her almost as soon as he took up with Chloë. It's not a prospect she relishes, with all its implications of half-siblings. A whole new set of circumstances to consider, another connection with Chloë for Thomas and Poll to handle.

They turn off the road and take the lane that leads to the house. Lily opens her window a fraction to catch a whiff of the sea. It's just after four, and so far the rain has stayed away.

They round the final bend, and there it is.

Poll

THERE IT IS.

The sight of it, the beautiful familiarity of it. She's taken unawares by the rush of emotion it conveys. A rise within her chest, a saltiness in her throat, a spring of sudden tears. She ducks her head, rummages in her bag for a tissue.

'Alright?' her mother asks, and Poll says yes, yes, pressing the tissue to her eyes, gathering herself together.

'I just need a minute,' she says, the words hidden and buried, but Mum seems to hear, and gets out of the car.

Poll leans back against her seat and closes her eyes and breathes. In and out, in and out. It's too much, the sight of it and the knowledge that Gran is gone from it, and the awful, awful thought that Chloë will soon be here, that they'll have to share it with her. She doesn't belong here, she has no right here, but she's coming and they'll have to put up with her.

She wanted Dad to come on his own. She wanted to pretend, just for a weekend, that Chloë had never become part of their lives. She'd thought there was a tiny chance that she and Dad might be able to be like they were before, but that's definitely not going to happen now.

After several minutes, when Mum has vanished into the house, when the urge to bawl has abated, she opens her eyes and takes it all in.

The trees are unchanged but the hydrangea bushes are overgrown. The railing around the veranda needs painting, the window frames too. It's showing its age, it has an air of neglect that breaks her heart to see – but it's still Land's End, still the place she loves, the place she remembers from two years ago, and twenty-two years ago, and all the years in between.

She opens the car door, and the pure air rushes in to envelop her. She gets out and walks slowly to the gate and takes in the ocean, spread out before her. Waiting for her to come and see it again. The beach, curving away to her right, the water pushing and pulling at the shore like it always has, like it always will. When she can't sleep in the city she travels here in her mind, to the rattle of the pebbles that soothes her and calms her and allows her to let go.

She returns to the car. She reaches into the back seat and hauls out her bag of bedding and climbs the steps to the house, feeling as if she's walking into the past. Her past.

Just inside the front door she stops.

The smells.

The faint whiff of damp, the delicate sweetness of old wood, the heady tang of long-unopened books, the saltiness of the sea. The beautiful composite scent of Land's End, still here, still blessedly unchanged. She walks slowly through the hall, taking everything in. Remembering what she never forgot.

There is the mahogany hallstand, a wedding gift from her grandfather's parents when he married into this house. There is the phone table with its marble top, there the spindly-legged chair in the corner, there the copper bucket for umbrellas, there the thin crack running diagonally through three of the small black and white floor tiles, caused years ago by a sewing machine in need of a service that slid off the trolley being used to transport it from the house.

Everything is as it was, no physical difference that she can see –

Wait.

Is there a new quality to the air, an indefinable change? Is that what causes her pulse to quicken, her skin to tingle with a wash of goosebumps? She comes to another stop just before the stairs, arms still wrapped around her load.

'Gran,' she breathes, lowering the bag.

Is it? Can it be? Is she imagining the presence of her grandmother, back where she belongs? She can almost feel her, almost see her – but is it wishful thinking? Is it just her overactive imagination, willing it to be true?

'There you are.'

Her mother emerges from the kitchen. Poll watches her pause, frowning, in the doorway. Maybe she senses it too.

'Are you alright, love?' she asks. 'You're very pale.' Not sensing anything then, her concern only for Poll. 'Is this hard for you? Is that it?'

'No, it's fine.' Poll will say nothing. It would sound ridiculous, the fancies of a young child. 'How are you?' she asks, remembering Mum's comments in the car. *I need you*, she said. *The others don't understand like you*, she said.

'I'm grand,' her mother replies, and indeed she looks unaffected. She's been back, of course, over the last two years. She and Joe made several day trips to check on the empty house, particularly in the winter months. But now it's different. Now her mother is dead. It must be hard for her.

'I've put you and Aidan in the green room – did I mention?'

'Yes. Great.' Poll stands at the bottom of the stairs and looks upward. Sees in her mind's eye Gran bustling down, arms laden with sheets and towels.

'I've to head back to the village,' Mum says. 'We forgot to pick up milk. I won't be long. I'll leave your case on the veranda.'

'OK.'

'The heat is on – and I've opened the bedroom windows, just for an hour or so. Air the place out a bit.'

'Right.'

When the sound of her mother's car has died away Poll climbs the stairs, bumping her bag of bedding along behind her. 'Gran,' she whispers again, and then more loudly: 'Gran. It's me, it's Poll. I've come back. I'm back, Gran.'

In the green room she holds a sheet by its bottom edge and flings it out over the double bed. It billows and drifts down: she tucks in the four corners, runs a hand along a centre crease to banish it – and as she does so, echoes return of her childish self doing exactly the same with Gran, summer morning after summer morning, year after year.

The sash window has a broken cord. Mum has propped it open with the same stick that was there when Poll was a child. They never slept in this room when they came on holidays: the green room was for paying visitors, out of bounds unless Poll was helping Gran to clean it after breakfast, when the people who'd used it had packed up and moved on. Poll would prop the window open with the stick before pulling off the sheets and pillowcases and bundling them with the towels on the landing.

She and Gran would make up the bed with clean linen and put fresh towels in the bathroom. Poll would flick Gran's feather duster around – real ostrich feathers! – alert all the while for anything the overnight people might have left behind.

Once she found a ring on the floor beside the dressing table.

Gold it was, or gold-coloured anyway, with a small red stone. Too big for her, too loose even for her thumb, but still she coveted it. Couldn't have it, of course – Gran posted it right back to the woman who'd forgotten it. But from then on Poll had kept an eye out, and hoped.

She sits on the edge of the bed now and slips off her shoes. Her city shoes, not wanted here. The bedside rug feels thin and rough under her feet, not soft like their pale grey bedroom carpet at home. But this rug was expensive once upon a time, shipped from America along with its counterpart in the room next door by Gran's sister Cora, a gift when Gran started up the B&B in the late seventies.

Cora was the only one of us who ever had money, Gran had told her. *She married a banker, Albert Finkleblatt, when she was twenty-seven and he was in his forties. He was as rich as anything; their wedding was the talk of Chicago. Cora was his third wife – you should have seen my mother's face when she heard that. The marriage didn't last though: poor Albert drowned only three years later when they were sailing in the Caribbean on his boat. Cora was left a rich widow but she never looked at another man, and I'm sure it wasn't for want of offers. There must have been plenty of gold-diggers sniffing around.*

Gran had had four sisters and one brother. For as long as she could remember, Poll was able to recite them in order from the top down: Maud, Gabriel, Pauline, Cora, Teresa, Kitty. Six children, just one boy among them. Kitty, Gran, was the only one to forgo the boat to America. *Maud and Gabriel went together, and they sent for Pauline the year after. Cora and Teresa followed, a few years later.*

Did you never want to go? Poll asked, picturing tearful embraces as trunks were loaded, promises to write, children lifted to be kissed goodbye, waving handkerchiefs as the ship pulled away, siren blaring. Passengers lined up at the rail for a last glimpse of Ireland before it disappeared over the horizon, often forever. *Did they never send for you?*

I couldn't go, my love, Gran replied, not a trace of regret in her voice. *Who'd have looked after our parents if we'd all left? Someone had to stay at home.*

None of her siblings had returned, even for a visit. She never saw any of them again. Maud and Pauline died in a boarding house fire, a month or so after Cora and Teresa's arrival in New York. Gabriel fell off the face of the earth for years after that, no word of him at all until Gran got a letter out of the blue from somewhere in Wisconsin: he'd been saved by Jesus, and was now working on a ranch in return for bed and board, and going from door to door in his spare time to spread the Good News.

The letter had been folded into a small blue Bible, along with a photograph. Thinner and hairier than Gran remembered, but undoubtedly Gabriel. Tragically, he was to die two years after that, aged just forty-nine, when a horse bolted and kicked him in the head. Saved once, but Jesus must have been busy the second time.

Cora survived into old age. She died ten years before her youngest sister in a retirement village in Arizona. No children to look after her, no niece or nephew, even: not one of the five emigrants left a child behind them.

Teresa, the second youngest, didn't stay long in the States. Two years after her departure from Ireland she wrote to say she was moving to Peru with a friend, Wilma, to work with orphan children in a home run by Irish nuns.

By the time she died, aged sixty-eight, the pair had covered most of the Central and South American countries, always looking after orphans. Teresa had met her Waterloo in Bolivia, swept away by a mudslide that also claimed the lives of several of her little charges.

A few weeks after that news reached her, Gran opened the door of Land's End and saw a tiny brown wrinkled woman standing on the mat, eyes swimming with incipient tears, and made the acquaintance, finally, of her sister's friend Wilma.

Father from Trinidad, mother from Cork. Working in a New York diner until she met Teresa and they joined forces, both attracted by the idea of a missionary life. *She was my world,* Wilma sobbed, over tea and a buttered slice of Gran's fruit brack. *We were everything to each other.*

And down all the years, with all the letters that had arrived unfailingly from her sister every six weeks or so, Gran had never guessed, never questioned the friendship that was, it would appear, something rather more than that.

Gran, the youngest of six, had outlived them all. She'd nursed her parents through their final years, and afterwards she'd married Robert Murphy, a local farmer who had waited patiently for her. *He moved in here,* she told Poll. *There was no way I was leaving this house. He knew that.*

The arrangement suited both of them. Robert's farm was just a few miles down the road, easily managed with Land's End as his base. Fifteen years after he'd walked Gran down the aisle and carried her over the threshold of the house she already inhabited (she insisted), and twelve years after he held his baby daughter in his arms for the first time, Robert Murphy dropped dead in the back garden with a paintbrush in his hand.

As a child, Poll revelled in her grandmother's stories, fascinated by tales of the grand-uncle and grand-aunts she'd never met, and the man who'd died years before he could become her grandfather. *Tell me again about Cora and Albert Finkleblatt's wedding,* she'd beg, Gran's memories far more compelling than the tale of an imaginary servant girl who went to a boring ball in shoes made of glass – glass! – and met a boring imaginary prince. Gran's stories were full of real people, full of real tragedies and triumphs. *Tell me about Abigail coming to visit. Tell me about Gabriel sending you the Bible.*

Well, Gabriel ... Gran would say, her gaze going far beyond Poll as she reached into the past and pulled out her recollections. And now Gran is dead, and the stories she shared with her granddaughter, and the scrapbooks she filled with photos that came to her tucked into letters from America, are all Poll has left of her.

But now she might be here in this house, or her spirit might be. Whatever was left behind when her body shut down might have returned home to Land's End. Poll so much wants to believe this.

'I need your help,' she tells Gran. 'I need you to stop me being afraid.'

Afraid of being happy – that's it, isn't it? Convinced, for some unknown reason, that she doesn't deserve it.

Through the open window she's aware of the soft rumble of the sea; she can smell its perfume. Gran will help her if she can. Before the weekend is out, if Gran has any say in the matter, Poll will know what to do.

She retrieves her weekend case from the hall and finds her swimsuit and changes quickly. She hangs her trouser suit in the wardrobe – silly choice for Land's End, where nobody dresses up: what was she thinking? She pulls on jeans and a blue top over the togs, and slips her feet into the yellow pumps she bought in a little market when she went to France last spring to meet Aidan's daughter.

We were young, he told her. Early on, their third or fourth date. *We were children ourselves. Before Loulou was a year old, we broke up. Éloïse moved back to France with her, to the little town she came from.*

Were you married?

No. Éloïse has married in the meantime though. He's French too. They have another daughter.

Loulou is sixteen now, quiet and not unfriendly. Petite and blue-eyed and fair-haired, with hesitant English and a grin that made her look younger, and Aidan's mouth and chin.

Poll also met Loulou's mother. To her relief, Éloïse wasn't the chic, beautiful Frenchwoman she'd been anticipating, but rather a fairly unremarkable creature, small and thin and not given to smiling. Perfectly styled dark hair, ramrod straight back. Wearing a heady scent and earrings that flashed green when she moved her head, and a grey shift dress with the nubby finish of raw silk. It might have cost a bit, but it didn't flatter her sallow complexion.

Looking down her nose at Poll, it felt like. Assessing her through narrowed eyes, checking her out quite openly and finding her wanting, if the dismissive attitude was anything to go by. Speaking mainly to Aidan in rapid French as Poll and Loulou sat by.

Oh, who cares about Éloïse, and what she may or may not think of Poll? Who cares about any of that, when Poll and Aidan might be on the brink of parting, when Poll might be plagued and tormented until she splits them up?

In the kitchen she unpacks the box of food Mum left on the table. Salmon steaks and salads, apple crumble and a large carton of cream waiting to be whipped. Five for dinner tonight instead of the expected four. Thomas and Aidan arriving tomorrow to make seven, the fullest the house will have been since the days of the B&B.

At the sink she fills a glass with water and raises it to her lips. The metallic taste catches her unawares, something she'd forgotten about. *Perfectly harmless*, Gran always said, and Poll and Thomas never minded it, but Dad kept a covert supply of bottled water in their room.

'Hello?'

She jumps, the glass almost flying from her hand. A man stands in the doorway, holding a battered galvanised bucket, his face covered with dismay at her reaction. 'Sorry, Poll, sorry, I thought you heard me coming in. The hall door was open, so I just ...'

Another thing she'd forgotten, the way people simply wander in when they see an open door around here. 'Gerry – you're very welcome. I was miles away. Will you sit down?'

'Only I heard,' he says, remaining on his feet, 'that ye were here, and I wanted to put my head in and see were ye alright for everything.'

Not an hour landed, the rural grapevine alive and kicking. They must have been spotted going through the village. 'We're down for the weekend,' she tells him, 'Mum and me, and Thomas and Dad and ... well, the rest are on their way. Just a kind of ... get-together. Mum's idea. Just to ... remember Gran.'

He shifts his bucket to allow his right hand to make a swift approximation of the sign of the cross. 'Kitty, God rest her. Great neighbour. Place was never the same without her.'

'... You were very good to come all the way to the funeral.'

'Not at all, not at all, wanted to pay my respects.' He sets the bucket on the edge of the table. 'A few spuds there, that's all.'

'Thank you, Gerry, that's very kind. Will you have tea? Mum is gone for milk – she'll be back any minute.'

But already he's edging away, palms raised. 'No, no, I won't stay. Ye'll be getting ready for the dinner. Tell Lily I said hello. I might see ye over the few days.' And he's gone, as suddenly as he came.

The potatoes are slightly larger than table-tennis balls, and covered with a wafer-thin biscuit-coloured skin to which small clods of dark brown soil still attach. Poll dips her head to inhale their thick, honest smell. She imagines Gerry pushing his fork into the soft ground and lifting them from the earth. She adores new potatoes, loves their waxy yellow flesh, the fresh delicate taste. So often they enjoyed them here, boiled for a few minutes in their skins and topped with a slice of the salty butter that Gran used to churn by hand.

Gerry must be in his late sixties now, maybe a bit older. His farm had doubled in size when he bought the land from Gran after Granddad died. A good-looking man in his younger days, the black hair washed grey now, the features beneath it grown craggy and weather-beaten, but still a warm light in the hazel eyes, still a face that commands attention.

Never married, though, never a woman in the running, as far as Poll is aware. Did she have a little crush on him, long ago? She fancies she did. She and Thomas had spent so much time on Gerry's farm as kids: safe enough in those days to let the two of them ramble off together from Land's End, with strict instructions to go straight to the farmhouse. She dimly remembers Thomas holding her hand all the way, probably on Mum's direction too. Half a mile up the road at the most, but to her small self it probably seemed like a marathon.

Poor Gerry had had great patience with them, never hunting them away, showing them how to scatter feed for the hens, and where to look for the carelessly laid eggs, only admonishing them gently when they slid down his haystacks, messing up his carefully sculpted mounds.

She can't remember when she lost interest in the farm. She's fairly sure she was still young, no more than six or seven. Maybe she simply outgrew it; maybe helping Gran at Land's End began to appeal more. Thomas continued to go there for another while, heading off after breakfast most days, but eventually he grew out of it too, and their only contact with Gerry after that was the occasional conversation if they met him on the road, or after Mass on Sundays.

A memory drops into her head, Gerry taking her and Thomas for a spin around a scalped field once on his tractor. She couldn't have been more than four or five but she can recall the thrill of it, like a ride in a fairground bumper car. Mum nearly hit the roof when they went home and told her, in their innocence. Wanted to go around there and then and let Gerry have it, but Gran talked her out of it, promised to have a word with him herself.

Maybe that was why Poll stopped going to the farm: maybe Mum decided it wasn't safe for her any more. So long ago, so hard to remember.

She puts the bucket on a shelf in the scullery. The potatoes will be used tomorrow night, with whatever they end up having for dinner. They can pick up something from the supermarket, or maybe her father will bring dinner. It'll be steaks if he does – he loves his steak.

It's going to be so difficult to be civil to Chloë. It's going to be so hard to smile and be polite, to hide the feelings she can't banish.

She's your dad's choice, Aidan said, when Poll spoke to him of her resentment of Chloë. *Whether you like it or not he chose her, and they're together now. You're better off making the best of it.*

She'll have to try. She'll have to do her best to make the best of it.

She hears a car approach, and prays it's not her father's. Let her not have to endure them on her own, even for a few minutes. Let it be Mum back from the village, or Joe, having made an early getaway.

She slips into the sitting room and peers through the bay window – and to her relief she sees Joe's dark green Land Rover pulling up next to the trees. She watches him climb out, sees him raise his arms skyward in a stretch, tilt his neck this way and that to take the kinks out of it. He's more of a walker than a driver.

She goes to the front door and pulls it wide open. She smiles a welcome as she crosses the gravel. 'Joe – you made it.'

'Poll.' He hugs her like he always does, like he did the first time they met. It took her aback then – a friend of her mother's, a stranger to her till that moment – but she soon grew accustomed to it. Now she likes that he's a hugger.

'Good to see you,' he says. 'You're looking well.' He smells of oranges. She wishes he'd shave off his beard, or at least tidy it up a bit. 'I made my escape, I ducked away as soon as I could.'

'You're nice and early: Mum and I aren't long here.'

'And when are you expecting your dad?'

'Not till later. He's bringing Chloë,' she adds.

'Is he? I thought she had other plans.'

'Seems not.'

'Right so.'

No sign of resentment or dismay – why would there be? Chloë didn't move in with his father, Chloë didn't drive a wedge through his family. He hardly knows her.

He takes an army-green rucksack from the passenger seat and slings it across his shoulder. 'What have you done with your mother's car?'

'She had to go back to the village for milk. I'm surprised you didn't meet her on the way.'

'No sign of her. So how are you?' he asks, following her into the house.

'I'm fine, Joe. Leave your bag there, come into the kitchen.'

She likes him. Impossible not to, nothing to dislike – and he can hardly be blamed for the break-up of her parents' marriage, coming on the scene so long afterwards. She likes him but they're not close, not yet. Maybe when he becomes her stepfather, maybe when she gets used to that, they might connect on a deeper level. They might be able to recreate what she and Dad used to have.

Or maybe not that. No, probably not that.

'I'll put the kettle on,' she says, bringing it to the sink, 'and then I'll leave you. I want to grab a swim before dinner.'

His look of horror is almost comical. 'You're not serious? You're going *swimming*? It still feels like winter.'

'Oh, come on – it's not *that* cold. And it'll technically be summer in a couple of days.'

'Technically won't make it any warmer. I'm happy to bundle up in any weather and go walking – but swimming in the Atlantic, in anything less than a heatwave? Forget it. Have you a wetsuit at least?'

'Never wore one.'

He shakes his head. 'You're made of tougher stuff than me, and no mistake.'

They hear a car pulling up outside. 'That'll be Mum,' Poll says, and he goes out to meet her. From what she can see he gets on OK with Dad, but there's bound to be some awkwardness between them, isn't there? Mum and Dad were married for so long, and now here's Joe with Mum. Joe, at least, must feel a bit uncomfortable in Dad's company.

Was it such a good idea of Mum's, assembling them all here? Was it a bit ambitious, expecting them all to get along? Mum never gave a reason for the trip, just said she'd like it to happen. They'd all assumed, or at least Poll did, that she was feeling nostalgic about the place, now that Gran was gone.

Poll hears the murmur of her voice in the driveway, a short burst of answering laughter from Joe. She waits in the kitchen until they reappear.

'I met Karina in the supermarket,' Mum says, crossing to the fridge, depositing the milk inside. 'Couldn't get away. She'll drop over some eggs to us in the morning.'

'How is she?'

'As daft as ever. Just back from a week on some Buddhist island in Scotland. Chanting at dawn on the shore.'

'She's not a Buddhist, is she?'

'Not at all.'

'Gerry called,' Poll tells her. 'He brought potatoes. I put them in the scullery.'

'Oh, lovely. They're all so good around here.'

'Lily, your daughter is talking about going for a swim,' Joe puts in, scalding the teapot. 'Maybe you can make her see sense.'

Mum shudders. 'I wish I could. You won't go out of your depth, will you, Poll?'

'I told you I wouldn't.'

'And don't stay out long, or you'll get pneumonia.'

'I won't.'

Within minutes she's immersed in the cold salty water, skin tingling, every nerve ending alive, blood racing through her veins. She'd forgotten the joy of this, the absolute exhilaration. How can Mum and Joe not want to do it too? She strikes out in a fast, powerful crawl, watching the ocean bed fly past beneath her, instinctively finding the familiar rhythm with her breathing.

When she tires she flips onto her back, panting, and listens to the dull comforting roar of the sea in her ears. Above her, although the daylight hasn't yet begun to fade, she can see a single star piercing the sky to the north. Gulls wheel past, making for the shore.

She wonders if her father and Chloë will have arrived when she returns.

Thomas won't know about Chloë coming until he gets here tomorrow. He probably won't take any notice; he doesn't seem to have a view on her one way or the other. He dodges the issue whenever Poll tries to draw him out, says something noncommittal like it's none of their business, which infuriates her. Surely he can't approve though. Nobody could approve of that mismatch.

Poll remembers Chloë from school. They didn't hang around together then, nothing like that. For a start, Chloë was a year ahead of her – but even if they'd been sitting beside one another day in, day out through years of schooling, they wouldn't have found a single thing to say. They simply had nothing in common. They were like two different species, their lives light years apart.

Chloë was never in a gang. She wasn't part of any group at all that you could point to. Chloë was just ... Chloë. But she was never bullied in the way some lone girls were, girls who didn't ally themselves with at least one or two others. Nobody ever bumped against Chloë in the corridor, causing her to drop an armful of books. Nobody made fun of her; nobody sniggered at her behind a hand.

Even aged thirteen, which was when twelve-year-old Poll first became aware of her, there was an air of something about Chloë, a sort of dreamy assuredness that told you she never lay awake worrying about whether a boy liked her, or if her shoes were cool enough, or if anyone at all was going to send her a Valentine card. Right through the terrifying obstacle course of adolescence, through the handful of years when Poll was floundering about with the rest of them, feeling her way to her late teens, Chloë Richardson acted like she had everything figured out.

Now and again Poll would spot her around town at weekends, generally in the company of more than one male, most of whom looked older than her. She always seemed completely at ease, dressed in loose T-shirts or sweaters and perfectly faded jeans, a bandanna or scarf pulled carelessly through a tousle of shiny brown curls that were sliced through with gold. She looked, more often than not, as if she'd just climbed out of bed – and yet, she was so … *together*.

To Poll, she was the epitome of effortless cool, curving an arm nonchalantly around the waist of one of her companions, or threading a couple of fingers through someone's belt loop. Once Poll had observed her slipping a hand into the back pocket of a boy's jeans and leaving it there. Hinting, by this casual intimacy, that she might not have spent the previous night alone.

And now she spends her nights with a man old enough to be her father.

Poll kicks out, creating an arc of droplets. Energised by her swim, empowered by her race through the water, she resolves not to let Chloë get her down. One evening is really all she has to endure – tomorrow she'll do her own thing, keep clear of her as much as she can, and then Aidan will arrive to offer moral support.

A second star blinks on above her. A breeze blows a scatter of drops onto her face. She's getting cold. She flips onto her stomach and moves off in a smooth breaststroke, hugging her resolve, keeping her gaze on the big blue house as she swims, pulling it closer to her with every stroke.

Thomas

'WHAT KIND OF BREAD DID SHE USE? JUST REGULAR white?'

'I think so.'

'OK, that's what we'll use then. Pity we have no day-old stuff – it's better made with that. We'll have to make do with today's.'

They have no day-old bread because at the end of each afternoon Freda makes crumbs from leftover bits of loaves and freezes most of them to use in meatballs and fish cakes, or as a topping for macaroni cheese, or to stuff tomatoes and mushrooms. The rest she brings home for her bird table.

She butters half a dozen slices of white now and cuts them into triangles while Thomas greases a pie dish. 'I don't suppose you know if she flavoured it with cinnamon or nutmeg.'

'Haven't a clue.'

'In that case, we'll go for a bit of both. Give it a nice warm kick.' Freda hands him a spice jar. 'You can grate the nutmeg.'

'How much?'

'About a teaspoon.'

The idea of bread-and-butter pudding had come to him in

bed the night before, as his thoughts meandered back to their summers at Land's End. He recalled the wonderful food Gran would make for them: a warm loaf of griddle bread every morning; potato cakes for tea sometimes, fried on the pan till they were golden brown; gooseberry tarts with fruit from her own bushes; rock buns, crumbly and delicious.

And then he remembered her bread-and-butter pudding, served up without fail after every Sunday lunch. Tantalisingly spicy, the bread layers liberally sprinkled with plump raisins, the whole dish topped with a crunchy sugary crust and accompanied with a homemade custard that tasted nothing like the stuff Mum made from powder out of a tin.

Bread-and-butter pudding. He hadn't come across it since the Land's End holidays, hadn't thought about it for years. The memory of it made his mouth water.

As soon as he'd come in to work this morning he'd asked Freda if she had a recipe. Of course she had – and when he told her what he was planning, she offered to help him assemble it after closing time. *It'll only take a few minutes. You can bake it at home, and reheat it when you want it.*

He'll bring it to Land's End: it'll be his food contribution. He likes the thought of them eating one of Gran's dishes during the weekend, a kind of homage to her. *I'll bring a dessert for Saturday,* he'd told Mum on the phone, and when she asked what it was, he'd said he wasn't sure yet. She'll assume it's some leftover from the café.

He runs the small round nutmeg against a grater. 'You should put this on the menu,' he says.

'We could give it a go,' Freda agrees, cracking eggs into a bowl. 'Bit of retro. Bit of nostalgia.'

She'd given him a Mass card when he'd told her that his grandmother had died. *Sorry for your loss,* she'd said, her face full of sympathy as she handed it over, making Thomas feel even guiltier that he wasn't grief-stricken by Gran's death.

He remembers when he first began to wonder about Gran. It was on one of his solo stays at Land's End, six or eight months before she was taken to the nursing home. Over the course of a single conversation she'd asked him the same question three times. When he returned to the city and reported it to Mum, she'd brushed it off.

I wouldn't take any notice, she said. *She's getting older: absent-mindedness is to be expected.* But before much more time had elapsed it became apparent that it wasn't just absent-mindedness: it was something more sinister than that. Everyone began to notice the change in her, the steady deterioration, the falling-apart that was awful to see.

By the time Thomas visited again, a couple of months later, Gran's Alzheimer's had been diagnosed. A home help had been found for her in the village, a woman who came each morning and spent several hours at the house. Gran's conversations were more halting now, with frequent silences while she searched for a word she would always have known. She still recognised Thomas but she'd stopped using his name, stopped showing the interest in his life that she would previously have done.

Eventually her needs went beyond the capabilities of the home help, and the nursing home became the only option. The end of an era, he remembers thinking. He'd never known the house without Gran in it, *she*'d never known another home, and now she was gone from it. The inexplicable sadness of life.

But he finds he can't grieve for her, now that she's gone. He was very fond of Gran, but he can't mourn her death. He hated that she'd fallen victim to one of the cruellest diseases, hated to see what it did to her – but what he has largely felt in the weeks since she died is relief.

How can he not be glad that she's been set free from the foggy, bewildering place the world had become for her? How could it not be the best outcome, for her and for everyone else?

Imagine trying to explain that to Freda, though, whose big, generous heart puts him to shame. Imagine telling her he was glad Gran was gone.

'My favourite dessert as a kid,' she says, sprinkling raisins, 'was lemon meringue pie. The first time I ate it, I honestly thought I'd died and gone to Heaven. Pass over that nutmeg.'

He watches her stirring the spices into the sugar. She's a natural cook, rarely measuring her ingredients, seeming to know by instinct what will work. She regards artificial sweeteners and low-fat alternatives with deep suspicion – *Leave food alone*, she says, *don't mess with it* – and her creamy chowders and buttery cookies and luscious cakes certainly go down well with her loyal following.

She and Thomas had met in the hospital, where he was an unhappy porter and she worked in the canteen. *I'm opening my own place*, she told him one day, as he sat over the pot of tea she made for him during his break each afternoon. *I'm leaving next week. Wish me luck.*

He couldn't say he knew her well. She was a friendly face, one of the few people who seemed genuinely happy working in the hospital – but now she was about to leave it. More to make small talk than out of real interest, Thomas enquired as to the café's whereabouts.

It's at the corner of Market Place and Davis Street. There was a deli there before – you might remember it.

He remembered it. *I'll be living quite near there soon*, he told her. *I'm moving in with friends, to help them with their mortgage*. Finally leaving home, at the ripe old age of twenty-five.

You'll have to pop in, Freda said, *as soon as you're settled. I hope to be up and running in a few weeks.*

I will – and he did, not long after the café doors opened for the first time. He offered to take Sam and Matt, his two new housemates, out to lunch on their first day off together. *I know a place,* he said, so they tracked down Glorious Food and ordered bowls of French onion soup on which floated chunks of crusty cheesy bread, and followed it with an excellent berry and plum crumble.

I'd have more choices on the menu, Freda told them, *if I had someone to help, but I can't afford that yet.* Dark circles under her eyes – and yet her face shone with the same cheerfulness he remembered from the canteen. Maybe she was predisposed to be happy. He assumed opening her own café to be the realisation of a long-held dream, and he was glad for her. She was the kind of person you wanted to achieve her dream.

But glancing around the small space – just seven tables, and a counter by the window with high stools – Thomas saw two tables not yet cleared, and a crumpled paper napkin on the floor, and something else – a baby's soother? – poking out from behind a chair leg. She definitely needed help.

He thought about the hospital, where he'd been working for the best part of a year, where as a porter he was pulled at from all quarters. He thought about the tight-faced matron, who hadn't bothered to learn his name, and the fleet of harried nurses who 'borrowed' him whenever he appeared, and the patients who would call to him as soon as they spotted his uniform, looking for bedpans or water or extra pillows or blankets, none of which he was authorised to provide.

He imagined working in the little café with Freda as his boss, and there was nothing about the notion that didn't appeal to him. *Think of me when you can afford it,* he told her. *I'm not a cook, but I can do everything else. In fact, I suspect I'd make a very good general dogsbody.*

She gave him a grateful smile. *Wouldn't I love it, Thomas – but don't hold your breath. I'm barely keeping body and soul together here.* She rushed off to attend to another customer, and for the rest of the day his mind was occupied with finding a way to achieve what was rapidly becoming his new ambition.

The following evening he phoned home, and his father answered. *Could I borrow some money?* Thomas asked.

There was a pause. *How much?*

Enough to live on for a while, a few months, maybe more. You needn't give it all to me at once – you could do it weekly, or monthly.

Another few seconds ticked by. *What are you planning, Thomas?*

He told his father about the café, and Freda needing help. *As soon as she starts to make a profit she'll pay me, and I can start repaying you. It's just that it might take a while.*

You want to work in a café?

His father's tone was mild but he heard the unspoken criticism, heard the silent judgement. *I think I'd like it*, he said. *I know you hoped for better.*

It's not that, his father said, but Thomas thought it was exactly that. *How long has it been open?*

He closed his eyes. *Not long, a couple of weeks. But the food is excellent, and it was nearly full when I was there yesterday.* He didn't add that 'nearly full' meant four tables occupied.

And if it goes bust?

I'll get another job and pay you back, every cent.

Again there was a short silence. *And you really think you'd enjoy this kind of work?* Voice full of doubt, unable or unwilling to believe that anyone would opt for such a humble occupation.

I would. I know I would.

Thomas wasn't sure where the conviction was coming from.

He'd never worked in a café, or anywhere remotely similar. He wasn't even all that interested in food; if it was edible, he ate it in large amounts. But the more he thought about making his way to the little space each day, and having someone like Freda as his boss, the more certain he became that it was what he wanted.

Let me run it by your mother and get back to you – and in less than half an hour Thomas's phone rang.

What rent are you paying?

Thomas told him.

And you'd need living expenses on top of that.

Not much: I have a bit saved. His savings were modest, but his needs were few.

Right, his father said. *We got off lightly with only two years of college: we figure you can have this.*

I'll pay you back, Thomas repeated.

Let's not worry about that just now. How about we give it three months and see how it goes?

Three months felt a little ambitious. Three months to get her little café established, to be reasonably sure of its survival. Then again, how long could he expect his father to support him?

Great, he said, *thanks a lot*. He'd make it work.

The following day, aware of a quiet but insistent twinge of fear – what the hell was he doing? – he handed in his notice at the hospital. *Going on to better things?* his superior enquired, and Thomas replied, with far more assurance than he felt, that he'd been given an opportunity to go into business with a friend. The nerve of him, and Freda wholly unaware.

On his way home from work he called to the café again. It was approaching closing time, with chairs upended on tables and Freda mopping the floor, and the last of the customers departed.

Thomas, she said, her smile quizzical. *There's coffee in the—*

I haven't come for coffee, he told her. *I've come to offer my services.* He explained the situation, watching the smile drop slowly, watching her bewilderment increase.

You've resigned? My God – Thomas, I told you I couldn't pay you.

You don't have to, not right away. He told her of his father's pledge. *We have three months – we can do it, Freda.*

Her frown didn't budge. *But I can't have you working here for nothing – it wouldn't feel right. Maybe they'll take you back at the hospital if you explain that you made a mistake.*

She was going to take some persuading. *I didn't make a mistake,* he said. *I hate that job.* Until the words were out, he hadn't realised how true they were. *Look, this is my own choice, and I feel it's the right one – and my parents can well afford to support me for a while. They're both professionals, they're earning good money.*

That's not the point, Thomas. You really should have checked with me.

I couldn't, he said. *I knew you'd never agree.*

She made no response to this, only continued to regard him with dismay – and it suddenly hit him that she'd never actually asked if he'd like a job. He'd offered his services, in a vague sometime-in-the-future way, and she hadn't said no – but this was different. This was turning up unannounced and foisting himself on her. This was leaving her with little choice but to take him on, now that he'd burnt his bridges at the hospital.

How cavalier, how foolhardy his actions seemed now. She was right, of course – he should have thought it through more, should have come to her before resigning and told her what he was thinking. It would have given her the chance to explain – and no doubt she would have done it very kindly – that she really needed someone who could cook, or someone more chatty, or someone younger.

Someone different. Someone else.

I'm sorry, he said. *You're completely right. I shouldn't have assumed you wanted me. I'll find somewhere else* – but even as he was speaking, he was thinking, Where? What? Even as the words were forming, his heart was sinking slowly.

Oh Thomas, she said quickly, *you'd be my first choice, if I was in a position to take anyone on. You're honest and diligent: I can see that, and it's all I'd need. But I can't have you working for no money, I just can't.*

His mind was put at rest. All he had to do now was convince her to take him. *Listen,* he said, *how about we try it for a month, just one month? If it'll make you feel better I'll keep an eye out for other jobs, but let me come in for a month and see how it goes.*

Her face was still creased with doubt. *A month.*

One month – and if it doesn't work out, I'll find something else.

Promise?

I promise. But he knew it wouldn't come to that. He'd make himself indispensable. She'd come to rely on him; he'd make sure of it.

In the end she agreed, still somewhat reluctantly, to give it a go. Two weeks later – and just a week, if he'd only known it, before his parents were to announce their separation – Thomas left the hospital for the last time, and the following morning he started at the café.

And right from the start, after three different college courses in two years, after a subsequent series of jobs that were miles from a right fit for him, he knew he'd finally found his calling. He did everything in the café except cook. He took orders and served food and cleared the tables and washed up, and there was no part of any of it that he objected to. He was busy enough to marvel that Freda had coped alone for her initial few weeks, and to be reassured that his help had indeed been sorely needed. She fed him during the day – *I can do that at least* – and frequently sent him home with leftovers enough for three, much to Sam and Matt's delight.

His parents' surprise separation didn't impact on his working life: his father's weekly payments into Thomas's bank account continued. At the end of his first month, Freda raised the topic of his continuing lack of wages. *I still feel so bad about that. The café is barely staying afloat – I can't pay myself, let alone anyone else. I'm tempted to find you another job, just to ease my conscience.*

Don't even think about it, he told her. *I love it here. You're the one doing me the favour* – and she laughed and said in that case she couldn't be unkind enough to send him packing. They went on in this fashion, Freda expressing concern at his situation every so often, he reassuring, until finally the little café showed a profit, eleven weeks after he'd started, and she presented him with his first pay cheque.

I'm mortified at how little it is. I'll make it more when I can.

Nearly four years later his wages are still only two-thirds what they paid him in the hospital, and he hardly has a cent left over at the end of each month, but he rises every working morning with a smile on his face.

They're a good fit. They're comfortable together. She doesn't feel like his boss, never has.

His father refused to be repaid. *I don't need it,* he told Thomas. *I'm just glad you're happy in the job.* His parents have paid separate visits to the café – of course they were both charmed by Freda, who refused payment for their coffee and cake – but Thomas is well aware of their bemusement that their son has ended up where he is. No matter. He's content and solvent, and that will have to do them.

'Now,' Freda says, covering the dish with tinfoil, 'be sure to keep it upright on the way home – you don't want your liquid spilling out. Bake it at gas five for about forty minutes until it's set and the top is golden. There should still be a bit of give when you press down on it.'

'OK.'

'And here,' she produces a folded sheet of paper from her apron pocket, 'I wrote out the recipe for custard.'

'I was going to get a tin,' he tells her, just to see her reaction.

As expected, she looks scandalised. 'Thomas Cunningham, you can't ruin a good bread-and-butter pudding with custard from a tin – it's not a patch on the real thing. Didn't your grandmother make her own?'

'Yes, but she—'

'Look, it's really easy – all you need are eggs, milk and sugar, because I'm going to give you the vanilla extract and the cornflour. Promise me you'll make it.'

He agrees to give it a go, amused at her insistence. 'If it goes lumpy I'll know who to blame.'

'It shouldn't if you keep whisking while you add the milk – but if it does, you can just push it through a sieve, and nobody will know the difference.'

'The tricks of the trade.'

'Exactly.'

They tidy up and leave the café. Thomas pulls down the shutters and hands her the keys. 'Thanks a lot. I appreciate it.'

'No problem, happy to help. Thanks for today. Have a good night.'

The traffic is heavier than usual on his way home. The start of the bank holiday, everyone bent on escaping from the city. This time tomorrow he'll be off himself.

He wishes again that Chloë was joining them, even as he acknowledges how much Mum and Poll would object to her being there. He wishes she hadn't made separate plans for the weekend.

She's not the first object of his affection. In secondary school he'd lusted silently after Phoebe, a classmate's sister, for the most part of two years. They never officially met – Thomas wasn't friendly with her brother – but he was acutely aware of her. She was a year behind Poll in the girls' school down the road, and she had a Saturday job in her father's newsagent.

Thomas would visit the shop every so often. He'd approach the counter on trembling legs and buy a bar of chocolate he didn't want, hardly daring to meet her eye. She never gave a sign that she knew him, although chances were she recognised his face at least. Not exactly what you'd call the romance of the century.

In college it was Angela from Cork. Auburn-haired, brown-eyed, pretty Angela. She was in his film studies tutorial group: he looked forward to the class all week. She loved Woody Allen and Quentin Tarantino – and Geoffrey Matthews, a fellow student. Like Phoebe, she was hardly aware of Thomas's existence – he was rarely confident enough to contribute to the group discussions – but for a long time after he left college, and the torture of seeing her with Matthews had mercifully ended, an overheard lilting Cork accent would cause a small skip of his heart, and instantly conjure up her face.

With Chloë it's different. The others were rehearsals: this is the real deal. This is love, even if it's doomed love.

Has his father guessed? He doesn't think so. He fervently hopes not. And Poll or Mum? Has either of them any suspicions – or would the notion of Thomas harbouring feelings for Chloë be too ridiculous even to cross their minds? He can only hope it would.

He's never spoken to anyone about it. He could tell Sam if he wanted. Sam would understand, and not judge. He'd probably advise Thomas to cop himself on and find someone he had a realistic chance with – but he wouldn't laugh, wouldn't make a fool of him.

The thing is, Chloë is always really nice to him. The thing is, it sometimes feels as if she's … flirting with him. The way she looks at him, smiles at him. He'd swear once she winked at him. And she refers to his father as the old man, even in his presence. Dad laughs it off, it doesn't seem to bother him – but maybe it bothers *her*. Maybe the age gap is beginning to matter.

Thomas is not quite two years her senior. He's gangly and shy and qualified for nothing. He's not rich and not in the least good-looking, with none of his father's easy charm – but maybe she sees beyond all that. It's not impossible, is it? He's not completely unlovable, is he?

Her interest may well be a figment of his imagination, a notion conjured up from his four years of devotion – but it may not. The fact that she's not accompanying Dad to Land's End might mean something too, mightn't it? Maybe she really does feel an attraction to Thomas; maybe she's waiting for some sign that he reciprocates.

But of course he can't reciprocate. Of course he can't ever confess his feelings to her, not as long as she's with his father. All he can hope for is an end to her relationship with Dad. Maybe then, maybe after a long time has elapsed, she and Thomas could find a way to be together that wouldn't reopen wounds and cause a new family rift. It's a forlorn hope: it's an infinitesimal hope. He's well aware of that.

He reaches home. He fishes keys from his pocket – *Titanic* keyring – and lets himself in. He lights the oven for the bread-and-butter pudding, and while it's heating he goes upstairs and opens his laptop.

He listens to Massenet. He watches her.

Charlie

'SHOULD I PACK A HAIRDRYER?'

Her voice floats down the corridor. Three nights, and she's taking what sounds like pretty much everything she owns.

'You should.' He resists the impulse to remind her that they haven't booked into a hotel. He wonders what state the house is in, after being unoccupied for two years. Presumably Lily's been keeping some kind of shape on it.

He recalls one of his last visits there, when he and Lily brought Kitty away from it for the final time. Lily had met Joe by then but he hadn't moved in with her, hadn't yet become a fixture, and Lily couldn't bring herself to involve the children, so Charlie was called upon to be her support for this most heartbreaking of tasks.

He remembers Lily linking her mother carefully to the car. By then Kitty's physical health had begun to deteriorate along with her crumbling mind, and her walk, previously a long, powerful stride, had been reduced to careful little shuffling steps. He remembers waiting until she was safely installed in the back seat before packing quietly into the boot her small suitcase of clothes and the box containing the few personal belongings that were to accompany her to the nursing home.

The Bible from her brother; her wedding album; a rosary with beads of green stone that had belonged to her mother; her father's silver pocket watch, a woman's bobbing head that Poll had given her a few years earlier. Tragically, none of these meant anything to her any more, but Lily had chosen them to take along, maybe in the hope, or the belief, that somewhere in the cloudy dimness of Kitty's mind they would trigger the faintest of memories, and afford her some comfort.

Where are we going? she'd asked peevishly as he drove through the gateposts, and Lily answered brightly that they were just bringing her on a nice drive. Charlie watched Kitty's face in the rear-view mirror as they brought her further and further from her home, and he consoled himself with the thought that she was pretty much impervious to what was happening.

Her expression didn't alter throughout the journey. The same down-pulled mouth he'd become familiar with of late, the same creases between her eyes that had lodged there some months before. An awful blankness in the eyes themselves, a terrible emptiness, their intelligent sparkle gone for good.

And Lily, sitting beside her in the back seat, holding her inert hand all the way to the city. Lily, her face as empty as her mother's, barely responding to Charlie's efforts at conversation. Beating herself up, he didn't doubt, when her only crime was taking Kitty to a place of safety.

He was to return to Land's End just once more, when Lily told him she was going back to give the place a spring-clean, about a month after Kitty had left it. *I'll come,* he said, anticipating Chloë's disapproval – she resented his continuing solo visits there after he and Lily had separated – but still wanting to do right by Kitty, who'd been so good to him.

'Are you bringing a phone charger?'

'I am.'

Better not mention the lack of coverage at Land's End: safer to let on he'd forgotten about that.

He's glad she's coming, glad she changed her mind. Flattered when she admitted that she'd miss him too much.

She's out of sorts though: something has happened. A row with a pal, or a falling-out with her mother. She hasn't said, and he hasn't asked. Experience has taught him not to ask. By the time they're at Land's End she'll have forgotten about it.

He checks the time: gone half four. Impatience jabs at him. He'd told her four o'clock, but she's never been a fast packer.

He eyes his reflection in the over-mantel mirror, rubs a hand along his jawline, feels the sandpapery rasp of his stubble. Not in bad fettle for a man of his vintage. Bit scruffy maybe, grooming never his strong point, although Lily had always kept him in check. Could maybe chop the hair a bit, could certainly lose the belly flab. Eyes a bit bloodshot: lack of sleep to blame for that.

Better things to be getting up to in bed – and occasionally elsewhere. Chloë is gratifyingly passionate and uninhibited, and entirely unselfconscious about her body. She frequently walks about the apartment in the skimpiest of underclothes, and prefers to meditate and practise her yoga in the nude. He summons a mental image and immediately feels himself becoming aroused.

As if on cue she appears, looking distracted. She sweeps across the room to whisk a candle from the windowsill. She's packing a *candle*? He bites back the question, his desire abating as he glances again at his watch. Twenty to five.

'How long is the journey?'

'Two hours, give or take.' Must be the third time she's asked.

'We should get going soon, sweetheart, beat the traffic' – but she's vanished again. Maybe the candle is the finale.

Lily wasn't happy when he broke the news, which didn't surprise him. Bit of an experiment, all of them there together – and of course she and Chloë have the politely strained relationship that he imagines is typical of women in their situation. Interesting to see how it goes.

Poll and Lily will be there by now. He imagines them arriving, opening the front door, coaxing the big house back to life, and he itches to be on the road.

The car boot is already packed to capacity – along with their usual bedding, Chloë had insisted on bringing her grandmother's enormous patchwork quilt that normally only comes out in the coldest of weather. He's also fitted in half a dozen bottles of red, the fillet steaks he bought at lunchtime, and his modest weekend holdall.

What on earth is keeping her?

In the bedroom he finds her on the phone. 'I do,' she says, and 'I have, yes,' and 'I know, you told me.' He gestures questioningly towards her case, lying closed on the bed: she gives a curt nod and turns her back on him. He smothers a jolt of irritation – she could have told him she was ready, could have saved the phone call for the car – and hauls out the case.

He remembers her telling him a few nights ago that her mother is spending the long weekend in Budapest – or is it Bucharest? – with one of her boyfriends. Nadia is Swedish and seven years younger than Charlie. Attractive and well aware of it. Long hair, paler than her daughter's. Blue-eyed, tall and willowy, openly appraising him when Chloë brought him to meet her. A widow since her late thirties, husband killed in a workplace accident. Not short of male admirers since then, according to Chloë. Sleeps with all of them, he assumes.

As he returns to the apartment Chloë is emerging from the room. 'Ready,' she says, slipping her phone into her bag, giving him a smile that's gone as fast as it appears. Yes, definitely something up. Say nothing, wait for it to pass.

Almost immediately they're caught up in a snarl of cars, two slow-moving lanes of like-minded travellers bound for the outskirts and the road west. If this continues they'll miss the start of dinner, or keep the others waiting.

Joe will be there, and Poll. Charlie imagines the five of them around Kitty's big kitchen table, making whatever kind of conversation they can. Keep it light, steer it clear of anything that might inflame feelings. The weather, always a safe topic. The new cello he's thinking of investing in. The Scorsese film he and Chloë saw last week. The upcoming end-of-year concert in the college –

Or maybe not. No, he'll make no mention of that.

The concert was where Lily and Chloë had come face to face for the first time. It was a showcase each year for the students, a chance for them to perform in public, to have the experience of being onstage while they were still within the safe confines of the college. The audience, of course, was pretty safe too: in theory open to all, in reality the majority of the concertgoers comprised parents and families of the students.

Lily always came to these occasions: partners of the college faculty generally did. It doubled as a staff night out, with a late supper somewhere afterwards. Chloë, in her second year, had chosen Massenet's 'Méditation' as her performance piece. *She's good,* Lily murmured afterwards, and Charlie felt a swell of pride.

Nothing had happened between them at that stage: nothing was to happen until the following year. He admired her talent, that was all – or that was all he'd admit to.

As Charlie and Lily were leaving, they happened to encounter Chloë, also on her way out, violin case under her arm, a rust-coloured scarf slung around her neck.

Charlie introduced the two women. He can still recall the slight sense of unreality the occasion engendered, the tiny throb of guilt he was aware of as they shook hands. Was it an advance warning of his future unfaithfulness, a subconscious acknowledgement of the affair that he and Chloë were eventually, inevitably, to embark on?

Their conversation was unremarkable. Lily complimented Chloë on her performance; Chloë murmured her thanks and admired Lily's necklace. It was nothing, a brief exchange, over in a matter of seconds, but that was where they'd first encountered one another, where they'd first become aware of the other's existence.

Someone, one of the other students, had made a video of Chloë that night and stuck it up on YouTube: for weeks afterwards Charlie would watch, mesmerised, after Lily had gone to bed. He was appreciating the music, that was all – but night after night he drank in her grainy image, her green dress, her tilted, beautiful head. Eyes half closed as she played, mouth open enough to show a glimpse of her tidy, perfect teeth.

No, he won't mention the concert.

The two lanes of cars have now stalled completely: looks like they won't be getting out of the city anytime soon. Chloë leans forward to slot a CD into the car's player. Seconds later, the pretty-boy drug addict who used to date one of those leggy supermodels begins to sing. For such an accomplished performer of sublime music, Chloë's fondness for the banal sounds that so often blare from supermarket speakers bewilders and dismays Charlie. Cotton wool for ears, predictable harmonies, clichéd lyrics. No depth, no poetry, no magic. What can she possibly see in it?

A space opens up ahead. As Charlie moves forward, a car from the adjoining lane swerves in to fill it, forcing him to brake hard. He curses quietly, resists the impulse to bang on the horn. Idiot: one of the many idiot drivers on the road.

'We should have left earlier,' Chloë remarks.

It's all he needs. 'Whose fault is that?'

She looks at him, a tiny frown creasing the skin between her eyes. 'Mine?' An edge to the word.

'Forget it,' he mutters. Don't start a row, not now.

In response she leans forward and increases the CD volume. Doing her best to annoy him, waiting for him to complain. Miss him too much indeed – probably coming along just to cause trouble, changing her mind at the last minute so Lily would be put out, and Poll too.

He drums his fingers on the steering wheel. He inhales deeply, does a slow mental count to ten as he exhales. It does precisely nothing to improve his mood.

The day is grey and dull, with a low sky. It drizzled all morning, and there's more rain to come soon, by the look of it. He thinks longingly of a dip in the Atlantic, imagines the lungfuls of salty air he'll soon be enjoying: now *that* kind of breathing will do him the world of good.

'We have a gig next week,' Chloë says then.

He turns to her, surprised. She's staring straight ahead. 'Have you? You never said.'

'I've only just heard.'

The phone call. 'What is it?'

'A wedding.'

'A *wedding*? Don't they book the music months in advance?'

A tiny impatient click of her tongue that he doesn't miss. 'The first lot let them down.'

'Which hotel?'

'It's in Donegal.'

'*Donegal?*'

She throws him a look that would turn milk. 'People get married there too.'

God, she can be irritating. 'And they couldn't find any group closer than you?'

A shrug. 'Lawrence was contacted. That's all I know.'

Lawrence. That would explain it. Weakest link in the string quintet, plays the cello like it's a ukulele – but the only member with a household name for a father so he gets away with it. Lawrence is the one who gets them most of the gigs, the occasions hosted by those who want to say they had Tom Carthy's son – yes, *the* Tom Carthy – playing for them. And now here's another snob: a Donegal mother of the bride probably, looking for a way to get one over on her book club buddies.

The quintet isn't much of an earner. Even with the connection to Tom Carthy – a has-been, a one-hit wonder, if anyone had the guts to admit it – the group gets two or three gigs a month at the most, and the fee for each, split five ways, isn't remarkable. Between that and the pittance she gets from the theatre, Chloë can just about afford to keep herself in books and make-up. Just as well Charlie earns more than enough for both of them.

'Well, I hope they're paying your travel costs.'

'They're putting us up in a hotel, actually.'

'You're staying over?'

Another withering look. 'We're hardly going to come all the way back.'

He digests this in silence. A night apart after all.

'When is this happening?'

'Thursday.'

He might find out which of his buddies are free: be good to have an evening out with his own generation. They could go for a curry, few drinks afterwards. He'll give a ring around when they get back to town.

'What's up with you?' he asks then. 'Are you mad at me? Did I do something?'

She twitches a shoulder. 'Nothing's up with me. I just don't like being cross-examined.'

'What?'

'You – quizzing me about the gig. It's my *job*.'

'*Quizzing* you? I was just asking. Am I not allowed to ask now?'

'Oh, just drop it,' she says wearily. 'Just let it go, Charlie.'

'Fine.'

He won't win: he knows this from experience. He slides down his window. A minute later he raises it again, defeated by the exhaust fumes. The traffic inches forward, then comes to another halt. In the car ahead of them, the one that cut in, a young boy with close-cropped hair, no more than four or five years old, kneels up on the back seat and fixes Charlie with a challenging stare. Charlie stares back, stony-faced. Not in the mood for smiling right now, far from it. And shouldn't a child of that age be in a booster seat, or at least belted up?

The boy suddenly pokes his tongue out: rude little beast. Without thinking, Charlie reciprocates. The child pulls his mouth into a wide slit, tongue still extended, and crosses his eyes: again Charlie mirrors the image.

Chloë sniffs. 'Silly,' she says – but whether her comment is directed at him or the child isn't made plain.

'He started it. Little twat.'

'*Charlie*.'

'What? He *is* a twat. Can we lower the music?'

She turns it down a fraction, not enough to make any real difference. Still the line of traffic is stalled – how long will it take them to leave the city? In the car in front the child's expression darkens into a more threatening, teeth-bared grimace: once more Charlie reciprocates, feeling now a sort of vicious glee at the game.

'Stop it, Charlie. You'll upset him.'

'Upset him? You must be kidding. This guy's a pro.'

He adopts an even more threatening snarl, accompanying it with a raised fist that he shakes in the air. The child's head whips around – he seems to be addressing someone over his shoulder – and directly afterwards the driver's door of the other car is pushed open. A meaty-looking man climbs out and stomps back towards him, scowling.

What's this now? Charlie feels a small quickening of his heart. He lets his snarl melt away, drops his hand to grip the steering wheel. Everything tightening, something falling inside him as the other driver approaches.

'Uh-oh,' Chloë murmurs. 'Here comes Poppa. You're in trouble now.'

The man reaches for Charlie's door: in the nick of time Charlie stabs the button that engages the lock. He watches with mounting incredulity as the man wrenches at the handle, face contorted with anger. Can this really be happening in broad daylight, surrounded by witnesses, because of a few funny faces? Christ almighty.

'Charlie,' Chloë breathes, her voice changed now. '*Do* something!'

He shoots her a glare. '*Do* something? What do you suggest?'

'I don't know – stop him!'

The man begins to slam with the side of his clenched fist on Charlie's window. Chloë lets out a little frightened scream as the drug addict sings on. A black T-shirt strains across the man's chest, some motto on it that Charlie's shocked mind refuses to decipher.

'Come out, you *bastard*!' the man shouts. 'Come *out*, toe-rag!' With each thump, the car gives a shudder.

'Charlie!' Chloë cries, but this time he ignores her. His mouth is bone dry, face ice cold with fear, knuckles white on the wheel. Breathing has suddenly become an issue – his head is light for want of air. He's aware of a pressing urge to urinate: he prays he can hold it back.

Violence on the small screen, or the big screen, has never bothered him. He can watch all sorts of gruesome happenings – it gives him a kick, let's face it, a testosterone-fuelled thrill to see someone being beaten to a pulp – but this is different. This is personal, and it's terrifying. The man is short but solidly built, freckled arms thick as tree trunks. He'd demolish Charlie with a few well-aimed blows, no problem.

His attack on the car is becoming increasingly frenzied. 'Come out!' he yells, banging with all his strength at the window as Chloë whimpers, knees drawn up now onto the seat.

Charlie darts a quick glance out the passenger window. Traffic has completely stalled in the other lane too, no sign of movement, no possibility of escape from this maniac. He's dimly aware of faces turned in his direction from neighbouring cars, gaping out at the goings-on, delighted with a bit of bank holiday road rage to break the monotony of the gridlock. A story to amuse their pals later in the pub, or over the dinner table. Someone probably making a video, up on Facebook later. Has anyone even had the cop-on to call for help?

His phone. He slaps at his pockets and finds nothing – where is it? His jacket – no sign of it. In the boot, he remembers, the phone more than likely in it. Fat lot of good it is to him there. Beside him Chloë sits rigidly in her seat, white-faced, eyes huge, gaze latched on their attacker.

'Your phone,' Charlie snaps, jabbing at the sound system to shut off the god-awful music. 'Where is it?'

She doesn't react, doesn't seem even to have heard him. 'Phone!' he shouts. 'Call the police – do it *now*, Chloë!'

Their tormentor changes course, banging instead with both fists on the car roof, his features contorted with rage. '*Out!*' he roars. 'Come *out*, you dickhead!' The sound of his pounding on the metal is enormous, booming. Chloë dips her head onto her knees. 'Oh God, oh God, oh God,' she whimpers. 'Make him stop, make him stop.'

This can't be happening. This is ludicrous, ridiculous. Why is nobody doing anything? 'Call the police!' Charlie shouts again – still she doesn't react. He unbuckles his seatbelt and lunges for her bag, sitting in the well of the passenger seat, and thrusts it at her. 'Find your *fucking* phone!' he yells. '*Now!* Do it!'

When she makes no move to take it, her stare remaining fixed on the man outside, Charlie curses loudly again and upends the bag, toppling its contents. He scrabbles on the floor, scattering tubes and tissues and purse and pen as the man continues his relentless pounding on the roof. Where the *hell* is it?

It's nowhere. He finds no phone. He sits back, heart hammering, blood racing. What now? He looks out again, meets the man's enraged stare. This can't go on – he has to do something. He presses the window-release button for a millisecond – '*Don't!*' Chloë screams, finally reacting. Charlie ignores her as the glass slides down an inch.

The man immediately shoves his fingers into the gap and tries to force the window further down. His bitten nails are rimmed with black. 'You cowardly bastard,' he yells, 'making faces at a kid! Trying to frighten my boy!'

His words ride into the car on a blast of coffee. A drop of spittle hits Charlie's lip – he rubs it off. 'For God's sake,' he replies, as steadily as he can manage, 'you're overreacting.' Hearing his too-high middle-class voice speaking middle-class words. 'It was a bit of fun, that's all. Your boy wasn't frightened – he's the one who started it.'

But the man isn't listening; he's beyond listening. He continues to put pressure on the glass, pushing on the window, grunting as he leans all his weight on it, doing his best to shove it down – dear Jesus, if he gets it open wide enough to put a fist in, that'll be the end of Charlie.

'Come *out*!' he roars, aiming a kick at the door, lunging with his whole body now at the car, causing it to lurch violently. Chloë lets out another terrified scream.

How long has this nightmare lasted? It feels to Charlie like an eternity. Someone must have called for help: surely somebody must have. 'Look, just stop!' he shouts. 'Just stop this, just *stop*!' His guts are churning, his mouth so stiff with fear that he can hardly form the words. From the corner of his eye he spots the child who started everything, watching the proceedings blankly, open-mouthed.

The traffic in the next lane inches forward, half a car length, then begins to move more steadily. A horn toots once, somewhere behind Charlie. The angry man swings around to glare in the direction of the noise: it isn't repeated. Charlie jabs at the window button again, nudging the glass up a fraction this time, capturing the man's fingers.

'*Oy!*' He yanks them out, newly enraged. The car shudders as the man's body slams into it again and again, prompting

Chloë to give repeated shrill screams that make Charlie want to squeeze her throat shut.

A volley of horns erupts suddenly behind them, several horns now. Trying, maybe, to put pressure on the thug, to force him to leave Charlie alone. The blare causes something to snap in Charlie. He feels the blood rush to his head, the adrenalin pump through his system.

'For *fuck*'s sake!' he yells, through the tiny gap in the window. 'Just *fuck* off and leave us alone!' He puts the heel of his hand on his own car horn and holds it there, adding to the cacophony.

The passenger door of the car in front is thrown open abruptly: a hard-faced woman emerges. 'Get in!' she yells. 'Come on, leave it!'

The man gives a final thump to Charlie's window before abruptly wheeling back towards his car. Charlie watches, hardly daring to hope. Is that it? Can that be the end of it? He jabs at the window button with a shaky hand, closing the gap.

The volley of horns behind him continues, a discordant chorus of tones and rhythms. To Charlie's vast relief he sees the man climb into his car and slam the door – and a second later he moves off, giving a sustained blast of his own horn. From the rear seat the little boy raises a middle finger at Charlie, grinning gleefully as he's borne away. A perfect little thug in the making.

Charlie unclenches his hands: they're wet with sweat. He wipes them on his jeans. His armpits are similarly damp; his shirt clings unpleasantly to his back. He takes a ragged breath and lets it out again. He repeats the process, ignoring the horns that continue to blare behind him.

He wipes a sleeve across his forehead and turns to Chloë, still curled into a ball in her seat, arms wrapped tightly around her knees, head bent.

'OK?' he asks, his mouth stiff with tension.

No reply, no reaction.

The car is still running. His legs shake violently as he presses down on the accelerator and releases the clutch. He pulls jerkily into the kerb and cuts the engine again, letting the line of cars move on without him.

He reaches for Chloë's hand: she shrinks from him.

'Hey,' he says. 'Come on. I'm on your side, remember?'

Still nothing. He leans down into the well and retrieves her bag and replaces its contents. She shies away from him again when he offers it to her, so he sets it back into the well.

He opens his door and steps out cautiously, praying his legs don't give way under him. The traffic is flowing slowly past, any witnesses to the attack well gone by now. Not a single person stopped. Nobody got out after the man drove off to check that they were OK. Thanking their lucky stars, no doubt, that it was Charlie in the firing line rather than them. Beating a retreat as soon as they could.

He examines the car. Several sizeable marks on the door where it was kicked, lesser dents on the roof from the force of the man's fists. No comeback for Charlie: in the heat of the attack it never occurred to him to look for a licence number. He tries now to recall the make or even the colour of the other car, and finds that he can't - and he very much doubts that Chloë will remember either. Not that he cares: right now he just wants to forget it.

He walks slowly around to the rear and slumps against the boot, bracing arms on thighs, filling his lungs again and again. He feels weak, as physically drained by the incident as if he'd just run a marathon. Out of nowhere it came - without warning they were under siege. So quickly it happened.

When he feels a little steadier he walks up and down the path, catching the sour waft of his sweat as he peels his shirt away from his back. He tries to collect his thoughts, tries to shake off the residual fear that clings to him. A small brandy might help: they could stop at a pub once they get to the outskirts. They'll definitely be late arriving at Land's End now anyway – another ten minutes or so isn't going to make much difference. Shame he can't let Lily know, given the lack of coverage at the house.

Chloë remains hunched in her seat. He regards her bowed head through the window, the achingly vulnerable line of her neck. He shouldn't have yelled at her, regardless of how justified he felt, how under pressure he'd been at the time. She was scared out of her wits, unable to help. He recalls their snappish exchange just prior to the attack: that won't have helped either. A brandy will do her good too.

He switches his focus to Land's End. He imagines sitting on the veranda with a glass of something, watching the darkness fall. The image gives him renewed strength. In a couple of hours they'll be there, and this will be far behind them.

He gets back into the car. He inspects the smudges the man's fingers have left behind. He slides the window down halfway and wipes at them with the chamois he uses to clear the windscreen. He scrubs hard on both sides of the glass until all trace of them is gone.

He stows the chamois and turns to Chloë. 'Sorry I shouted at you,' he says, but she keeps her head down and says nothing at all.

'Chloë, I wasn't thinking straight. I panicked; I hardly knew what I was saying. I thought he was going to hurt me. He would have, if he'd got hold of me – and maybe you too. I'm sorry I took it out on you, but you must know I didn't mean it.'

Still the silent treatment. He doesn't deserve it.

She'll come round. Give her a while.

They sit. A minute passes, two minutes. Can it only be twenty to six? It seems like hours since they set off. They remain without speaking, without music, while the holiday traffic moves past slowly, paying them no attention at all.

Finally, Charlie turns the key in the ignition again. He indicates and swings the car back into the line of traffic.

Chloë lifts her head. 'Where are we going?' So quietly he hardly hears.

He shoots her a glance: still so white and frightened-looking. He forces a smile. 'What do you mean, where are we going?' He reaches out, places a hand on her arm. 'To Land's End, of course.'

She snatches her arm away, looks at him wild-eyed. 'What? No!' Her voice suddenly high and quivering. 'I can't – I don't want to! I want to go *home*! You must take me *home*!'

'Chloë—'

'No!' She fumbles with her seatbelt. 'No, I can't go – you can't— Stop the car! *Stop* it!' The belt releases with a click; she turns and pulls at the door handle.

'Chloë – what are you doing?' He grabs her with one hand as he swerves towards the kerb and brings the car to a clumsy halt, causing another driver to hoot.

'What the hell?' He holds her: she thrashes against him but he hangs on. 'Chloë – I've stopped, look, we're stopped. It's over, Chloë. He's gone. We're OK. We're OK, he didn't hurt us.' She keeps trying to pull away – if anyone looked in they'd think she was being attacked. 'Chloë, please stop this, please *stop*. It's OK, nothing is going to happen to you.' He keeps talking, keeps hoping to God he can somehow calm her down sufficiently to change her mind about the trip.

They're going. They have to go. He has to go, he has to persuade her – but first she must be composed.

Eventually her struggles diminish, and she starts to weep. 'I don't want to. I can't,' she insists, letting the tears fall. 'I can't, I just can't—' Her head is shaking from side to side, hair tumbling. The worst of her panic is over, but her resolve is still strong. 'Take me home,' she begs. 'Please, Charlie. Just take me home.'

'But sweetheart, this is just what we need now. We need to get away from—'

'No!' Immediately she rears up again, and again he grabs at her.

'Chloë, everything's packed, we're all set, and the sea air—'

'*No!*' Her struggles resume in earnest - and he sees to his despair that he must admit defeat. The trip is not going to happen. They're going nowhere. How can they, with her so determined not to?

'OK,' he says. 'I'll take you home.' His heart leaden as she instantly relaxes in his arms. 'We'll go home, if that's what you want.' His last chance to see Land's End gone, thanks to that bastard and his brat of a kid. He turns the car around, utterly defeated, as Chloë sits quietly now, blotting her wet cheeks with a tissue she takes from her bag.

He needs to let Lily know not to expect them - but how? He'll just have to leave a voicemail message, and hope she picks it up at some stage. She'll surely try to call him when they don't appear, although she'll have to go almost as far as the village to do it - but he should make the effort to get in touch before that.

What'll she think when she hears they're not coming after all? He imagines she'll be pleased, on balance. Oh, what does it matter what she thinks? What matters is that he's not going.

He mustn't blame Chloë. She was traumatised by what happened, and Charlie yelling and swearing at her didn't help. He must keep his patience, must not make her feel guilty.

On the way home he becomes aware of a gnawing hunger. 'You want to stop for food?' he asks, but she shakes her head. He tries to recall if there's anything in the fridge – and then he remembers the steaks that were destined for Land's End, sitting in a box in the boot.

He thinks about a seasoned steak sizzling in butter on a hot pan, a mound of onions softening and turning golden brown beside it, the bottle of Bordeaux he'll open to wash it all down, and the bowl he'll fill with scoops of Ben and Jerry's for afters.

It doesn't help. None of it helps. All that matters is the ruined weekend, and the heart-wrenching possibility that he may never see Land's End again.

He drives on, in the wrong direction.

Lily

THEY WAITED TWENTY MINUTES, THEN ANOTHER TEN, and another ten after that. When there was still no sign of them Lily plated up five servings of salmon and stowed two in the fridge. *We'll go ahead,* she said, doing her best not to sound as annoyed as she felt. Bad enough to foist Chloë on her at the last minute: unforgivable to keep them waiting like this. He knew dinner was at seven o'clock: you'd think he'd at least have made sure they arrived on time.

The three of them ate salmon and salad and followed it with apple crumble as the sky turned slowly from white to grey to purple to navy outside the kitchen window. Poll's swim had done her good: she came back smiling and exhilarated, even if she also looked frozen through. She showered and changed and returned downstairs to chat throughout the meal, no doubt making the most of their time without the new arrivals.

Half past eight. Nine o'clock. Half past nine. By then they'd washed up, Joe had lit the sitting-room fire and Poll had set out the Monopoly board on the coffee table, although none of them suggested actually starting a game. Instead they sat in front of the television, waiting for the sound of car wheels on gravel, the sweep of headlights through the window – but nothing happened.

And now it's a quarter to ten, and finally Lily gets to her feet. 'I'll go to the village,' she says. 'I'll have to ring him and see what's delaying them.'

'I'll come with you,' Joe says, rising too – but she tells him no, no need, she won't be long. 'If I'm not back by ten …' She stops, unsure of how to finish it.

If she's not back by ten it will mean that something has happened to them. It will mean that she has to stay where she can use her phone, where she can do whatever needs to be done, contact whoever needs to hear from her, be contactable herself in the event of an unfolding emergency. They shouldn't have been so quick to disconnect the landline when Mam moved out of the house.

'I won't be long,' she repeats, conscious of Poll's anxious expression. 'They'll be caught in traffic.'

But not even bank holiday traffic would have delayed them by this much. All the way to the village she tells herself it'll be something minor, something that prevented them from coming but nothing bad, nothing harmful to either of them.

You're good in a crisis, she's heard more than once. It's not always presented as a compliment. Good in a crisis can mean unfeeling, can mean not swept away by emotion when everyone else is. Good in a crisis can mean bad at empathy; can mean too concerned with the practicalities to comfort whoever needs it. Everyone wants someone who's good in a crisis when a crisis is actually under way – but the rest of the time they can be regarded as cold fish.

She hasn't cried since Mam died, not once. What kind of person doesn't cry when she loses her mother? Poll wept at the funeral – she produced enough tears for all of them – but Lily remained dry-eyed throughout the entire ceremony. What does that say about her?

She passes Karina's gate for the fourth time that day, its metal points standing out starkly now against the softer blackness of the night. Karina wouldn't be much good in a crisis – she's too scatterbrained to be relied on – but she'd hold the hand of an injured party, she'd sit beside them till help came. She'd be good at that.

Lily's phone emits a series of beeps as she approaches the village. Coming back to life, reminding her of the world beyond Land's End. She pulls up outside the supermarket on the main street and turns off the engine. She retrieves her phone from her bag and holds it in her lap, suddenly afraid to check whatever communications are waiting for her. What if something *has* happened to them? What if they've been in an accident?

What if Charlie is dead?

Oh, for goodness sake. She squints at the screen in the half-dark. *One missed call,* she reads, below the voicemail icon. The number is Charlie's. Not dead then, if he was able to leave her a message. Assuming he was the one who left it, of course. It could be Chloë, using his phone because she wouldn't have Lily's number in hers.

It's not Chloë.

Really sorry to cancel at such short notice, but something's come up and we won't make it. I don't want to go into it here but I'll call you on Tuesday. Enjoy the weekend.

She deletes the message, lowering the phone slowly as she raises her other hand to answer the salute of a man passing by on the path. One of the McGinns, she thinks, but she'd know the older generation better, his father and his aunts.

Something's come up. What could have come up in the time since she spoke with him? Only a few hours ago he was on the phone, talking about steaks. Saying he was looking forward to seeing Land's End again.

They've had a row, he and Chloë – but as soon as this occurs to her, she dismisses it. If they'd fallen out he'd have come on his own, like he'd been planning. A row would be all the more reason to put distance between them.

Something's happened to Chloë's mother, then: that might stop them. Or there's some emergency with the music college, although she can't think of anything so urgent that it couldn't wait till after the weekend. His car has packed up, maybe – but no, he'd have said.

She stops trying to figure out the why, and considers the implications of not, after all, having the two of them to stay. Obviously, Chloë's absence is a welcome development – but she would have liked Charlie to come, for Poll's sake if for no other reason. Give them a chance to reconnect without Chloë around.

And no steaks now for tomorrow night's dinner. She'd been looking forward to a fillet being dished up to her.

But on balance it's best. On balance it's good news.

She should acknowledge the message, let him know she's picked it up. Instead she stows her phone back in her bag with a perverse sense of satisfaction. Do him no harm to wonder, backing out at the last minute like that. She turns the car for home, still feeling a mixture of annoyance and relief.

Driving back, she wonders what Chloë would have made of Land's End. Probably would have thought it old and shabby, which it is. Charlie always loved it, though. She can still see him winding down his window on this very stretch of road at the beginning of each holiday. *Smell the sea!* he'd urge the children. *Smell the Atlantic Ocean! Nearly there!*

All the family traditions, all the shared memories pushed

aside when he'd told her it was over – and while she was still struggling to come to terms with it, Lily had had to break the news of the split to Mam.

True to form, her mother had spoken her mind. *You're both far too old for such nonsense: what on earth has brought this about?*

Love, Lily thought – or rather, the loss of love, the lack of love. She said nothing, of course: the mention of the word would have had her mother raising her practical eyes skyward. They were one of a kind, Mam and her. Good in a crisis, bad at emotion.

She's almost back at the house when it hits her: Charlie won't be here tomorrow night when she breaks her news. Not that it really matters, with his connection to Land's End pretty much severed at this stage. She'll let him know though, when she returns to town – with all his past associations here, it feels right that he be told what she's planning to do with the place.

'They're not coming,' she tells the other two, and sees the twin expressions of relief in their faces. Charlie and Joe get on well enough on the rare occasions they meet, but the prospect of spending an entire weekend under the same roof as Lily's ex was probably something Joe hadn't been relishing, although he'd said nothing.

They open a bottle of red. Not bad for €7.99: how did they manage before Lidl and Aldi came along, putting it up to Tesco and the rest? They play an hour of Monopoly before Lily bows out, donating her properties to the other two.

'I can't keep my eyes open,' she says, which is almost true. The whole truth is that she wants to be alone. She feels the need, for whatever reason, to be alone right now.

'I won't be long,' Joe says.

'Take your time.'

Upstairs she undresses quickly and slides between the sheets she brought from the city, the bed creaking loudly with each shift of her body. The mattress is softer than the one at home, with a dip towards the centre.

The bed she was born in, fifty-two years ago. Maybe even the same mattress. She's still unsure how she feels about sleeping here, in the room that she's always associated with Mam. She tries to recall what Poll asked her earlier in the car, something about where she thought her mother had gone, and Lily had fobbed her off with something vague, a better place or some such nonsense.

'Where are you?' she asks, and no answer comes from the darkness. Of course it doesn't.

The hot-water bottle she filled before dinner has lost much of its heat, but she can't be bothered to refill it. She cradles its lukewarm heft, knees drawn up, eyes closed, listening to a soft hooting outside the window.

It frightened her as a child, that sound. Even after she knew it was only the harmless song of the owl – a long-eared owl, her father told her, most likely nesting in the copse of trees at the bottom of the garden – it still conjured up an image of a hooded man walking slowly across the back lawn to stand beneath her bedroom window, filling the air with menace.

She often looked for the owl by day. She searched the branches of the trees till her neck hurt from looking up, but she never found it. She wonders if this owl is a descendant of the one that frightened her childish self. How long do they live? She has no idea. She imagines generations of owls all nesting in the same trees, observing the comings and goings of the humans below, witness to the various changes over the years. Did an owl look down when her father dropped his paintbrush and folded to the ground?

She slides an arm under the other pillow and finds Joe's

pyjamas. He always wears them, winter and summer. Charlie sleeps – slept – in boxers and a T-shirt, never went near pyjamas. She wonders sometimes if she deliberately tried to find someone the polar opposite of Charlie. Was her subconscious, wary of another failed relationship, urging her towards the safety of Joe?

Joe *is* safe. Nothing wrong with that: safe is good. He's dependable and trustworthy, and he loves her, and her children approve of him. She has no complaints.

Won't feel it now till the wedding. Second time around for both of them, Joe's first wife killed in a road accident six years before he met Lily. No children, although they were married for over twenty years. He hasn't offered an explanation for that, and she hasn't asked.

The minutes pass. No more from the owl, gone off to hunt further afield. No noise from below stairs, the sitting room located on the far side of the house. A few creaks, a few rattles, the building shifting and settling, sounds that hold no fears for her.

She imagines Mam pottering about the room in the evenings, putting on cold cream, getting into her nightdress. Setting her alarm for half past six, giving her time to bake the griddle bread and fry the sausages before her paying guests awoke.

Eventually her eyelids grow heavier, and sleep comes.

Poll

SHE CAN'T SLEEP. SHE LIES ON HER SIDE, FACING THE window. She hasn't drawn the curtains: how can she block out the stars? She remembers as a child how in awe she was of the night sky at Land's End, how magical it seemed with its countless glowing pinpricks. She assumed, until she learnt otherwise, that stars only shone here – she'd never been aware of them in the city sky – just like she'd believed, when the sun dipped beneath the horizon at dusk, that it was sinking slowly into the ocean.

Childish fancies, long dismissed – but she still loves the sky at night here, still can't bear to shut it out with curtains. Tonight she can't see a moon in the patch beyond the window, just hundreds and thousands of stars, each with its fixed place in the firmament.

Her hair smells of the sea. She gave it a quick rinse in the shower after her swim but she didn't shampoo it, not wanting to banish the sea scent completely. Her swimsuit hangs alone on the washing line in the back garden. Tomorrow she'll swim again – if Thomas arrives with time to spare before dinner she'll take him with her. She's glad Dad taught them so young: if she ever has children she'll do the same.

She thumps her pillow, turns onto her other side. So many memories this place evokes. They're a mix of happy and sad, a jumble of the past, the long-ago and recent past.

She recalls Thomas collecting shells each summer, remembers his fascination with their whorls and curves and colours. She can see him scrubbing each one with an old toothbrush in the basin that Gran would fill with hot water, and drying them carefully with a towel before displaying them on the windowsills of their bedroom. He always returned them to the beach at the end of the holiday, putting them back where they belonged.

The night is chilly: she pulls the duvet a little higher. This room became Mum and Dad's, after Poll and Thomas stopped coming on family holidays. Mum and Dad still made the trip here each summer, still stayed a good month with Gran. As solid a partnership, Poll had thought, as Laurel and Hardy – until they'd taken her and Thomas out to dinner and announced they were splitting up, just months after Poll had organised the surprise party for their silver anniversary.

And now Mum is in the next room with Joe, and Dad …

At least Chloë isn't coming. The relief that had washed through her when Mum said it had made her realise how much she'd been dreading it. Kind of a shame he's not coming though, on his own like he'd planned.

Beyond her hot-water bottle the sheet is icy. She wishes she'd thought to pack bed socks. She misses Aidan, misses his warmth beside her, the way he sometimes reaches out to pull her close in the middle of the night, even in his sleep. This is what it will be like, night after night, if she splits them up. This is what she'll face if the demons get the better of her.

And if she and Aidan come to an end, she'll have to move out of the apartment – and what then? Back to the house she grew up in, which Joe now shares with Mum? And what of her pottery? Who'll sell it if the gallery becomes a place she can't associate with? Oh, such a mess their parting would cause, such upheaval, in her heart and in her life.

It can't happen. She can't let it happen.

She throws back the duvet, tossing her thoughts aside with it. She slips her feet into shoes and finds her green jacket in the wardrobe and pulls it on over her pyjamas. The landing is in darkness but she feels her way easily to the stairs and descends quietly, her fingertips sliding over the little knobbles of the wallpaper.

In the sitting room she takes a cushion from the rocking chair. She opens the front door softly and crosses the veranda to settle on the top step, where she and Thomas have sat on so many nights. She wraps her hands around her knees and looks up – and there's the moon, just a tiny narrow crescent, a C pulled from the alphabet to hang in the sky, but there. She hugs her knees and remembers mugs of hot chocolate.

A pink marshmallow for Poll, a white one for Thomas, floating on a generous dollop of whipped cream. She hasn't had hot chocolate in well over a decade, but she remembers the heavenly gooiness of the melting marshmallow. On warm summery evenings the two of them would sit here with their mugs, right here, watching the sun go down with Mum and Dad and Gran, and whichever B&B guests chose to join them.

An owl hoots somewhere above her. She'd forgotten the owls, how they were always part of the evening soundtrack here. She loves the music they make, so soft and mellow. When she was a young girl they'd lulled her to sleep on many a night. The bats they shared the sky with had unnerved her with their high-pitched cries and sudden swoops, but never the owls.

A creak behind her makes her turn – but nothing's there. She pulls her jacket more tightly around her. Not afraid – she could never be afraid here. It's just the cold making her shiver, just the night air causing a tremor to pass through her.

Aidan will be in bed now, sleeping under the single duvet from the spare room, their double here with her in Land's End. She pictures him curled up, glasses and book and phone on the bedside locker. Or maybe still awake, missing her as much as she's missing him. *Be good,* he said, kissing her goodbye. *No running off with a fisherman.*

More farmers around Land's End than fishermen, she told him. Plenty of farmers here, the surrounding fields full of crops or animals. Gerry Flaherty tilled his land, grew wheat and barley, never kept livestock, only hens – and he had a dog too, didn't he, years ago? A collie mixed with something else, or maybe a few other something elses. What was he called?

She conjures up the black and white face, the low, barrelly body, the comically long ears, the always-wagging bush of a tail – and out of the image comes the name: Clarence. Made her sneeze whenever he came too near, so she had to keep her distance. Not a working dog, with no sheep to herd. Trotting around the yard as she and Thomas chased one another in and out of the barn, or dozing by a haystack in the sunshine, like a canine version of Little Boy Blue. There was a cat too, a skinny ginger thing that didn't have a name, or none that Poll ever knew. Spent most of its time in Gerry's kitchen, sprawled on an old blanket in the corner.

And also in the kitchen was Gerry's mother. Poll had forgotten her, the thin silent figure in black, invariably sitting in a wing chair by the range, a blanket tucked around her. Paid Poll and Thomas no attention on the rare occasions that they strayed inside. Died when Poll was still too young to have anything but the cloudiest recollection of her.

She shivers again: better go inside before she freezes. In the kitchen she fills the kettle and tiptoes upstairs to retrieve her hot-water bottle. While she waits for the water to boil she nibbles some of the leftover salmon, although she was three pounds up last time she braved the scales. Thomas eats all around him and he's skin and bone: she looks at a cake and gains a pound.

From the corner of her eye she sees a movement. She turns to watch a tiny field mouse scampering across the kitchen tiles before disappearing through the gap between the cooker and the wall: another feature of Land's End that she'd forgotten.

'Look, Gran,' she says softly. 'They're still here.'

Gran waged a running battle for years with the mice, putting down traps baited with cheese, setting poison in jam-jar lids by the gaps and cracks, giving chase with the broom whenever she spotted one. Once in desperation she borrowed Gerry Flaherty's cat, even though she didn't believe in allowing cats into a house – particularly in a kitchen – but he was too old by then, or too lazy, to do more than snuffle around the room before settling down to wash himself.

Nothing worked. Gran never won the war of the field mice. Year after year, a fresh crop of little brown creatures showed up to drive her to distraction. Poll secretly applauded each time they got the better of her, each time a raided trap was discovered, and no body found. Sweet little things, not deserving of a horrible death. Mum isn't a fan of them either – if it has any sense, this one will keep out of her way while they're here.

Back in bed she closes her eyes determinedly. Twenty-five past two, the kitchen clock said; she can't remember when she was last awake this late.

And then, out of the blue, she hears her grandmother's voice.

Don't put pepper on those shoes.

As clear as anything. She sits up.

The words make no sense, but the voice is exactly as she

remembers it, loud and deep and a little strident. It *was* Gran's voice, even though it can't have been.

She strains to hear more, but no more comes. She lies down again slowly.

Don't put pepper on those shoes. No sense to the words – but maybe there's not meant to be. Maybe it's the voice that's important, not what it's saying.

Outside the window, the owl hoots. Eventually it lulls her to sleep.

SATURDAY, 29 APRIL

Thomas

HE DELIVERS ORANGE JUICE TO THE WRONG TABLE. Twice he serves coffee instead of tea. He completely forgets a scrambled egg order.

He apologises again and again. He can't think straight. All night, try as he might to rid himself of her, his head has been buzzing with thoughts of Chloë.

'Peace at last,' Freda says, when the breakfast crowd has moved on and the café has emptied out and Thomas is restocking the cutlery trays for lunch. She seems subdued today, not her usual cheerful self. Maybe she's annoyed at him for being so clueless.

He drops teaspoons into their section. 'Sorry, I'm a bit – distracted today.'

'I can see that,' she says, but not in a mean way. 'Don't worry about it.' Stacking clean mugs by the coffee machine, pausing to shove a sleeve up past her elbow in a way he's seen her do so often.

He rolls forks and dessertspoons into serviettes. Say something. Snap out of it.

'I baked the bread-and-butter pudding,' he tells her.

'And how did it turn out?'

'OK, I think.'

'That's great,' she says. Her smile diluted, its brightness dimmed. 'I'm sure they'll enjoy it.'

'Hope so.'

He looks out the window at the rain that's been falling steadily all day. In a few hours he'll be on the road to Land's End. He wonders how the weekend will go, how he'll manage to spend two days and nights in his father's company, given his predicament.

And beyond the dilemma of his feelings for Chloë something else is niggling at him, something is prodding at the edge of his consciousness. He puts the last cutlery bundle into the tray as the door opens to admit new customers.

And for the following few hours, as he pours coffee and fills bowls with soup, as he takes money and clears tables, the feeling that he's forgetting something remains one infuriating step ahead of him, pulling away just as he's on the verge of grasping it.

Charlie

ALL EVENING SHE SULKED, PUNISHING HIM FOR daring to raise his voice to her. Once they got home she started in on him, the minute he'd finished trudging from car to apartment, replaying his earlier movements in reverse order.

You shouted at me. You swore at me. As if that was all that mattered, as if the fact that his car was being attacked at the time by an enraged thug, and that he, Charlie, was in real physical danger, counted for nothing.

He felt most aggrieved. He'd given up his weekend for her, and this was the thanks he got. He'd forfeited the trip he'd been anticipating with great pleasure, and she couldn't see beyond a few swear words. *I was under pressure. I thought he might attack you too.* How many times?

Why would he? I hadn't done anything.

That's beside the point. There was no knowing what that idiot might do, he was so mad. Look, I get that you were afraid, honestly I do – but I think you're being a bit oversensitive.

Her phone, as it turned out, had been right beside her in the door pocket all the while. Anyone with a bit of wit would have grabbed it and pressed 999 as soon as the attack had begun.

She finally ran out of steam. After turning down Charlie's offer of a steak – how can you possibly *eat*? – she stalked off to bed without saying goodnight. While his dinner was cooking, Charlie tried putting in a call to Lily, but all he got was her recorded voice telling him to leave a message, so he left one. Didn't go into the whole saga, couldn't face it. Time enough when she got back.

After dinner he sat on, nursing the last of the bottle of Bordeaux he'd opened, and cursing the whole stupid mess. They should have been at Land's End by now, having after-dinner coffees on the veranda, or strolling to Sully's for a pint. He'd have had his swim; Poll might even have joined him. Instead here he was drinking alone, drinking too much alone, with a cranky girlfriend and a damaged car.

If they'd left the city earlier, if she hadn't taken forever to pack, they'd never have encountered the thug and his thug-in-waiting son. If he'd taken a different route, headed for the bypass instead of going the old way through the city centre, all this would have been avoided. If Chloë hadn't changed her mind about accompanying him he'd have left earlier, far earlier, and got there in plenty of time.

Fat lot of good they were now, all his ifs.

There was no response from Lily, but she must have got his message: she'd have been in touch otherwise. No doubt she was taken aback at the second change of plan, but she'd also be relieved that she didn't have to put up with Chloë for the weekend. He wished *he* didn't have to, if she was going to stay mad at him.

By the time he made his way to bed she was asleep, or giving a very good impression of it. He kept his distance, hoping to God she'd have thawed by morning – but when he woke with a headache soon after nine, she'd already vanished. Saturday was the day they had a lie-in until eleven or so: clearly that hadn't appealed to her today.

In the kitchen he looked for a note, and found none. Gone off to moan to one of her friends about him, or to spend some of his cash in one or other of the city's boutiques. He washed down three paracetamol with coffee, and filled a bowl with muesli he didn't want, his movements sluggish. After he'd eaten what he could he brushed his teeth and got dressed and drove across town to Philip, the mechanic who'd serviced his cars for years.

He showed him the damage: Philip whistled. *Who did you annoy?*

Charlie gave him the gist. *Can you take care of it?*

I can, but not till Tuesday. I'm up to my eyes for the rest of today, I'm afraid.

Tuesday, three days away. At least the car was perfectly roadworthy; a few dents didn't affect its performance. Not that he had any travel plans, now that Land's End had been written off.

See you Tuesday, then, he said, and got back into the car.

And in the act of putting the key in the ignition, he stopped.

Why should the entire weekend be lost? Why couldn't they go to Land's End today? Chloë would probably take some persuading – but the more he thought about it, the more sense it made to him. Why *shouldn't* they go? Why should she deprive him of this? She must be over it by now, surely. Bit of retail therapy was all she needed.

He felt his spirits lifting as he drove away from the garage. They could be on the road as soon as she reappeared, nothing much unpacked last evening. He wouldn't be able to let Lily know, unless he sent another message that she might or might not get – but couldn't they just turn up? With two couples and

Thomas there was going to be at least one bedroom free, even if there'd been a reshuffle after he and Chloë had cancelled.

They could still go. Nothing was stopping them. They'd still have two nights there. All he had to do was persuade Chloë.

On the way home he stopped at a newsagent's and bought a paper. As he approached the door on his way out he stood back to allow a woman to enter.

Charlie, she said, and he did his best – she was familiar, yes, he'd met those big teeth, that pointy chin before – but nothing came.

Gloria. Her smile dimming a fraction. *I play with Chloë in the quintet. I'm the viola.*

Gloria, of course. Gloria and her viola – how could he have forgotten? Gorilla, Chloë called her, although he wouldn't have said she was that large. *Sorry, a little too much wine last night. Brain still a bit mushy*.

She laughed, the shrillness of it making his toes curl. *How's Chloë's brain?*

Fine – she was far more sensible, had an early night.

That's good.

A beat passed. He edged towards the door. *Well …*

You haven't any gigs for us, have you? We're having a terrible dry spell! Another raucous laugh, drilling nails into his temples.

Aren't you going to Donegal next week?

Donegal? She stared at him, frowning-smiling. *Why would I go there?*

The group, I mean. The quintet. I thought Chloë said there was a wedding.

Wedding? I've heard nothing about a wedding – unless the rest of them are sneaking off without me! A fresh peal of laughter that almost undid him.

I must have got it wrong then, he said, putting a hand to the door. *We'll blame the wine again. And now you'll have to excuse me – she's waiting for her paper*. Holding it up, Exhibit A.

Well, tell her I said hi.

Will do.

He puzzled it out on the way home. Chloë *did* say Donegal, and it *was* next week, he was sure. Thursday, he'd bet anything she'd said Thursday. Gloria must have missed a rehearsal.

But wouldn't Lawrence have rung her to let her know about Donegal? Wouldn't he have had to make sure that everyone could manage an overnight trip before he said yes to the gig?

Unless there wasn't a gig.

But why would Chloë invent it? Why would she want a night away from him? Couldn't she have had three this weekend, if it was just space to herself she needed?

It didn't make sense. He'd ask her about it later – but his priority now was to get her to agree to his new travel plan.

Hello? he called on entering the apartment, and nobody answered. He tried her phone, and got only her voicemail. He paced the floor, impatient now for her to reappear. He repacked his toilet bag and returned it to the case he hadn't yet unpacked – and there was Chloë's case, also practically untouched. All he had to do was load up the car.

He tried her phone a second time, and again got only her recorded message. *Come home*, he said. *There's something I need to run by you.*

Eleven o'clock came and went. His impatience veering towards anger, his headache still in place, he tried her number again, and again got nowhere. *Leave a message*, Chloë said, but this time he didn't trust himself not to say something he'd regret.

And now it's heading for noon, and there's still no sign of her.

He sits in the living room, leafing through the newspaper, anger curdling his insides. Time passes, his anger increasing – and finally, at ten to one, he hears her key in the door. He drops the paper and gets to his feet and meets her in the hall.

'Where've you been?' Careful to keep the accusation out of his voice. Concern, not accusation. Not yet.

'Out.'

She drapes her jacket on the radiator. She knows he hates when she doesn't hang it up. He counts to ten as she tosses her key onto the windowsill and walks ahead of him to the kitchen. Easy does it. Think of Land's End. Keep calm.

'Chloë, I'm really sorry about yesterday. You know I'm sorry, I've said it over and over. Don't you think it's time you forgave me?'

She drops a green teabag into a cup and throws him a look that's still full of resentment.

'Sweetheart, I hate myself for shouting at you. If I could turn the clock back, I would.'

She fills the kettle, plugs it in. Rakes hair back from her face. 'You were trying to ring me,' she says. Managing somehow to make it sound like he'd committed a crime.

'Darling, I've just had a thought.' Easy does it. One step at a time.

She narrows her eyes.

'I know you were too upset to go to Land's End last evening, and I can understand that, truly I can.'

She leans against the worktop, folds her arms.

Here goes. 'But I really think we should go today. We can't let that idiot ruin an entire long weekend.'

She scowls. '*You*'re the one who ruined it, by taunting that little boy.'

With a great effort of will, he resists the temptation to snap a retort. A tense silence settles between them. Hold your patience, Charlie tells himself. Don't lose it. She hasn't said no.

The kettle bubbles and boils and clicks off, and when she doesn't react Charlie fills her cup and sets it on the table. 'Sit down,' he says, but she stays where she is.

'Why don't *you* go,' she throws out, 'if you're that keen?'

He's sorely tempted. He could fire his bag into the car and head off within minutes. Serve her right. Leave her alone to get over her terrible trauma, or her annoyance with him, or whatever is turning her into such a bitch. He could leave her to her meditation and her yoga and her green bloody tea. Be a relief, if the truth were told, to get a break from her.

But he can't arrive without her, not after telling Lily yesterday that she was coming. He can't tell them about yesterday's attack and say she was too upset to accompany him: he'd be the worst in the world for leaving her on her own. And neither can he admit that they had a row and she refused to come; he couldn't take the pity – or worse, the amusement – the admission might cause.

Lily would know anyway, whatever he said. She's never been easy to fool. She'd know and he couldn't bear that, he couldn't tolerate her silent *knowing*, so he swallows his resentment and grovels some more.

'Darling, of *course* I wouldn't go without you, not after what happened. I can see you're still upset – but that's precisely why I think it would be a good idea. A change of scene, a couple of days by the sea, would do you the world of good.'

She nibbles on her bottom lip.

'Don't you think it would be better than staying here, where it happened?'

She lifts a shoulder. Still not saying no. He forges on: 'It's in a beautiful location, very peaceful, and the beach is literally on the doorstep. I wish you could see it. I'd love to show it to you, and this will probably be the last chance I get.'

He puts a hand under her chin, tilts it towards him. Looks into her eyes, waits until she looks back. 'Some lovely walks too – and bicycles if we felt like a cycle.' Are the bicycles still there? He has no idea. 'Or you could just curl up by the fire and read, if you'd prefer. You could do exactly what you wanted.'

She gives a heavy sigh, turns her head away – but the idea is up for consideration. He can feel it.

'Wouldn't you like to get out of the city? Think of the fresh air – and the night sky is amazing, with no light pollution.' He laughs lightly. 'We could go skinny-dipping in the moonlight, after the others had gone to bed.'

'*Skinny dipping?* In this weather?'

'Well, maybe not – but the beach is gorgeous just for walking on.' What else? 'And the villagers are all so friendly. I'm sure they'd love to meet you.'

A blatant lie. He can't think of a single villager who'd love to meet the woman who replaced Lily in his life. Lily, who'd grown up at Land's End, who was one of them. He wasn't exactly flavour of the month there after the split; that was made plain. They still saluted him, most of them, when he encountered them on the street, but the greeting was often cooler.

'I can see *you* have your heart set on it.' Still sulky, still pouting, but coming round.

'Well, I *would* love it, but only if you come with me. I think it would be good for us, Chloë. I really do. It would help us move on from what happened, I know it would.'

And in the end, he gets his way. In the end, she gives in. Reluctantly, resentfully, but she agrees to go. It's enough for him.

He begins repacking the car before she can change her mind.

She makes no effort to help, standing by, arms folded, while he does it all. When the alarm is set and the apartment locked up she gets in without comment and opens a book. He's too happy to care. She'll get over it. By the time they arrive she'll be herself again, or close enough.

Ten to two. Even with traffic, they should be landed by half four.

He starts the engine. He resists the urge to whistle.

Chloë

SHE'S STRUNG OUT LIKE A JUNKIE RIGHT NOW. NO matter how many times she reads them, the words on the page make no sense. She can hardly look at Charlie without wanting to bite his head off, or burst into tears, or both.

The more she thinks about it, the more it kills her. She's going to have surgery. She, who hates pain, and blood, and needles, is voluntarily placing herself on an operating table. She will be anaesthetised; her body will be invaded while she's unconscious.

She tortures herself by anticipating Thursday in all its awful stages. The drive to the airport with Abby, who will probably want to make inane conversation all the way. The large brandy she will order in the departure lounge at ten in the morning, surrounded no doubt by business-suited men, at least one of whom will try to catch her eye or attempt to chat her up. The second brandy she will drink on the plane – because whatever they said about fasting from midnight on Wednesday, she has no intention of going into that clinic stone cold sober.

She doesn't want to think about what will happen once she steps through those doors. Thinking about it makes her want to throw up – but it's all she can think about. The scalpels, and whatever other instruments of torture will be involved. The pain afterwards, because of course there will be pain. The effect it might have on her mind as well as her body. All this runs through her with the quiet menace of a malignant tumour.

The cruel irony of coming under attack in the car yesterday, when she was still trying to get her head around what she'd set in train. The bad joke of finding herself in such a ghastly situation, just as she was trying to banish all thoughts of another.

If it hadn't been for Thursday, she could have coped. The assault, or whatever you'd call it, was over relatively quickly. Their attacker drove off and they survived without a scratch, and Charlie losing it and swearing at her was only to be expected – but to have it happen when she was already in bits was too much. It totally threw her, sent her over the edge, turned her into a hysterical ninny. All she'd wanted to do was go home. She couldn't bear the thought of facing his family in the state she was in.

This morning she was no better. After a night of fitful sleep she'd sneaked from their bed and dressed in the bathroom and slipped out. She'd spent the morning wandering around town, looking but not seeing the shop windows, stopping at some stage for a cup of green tea that burnt her tongue when she sipped it, and a scone that might as well have been made of clay for all the pleasure she took from it.

Her phone rang. She looked at Charlie's name and listened to the rings until it stopped. *Come home*, he said, after his second attempt. *There's something I need to run by you*. Her first thought was that he'd discovered her lie about Donegal, but it was only that he still wanted to go to his precious holiday home.

Should she come clean? Should she tell him? No – she couldn't. That wasn't an option. But a nugget of guilt was festering inside her, a shard of remorse that she was going to carry out this act with him all unawares.

So she gave in. She agreed to go because she wanted to make it up to him in some way – and here they are, on the road for the second time, heading towards Poll's silent resentment and Lily's standoffishness and Thomas's mooning. None of that will bother her – she has more to worry about than Charlie's failed family. She'll do her own thing. She'll tolerate their company when she must, and avoid it when she can – and who knows? It might just clear her head to be out of the city, like he says.

'Traffic is light,' he remarks.

'Mm.'

How badly he hides his delight at having got what he wanted. She itches to slap away his smugness. No, she wants to curl into his arms and beg him to protect her.

She keeps her eyes on the page she can't take in, and wills Thursday never to come.

Poll

AT THREE O'CLOCK, TIRED OF WAITING FOR THE RAIN to stop, she and Joe pull on raincoats. 'Will you not come?' she asks Mum again, but Mum waves them off, preferring to stay by the fire with her crossword. 'If you pass a shop, we could do with a few tomatoes,' she says, so Poll decides to bring Joe on the big loop: around by Sully's, over the Hill Road, down by the old creamery and the GAA grounds and into the village from the far side. From there they can pick up a lift, or walk home if nobody obliges.

They set off, heading away from the sea. Rain slaps onto her face, borne by a stiff breeze. She'd woken late to the sound of drops pattering on the window. She'd lain in bed and considered a swim: what would the rain matter, when she was going to get wet anyway? – but then she remembered her swimsuit, still hanging on the line outside. Tricky enough wriggling into wet togs on a warm summer's day: another thing entirely on a chilly April morning, even if it's closer to May than to March. Maybe later.

She'd gone downstairs to find Mum and Joe sitting with a stack of old photo albums at the kitchen table.

There's tea in the pot, Mum said, so Poll poured a cup and took an album from the stack and leafed through the spotted pages filled with sepia white-bordered snaps. There were her great-grandparents, he the builder of Land's End, she an assistant in the local drapery shop, having travelled from her native Cork to take up the position. Both formal and unsmiling on their wedding day, looking happy in photos not encouraged in those days.

Another page, and here came their children, Gran and her siblings, propped up in their turn in the same enormous pram, bonneted and grave, or standing stiffly as toddlers or youngsters. The girls' hair, dark and bushy all, captured and tied with wide white ribbons, Gabriel's shorter, combed and oiled. His little trousers, anchored with braces. His chubby knees, his socks pulled high, his shoes small and shiny and buckled. His hopeful smile, heedless yet of the tumultuous years that lay in wait for him on the far side of the Atlantic.

Another page, colour snaps now, sent home in letters from America over the years. Cora and Teresa on the day they landed, standing by the ship in New York harbour, wearing identical excited smiles. Teresa's beautiful dark eyes, Cora's curls beneath her neat little hat, waiting to bewitch one Mr Finkleblatt – and there they were on the following page, Cora and Albert, having found one another. Both broadly smiling, his arm about her waist. Her gorgeous coral dress, his tuxedo. *A night out*, Gran said. *The opera, I think it was*. Albert, fair and slim, round glasses like Lennon's sitting on his long nose, looking proud as Punch to have landed his Irish colleen, mercifully ignorant that they were to have such a short time together.

And towards the end of the album there was a leap forward to one of her and Thomas, aged about four and six, standing outside Fox's, eating their Sunday-morning ice-cream wafers.

Poll in a blue dress dotted with yellow – yes, she thinks she remembers it – and little white sandals, a beam of pure happiness on her messy face. What had happened to snatch it away and leave a world of uncertainty and anxiety in its place?

She ate toast and drank tea and leafed through the past as the rain fell outside. Later she played gin rummy and Trivial Pursuit with the other two, and counted the hours till Aidan's arrival. At half past two they had bowls of soup with crackers and cheese, and at three she and Joe bundled up and headed out.

As they walk she identifies the various old farmhouses and landmarks that dot the area. A mile from Land's End she indicates a partially constructed six-foot-high stone wall, twenty or so feet in length, that emerges from one of a pair of giant pillars. 'This was supposed to be the entrance to an exclusive holiday village,' she tells Joe. 'The developer got this far before he went bust. It was the start of the crash, around 2008. It looks really sad now, doesn't it? An entrance leading to nowhere.'

'Bad timing. Someone might take it on again though, now that things are improving.'

'They might. It would be good if something was done.'

They walk past the rundown home of the reclusive painter who won some big art prize a few years ago, and refused to accept it. 'Nobody knows why he turned it down. Gran said he was always very odd, even as a young boy.'

They pass the skeletal remains of the small house that went up in flames many summers ago, taking its two elderly bachelor brother inhabitants with it. 'We were here for the funeral – the church was packed. I would have been nine or ten at the time, I think. I remember the absolute silence in the churchyard when the coffins came out.'

They walk on as the soft rain continues. Her face feels slick with it; water runs along the slope of her nose and drips off the tip. She doesn't mind; she pulls down her raincoat hood to let it bead on her hair. Rain like this is calming, falling gently as it does.

In the village supermarket they buy tomatoes and chocolate and two bottles of dubious-quality wine, and half a dozen mandarin oranges for Joe, who can't do a day without at least two. 'As addictions go, it's not a bad one,' he says, and Poll has to agree.

On the road home, the rain having cleared at last, Poll indicates Karina's gates. 'She inherited the house from a grand-uncle or something. She only keeps up about a third of it – the rest is pretty much derelict.'

'Karina – that's the American woman who brought us the eggs this morning?'

'Yes. She's lived here for over forty years, but she still sounds like she just got off the plane. She used to play the banjo when Thomas and I were small. She'd bring it to Land's End some evenings, and she and Dad would play together.' She laughs. 'Can you imagine a cello and a banjo?'

'Not easily.'

'They actually sounded really good together – or we thought so at the time.' She points to the cemetery across the road. 'Have you taken a walk in there yet?'

He nods. 'Your mum brought me, last time we came down.'

Poll regards its high wall. 'Pretty much all her people are there.' Pause. The wall blurs. 'Apart from Gran,' she adds. 'There wasn't room for her.'

'Too bad.'

A single tear rolls down her cheek. She flicks it away. 'Come on – Mum will be wondering where we are.'

They walk on. 'You miss her,' he says lightly.

'I do.'

He never got to know Gran. He wasn't hidden from her like Chloë was, but by the time he was introduced to her, a few weeks after Poll and Aidan officially became an item, she was slipping from them. You could still just about hold a conversation with her – a short one, an uncomplicated one – but all memory of it would wash out of her mind five minutes afterwards.

And just before Christmas, when she was told of Joe and Mum's engagement at a specially convened family dinner – they'd taken her out of the nursing home for the occasion – she'd gone beyond even the simplest conversation. The words clearly meant nothing at all to her.

Lily showed her the ring: she looked at it blankly before casting around the table in the manner of a small child searching for a familiar face. *Is it time to go home yet?* she asked, in a voice that had grown progressively more querulous over the preceding year. By then, the nursing home was the only home she recognised.

Curiously though, she never forgot who Dad was. As her illness gained hold she began to mistake Mum for her long-dead sister Pauline, and Poll was often called Lily, much to *her* dismay – but Dad remained Charlie to the end. That he'd been married to Gran's daughter, was technically still married to her, might have been left behind somewhere, everything else about him might have slid away from her, but his name had lodged somewhere in the quagmire that had become her brain. He was there with the rest of them when she died, as much a part of her family as he'd been when he and Mum were still together.

They approach a field of cows. Black heads lift as they pass.

'Joe,' Poll says. Feeling her way, not wanting to alarm him. 'I know this might sound a little … It's just that I've had the sense, ever since I walked into the house yesterday, that Gran is … that she might be still at Land's End. Isn't that weird?'

He considers. 'Maybe,' he says. 'Maybe not. Who knows where we go after here? Who knows what the next place is like, if there *is* a next one?'

'It was her only home. She never lived anywhere else. She loved it.'

'Well, then,' he says, and she waits for more, but nothing more comes.

'So you think she might be back there.'

'She might well be,' he says. 'Indeed she might.'

No awkwardness, no embarrassment. No sidelong glance as if she needs to be humoured, or to have her head examined. Accepting what she said with no judgement.

She tucks her arm into his. They turn down the lane that leads to Land's End, her feet beginning to complain now, just a little.

And at the end of the lane, there is her father's car.

Lily

THEY CAME. THEY'RE HERE.

When she heard the car she thought it must be Thomas or Aidan, having got away early.

Wrong. Not Thomas. Not Aidan.

She watched from the sitting room as Charlie got out. Were there dents in his car? Had he been in some kind of accident? Was that why they didn't come yesterday? And was he alone now? She couldn't see if anyone was sitting on the passenger side.

He was opening the boot as she walked out.

You came after all.

To give him his due, he had the grace to look embarrassed. *I had no way of letting you know. I could have left another message, but –*

It's fine, she said. *Glad you could make it after all. What happened to your car?*

He hauled out a case. *I offended the wrong driver is what happened. I'll fill you in later. I hope we're not messing things up by arriving unannounced.*

We?

The passenger door opened then, and out she came. Paler than usual, Lily thought, although it was a while since they'd met. Swathed in a blue wrap. Tucking hair behind an ear, giving a lightning glance to the house before turning on a stiff little smile for Lily.

Chloë – welcome to Land's End, Lily said, every word an effort. *Charlie can show you around*. Damned if *she* was going to act the tour guide.

Actually, the child replied, the smile vanishing, *I'm really tired right now. I'd like to lie down, if that's OK.*

Of course, Lily said smoothly. Whatever little madam wants. *Charlie, you're in the back double. I'll leave you to settle in*. She turned away without waiting for a response. She returned to the sitting room and resumed her seat. She listened to the sounds of them going upstairs, and Charlie's subsequent journeys up and down. No help from his exhausted lady love.

Now, fifteen minutes later, he hasn't reappeared. Settling in the poor baby, making sure she's got all she needs. Or maybe they're up to—

No.

She would rather not go there.

She can't concentrate on her crossword. She shouldn't have invited them, either of them: why had she felt obligated? Yes, he'd remained close to Mam, he'd visited her right to the end – but so what? Nobody had twisted his arm; he'd *wanted* to. Lily owes him nothing at all – and from the day he walked out on her, Land's End stopped being any of his business.

She gives up trying to solve the clues. She closes the book and crosses to the window. Where are Joe and Poll? What's taking them so long? She dreads Poll's discovery of the new development, but she still wishes they were here, particularly Joe, who could be relied on to make conversation.

At least the rain has stopped. Could be a nice enough evening. She might suggest a stroll to Sully's after dinner. Better than sitting around here, trying to pretend they're one big happy family.

Footsteps sound finally on the stairs. Let it go, she tells herself. Be nice. What's he done but take up your invitation? 'In here,' she calls, and Charlie elbows the door open, cradling a cardboard box of wine bottles with red foil tops. 'Will I pop a cork?'

'Good idea.' Not yet six, not long after five if you were being specific, but it's a holiday weekend, isn't it?

From the kitchen she hears the squeak of the cork being hauled upwards – no screw tops for him – and the small hollow pop as it comes free. A short pause, a clink of glasses, the soft glug of liquid.

He returns and hands her a glass. The wine is so dark it's almost black. She notes, not for the first time, the thickening around his waist, the new flabbiness under his chin. If they were still together she'd be urging him to exercise more, bringing him out on evening strolls.

'Where are the others?'

'Gone walking. They shouldn't be long.'

'No sign yet of Thomas or Aidan?'

'No – I'm not expecting them till dinnertime.'

He places his glass on the mantelpiece and crouches to add a couple of sods of turf to the fire. Didn't take him long to make himself at home. Again she tells herself to be pleasant: this *was* his home, summer after summer. He was a good help to Mam while they were here, keeping the grass cut and the shrubs trimmed. Paying Terence Mulcahy for a load of turf, arranging for Bernard Ryan to come and clean her chimneys. Checking the attic for signs of bats or mice, or worse.

His hair is longer than she likes it. Chloë must prefer it long. She sips her wine and tastes black cherries and something darker, earthier. She always liked the wine he chose.

'Tell me about the car,' she says.

He drops into the chair across from her and tells her of a small child making faces through a car window, and a parent angered when Charlie reciprocated. He makes little of the incident – 'We were OK, the car got the brunt' – but the violence fills Lily with alarm.

'Didn't anyone try to stop him? You were stuck in traffic – there must have been lots of people who saw it.'

He gives a bark of a laugh that has no amusement in it. 'He wasn't the kind of character you'd be inclined to approach, believe me. I couldn't blame anyone for not intervening – *I* wouldn't have.'

She tries to picture it. The two of them trapped in the car, at the mercy of some raging goon. She imagines the brute force it must have taken to cause those dents. She wouldn't consider herself a coward – she's had to stand up to some pretty aggressive characters in the course of her work – but that kind of mindless violence would, she thinks, reduce her to a cowering wreck.

'Chloë must have got a fright.'

He shifts in his chair, takes a swig from his glass. 'She was pretty upset.'

'Did you call the guards?'

'No – I couldn't get to my phone, and Chloë couldn't find hers.'

'But afterwards?'

He shrugs. 'What was the point? Neither of us thought to get his reg.'

'So you just went home? You didn't report it? Charlie, he did damage to your car: he can't be allowed to get away with that.'

He throws her a look. She knows that look. That look says drop it. That look says back off.

She doesn't back off. 'But there were so many witnesses. Surely one of them must have—'

'None of them did anything,' he says, loudly enough to stop her. He sighs heavily, pushes hair from his forehead. 'Lil, nobody bothered to stop and see if we were OK when he drove off. Anyway, what difference would it have made if they had?'

'Someone might have got his registration. Now he'll get off scot-free, and you'll have to pay for damage you didn't cause. It just seems so unfair, Charlie.'

'I'll get over it.' He takes another sip, settles into his chair, stretches his legs towards the fire. 'To be honest, I just want to forget about it, now that I'm here. It's good to be back, Lil.'

She softens. He always loved this house. She thinks again about the decision she's made. She could tell him now - because of course she'll tell him, she wants him to know - but something stops her. Not now, not when he's relaxing.

'The wine is nice.'

'Bordeaux.'

She smiles. So predictable. A silence settles between them. It occurs to her that this is exactly how they used to be: this is precisely where they used to sit after the children outgrew the family holidays, and she and Charlie came on their own. He to the right, she to the left of the fire. Mam always preferred the rocking chair.

Before Dad died, before Mam began the B&B, this little room was the front parlour, used only at Christmas or for other special occasions. When the B&B started up this became their haven, hers and Mam's, with the larger back sitting room given over to the paying guests.

Her grandparents' gramophone still sits on a small table by the window, although none of their old records have survived. A crystal vase that they got as a wedding gift is on the mantelpiece, alight today with the yellow furze sprigs that Lily clipped from a roadside bush earlier.

The wall facing the window is almost completely taken up with a wide bookcase that holds her grandfather's collections, the complete works of Dickens and Chaucer and the like, each set bound in navy or maroon, the titles in faded gold lettering on the spines. On the wall to the left of the fireplace several silver-framed photos have been hung, everyone in them dead now, apart from Lily and her family.

Charlie swirls his glass, shifts his position again. 'She's been mad at me since it happened, Lil. I shouted at her, swore a bit. I just wanted her to find her phone. It was in the heat of the moment, but she can't see that.'

Don't, she thinks. Don't bring me into your domestics. 'Oh dear,' she says lightly, because some sort of response seems to be expected. 'Trouble in Paradise.'

He says nothing. He lifts his glass.

'Sorry,' she says, after a beat. 'That was glib.'

'She's being far too sensitive. I had this thug doing his best to break into the car and thump the life out of me, and she objects to a few F-words. It's hardly fair.'

Is he seriously looking to her for sympathy? She lets the silence lengthen, watches the turf redden and glow in the fireplace. Sees a ghost image of Mam bending to throw in another sod. 'Maybe I'm not the one you should be talking to,' she says then. 'About this, I mean.'

He turns to look at her. 'Sorry. You're right.'

She holds his gaze for a few seconds. His eyes are bloodshot.

Not much sleep last night. Neither of them got much, she'd bet.

'Did you think of the steaks?' she asks, suddenly remembering them.

'The steaks.' His face changes. 'Damn,' he says quietly. 'I had them in the car yesterday. I unpacked them when we got home. I cooked one for myself and put the rest in the freezer. Damn it to *hell*.'

Poor Charlie, his weekend not exactly going according to plan. She pictures the steaks in his freezer – interesting that Chloë didn't have one. Stalked off to bed because nasty Charlie said rude words to her. 'Relax. We weren't expecting you, remember? We're having quiche – Karina arrived with a dozen eggs this morning.'

'Did she?'

'She did.'

'Is there enough for us? We can go out.'

'Don't be daft, there's plenty. Gerry brought potatoes yesterday too.'

'Are you sure?'

'Of course I am. Fear of us.'

'OK. I could take everyone to Sully's tomorrow.'

'Sully's – last of the big spenders.' Keeping the smile in place to take the sting out of it. 'Why don't we worry about tomorrow tomorrow?'

He sits back again. 'Thanks, Lil.'

'You'll have plenty of steaks when you get home.'

He tries to smile: it doesn't quite work. He drinks wine, lowers his glass. 'How is it, Lil?' he asks then. 'Being back here, I mean.'

The change of topic throws her. She thinks about it. She

recalls an odd feeling she experienced upon entering the house the previous day, as if something was out of sync, even though everything looked precisely as it should. She'd said nothing to Poll, in case it disturbed her.

'It's …' She trails off, shakes her head. 'I don't know … it's different. I can't explain.'

'Lil, it's your mother not being here any more,' he says gently. 'It's early days yet, it's only a few weeks.'

She nods slowly. 'That's probably it.'

'… Are you feeling OK, Lil?'

'I am. I think I am.'

A beat passes. A sod slips onto the stone hearth: Charlie reaches out with a foot and nudges it back. 'I miss her too,' he says quietly.

The admission touches her. It's an oddly intimate moment, broken by footsteps on the gravel outside. 'That'll be Poll and Joe,' she says, and Charlie sits up, eyes on the door. Wondering, no doubt, how he'll be received by his daughter.

She'll see the car. She'll have advance warning.

The door opens. It's not Poll.

'Hey there,' Joe says. 'You got here after all.' He crosses, hand extended. Good old Joe, can always be relied on.

Charlie stands, shakes his hand. 'How're things?'

'Grand. Can't complain. What happened your car?'

Charlie gives an abridged account of the attack.

'God almighty – I presume the guards were called.'

'Nope. No guards.'

'Where's Poll?' Lily puts in.

'Gone to get her togs – she's going swimming again.'

Hasn't come in to say hello to her father. Not a good start – but here she is, swimsuit in her hand. Thank goodness Lily thought to take it in before the rain began.

'Hi, Dad.' A tiny smile for him. It's something. 'Thought you weren't coming.'

'Poll, good to see you. Got here in the end, didn't want to miss it.'

Awful to hear the hearty tone in his voice, the cautious note in hers. Sad to observe the distance that's grown between them. Tragic not to know how to help.

'Mind if I join you for a swim?' he asks.

A second, two seconds. Please, Lily begs silently. Please.

'Sure. See you down there.' And she's gone, tapping up the stairs, yet to discover that Chloë is here too.

Charlie drains his glass and sets it on the mantelpiece.

'You're as mad as your daughter,' Joe says, 'swimming in this weather.'

Charlie grins, his humour restored. 'You should try it sometime, Joe – puts pep in your step. Lil, will I open another bottle, let it breathe before dinner?'

'Do, I suppose.'

'Right, see you later so.'

After he's left the room Joe sinks into the vacated chair. 'That girl of yours can walk – I'll give her that. We must have done ten miles. We got the stuff you wanted; it's in the kitchen.'

She looks at him. The normality of him, the lack of undercurrents with him. What a relief he is.

'Get yourself a glass of wine,' she says. 'Bring the bottle.'

Thomas

HE FOLDS A SHIRT AND PLACES IT ON TOP OF THE T-shirts. He adds shorts and jeans and underwear and socks. He fills his toilet bag with toothbrush and razor and shower gel and deodorant and aftershave. As he's about to close the case he thinks of his swimming trunks.

He can't remember when he last wore them. He scrolls back in his head and arrives at the solo trip he took to Guernsey one September while he was still working in the hospital. He hired a bike and cycled the length and breadth of the island – not difficult, nine miles by three, someone told him, at its widest part – and swam alone in the bays, ignoring the drizzle that persisted for most of his stay. Compared to the Atlantic, the Channel was balmy.

By the time he locates his trunks and turns to add them to the case Rasputin has settled there, curled up on his clothes. 'Sorry, boy.' He lifts out the cat and places him on the bed. Rasputin stretches unhurriedly – front half, back half – and leaps down, and stalks across the room to the door.

Thomas listens to the soft tap of his claws on the wooden stairs. Gone in search of the other two, who left for the airport and Austria last evening. *No sign of the Von Trapps*, Sam texted this morning, *but the sun is here. Off to do some yodelling in the Alps. Enjoy the gathering of the clan in the old homestead.*

Sam hasn't come out and said what he thinks of the trip to Land's End. He didn't have to.

What – everyone is going? Old partners, new partners, the whole kit and caboodle all mucking in together? Whose idea was that?

Mum's, Thomas told him. *And Chloë's not going, but everyone else is.* Careful, as always, to hop quickly over the mention of her.

Right. Pause. *But your dad will be there, and – what's his name again, your mum's guy?*

Joe.

Joe, right. Have you ever done this before? Stayed overnight all together, I mean.

No, first time.

OK.

He said no more, but the very act of not commenting told Thomas what he thought. Thomas can't see the problem. Dad and Mum are both well over the split, both settled with new partners – and with Chloë not there, Poll and Dad should be OK.

In the kitchen he takes the bread-and-butter pudding from the fridge. Looks promising, crunchy and golden on top just like Freda said, bit of a spring to it when he presses down. He wraps the dish in tinfoil and stows it carefully in the box that Matt's new running shoes came in. He carries it out to the car and places it in a corner of the boot, and packs his bedding around it. His case goes on the back seat, along with two six-packs of beer. It seems like a lot of stuff for a couple of nights.

He returns to the house and checks again that he's closed all the windows. He rattles kibble into Rasputin's dish and tops up his water. He pulls the front door closed and gets into the car, and all the while the thing that's been nagging at him throughout the day continues to pick at the edge of his mind.

Rasputin is sorted. Their neighbour Kellie will call in the morning to refill his bowl before she goes to work, and she'll be in and out over the weekend. Anyway, the cat is well able to fend for himself – they're aware that several of the neighbours already feed him leftovers when he slips out through the cat flap. It's not Rasputin that's bothering him, it's something else – but what?

Traffic is lighter than he'd anticipated: most travellers must have got away yesterday. He makes it to the outskirts without delay and pulls up at a petrol station and fills the tank. As he's paying, he spots a display case of Lotto scratchcards, and on a whim he asks for six.

He leaves the building and crosses the forecourt to his car.

'Sorry there—'

He turns to see a youth, mid-teens, cradling a large bottle of Coke.

'You wouldn't be going to Galway, by any chance?'

Grimy black tracksuit top, the collar of another visible beneath. Bagging denim jeans that could do with a good scrub. Immaculate, expensive-looking trainers on his feet, in stark contrast to the rest of his attire. Gaunt face, hollowed cheeks. An inch-long gash that looks recent on his left temple, held closed with three black stitches. Bloodshot scribbles in the yellowish whites of his eyes, lips dry and cracked. Brown hair cut close to his scalp.

'I couldn't scrounge a lift, could I? It would really help me out, man.'

Thomas doesn't want to say yes. He's never given a lift to

a hitcher in his life, has always been wary about picking up strangers – but how can he refuse now? The boy can't be more than sixteen, with the thrown-about appearance of someone who doesn't generally get to sleep in a bed at night, and the undernourished look of someone who rarely enjoys three square meals a day. Not exactly the passenger anyone would willingly choose – but Thomas can't say no, not when it's put up to him like this.

It won't kill him to help someone out. Call it his good deed for the day: Freda would be proud of him.

'I'm not going to Galway, but I can bring you most of the way.'

'Thanks, man, appreciate it.'

He opens the door and scoots into the passenger seat. As soon as Thomas opens the driver's door he's hit with a strong wave of the boy's unwashed stench. He peels off his jacket and tosses it onto the back seat, next to his case. He slips the Lotto tickets into the cubby under the steering wheel and winds his window halfway down, even though it's still raining. Seventy miles or thereabouts of dual carriageway until he turns off the Galway road: an hour and a bit, barring hold-ups. Rain or no rain, he'll need fresh air.

He starts the car and moves off towards the exit. 'Not a great day,' he says, wondering what they'll talk about once they've used up the weather.

No response. He glances left and sees that the boy has tipped back his head and closed his eyes. Exhausted maybe, after sleepless nights on the street. Just as well: no need to hunt for conversational topics.

He goes to turn on the radio and stops himself. He wonders what the boy's story is, how he came to be in such a state. His dishevelled appearance would suggest a habit of some kind, drugs or alcohol: something that makes healthy food less of a priority and pushes personal hygiene into the background. The bottle of Coke lies at his feet: hardly a balanced diet.

Thomas might offer him a few euro when he drops him off – could he suggest that he uses it to buy proper grub, or would that sound patronising? Should charity come without attached conditions?

Freda would say it should. She'd feed this boy unquestioningly, or give him what change she had if he looked for it. Wouldn't expect any thanks for it either.

Freda.

Freda's birthday.

Today is her birthday. Today is her thirtieth birthday.

It comes to him in a rush, scattering his thoughts. He forgot her birthday, forgot it completely. He forgot to surprise her with a few candles in a cake, forgot to get everyone in the café singing like he'd planned. Didn't even buy her a bloody card. Didn't even wish her a happy birthday.

He's angry with himself. He should have put a reminder into his phone. No, he shouldn't have needed to do that – it's only a couple of days since she mentioned it. How utterly thoughtless of him to have forgotten it.

No wonder she was quiet all day. She wasn't tired, she was disappointed. She wouldn't have expected a cake, or even a card. She'd have been happy if he'd just acknowledged it, if he'd simply made a reference to it, but he'd been too preoccupied, too obsessed with himself and the weekend and his impossible situation with Chloë.

He'll make amends. He'll get her a belated gift of some kind next week. He's clueless when it comes to choosing presents, but Poll might help.

An hour into the journey the rain begins to lighten, then

finally stops altogether. His passenger remains unmoving, his body odour thick in the air. When was the last time he had a shower, or even a wash in a public toilet? When did he last change his clothes? The car will have to be given a good airing after this – no better place than Land's End, where the sea breeze can sweep through it.

After what seems like an awfully long time – no radio to distract him – he spots the roundabout ahead where he must turn off the Galway road. He moves to the right lane and takes the third exit, and pulls in to the grassy verge. The dashboard clock shows six twenty-five: he'll be in Land's End around seven. Just in time for dinner.

'We're here,' he says. 'This is where I have to drop you.'

The boy's eyes immediately snap open. Was he feigning sleep all along, or has a life on the streets trained him to wake abruptly?

'Go back to the roundabout and turn right,' Thomas tells him. 'You're about twenty minutes from Galway. There's plenty of traffic – you shouldn't have a problem getting another lift.' Although this is doubtful, given the state of him.

He waits for the boy to open his door, but that's not what happens. Instead, he unclips his seatbelt and reaches inside his tracksuit top and draws out a knife with a long thin blade.

At the sight of it, Thomas's heart jumps.

'Sorry, man,' the boy says. Not sounding sorry. Sounding, if anything, bored. A slight smile on his lips, even.

Everything in Thomas seems to melt and dissolve. His face floods with heat. He looks from the weapon to the bland expression of the boy. He opens his mouth to speak: nothing emerges.

'I need your car, man – and your wallet too.'

His car, his money. Thomas finds his voice. 'I gave you a lift.'

The boy's expression hardens into a sneer. 'You want a round of applause, is it?' He jabs the air with the knife – Thomas rears away from it, his back thumping against the door. 'Come on, man.' Harder tone now, another jab. 'Don't make me cut you. I will, I swear it. Give us the wallet and get out.'

What can he do? The boy could be on something. He could be unpredictable, his judgement skewed. No knowing if he'd really carry out his threat – but how can Thomas take the chance?

Cars drive past. He wants to alert them, but he's afraid to risk it. Seeing no alternative, he takes his wallet from his shirt pocket – he was going to offer money! – and hands it over silently, thinking of the eighty euro cashback he asked for when paying for his petrol.

The wallet is rammed into a jeans pocket. 'And your phone.'

'I haven't got it.' Praying it doesn't choose this moment to ring. 'I left it at home.'

'Like fuck you did.' Thankfully, he doesn't pursue it. 'Get out so. Go on, get a move on.' Swiping again with the knife, missing Thomas's face by inches.

'Let me take my stuff,' Thomas says, indicating the case on the back seat. 'There's nothing valuable in it.'

But the boy is already clambering over the gear stick, waiting to claim the driver's seat. Up close, his stench is even more awful. 'Bet your phone's in it though. Get the fuck out, man.'

'Give me my jacket at least,' Thomas pleads. 'It's going to rain again.'

'*Fuck* your jacket,' the boy retorts, knuckles white on the knife handle. 'Get the *fuck* out.' Another jab. 'Go on, or I'll *fucking* cut you to ribbons.'

Thomas opens the door, mind racing. Could he flag a passing

car now? Is there still a chance to stop this outrage happening? But as luck would have it, no cars pass as he steps out, and those on the roundabout are too far away.

At the last minute he reaches back in and tries to grab the keys from the ignition, no plan in his head other than to stop the car being taken – but the boy gives a shout, and lunges with the knife, and Thomas pulls his hand back sharply, barely avoiding the blade.

The door is slammed closed. The knife is tossed onto the passenger seat; the boy guns the engine and whips the car around with a screech of tyres. He lifts a hand to wave, grinning, before skidding off, causing a hot wave of anger to flood through Thomas. He watches, blood racing with rage and shock, as the car heads into the roundabout and takes the road for Galway. *His* car.

He tallies up what he has just lost. A tank full of petrol, or almost full. Nearly a hundred euro in cash, including the money that was there before he got the cashback. His bank cards, his jacket, his suitcase of clothes and toiletries. His house key, attached to the same ring as the one for the car. What else?

The beer. His bedding in the boot. The bread-and-butter pudding.

What must he do? He can't think straight. He paces the grass verge, trying to focus. Without his jacket it's chilly.

His phone: he whips it from his jeans pocket. He must call the guards, report the crime – but he sees to his dismay that the battery is almost empty. His charger, of course, is in the case, not that it would help him now.

He might only have minutes left on it. If he uses up those minutes on a call to the guards he won't have any way of contacting anyone else. The guards will hardly send a squad car out for him, even if he tells them he's stranded. He needs to call someone who can come and pick him up – but who?

No mobile signal at Land's End, so they're no good to him. Not that he wants to go there now – not much point to it, with no change of clothes and no money – but he can't stay on the side of the road, and Land's End is nearer than home.

And then he remembers Aidan, headed there like himself this evening. Would he have left the city before Thomas? Would he have shut the gallery early, and already arrived?

Maybe not. Maybe in this regard at least, fate will be on Thomas's side. He scrolls quickly through his contacts and presses Aidan's number. He listens to the rings, praying for the call to be answered, praying that they're not disconnected before Aidan picks up. If that happens, his only hope will be if Aidan is on the road, and due to pass this way at some stage. That, or hitch a lift, which he's never done in his life.

He's in luck. 'Thomas – everything OK?'

'Aidan, I'm almost out of battery.' He rapidly gives his location, and the bones of his quandary. 'Are you en route?'

'I am, about fifteen minutes away from you, I'd say. Sit tight.'

Fifteen minutes – could have been a lot worse. It strikes him after he hangs up that he and Aidan should have arranged to travel together. Why did neither of them suggest it? This whole mess would have been avoided – even if they were unlucky enough to encounter the teen, he'd hardly try to hijack a car with the two of them in it, regardless of how high he was. And Thomas could have come back on Monday with Mum or Dad, or with Aidan and Poll.

He suddenly recalls the six Lotto tickets he bought at the petrol station. He sees them in his mind's eye, tucked into the cubby under the steering wheel. The thought of the youth scratching them, maybe winning money on them, increases Thomas's fury.

The guards. He must ring them quickly – but as he dials 999 his phone gives a single sustained beep, and directly afterwards his screen goes black.

A minute later, the rain begins again.

Charlie

HE'D FORGOTTEN THE DEPTH OF HIS FEELING FOR THE place. As soon as he turned into the driveway, the instant he set eyes on the house, the love came rushing back, warming him like an embrace.

We're here, he said to Chloë, and she lifted her head from a biography of Morrissey - a singer whose voice Charlie couldn't abide - and regarded the house.

It's big, she said, and nothing else. It shouldn't have disappointed him - she didn't know the house like he did, she couldn't be expected to enthuse - but it did. He turned away from her and drank it in.

It looked precisely as he remembered it, or almost. The hydrangeas could do with a bit of cutting back, the place was crying out for a fresh coat of paint, but by and large it was the house he saw when he closed his eyes at night.

He opened his door and stepped from the car. He inhaled the glorious pure air, filled his lungs with it. This, all of this, he'd missed. His gaze fastened on the window of the green room. He hoped that was where Lily had put them so Chloë could get the sea view. He reckoned she'd have wanted to show off the house to Chloë, to let her see it at its best – and she might also have wanted to remind him of what *he*'d have continued to enjoy if he'd stayed with her.

He was wrong. They're in a back room, with no view of the sea. It's another disappointment, but a minor one. He's here, that's all that matters.

But he's cold, so cold, after the swim. His hands are frozen; his teeth won't stop chattering. *You first,* he said to Poll when they got back, and now, ten shivering minutes later, it's his turn for the shower.

The mirror above the sink has steamed up. He rubs it clear with his towel and sees a tousled mess of greying hair, a chalk-white craggy face, lips a rather alarming shade of bluish-purple.

How old he looks. All those lines. When did they happen?

What does she see in him?

He turns on the shower over the bath. He peels off his sodden togs and steps in. He'd forgotten the feeble flow of the water here, but it's blessedly hot. He stands underneath it, feeling the warmth returning slowly to his body, spreading out to his fingertips, working its way down to his toes.

When he's fully thawed he swipes the bar of soap from the sink, humming Beethoven's Fifth – da da da *daaah,* da da da *daaah* – and washes the salt from his skin. He'll sleep tonight, always sleeps like a baby here.

Good to get the swim in with Poll just now, even if they didn't do too much talking. Even if, when they did, their remarks were studied and careful. She asked about the car; he enquired after her work. The gallery was mentioned, and a film he'd seen that he thought she'd like. She told him of a recent chance encounter with a mutual acquaintance. Nothing that dipped below the surface, nothing that suggested a shared past, a blood connection.

Good just to be with her though, good to have her to himself. He can't remember when that happened last. They might do it again tomorrow – didn't he hear a good forecast for Sunday?

He hopes she's OK with Chloë being here. He doesn't think she's aware of her presence yet. He made no mention of it when they were swimming, too cowardly to risk upsetting the fragile equilibrium of their exchanges. He hopes she's not annoyed when she finds out.

He wishes she'd learn to accept him and Chloë. He wishes he didn't have to keep tiptoeing around that with her. Has he committed such a crime, falling for someone so much younger? Yes, he can see how it might be a little uncomfortable for her that she and Chloë are so close in age – but is he to be punished for the rest of his life for following his heart, regardless of where it had led him?

Poll and Aidan have been together what – two years, is it, or a bit longer? Lily could tell you to the day. No sign of them getting married. He wouldn't mind an old fogey like him being slow to go again, but it's a bit sad when the young ones seem to have lost interest in the institution. Going out of fashion, it would seem, to promise in front of witnesses to spend the rest of your lives together.

Or maybe he and Lily had put her off marriage. It's a depressing possibility. Why would she aspire to something that had ended in failure for her parents?

He steps out and dries himself. His towel is one Chloë bought a few weeks earlier, along with two others. It's grey and soft and wonderfully thick, and probably cost far more than he would have spent. He's learnt not to scrutinise his credit card bills too closely.

He wipes the mirror and opens the window and leaves the bathroom. Without thinking he makes for the family room, located at the top of the stairs. As soon as he opens the door he realises his mistake.

He stays put, reacquainting himself with the familiar space. This is the largest of the bedrooms, where Kitty slept as a small girl with her four older sisters, before they graduated in turn to more private quarters. This is the room that was set aside two generations later for Charlie and Lily and the children when they came on holidays.

He casts his mind back, recalling the many, many nights they'd spent in the room. There are the bunks where Thomas and Poll slept, nestled into the alcove created by the chimney breast; there the bed he and Lily shared, on the opposite side of the room. There is the chest of three generous drawers, and the double wardrobe that accommodated the rest of their summer clothing.

The two windowsills are bare now but he can see, as if they were still there, Thomas's annual shell collections spread over both. A canvas bag used to hang from the wardrobe-door handle, holding their buckets and spades and fishing nets; a jumble of flip-flops and sandals lived beneath the bottom bunk; tubes of sun screen, antiseptic cream and bottles of calamine lotion were set out on the chest of drawers.

Their suitcases, piled onto the wardrobe. His books, stacked on the locker. His cello, resting in the corner. Lily's white straw sunhat, thrown over one of the bed knobs.

He sees it all again in his mind's eye. The four of them together, Thomas and Poll tucked up safe and sound with their parents. He remembers lying in bed, listening to the small noises of them sleeping across the room, the whimpers and sighs and chuckles of their dreams, before drifting to sleep, twined around Lily. He remembers waking in the morning – very early in the morning – when one or both of his children pattered across the floor to clamber sleepily into the double bed.

They were happy then, the four of them. He took their happiness completely for granted, and never envisaged a time when everything would change, and their comfortable little unit would be no more.

He closes the door softly and opens the next. The curtains haven't been drawn: Chloë is not a fan of closed curtains. It took him a while to learn to sleep with the night uncovered.

He pads in quietly, shutting the door with a soft click. She's curled in the bed, pretty much buried beneath the covers; a tumble of hair on her pillow is all that's visible. *It's cold*, she'd said while he made the bed. *So cold here*. Shoulders hunched, rubbing her arms.

The heat is on, he'd pointed out. *Old houses are hard to warm up.*

You should have told me.

He should have told her what? That a house she knew was nearly a hundred years old would be colder than their modern double-glazed apartment? He's getting fed up with her. Scarcely a word to Lily on their arrival, no condolences on her mother's death, no thanks offered for the invitation to Land's End. And the one bathroom for everyone, when she made that discovery, hadn't gone down well either. Wait till she tries to use her phone.

It would have been best to come alone.

He spreads his togs on the radiator and crouches to get clothes from his case. Rain falls steadily, pattering on the room's two windows. He hears a rustle from the bed and turns to see her rising onto an elbow to regard him solemnly.

'Hi,' he says.

'Hi.'

'I had a swim with Poll.'

She shudders. 'In the rain?'

'It didn't start until we were out.'

Her face is soft from sleep, her cheeks faintly flushed. He's always loved the way she looks just after waking. He pulls out boxers, jeans, a sweatshirt. Maybe he should go to her, maybe they need to let their bodies bring them together again, let the act of sex banish the ugliness of yesterday.

But they are under the same roof as his ex-wife. They are in the house where he and Lily had sex many times over the years, stealing upstairs in the afternoons when the children were elsewhere with Kitty. Turning the key in the lock so they wouldn't be disturbed.

Chloë hadn't accompanied him to Kitty's funeral, hadn't asked him if he wanted her there. It was probably best that she hadn't gone, but it still rankled a little that she didn't suggest it. And now here she is in Kitty's house, showing precious little regard for it. Here she is in the house of the woman who became like a second mother to him when his own died, the woman who was big enough to forgive him for separating from her daughter.

The woman who was never told of his relationship with Chloë because she would have disapproved; she would have thought less of him.

He steps into the boxers. He pulls them up, lets the towel drop. 'I'm going to give a hand with dinner,' he says. 'I'll call you when it's ready.'

'Fine.' She sinks down, disappears again beneath her grandmother's quilt.

He finishes getting dressed and leaves the room quietly.

Poll

'JUST AS WELL WE DIDN'T COME FOR THE WEATHER,' her mother remarks, standing at the sitting-room window as the rain beats against the glass. That shade of blue suits her. The cut of the dress shows off her trim figure. 'That rain will make the traffic worse for the others.'

Poll makes no reply. Aidan promised faithfully he'd close the gallery an hour early. Even with heavy traffic she would have thought he'd be here by now. She tried phoning him from the supermarket when Joe was paying for their purchases, but the call went straight to his voicemail. *Looking forward to seeing you*, she told him. *Drive carefully.*

The door is pushed open and Joe enters, his arms piled with black turf sods. 'Forecast is good for tomorrow,' he tells them, tipping the sods into the waiting wicker basket, brushing his jumper clean. 'They're talking about nineteen degrees.'

Her mother looks doubtful. 'Nineteen degrees in April?'

'That's what they're saying.'

The fire, tended since noon, flickers in the brick fireplace. A pair of brass floor lamps topped with cream-fringed shades stand like sentries in opposite corners of the room, throwing out twin circles of muted light. Poll is in the rocking chair, always her favourite. She remembers sitting here on Gran's lap on rainy afternoons, playing I Spy while Thomas and Dad made Lego houses on the floor.

Outside the daylight is fading, the night ushered in more rapidly by the leaden sky. Hard to imagine warmth tomorrow, hard to believe the sky might actually have some blue in it, but they'll live in hope.

Her father appears in the doorway, wearing one of Gran's aprons. His hair is combed back from his forehead. 'All set,' he says, looking pleased. He carries a glass with red wine in it.

'Oh, good. Joe, put a few sods on the fire to hold it.'

'Are we not going to wait for the others?' Poll asks.

'Oh, I don't think there's any need – they won't mind. Poll, would you tell Chloë dinner is ready?'

'I can do it,' Dad says quickly, but Poll is already up, not looking at him as she makes for the stairs. Mum was happy to wait for ages last night when she thought he and Chloë were on the way, but she can't hold on five minutes for Aidan and Thomas.

Of course that's not really what's annoying her. What's really annoying her is that *she*'s here, after the relief last night of thinking they'd been spared.

He told you she came? Mum asked, when Dad was in the shower. No, he hadn't. He hadn't bothered to tell her while they were swimming – or maybe he'd been too chicken to tell her. Maybe he'd been happy to let Mum do his dirty work for him.

At least Aidan will be here soon.

She should have waited until today and come down with him.

She climbs the stairs unhurriedly, aware of Dad watching her from below. She will smile. She will be polite if it kills her.

She won't give the smallest sign that she's in any way put out, but she will *not* be friendly.

She taps on the bedroom door.

'Yes?'

'Dinner's ready.'

A patter of steps. The door is thrown open.

Chloë wears a tunic the colour of cornflowers that falls to mid-thigh, a dark blue wrap thrown over it. Slim grey trousers beneath, little black pumps studded with gold on her feet. Threaded through her hair, pulling it up into a careless bunch from which rogue curls tumble, is a narrow scarf in a paler shade of grey than the trousers.

Her eyes are framed in smudgy black, her lips painted a pretty shell pink. Her skin is luminescent.

Next to her, Poll feels dowdy and fat. The patterned top that Aidan loves, the linen pants that pick up the green of the top, suddenly seem loud and tasteless.

'Hi,' Chloë says. 'Long time no see. Sorry about your gran.'

'You didn't come to the funeral.'

It slips out. She had no idea it was going to. She didn't even want her at the funeral – and yet out it comes. Blunt. Accusing.

Chloë's rather bland expression doesn't change. 'I didn't think I needed to, since I never met her.'

'And yet here you are in her house.'

Scalp prickling, palms hot. So much for being polite. So much for not showing how seriously put out she is that this *person* had the gall to come here.

A beat passes. 'Actually, I was invited here. Your mother invited me.'

Her tone gone a bit steely now. Staring steadily at Poll. There's a challenge in the stare. *I'm able for you,* the stare says.

Poll is able too. Poll is more than able.

'Dinner's ready,' she repeats, and turns for the stairs with a knot inside her.

At dinner there's a new tension. It's in her mother's brittle smile, her father's forced laugh. It's in the overly polite conversation, and the small silences between remarks before someone rushes to fill them. Joe alone seems unaware of the atmosphere, or maybe he's choosing to ignore it.

Poll picks at the wedge of quiche on her plate, ignoring the steaming bowl of Gerry's potatoes. The sea air usually gives her such an appetite, and today she got more than her share of it, with the long walk and the swim with Dad afterwards. She should be ravenous, but she's not.

Being here is a jumble of happy and sad. Everywhere she goes in the house she sees Gran, or an echo of her. Folding back a bedspread, mopping a floor, chopping carrots, polishing a banister. In the act of closing Thomas's bedroom window earlier she glanced out and there Gran was, or there her ghost was, rolling the hand mower across the grass.

These sightings, these fancied sightings, don't frighten her. They're a reminder of her loss, of course – they say to Poll, *This is what you had, and what you no longer have* – but they also bring good memories flooding back, memories of when Gran was healthy and strong, and running the B&B every summer was no bother to her.

She can't *connect* with her, though, can't feel that Gran knows she's there. Can't decide whether she's imagining the whole thing, just because she wants it so much.

And swimming with her father was sad too. So much has changed between them since he and Mum broke up. They tried, both of them tried, while they swam together in the sea. He tried a little harder maybe, but the chasm between them remained wide.

'Wine?' her mother asks, the bottle poised above Poll's glass, but Poll shakes her head. Not in a wine mood, too jumpy until Aidan arrives.

'Salad?'

Chloë, seated across the table, is offering her the bowl. She hasn't said one thing, not a single solitary thing, to Dad since she entered the room, since she sailed in like the lady of the manor. Gushing at Joe, saying she hadn't seen him in so long, but not so much as glancing once in Dad's direction.

There are rings of red onion in the salad that Poll will have to fish out. Did her father forget that she hates raw onion, that a portion of salad was always set aside for her before it was added? Or did he remember and not care?

'Charlie tells me you went swimming,' Chloë goes on.

Charlie tells me – how it grates. Making a point of mentioning him, driving home the fact of their togetherness. Pretending to be friendly with Poll in front of everyone else.

'Yes,' Poll replies, conscious of her mother's wary glance. On tenterhooks for fear of Poll losing the rag and disgracing herself.

'You might join them tomorrow,' Joe puts in, twinkling at Chloë.

She laughs. High, false. She all but bats her eyelashes at him. 'I'm afraid I don't swim.'

'Yes you do,' Dad puts in. 'You swam last year when we were in Greece.'

'I didn't say I *can't* swim, I said I *don't*. Not in Ireland.' Her tone cool, her smile drifting away. Not looking at Dad while she addresses him.

He makes no response, just resumes eating. In the short silence that follows, Lily's knife scrapes across her plate. Joe clears his throat, makes a big thing of helping himself to more salad. Finally feeling the tension, maybe. The air's so thick with it, it's a wonder they can breathe at all.

'The other two are late,' Poll remarks, just to break into the quiet. 'They should have been here by now. Aidan said he'd leave early.'

'Maybe the gallery was busy,' Chloë replies. 'He'd hardly close early if someone was about to drop a small fortune.'

Another wide smile, but everything she says feels like it's studded with thorns.

'I wouldn't worry,' Joe says. 'Rain always delays things. They'll be here soon.'

'Hope so.'

They finish dinner and move on to the remains of the apple crumble, and after that they drink coffee and take out the mint chocolates Joe brought, and still no sign of the other two. The candles Mum stuck into Gran's old china holders dribble wax down their lengths: a few errant drops spatter the table. Conversation remains sporadic; short exchanges followed by what feels to Poll like increasingly edgy bouts of silence. Finally, unable to bear it any longer, she pushes back her chair.

'I'm going out to the veranda. I need some fresh air.'

'Poll, you'll freeze out there,' her mother says. 'And you'll have nowhere to sit with the chairs in the shed.'

'I won't stay long.'

'At least take my shawl: it's on the bed.'

So she climbs the stairs for the umpteenth time and opens the door to the room that was Gran's. Her first time to enter it since their arrival, fearful of what it might do to her heart, but here she is.

She stands. She looks around. It's familiar, but changed.

The high mahogany double bed is covered now with Mum's

duvet, but Poll remembers a blue candlewick bedspread, a bolster pillow, a folded plaid rug.

There's the big wardrobe in the corner, and the chest of drawers next to it against the end wall. There's the pink padded chair by the window, where Gran would sit with a piece of knitting while Poll had doll tea parties on the bed. When the soft *click-click* of the needles halted Poll would glance up and catch her, hands stilled, looking quietly out at the sea. Remembering, maybe, the brother and sisters who had sailed across it and never come home.

The dressing table is missing its lace runner. Poll remembers Gran's various bits and pieces laid out on it. The squat glass jar of her face cream, the single gold tube of pink lipstick - always the same shade, something Candy it was called. The powder compact with its flat round pad, putting Poll in mind of the mushrooms that would appear overnight under the trees at the end of the garden during damp spells. The fluted perfume bottle whose contents smelt of the lavender bush beside the shed. The shell-encrusted jewellery box that Mum had made for her long ago, while she was still a girl in school.

Poll runs a hand over the knobby surface of the woodchip wallpaper, painted over in cream for years: how many coats has it had by now? She regards the pair of man's check slippers at the foot of the bed. Yes, Joe would be the type to bring his slippers on a weekend break. Dad, as far back as she can remember, never owned a pair: around the house he wore canvas shoes, winter and summer.

She crosses to the bed and sits on the edge. Through the open door she can hear voices rising faintly from the kitchen, a sputter of male laughter. She conjures up an image of Gran sitting on a stool before the dressing table, spraying perfume onto her wrists, taking a string of pearls from the jewellery box to drape around her neck.

'I need help,' she says. The words sound startlingly loud in the silent room. 'I need your help. I wish I knew if you were really here.'

She listens, hears nothing. After another minute she rises. She gathers up Mum's shawl – mint green cashmere, beautifully soft and light – and makes her way back downstairs and out through the front door. The veranda seems so long and empty without its complement of wicker furniture. If tomorrow is nice they should take it out.

The rain has stopped, for the moment at least, but the evening remains damp and chilly. She imagines a pile-up on the dual carriageway, screaming bloodied bodies trapped in twisted metal. In this weather it could happen so easily, everyone in a rush, roads slick with rain. All it would take would be one idiot on his phone, veering unaware towards the car in the next lane —

Stop. Cut that out. He got delayed, that's all, caught up in the snarl of cars leaving the city for the long weekend. He'll show up full of apologies for being late. Thomas too, part of the same slow exodus. They should have travelled together, she thinks suddenly. Why did neither of them suggest it?

She draws in the cool air. Everything's freshly washed – that was how Gran always put it after rain. Leaves shiny and dripping, gravel gleaming. Darkness closing in, the gulls silenced for the day. The sea a shining mass, quiet and calm, barely a ripple to disturb its surface.

She gets a whiff of Mum's flowery scent from the shawl. The wooden railing is beaded with drops; its white paint is flaking. She could do it: she could come down during the summer and paint it a pretty duck-egg blue, or maybe a dove grey. If she and Aidan part, it will give her something to do, something to take her mind off the ache of his loss.

Maybe she could move down here, rig up a studio in the

shed, find a new stockist for her heads. She could become the reclusive potter, like the artist a few miles away who rarely shows his face in the village. Yes, that might work. She could talk to Mum, see how she felt about Poll moving in.

She doesn't think she'd be lonely – or not any lonelier than in the city, surrounded by people she can never allow to love her.

She walks the length of the veranda. Fifteen paces it takes her. When she was small it seemed enormous, a mile long.

A sound in the distance – a car? She returns quickly to the steps, straining to hear. Yes, definitely a car – coming this way. She can see the beam of its headlights now on the road, cranes to make out the shape of it as it draws closer. Thomas or Aidan?

As it turns into the drive she recognises the Saab with a joyful leap of her heart. She watches it pull up behind Joe's Land Rover – and then she can't help herself. She flings off Mum's shawl and tosses it onto the railing. She races down the steps and reaches the car as he gets out. She throws herself into his arms, almost knocking him sideways.

'Hey –' He grabs at his glasses, catches them as they're about to fly off. 'Steady on there, Poll!'

'I thought something had happened to you.' Clinging to him, pressing her face into the crook of his neck, inhaling his smell. Not wanting to lose him. 'You're late, I was scared, we were all worried. Why are you so late?'

She feels his arms going around her – oh, the comfort of them, oh, the bliss of his embrace. 'Poll,' he says gently, 'something *did* happen, but not to me.'

She hears the passenger door open. Astonished, she lifts her head to peer over Aidan's shoulder.

'Thomas,' she says.

Lily

HE HAD A KNIFE.

He threatened her son with a knife.

Some lowlife, some scumbag forced her son out of his own car at knifepoint. After Thomas had shown him kindness, after he'd taken him in, this delinquent was prepared, presumably, to hurt him. Maybe even prepared, if he had taken enough of the wrong kind of substance, to kill him. She shuts off that thought, unable to countenance it.

The anger she feels towards Thomas's attacker, towards this sorry individual she's never met, is primeval and ferocious. The rage, the hot, gut-burning fury comes from deep in her core, born of a mother's single-minded blind instinct to protect her young, even when they're not young any more. Thinking about what the boy did to Thomas, and what he might have done to him, curls her hands into fists, tightens every muscle in her face. She'd kill him, no problem, if he'd caused Thomas any real harm.

She imagines lashing out, giving full rein to her anger. Kicking and punching and clawing, doing what damage she could to him. She imagines putting her hands around his neck and squeezing with every ounce of her strength, watching the skin of his face become purple and mottled, watching the focus leave his eyes.

First Charlie, now Thomas. It feels like her family is under attack. Is Poll next? Is she herself next? Are they safe here?

Of course they're safe. It's coincidence, that's all. Lots of traffic during bank holidays, delays and tempers running high, plenty of opportunities for those with badness on their minds.

As the two new arrivals eat, the rest of the story comes out. Aidan picked up Thomas after the incident, wet through on the side of the road. They reported the crime from Aidan's phone, and were told that Thomas should call to a garda station the following day to make a full statement. They made a brief stop at a pub so Thomas could change his clothes and drink a hot whiskey.

His wrists poke from the sleeves of Aidan's sweater; the tracksuit bottoms are similarly too short. Only Joe's slippers, which were offered to him on arrival, fit perfectly. His sodden clothes are drying on various radiators.

Lily watches as he eats the quiche that was kept for him. She wants to hold him. He looks shell-shocked, bewildered. She wishes, like she so often wishes, that he had somebody special, like Poll has Aidan. Like she has Joe.

His phone is hooked up to some charger or other, even though it'll be of precious little good to him here. His shoes have been stuffed with newspaper. Poll, the only driver who didn't have wine, took her mother's car to the village so she could call the emergency number – thankfully stored in Dad's wallet – to report the theft of Thomas's bank cards.

They've made up his bed with the spare sheets Lily brought along, just in case, and a heavy, ornate patchwork quilt donated by Charlie and Chloë. A T-shirt of Charlie's, emergency nightwear, has been wrapped around a hot-water bottle.

The closest garda station is back in Galway, around forty-five minutes' drive away: Aidan or Charlie will ferry Thomas there tomorrow afternoon. They're doing what they can for him, attempting to minimise the trauma of what happened, and still Lily feels impotent, and furious.

And beneath that rage she is conscious of a continuing scratching irritation at the presence of Chloë at Land's End. There is no logic to her annoyance – the girl was invited, yes, yes – and still she resents it, still it offends her.

And Chloë herself has no great wish to be here either, by the look of her. Silent and sullen for much of the meal, except when she was flirting with Joe, or trying to get a rise out of Poll. Why on earth has she come?

She's clearly still annoyed with Charlie, after he dared to yell at her yesterday. Hardly looking at him, snapping if he dares to address her, seeming not to care what the rest of them are making of it. Lily itches to shake her hard, to tell her to grow up and stop being such a spoilt, sensitive brat.

And her hair, tethered in that ridiculous scarf. She looks like some kind of hippie charlady. Skinny as a waif too – how can Charlie possibly find that attractive? Look what a lovely normal figure Poll has in comparison. She could stand to lose a few pounds maybe, but that's better than looking like someone from the Famine.

Thomas got a land, it was quite obvious, when he saw her. Not expecting her, of course. Hadn't been informed of her change of heart yesterday. Hard to know what he really thinks of her and Charlie, he's such a closed book, but he surely disapproves, even if he goes to dinner with them to keep the peace.

Oh, stop it, she tells herself wearily. Stop obsessing, stop letting them ruin the weekend.

She looks around the table. Everyone assembled now, no one

left to arrive. She should make her announcement while they're all here, all together – but now is not the right time, with Thomas still getting over what happened, and her silently fuming. She'll wait till tomorrow night, when things will surely be calmer.

She tips what's left of the wine into Aidan's glass and looks enquiringly at Thomas. 'You want Dad to open another?'

He shakes his head. 'Thanks, I'm OK.'

'I was thinking,' Charlie says, to nobody in particular, 'of walking to Sully's for a nightcap.'

'Count me out,' Lily says immediately. Last thing she wants now, traipsing in the dark to the pub. Not in this mood.

'Me too,' Chloë puts in. 'I'm going to have an early night.'

Lord, more sleep: what's wrong with the creature?

'I take it Sully's is a bar,' Aidan says.

'It's the nearest to here,' Lily tells him. 'About half a mile away.'

'How about it, Poll – will we go?'

'Why not? Thomas, will you come?'

Another shake of his head. 'I'll pass, not really up for it tonight. Maybe tomorrow.'

'I might tag along,' Joe says, throwing a quick glance at Lily. 'You wouldn't mind?'

'Of course not,' she replies, more tartly than she'd intended. He hardly needs her permission to go for a drink.

Within twenty minutes, after clearing the table, and hunting for and eventually finding a pair of torches, they're ready to go. 'Leave the washing-up,' Charlie says. 'We'll sort it when we get back.' Knowing quite well that Lily can't bear to have dirty dishes lying around: serve him right if she *did* leave them.

Somewhere along the way Chloë vanishes, saying goodnight to nobody. No wine for her at the meal, a cup of her own green tea afterwards: such a clean-living little madam. No offer of help with the washing-up either, happy to leave it to Lily and Thomas.

When it's done Lily makes a pot of tea and they take it through to the sitting room, which is cosy from the fire and aromatic from the turf. Was there ever a time at Land's End when turf from Mulcahy's bog wasn't stacked up against the gable wall of the house – or in more recent times, bagged like the coal and stored in the shed?

Mam always loved her fire. Winter and summer she'd have one lighting each evening in both sitting rooms, much to the delight of her American guests. Of course, an open fire became a thing of the past towards the end, when she couldn't be trusted not to burn the house down. She didn't take to the electric one Charlie installed in the grate, and Lily couldn't blame her: awful soulless thing.

She wonders where it is now. What did they do with it after Kitty went to the nursing home? Charlie must have moved it to the attic when they came to tidy the place up, a month or so after Kitty had vacated it.

Thomas adds fresh turf to the fire. Lily brings his shoes in from the kitchen and places them at the edge of the hearth. 'How are you feeling?' she asks him.

'Better. The food helped.'

She takes her usual chair. 'What a horrible, horrible thing. I so wish it hadn't happened.'

'Me too.' He gets up, brushing at the knees of the ill-fitting tracksuit. 'I hope you didn't feel you had to stay behind to look after me.'

'Not in the least. I'm not in a Sully's mood this evening.'

'No?' He gives a small smile, folds his arms as he looks down at her. 'That's probably my fault.'

'Indeed it's not. I mean, of course I'm upset about what

happened' – a glance towards the door, a lowering of her voice – 'but to tell the truth, I'd much rather Chloë wasn't here. It's annoying me that she is.'

A beat passes. He lowers himself into the rocking chair.

'I know I invited her, I'm just … I was just taken aback when she came, that's all. When we weren't expecting her.'

Again he makes no response, just pushes the floor with a foot to set the chair rocking gently. He's right, of course, not to pursue it.

'Do you remember?' she asks, more to change the subject than anything else. 'We had a timetable for that chair, for you and Poll. To stop you arguing over who got to sit in it.'

He laughs. 'Really?'

'Every twenty minutes, I think it was.'

'Funny.'

A short silence falls between them. After a bit, Thomas goes to say something, and then stops. Lily waits.

'When it happened,' he says, 'the car thing, I mean, I wanted to turn around and go home. I really didn't want to come here.'

'I can understand that.'

'Yes … but now that I'm here I'm glad I came. It's nice to be back.'

'That's good.'

They sip tea while the fire flickers. 'What did you do today?' he asks.

'Me? Oh, nothing much. Karina Clery dropped in eggs this morning, hence the quiche. She stayed for a coffee that lasted a couple of hours – you know how she can talk. Had a stroll on the beach when she left, until the rain came. Spent most of the afternoon in here, doing my crosswords and dozing.'

'Recharging the batteries.'

'Exactly.' She sips more tea. 'I hope you'll sleep tonight. I hope you won't be brooding.'

'I'll do my best.'

'Keep telling yourself he only got the car, and stuff that can be replaced. The main thing is you're OK.'

'True.'

'Remind me to refill your hot-water bottle.'

He smiles. 'Mum, I think I'll manage that. I'm a big boy now.'

Of course he will. Of course he is. Mothering habits die hard. Her mouth stretches into a yawn.

'You're tired,' he says.

'I am, a bit. The sea air.'

So pale and thin his ankles look. Couldn't put weight on him as a child, for all the potatoes and pies she filled him up with. Poor Poll only has to look at food. Hardly fair.

They lapse into an easy silence. As she stretches her legs towards the fire, memories float about in Lily's head. Poll's first fallen-out tooth under her pillow at Land's End. Thomas's broken wrist after a tumble from his bicycle. A ragged doll washed up on the beach, instantly adopted by Poll, a new outfit knitted for it by Mam.

She goes further back, to her own girlhood. She recalls the creamy top from the glass bottle of milk, poured as a treat each morning onto her porridge. A beloved green velvet coat, worn only on Sundays. The small bumps of nettle stings on her calf, rubbed with a dock leaf by her father. The excitement of her aunt Cora's parcels coming from America, wrapped in brown paper and fastened with tightly wound string.

Sadly, quite often, the contents were a dreadful disappointment. Neatly folded dresses that rarely fitted properly, dolls with china faces that she found unnerving. A bright green knitted hat once, horrible bobbly thing. Mercifully,

Mam agreed it was awful, and it was passed on to a village family with more small heads than hats to cover them.

But sometimes Cora got it spectacularly right. A pair of red woollen tights with black polka dots that Lily wore incessantly even though they were at least two sizes too big, causing them to sag at the crotch, to need constant hoicking up. A doll's tea set that literally took her breath away the first time she saw it, flowery blue and white, complete with miniature napkins in matching fabric. A pair of Stars and Stripes hair slides, exotic enough to make her the envy of the school playground for at least a week.

She remembers her mother's delight when her brother Gabriel, missing for years, finally made contact from somewhere in the middle of America. It wasn't long after Lily's father had dropped dead – a few months, no more, everything still tainted with grief – but on the day Gabriel's letter arrived Mam had smiled properly for the first time since becoming a widow.

The Bible Gabriel sent along with the letter had sat on the kitchen dresser for months afterwards. It was opened every evening after dinner, and a verse or two read aloud by one or other of them. A silver frame was bought for the photo contained within its pages.

Sepia-tinted, slightly out of focus. A thin dark-haired bearded man, standing arms folded by a fence and squinting into the sunshine. A check shirt and worn baggy trousers, and a broad smile. The photo was hung in the hall, where it still is. Uncle Gabriel, whom she never met but who has Mam's smile.

She remembers too her mother's wild weeping, just a couple of years after that, when a telegram arrived from Cora with the news that Gabriel was dead. Hadn't seen him in so many years, but still Mam's only brother's death broke her up. Almost four decades ago, but Lily can still recall how cruel it had seemed to her at the time. Why give him back to his sisters after so long, only to whisk him away from them again? As cruel as snatching Dad from Lily and Mam without warning.

'What's it like for you, Mum? Being back here – after Gran, I mean.'

The question breaks into her reverie. It takes her a few seconds to climb out of the past and make sense of it. 'It's … different. It feels a bit different. I suppose it's bound to be, now that—'

She breaks off, surprised by a sudden tightness in her throat, a hot sting behind her eyes. What is this now?

She blinks and tries again. 'Now that she's gone, I mean.' She clears her throat, blinks some more. How silly, she thinks crossly. What nonsense, to find herself on the verge of tears. All that remembering, it'll be. All that delving into the past, dwelling on the deaths and the losses.

She becomes aware that Thomas is looking at her with concern. 'Are you OK, Mum?'

'I'm fine.' She drinks tea too quickly, feels it burn its way down. It steadies her. 'I'm fine,' she says again. 'Just a bit tired. I might head up, actually, if you don't mind.'

'No, of course not. I won't be long after you. Sleep well.'

Ten minutes later, face washed, teeth brushed, she's beneath the duvet in her mother's bed, knees drawn up, hot-water bottle cradled in her arms.

Is she doing the right thing, letting Land's End go? Is she mad, parting with the place she's always called home? It makes sense, though, doesn't it? Because everything has changed, now that Mam is dead and Charlie is gone, and there's no reason to hold on to it any more. What else can she do but say goodbye to it?

They were to retire here, she and Charlie. They were to see

out their days here, if they were lucky enough to keep their wits and their independence to the end. It would have made perfect sense, both of them loving Land's End like they did. But now that's not going to happen. The alternative is her and Joe living here, and she can't see that.

Joe isn't connected to Land's End: he has no history with it. Until this weekend he'd never spent a night under its roof. He can't be expected to love it the way she does, the way Charlie does. Did.

No, still does.

So the house would be empty for much of the time. Of course she and Joe would visit sporadically, and presumably Poll and Aidan and Thomas would too. They'd spend time here, separately or together. Weekends, maybe a week at Easter, maybe longer in the summer – but inevitably, with nobody keeping a full-time eye on things it would fall into slow and possibly unnoticed decline, and by the time it did become apparent, it would surely require the kind of work she wouldn't be able to afford. Joe would want to help, but she couldn't have that – and anyway, his salary was nowhere as good as Charlie's.

So her only option is to sell up, let it go to someone who'll look after it and love it as it deserves to be loved. Of course it will be a wrench, for all of them, but it's the only rational course of action.

She hears Thomas coming upstairs, hears the toilet flush, the water run. Does he even have a toothbrush? Again she feels a stab of sympathy for him, a surge of anger towards his assailant. She recalls the feeling she had downstairs when he asked her how it was to be back here, the almost irresistible urge she'd felt to weep. The year has been a tough one, with the various school challenges, and Mam's death, and the pressure of the wedding hanging over her.

Maybe they could postpone the wedding, just for a few months. Maybe it's a bit soon after Mam. They could wait till Christmas, couldn't they? Where's the rush? Joe might be a bit put out – he's keen to make an honest woman of her – but if she explained she wasn't feeling up to it he'd understand.

Two years in June since they met, their teams up against one another in a golf tournament that was open to all of the city's courses. He bought her a drink in the clubhouse after her team had beaten his. *To show there are no hard feelings*, he'd said.

She'd thought he was sweet, and she liked that he was a vet. It was gratifying to be wanted again after the heartbreak of Charlie, and a relief not to feel she'd have to live the rest of her life alone, the spare at every dinner party, the object of pity among her married friends. It was lovely to be part of a couple again, to fit in again.

The house falls silent, only the usual familiar creaks to be heard. She thinks of Thomas in one of the back bedrooms, Chloë in the other. Shame those two didn't pair up. Would have made so much more sense: a year or two between them, no more. But of course they'd be a disastrous pairing. Chloë would run rings around poor Thomas – he'd never be able for her. Anyway, she's not his type, far too uppity for him.

She cradles the hot-water bottle; she clings to it like a lover. At length, she drifts to sleep.

SUNDAY, 30 APRIL

Thomas

IT IS A COUPLE OF MINUTES BEFORE SIX IN THE morning on the last day of April, and only beginning to be light. Twenty-nine-year-old Thomas Cunningham stands on ice-cold rounded stones at the edge of the Atlantic, wearing nothing at all and trying not to shiver. The early-morning air is chilly: the water, grey as steel, is a thousand times colder. Each small eruption of a wave onto his bare feet is a shock that causes his whole body to tense.

He is light-headed with tiredness, his eyes burn with it, but his head is too full for sleep. His head is full of a hard-faced youth pointing a knife at him and ordering him from his car.

What sleep he did get, over the course of the endless night, came in short bursts, snatched unsatisfying losses of consciousness. Through some nightmarish trick of his overtired imagination he was taken, over and over, to a point beyond yesterday's drama, to the excruciating white-hot pain of the knife blade plunging deep into his chest, to the arc of blood that chased after it as it was yanked out.

After each of these awful episodes he would wake, heart pounding, sweating, too weary to turn on the light and read the newspaper he'd brought upstairs, too exhausted to do anything but drop eventually into another spell of unconsciousness, where the same horrible scenario awaited him.

Finally, on yet another abrupt heart-hammering awakening, he'd had enough. It was still pitch black outside, not even an inkling of light leaking through the window's summery curtains. In the first confusing seconds of wakefulness he couldn't place his surroundings. The bed, he knew, was not his, yet the air around him smelt familiar. He fumbled for his bedside lamp and found the on switch.

The room sprang into being – and still his befuddled mind refused immediately to recognise it. He registered a patterned paper – ferns, lilies – on the walls; a chair on which were draped unfamiliar clothes; a cream-painted dressing table with a spotted mirror and ornate legs; a smaller table by the window holding a china basin and a jug in a matching flowery pattern. Land's End, he finally realised – the knowledge slotting into place, along with the fact that Chloë was sleeping in the next room.

No: he pushed her away. He couldn't deal with her now, couldn't face the memory of his shock at her presence when he'd walked into the kitchen, nerves still stretched taut after what had happened. Couldn't dwell on the fact that she had come after all, that she was here after all – and now he was trapped with her, his only means of escape snatched away yesterday. Trapped but still wanting her, the incessant push-pull of the feelings he shouldn't have.

He reached for his watch. He blinked until the digital display came into focus. Five fifty-one: dawn couldn't be too far away. He threw aside the heavy quilt and swung out his legs, shaking his head free of its horrible imaginings. He had to get up; he had to do something to drag himself out of that ghastly night.

He shed his father's T-shirt and pulled on Aidan's borrowed clothes and emerged barefoot onto the landing, his tired muscles protesting wearily. In the bathroom he emptied his bladder and stole a towel. He tiptoed down the stairs and retrieved his shoes from the sitting room and yanked out the wadded newspaper Mum had stuffed them with. He slipped them on, not bothering to tie the laces. They felt a little damp still, but he couldn't take Joe's slippers onto the beach.

He opened the front door and stepped outside. He stood for a few moments on the veranda – yes, the first hint of dawn was now evident in the sky, a ribbon of paler grey marching along the horizon, pushing light upwards. He left the door slightly ajar and made his way down to the beach. A couple of metres from the shore he shed his clothes quickly, before he could change his mind.

And here he stands now, here he hovers by the water's edge, still half asleep, toes curled, rubbing his hands together so quickly they blur. *Get in fast,* Dad always said. *Don't delay. The longer you wait, the harder it will be.* He takes a deep inhalation and plunges into the sea, leaping through it at first in giant bounds, gasping at the icy drops that fly up and slap against his warm skin.

When it becomes too deep to jump over he wades on, shivering but determined as the water climbs up his body, as the rounded pebbles on the sea floor collapse a little beneath each of his footfalls, as they give way eventually to sand. When he's deep enough he plunges in, giving a loud triumphant whoop as he's fully immersed.

He's never swum naked before. It never crossed his mind to do so, anywhere he might have had the opportunity – but with his togs gone along with the rest of his luggage, he doesn't have a lot of choice. He discovers, to his mild surprise, that he enjoys the sensation. There's something very liberating about moving through water without any clothing. No constriction, no barrier between his skin and the sea. He feels somehow more alive, more buoyant, his gangly limbs more graceful.

As he swims on, as he breathes and dips and glides, he begins to feel his spirits lifting. Isn't there something about exercise producing happy hormones? A natural feeling of euphoria caused by energetic movement – and this is about as energetic as it gets. He lets out another *whoop!* as he swims, tasting salt water as it rushes into his open mouth, tossing his head to tumble it back into the sea.

With his uplifted mood comes new resolve. He won't, he decides, dwell on the loss of the car. It's an inconvenience – and it was infuriating to lose the rest of the stuff, not least his favourite shirt – but it's not the end of the world. He walks to work, so it won't affect that. And the guard he spoke with on Aidan's phone last evening told him that the car, anyway, would most likely be found. *We'll check the usual estates. It might be damaged, but unless it was used in a crime he probably won't bother burning it out.*

If he's wrong, and no trace of the car is found, or if it *is* burnt out, Thomas vows to put the episode from his mind and never think of it again. Sam will find a replacement easily enough for him if the original doesn't reappear.

He swims on, his mind turning now to his mother. He can't recall ever seeing her cry, not once – but last night she came pretty close. He felt helpless, embarrassed at her display, or almost-display, of emotion. His relief when she went to bed, so he wouldn't have to deal with her sadness, makes him ashamed now.

He'll take her out to dinner when they get back, just the two of them. He'll call to see her more often than he does. He'll be a better son. He's glad she found Joe: must have been tough on her own after so long with Dad.

Above him the sky continues to gather light, its banks of sludgy grey shot through with slashes of lavender and deeper purple and pink, and occasional splotches of luminescent yellow that he decides are a hopeful sign. They're due a bit of sunshine after the rain of yesterday.

A sole gull flies overhead, a dark blob against the sky, an early riser like himself. He's not usually up this early on Sundays though – at home he relishes his Sunday morning lie-in, often not stirring till nearly noon.

They're going to Mass today. He hasn't been inside a church in quite a while – he fell out of the habit somewhere in his early twenties – but this morning is for Gran. The church in the village is small and old: he remembers liking the smell of it. The incense, probably.

After lunch he and his father, or he and Aidan, will take the road for Galway and find the police station he's been directed to. He doesn't relish the thought of rehashing what he'd rather forget, but it must be done.

He's still getting used to being back at Land's End. He told Mum last night he was glad he'd come, and notwithstanding the turmoil of Chloë's unexpected presence, he meant it. He's remembering what he'd forgotten, grabbing back snatches from all the holidays spent in this place.

The family room at the top of the stairs, he in the top bunk, Poll below. Playing Twenty Questions until one of them dropped off.

Walking with Mum or Dad to the village – how far it had seemed! Spending his pocket money on gobstoppers and packets of sherbet in Fox's, or splashing out now and again on a brown bag of chips from the Jolly Fisherman.

Building castles on the bigger beach, the sandy one on the far side of the village. He preferred their beach though. As a small boy he had believed it to be theirs, until he asked Gran once why she allowed others to use it so freely. *Nobody owns it*, she explained. *We're just lucky we're the closest.*

Time to head back, the cold beginning to bite. As he turns, an incident from yesterday pops into his head, something he didn't include in his telling of the tale last evening. In the aftermath of the car being snatched, as he waited dejectedly in the rain for Aidan, an approaching car slowed and pulled up beside him. A black expensive-looking saloon, Kerry registration. A window slid halfway down, sending out a waft of warm air.

You need a lift somewhere? the driver asked. Shirt and tie, middle-aged, balding. Jazz on his radio, suit jacket hanging from a hook above the back window. Thomas thanked him and said no, he was waiting for someone. He didn't explain his lack of a coat in the rain, didn't say anything about the car being taken from him. Didn't have the heart to put it all into words.

The man reached into the well in front of the passenger seat and brought up a folded black umbrella. *Here,* he said, *at least take this.*

What? No, I –

Take it, he repeated. *I have another in the boot.* So Thomas accepted the umbrella and thanked him again, and the man waved a hand in acknowledgement before sliding up his window and driving away.

Nice of him to stop and do what he could to help. Good of him to remind Thomas that kindness existed, that some souls could still be trusted to do the right thing. The umbrella, he recalls, is still in Aidan's car. Thomas will reclaim it, hang on to the reminder.

The shore draws closer. Must be about half six now, still too early to expect anyone else to be awake. He's weary from the unaccustomed exercise, allied with the lack of sleep. He'll make tea and bring it upstairs, and maybe nod off for another couple of hours.

The blue façade of the house stands out against the more muted greens and yellows and browns of the surrounding countryside as he approaches the shore. He wades from the sea, eager now to get dressed. He pats the water quickly from his skin and clambers into the tracksuit bottoms. His own clothes will be dry by now – good to get back into things that actually fit him.

He pulls on the borrowed sweater and steps into his shoes. He sprints along the beach and hops up the steps and jogs across the driveway. He enters the house and pauses in the hall, listening for sounds, hearing nothing but his own accelerated breathing.

He enters the kitchen.

'Hello Thomas.'

She leans against the radiator, a steaming cup clasped between her hands. She's swaddled in several layers – blue, lavender, lilac – that wind around her slender frame. Her hair is unpinned, flowing past her shoulders in a glorious tousle. Her lips are pale and unpainted, her eyelids bare of their usual shadow.

Her eyes are huge, and dark beneath. She looks young, and very tired, and beautiful. The sight of her, so unexpected, throws him like it threw him the night before.

'I was on the beach,' she says. 'I saw your things. Couldn't you sleep either?'

She was on the *beach*? 'No.'

She gives a shiver. 'Don't know how you could swim in this

cold. You must be very hardy.' She sips from her cup. 'I had to make tea, to warm up. There's water left in the kettle.'

'Thanks.'

He drapes his towel over a chair, conscious of how dishevelled he must look, a frozen scarecrow. And the clothes, horrendously ill-fitting. In silence he flicks the switch on the kettle and drops a teabag into a cup. He feels her eyes on him, the knowledge making his movements clumsy, his cold skin tingle. The room smells faintly of last night's dinner.

'Sorry about your car,' she says.

'Yeah.'

'Strange that we both had scary car experiences, isn't it?'

He glances at her, sees the ghost of a smile. Tries to match it, but his mouth feels stiff.

'At least we still have ours,' she adds.

Ours.

This is what she looks like immediately after waking. This is how she would look if he had lain beside her all night. If he'd woken, and she'd woken, and they'd turned to one another.

He makes tea and stirs in sugar. He takes milk from the fridge. When have they ever been alone together? Never, he thinks.

He will grab his chance now. He will tell her now how he feels, and to hell with the consequences.

Do it. Do it.

He dribbles milk into his cup. His hand is shaking, with cold or with fear. His heart bangs painfully, his throat is tight. He feels sweat pop out on his palms and forehead. 'Chloë—'

'Why is it so cold here?' she asks. At the exact same instant their voices collide.

He stops. The words stick somewhere inside him. Hammer, hammer, hammer goes his heart, trying to break out from his chest. How can she not hear it?

'Don't you find this house cold? I know the heat is on, but I'm still frozen. Charlie says it's me.'

Charlie.

She's with Charlie. She's with his father.

He becomes aware that she's waiting for a response. 'It's an old house,' he says. 'I suppose we're used to it.'

'That's what he says.'

He stirs his tea. The clink of his spoon against the cup is too loud.

She pushes away from the radiator, sets her cup in the sink. 'I'm going to try to get more sleep. I'll see you later, Thomas.'

'Right.'

When she's gone he hangs his towel on the radiator and rinses her cup and leaves it to drain. He stands by the sink and looks out at the approaching day and calls himself every name under the sun.

Back in his room he sheds his clothes again and crawls under the heavy quilt. His hair is still damp: he's too tired to care. He closes his eyes and tries to relive the swim, tries to recapture the exhilaration he experienced as he travelled swiftly, unfettered, through the water, but it's gone. It's been pushed away by the brief exchange in the kitchen.

He almost did it, almost lobbed the nuclear bomb. She stopped him – but was it accidentally, or because she sensed what was coming and didn't want to hear it?

Will he ever get another chance like that?

Does he want it? Can he risk it? So much to lose, but everything to gain.

Just before seven, as the first faint rays of sun fall slantwise onto the Atlantic, he drops back to sleep, sinking this time into blessed oblivion, his tea cold and forgotten on the dressing table.

Charlie

'WHERE WERE YOU?' HIS TONGUE FEELS THICK WITH sleep. 'I woke and you were gone.'

He gets no response. The mattress dips slightly to accommodate her weight as she settles back beside him. Her foot brushes his calf; he feels the chill of it.

'Where were you?' he asks again.

'At the beach.'

'The *beach*? It's the middle of the night.' Or barely dawn: the sky, what he can see of it, is still more dark than light. 'What time is it?'

'Ssh. It's early. Go to sleep.'

He closes his eyes obediently, but she has disrupted his dream, whatever it was. He casts about and recovers a piano. His dreams often tend towards the musical. Yes, a piano. In a field, wasn't it? Some sort of open space, and he was playing it – he doesn't really – and someone was singing. He fancies it was Lily, who claims she can't, who in all their years of their marriage never once sang in his presence. He tries to snatch back the essence of the dream, but it disintegrates and floats away.

'Thomas was there,' she murmurs, a half-whisper that he barely hears.

His eyes snap open. 'What? Thomas?'

'Mm.'

He rolls over, looks into the pale moon of her face. 'Thomas was on the beach?'

He hears the stretched breath of her yawn, smells the staleness of her exhalation. 'Swimming.'

'Thomas was *swimming*?'

'Ssh. I'm tired. And *cold*.' She drags the duvet more tightly around her.

'Is he still there?'

'I don't know.' She turns away from him, bringing more of the duvet with her. Dismissing him.

He listens to her breathing as it becomes slow and even. So quickly she falls asleep, like a little child, or a baby animal. He lies beside her, his desire for sleep having deserted him, debating whether to go and investigate.

Why would Thomas go swimming alone at this early hour? He's an able swimmer, certainly, and the beach is a safe one with no strong currents – but still. Thomas and Poll were warned against solo swimming as children; they had it drilled into them. Yes, Charlie does it himself, he's often swum alone, but he's older and stupider, no great loss to anyone if he got a cramp and shuffled off his mortal whatever.

He hears a sound – or does he? He listens, unmoving. The soft *tap tap* of someone ascending the stairs. The tiny click of a nearby door opening, the second click of it closing.

Thomas, returning from his swim to the room next door.

His son, the college drop-out. Waiting tables and mopping floors in that poky little café. Never in a relationship, or none that he's admitted to. Sharing a house with a gay couple – so who knows which way his own inclinations lie? Old enough now, more than old enough, to have come out to his family, but he hasn't.

Precious little in the line of savings, you'd have to assume, from the dead-end job. Heading for thirty in November, born five and a half months after Charlie walked Lily down the aisle.

Thomas, their little accident.

He closes his eyes and turns over – but the past refuses to let him sleep again. The past insists on being revisited.

I'm late, Lily told him.

It was March. They'd met the previous September, after Charlie had joined the staff of the school where she taught, after numbers had dropped in his old school and he'd become surplus to requirements. Music teachers, he was discovering, were deemed more dispensable than people who taught the real subjects, or those deemed real by the world of academia.

In October he asked her out. In December they slept together for the first time. After that, it was pretty much any chance they got, in the apartment he shared with a colleague from his old school, or in the house she was renting with two friends.

They were careful – they weren't stupid. He was twenty-seven, not a lustful teenager who didn't know or care how to stop babies coming. They used protection, they never took chances – and one night towards the end of February the protection split, at a crucial stage of the proceedings. And a fortnight later, Lily was late.

The timing was disastrous. He was studying for a master's in music with his eye on a job in third level, with more money and security, and more prestige. Lily was just gone twenty-two, in her second year of work, still enjoying the independence that a job and a salary brought along. A baby was not on either of their agendas, not then.

They talked about it. They weighed up the options. They agreed that it was too early in their relationship, just five months since their first date. Maybe they would stay together, maybe they'd opt to spend the rest of their lives with one another, but it was too soon to decide that, wasn't it? They couldn't let a baby shape their entire futures, could they?

In the end a flight to England, and a clinic in London, was deemed the most sensible course of action. Lily consulted with a friend whose sister had taken that road some years previously, and got the necessary information.

St Patrick's Day was obliging them by falling on a Tuesday that year; the school was also taking the Monday off, making a long weekend of it. Arrangements were duly made. Lily told her mother, who'd been expecting her home to Land's End for the few days, that Charlie had invited her to a friend's wedding in London. A group was going, she said, and making a holiday of it.

Charlie's parents were told that he was staying put in the city to study over the break; this they accepted without question. His mother in particular was fully behind his decision to pursue a master's, and his father, recently diagnosed with cancer that was to kill him well before the end of the year, only expressed a hope that Charlie wasn't working too hard. *Remember to have a bit of fun too,* he said on the phone, and Charlie imagined his dismay and disappointment if he knew what they were planning. Nothing fun about it.

Everything was set, her appointment made for the Monday. Early on Sunday morning he collected Lily in the Mini and they drove to Shannon airport. She was quiet; he'd expected that. He felt out of sorts himself, wary of what was ahead of them. He just wanted it to be over, wanted to resume the life this pregnancy had halted. He also felt protective of her, and obscurely guilty that he was somehow failing her now. But this was what she wanted, wasn't it? This was what they both wanted.

Wasn't it?

In the departure lounge he bought tea and overpriced scones. He ate his without pleasure; Lily picked at hers before eventually wrapping it in a serviette. *Might feel like it later*, she said, trying to smile. For the entire plane journey she stared at the same page in her magazine while he struggled through the *Irish Times* crossword that was usually no bother to him.

They touched down in London. He retrieved their bags from the overhead bin and walked ahead of her down the steps to the tarmac. He stood waiting at the bottom: every other passenger disembarked, but she didn't appear.

He left the bags on the ground – who was going to take them? – and mounted the steps again. He presented himself to the same stewardesses who had smiled goodbye to him minutes earlier. *My girlfriend*, he said, peering down the aisle. *She hasn't come out* – so one of the hostesses led him back and there Lily was, sitting where he'd left her in seat 11B. Pale, calm, silent.

He took 11C and reached for her hand while the stewardess moved a discreet distance away. *Sweetheart, come on*, he said gently. *You have to get off now, everyone's gone.*

She turned to him. *I can't do it*, she said. *I can't.*

Lily, we talked about it. We agreed that this –

I know – but I can't. I just can't.

So in the end, they didn't. They took the tube into London and dropped their bags into the small hotel he'd booked for a couple of nights, and they spent the rest of the day in St James's Park, walking in the weak sunshine, resting every now and again on a bench.

And they made a new plan.

We'll get married, he said, as they stood on the Blue Bridge, as she crumbled her leftover scone and threw it to some ducks in the lake.

She turned to stare at him. *Charlie, you don't have to do that.*

I want to.

He was twenty-seven. It was time he settled down. They were both employed, both in permanent pensionable jobs that might be put in jeopardy if they simply lived together without marrying. He was fairly sure he loved her, and she professed to love him, and she was having his baby.

It was the right thing to do.

Do you want to? he asked. *Get married. Do you want to marry me?*

Her eyes travelled around his face, settled on his mouth. *I think I do,* she said slowly, *but I wish it wasn't … like this.*

He wore a gold signet ring on his little finger that his parents had presented him with on the day of his graduation. He slipped it off and dropped to one knee.

Charlie—

Lily Murphy, will you do me the very great honour of becoming my wife? Presenting the ring, sliding it onto her finger. Too loose, of course. *Will you overlook the fact that it's happening earlier than we thought it would, and just marry me anyway, if I promise to do right by you and our child?*

She bit her lip. He saw she was on the point of tears. He stood up and gathered her into his arms. Broad daylight, tourists walking around them, pretending not to see. Big Ben ahead in the distance, Buckingham Palace behind them.

Do you want to? she whispered into his ear, clinging to him. *Honestly?*

I do. Honestly.

You're not just saying that?

I'm not just saying that. He paused. *I do need to make one thing clear though.*

She drew back. She searched his face, her eyes brimming. *What?*

I'll want my ring back. You can't keep it.

A beat passed. A single tear rolled down her cheek. He thumbed it away. She made a sound halfway between a laugh and a sob, and nestled into him again.

By the time they returned to Ireland it was settled. They would marry as soon as they could organise it. She wanted it to be in a church; he wanted the same, for his parents' sake more than for his own. All they had to do was break the news.

Easier said than done. Both mothers hit the roof.

She trapped you, his mother raged. *Oldest trick in the book: get pregnant, force the man to marry you. What do you know about her? What does her family do?*

Her father is dead. Her mother runs a B&B on the coast.

A B&B!

He changed tack. *Lily is a teacher, like me.* She could hardly object to that.

She didn't, exactly – but it didn't make things any better. *All very well for her then, nice short day, nice long holidays to look after her child – but what about you? You have ambitions. You're going places, Charlie. You're aiming higher than a secondary school. This will put a stop to all that now.*

It won't. I'll still be able to do the master's. He wasn't a bit sure about that. He still wanted to, but would it be feasible now?

With a baby in the house? Have you any idea how much a child costs, and how much work is involved? And where are you going to live? Have you thought about that? And on and on, unable or unwilling to see that the blame didn't rest entirely with Lily, that it had taken two to make her first grandchild.

And Kitty, when her turn came, wasn't much easier.

Why weren't you more careful? she demanded, when Lily left her alone with Charlie and went to check on the lamb chops she was cooking to mollify her mother. *You're older. You should have been the responsible one.*

Charlie began to explain about the split condom: she cut him short.

For goodness sake, I don't need the gory details. The question now is: do you love my daughter?

Yes, I do.

He was sure he did. It felt like he did. He missed her when she wasn't around; he enjoyed their time together. She was thoughtful and loving and intelligent. They were sexually compatible. Didn't all that point to love?

Kitty wasn't finished. *How do you propose to manage, with both of you working? I hope you won't expect Lily to give up her job.*

Of course not. We'll work something out.

They did work something out. They coped – thanks in no small part to Kitty, who proved a godsend in the end, putting herself at their disposal once her B&B closed at the end of summer. Installing herself in their rented flat for a few days when Thomas was born, declaring herself perfectly happy to return anytime they needed a break, anytime they wanted to escape together for a night or two.

They took to spending the odd weekend at Land's End: Kitty would wave them off each Sunday with enough food for a week, would urge them to return soon. *Come for the summer holidays,* she told them. *I'll set a room aside for the three of you.*

Eventually his mother came around too – although she and Lily never grew close in the way Charlie and Kitty did. Hardly surprising, given the precious little time they were afforded to bond, with his mother nursing his father through the final stages of his illness for the first few weeks of Thomas's life, only to succumb to the same lung cancer before her husband was cold in his grave. She died less than two years following her diagnosis, while Lily was pregnant with Poll.

But for all its traumatic beginning, for the upheaval it caused on both sides, his marriage worked. Did he truly love her when they started out? He can't be certain now, so many years later. But he stood by her, he walked her down the aisle. If what he felt for her wasn't exactly love, it was a good approximation of it – and in the years that followed, his regard for her grew and deepened.

He can honestly say they were happy for more than two decades. Largely happy. They had their ups and downs, plenty of those along the way: what couple doesn't? Lily went through a rough patch in the weeks after Poll was born, prone to bouts of inexplicable weeping, plagued, despite exhaustion, with insomnia. He did what he could to help, but he had his own challenges, preoccupied at the time with tying up his mother's affairs and finally putting the finishing touches to his thesis. Not a good time for them, but they weathered it.

And there were more hiccups, more occasional tumbles off the road as the children grew up and the years passed – but on the whole they were OK. In many ways they were the perfect couple, solvent and successful, with the father-mother-boy-girl family so often held up as the ideal. And if he wished for more excitement every now and again, he'd tell himself to cop on and count his blessings.

And then a new student called Chloë Richardson had enrolled in the music college, and she reminded him of what he had forgotten – and all that he and Lily didn't have was thrown into cruel relief. Even then he might have done nothing, might have juggled his comfortable marriage and the excitement of Chloë until the affair had burnt itself out, until she became bored with someone so much older, and moved on – but Chloë had had a different plan. Chloë, for all her youth, knew exactly what she wanted. Within a year of their affair she was demanding that he choose – and he, in thrall, chose her, and brought his marriage to an end.

And so far, so good.

Is it love? For sure it is. For all their differences, not least the years that yawn between them, he remains devoted to her. In turn she's impatient, discerning, selfish, thoughtful, funny, tactless and charming. She undoubtedly infuriates him at times – she's coming close right now – but even that brings its own excitement. For better or worse, he's more alive when he's with her. She's part of him in every way.

Did he ever feel like this with Lily? Did she light him up with a look, make his heart melt with a smile, or a kiss? He can't say, it's too long ago to be sure – but if he had, would they have lost it? Would he be with another now?

He places his palm against Chloë's warm naked back: she sighs in her sleep but otherwise doesn't react. Four years in August they'll have been together – officially together, after the furtive, thrilling year of their affair. Will they still be a couple twenty years from now, even ten years from now? A decade on he'll be looking at seventy, and Chloë will be a woman in her prime.

He wouldn't lay his last shilling on it. He'll have his work cut out to hang on to her.

He intends to enjoy it while it lasts.

He lies beside her, watching as the sky turns slowly from grey to white to blue, until the scorched nutty smell of coffee creeps into the room. He leaves the bed, and his sleeping lover. He pulls on his clothes of the day before and runs fingers through his sleep-ruined hair. He leaves the room and makes his way downstairs.

Poll

'MORNING,' HE SAYS. 'YOU'RE UP EARLY.'

She wasn't expecting it to be him. She thought it might be Mum or Thomas, the two other early risers in the family.

'I smelt the coffee,' he says.

He's dressed in the same things as yesterday, royal blue sweater with navy at the neck and waist, and the usual jeans. When he's not at work he lives in jeans. He's unshaven, his chin bristly and grey. Pouches of skin beneath his eyes, deep lines radiating from the outer corners. A hint of a hunch in the shoulders.

In a few years he'll begin to be an old man.

He indicates Gran's stainless-steel coffee pot. 'Will I make more, or ...?'

'There should be enough.'

He takes a cup from the dresser. 'You need a refill?'

'No, thanks.'

He adds milk and stirs, ignoring the sugar bowl. He always took two spoons, thwarting Mum's intermittent efforts to reduce it to one. Watching his weight maybe: hard to miss the thickening around his middle when she saw him in his togs yesterday.

Chloë might have complained.

He comes to stand beside her at the window. He's Aidan's height, a couple of inches taller than her. She catches a whiff of Chloë's flowery perfume: she raises her cup to banish it.

'I wonder,' he says, looking out, 'what'll happen to this place now.'

She shrugs. 'Nothing much. Mum and Joe will come and go until they retire, and then ...'

What *will* happen to it? Who knows? She thinks again about coming to live here herself. Waking up alone every morning in the green room, just a ghost for company.

'End of an era,' he says.

End of an era four years ago, when he and Mum changed everything. End of an era two years ago, when Gran left her home for the first and last time.

'I hope he doesn't change things – Joe, I mean. I hope they don't try to modernise it.'

She turns to him. 'What's it to you now?' she asks, the question sounding nastier, more uncaring, than she'd meant it to. 'I mean, you won't be here again, will you?'

He meets her gaze for a second. 'No,' he says mildly. 'I don't imagine I will.' He ducks his head to blow on his coffee. He takes a sip, turns back to the table to stir in more milk. 'You like it strong,' he says. 'I forgot that.'

She's sorry for the remark, but unable to tell him so. In the silence that follows, a gull gives two shrill cries – or maybe it's two gulls, saying hello to one another. The sky is a uniform pale blue, not even a wisp of cloud. Going to be a better day than yesterday.

'Thomas was swimming earlier,' he says then.

She's surprised. 'Earlier than this?'

'Around dawn, it must have been. Chloë saw him. She was on the beach, she couldn't sleep.'

Poll drinks coffee and thinks about Thomas and Chloë on the beach at first light. No, Thomas in the sea, Chloë on the beach. Still hard to picture it.

'Mum wants us to go to Mass today,' she says. 'For Gran.'

'She mentioned it.'

'The four of us, I mean. Not the others.'

That definitely comes out the way she wants it to.

Her father opens his mouth, closes it again. Opens it again.

'I'm sorry, Poll,' he says gently. 'I know it's not been easy for you.'

She moves away, because she has to. She lifts the pot too quickly to refill her cup and splashes a little onto the worktop. Not been easy to see her father make a fool of himself with a girl of her age. No, not been easy at all.

'Losing your gran, I mean, when you were so close. Must be tough for you, being here now.'

Ah. She should have known. As far as he's concerned, he's done nothing wrong. 'I'm going to sit in the garden for a while,' she says. 'See you at breakfast.' Cup in hand, she moves towards the scullery door.

'Poll …'

Her gut clenches. Don't, she thinks. Don't ask me to give Chloë a chance. Don't say you still love me. Don't go anywhere near that.

He doesn't. 'Will you be warm enough?' he asks.

'I'll be fine.' She wears Aidan's jacket over her pyjamas, and nothing on her feet but a pair of socks. She should have more on – the cold tiles are making her toes curl – but the garden is better than here. The garden is better than trying to dance around the fact that they have no real connection any more.

He drains his cup, drops it into the sink. 'I'm off anyway,' he says – and something about the stoop of his shoulders makes her feel ashamed again.

'We might go for a swim later,' she says. 'Looks like it's going to be a nice day.' She can do that much.

The smile he gives her is grateful. It makes her feel worse. 'That would be great,' he says. 'After Mass maybe.'

'Yeah.'

There are sounds above them. Steps across a floor, a door opening.

'Better go,' he says, 'if I want to grab a shower before the rush. Thanks for the coffee, love.'

She listens to the soft thud of his feet on the stairs. She takes her coffee through the scullery and out to the back garden. Here the sky is an even more marvellous wash of blue, the sun climbing up from behind the hills in the east. Going to be a wonderful day – but the early-morning air is still sharp enough for her to pull Aidan's jacket more tightly around her.

The coffee is stronger than she'd intended it to be. She feels it zinging through her, rushing to all her nerve endings, washing away the fuzziness left behind by sleep.

She slept so well, the sea air doing its job, no dreams to trouble her, or none that she remembered. Presumably Aidan had a good night too – he was still sleeping soundly when she tiptoed from the room in need of coffee.

He likes the house. She gave him a quick tour after dinner, while everyone was still concerned with Thomas. *I can see why you love it*, he said, pulling her close to drop a kiss on her cheek. *It's got real character*. Later in the pub he was in high spirits, insisting on a darts game even though he's rubbish at it.

Anyone looking at them would think everything's alright. Anyone looking at her wouldn't dream of the battle going on most of the time in her head.

She perches on the cast-iron seat outside the kitchen window and cradles her cup, and listens to the birdsong. The grass beyond the patio is beaded with dew. The long and ugly metal shed has a weary look about it, windows opaque with cobwebs, walls pitted with rust stains. The shrubs that border the lawn have all grown unruly with neglect: Gran would have hated to see them like this.

A toilet flushes. Minutes later, the shower runs. The house is waking. She should get dressed, but she's reluctant to leave the peace of the garden. She glances up to the curtained window of the room her brother is occupying, and thinks of him swimming alone in the sea before the sun came up.

She'll drive him to Galway later; she'll borrow Mum's car. She'll tell the others she'd like to do it. Aidan won't mind being left to his own devices for a couple of hours; he'll find plenty to do.

She and Thomas don't spend enough time together, given that they're each other's only sibling. She should drop into the café more often; she could choose a quiet time when he could sit and chat for a few minutes. She's glad he finally found a job he likes, after his wasted years of college and subsequent efforts to settle on something he really wanted. Took him long enough, but he managed it in the end.

She wouldn't in a million years have put him in a café – he can't cook to save his life – but he seems perfectly content there. It's a cosy enough little spot, if not exactly trendy. Then again, nobody could ever accuse Thomas of being trendy. And a person would have to be made of stone not to get along with Freda.

A distant bell sounds, the clang of its peals carrying easily across the morning stillness. The summons to first Mass for the early risers. The church used to be full when they went as children to the later one with Mum and Dad and Gran, people in colourful summery clothes filing up at communion time, a mix of tourists and locals.

The priest had a beard: that's her only memory of him. He looked a bit like the picture of Jesus in her religion workbook, except his hair was shorter.

She hears the throaty *put-a-put* of a tractor coming from beyond the garden. Gerry, getting a head start on the good day. The farmers have to grab the good days, even if they happen to be Sundays.

She hears approaching footsteps. Her mother appears at the back door. 'Poll. What a glorious day.'

She wears a lilac fleecy dressing gown that looks familiar – fabric-covered buttons, a flower embroidered in darker purple on the left front, its green stem winding down almost to the waist, spear-like leaves erupting from it now and again – and thick grey socks with flecks of black, too big to be hers. Her hair is matted on one side, the corresponding cheek pink and creased from her pillow. She looks younger.

'I needed coffee,' Poll tells her. 'There's some inside – although it might have gone cold by now.'

'I'll make fresh in a while.' Her mother leans against the door jamb, finds the dressing gown pockets for her hands. 'That fuchsia,' she says, nodding at it. 'My father planted it a year before he died.'

Poll looks at the bush, off to their left, the clutch of tiny drooping red and purple flowers. *Deora Dé* in Irish, tears of God. She never knew her grandfather planted it. 'What was he like again? Remind me.'

'Oh,' her mother says quietly, and nothing else.

When the silence stretches, Poll turns back and sees her pressing the heels of her hands to her eyes. 'Mum? You OK?'

'For Heaven's sake,' she says quickly, giving a little toss to her head, squeezing the bridge of her nose between index finger and thumb. 'It's just … coming here, *being* here now … maybe it was a bit soon …' She frowns, gives another small shake to her head. 'Oh, I don't know what I'm trying—' She breaks off to fish for a tissue in the pockets of the dressing gown. Makes a bit of a production of blowing her nose.

Poll slides along the seat. 'Sit down,' she says, and her mother obeys. She clasps the seat's cold edge with both hands, looking not at Poll but towards the bottom of the garden.

'It's *unsettled* me,' she says. 'I'm unsettled, that's all it is.' As if to demonstrate she shifts her weight on the seat, brushes at something on the dressing gown, plunges her hands back into the pockets.

'So,' she says, 'last night.' Turning to fix Poll with an awful forced smile, her nose tipped with pink. 'How was it? How was Sully's?'

'It was fine. We met Nancy and Bernard Cahill.'

'Were they out? How was poor Nancy?'

'Fine. She was asking for you.'

'Their son died - did you know? Must be coming up to six months now. Their only boy, killed crossing the road. You wouldn't have known him, he was years older than you.'

Poll knew him. Such a crush she'd had on Danny Cahill. Eighteen or so to her ten, working for a summer behind the counter in the village chipper before he went off to uni. The merry brown eyes of him, the coal-black hair. Juggling battered sausages to make her laugh. Calling her and Thomas the city slickers, but not in a mean way.

'I remember you telling me,' she says. 'You went to the funeral. I would have gone with you, only I had that bug.'

'Oh yes.'

She remembers quietly mourning him as she lay in bed, her stomach cramping horribly. All that fun, all that merriment gone.

'Poor Nancy,' her mother says again.

They lapse into silence, broken intermittently by the tractor, and the continuing chirruping of birds. Poll sips coffee, but it's gone cold.

'It could do with a little attention,' her mother remarks. 'Couldn't it? The garden.'

'I was thinking the same myself. I could ask Aidan to cut the lawn later – we could borrow a mower from someone.'

'Do not: I wouldn't dream of having him work this weekend. I'll get someone from the village to cut it, next time I'm down.'

'He wouldn't mind, Mum. I'm sure he wouldn't.'

'No, Poll – he's a guest. This is his holiday.'

Another pause. A robin hops his way across the grass, stopping briefly to look up at them, head tilted. Wondering who's encroaching on his territory, it looks like.

'Anyway, I thought Aidan was bringing Thomas to Galway.'

'Actually, I'd like to do that, but I'd need your car – Aidan is a bit funny about anyone driving his.'

'Of course you can have mine. Go easy on the road.'

'I will.'

Her mother pleats the belt of the dressing gown. 'Aidan likes the house?'

'He does. He says it's got character.'

A small laugh. 'It certainly has.'

The sun is climbing higher, the air softening a little. The tractor is still coughing.

'Gerry's up bright and early,' her mother remarks.

'He's been at that a while.'

'Shame he never married, isn't it? I used to think he had an eye for your grandmother.'

Poll looks at her in surprise. 'For Gran? Did you? Wasn't he much younger than her?'

'Not that much – seven or eight years only. I'm not sure he'd have been able to handle her, though.'

Poll tries to imagine Gerry and Gran together. Yes, she might well have bossed the poor mild-mannered man to distraction. 'What'll happen to his farm? When he dies, I mean.'

'Oh, the cousin, I suppose. He lives in Belgium, I think, or Holland, somewhere over there anyway. A second cousin, or maybe a third, I forget. He came home when Gerry's mother died. What's this his name was? Something unusual. He had sideburns, nasty bushy things. You wouldn't remember him, you were too young.'

A seagull wheels lazily, directly above them. Something rustles in a bush. A small tremor runs through Poll: her grip instinctively tightens on her cup. *Someone walked over my grave.*

'Do you recognise this?' her mother asks then, touching the collar of the dressing gown. 'I found it yesterday, folded on a shelf in her wardrobe. I thought we'd cleared everything out.'

Poll nods slowly. 'I knew I'd seen it before.' It comes back to her. One time Gran had been sick, flu or something, the only time Poll recalls seeing her not fully dressed. She appeared in the kitchen in the dressing gown, flushed and shivering but bent on making breakfast for her paying guests. Mum had to practically chase her back to bed.

'We did the breakfasts,' Poll says. 'For the visitors, that time she was sick. We did them for a few days, the two of us. I burnt the porridge the first morning.'

'Did you? I have no memory of that.'

'Why didn't it go with her to the nursing home? The dressing gown.'

Her mother shrugs. 'I thought I'd packed it, but when we got there I discovered it was missing. I bought her a new one.'

'Yellow.'

'That's right.'

Poll didn't accompany them, the day Mum and Dad drove to Land's End to take Gran away. It was never said aloud, but everyone knew she'd never be going back. Poll herself had been to Land's End a week before. She'd gone to spend the night, ostensibly to tell Gran about Aidan – none of the rest of her family knew about him yet – but really it was to say goodbye to Land's End, knowing she wouldn't be seeing it again, at least for the foreseeable future.

Gran was spending pretty much all of her days indoors by this time, with a trio of village women on a rota to clean and feed her, and to sleep in the house at night. The arrangement was temporary, just until a place in the nursing home could be found for her. It was their only option, Poll could see that, but it was still heartbreaking to think of her moving to some anonymous place, being cared for by strangers.

I've met someone, she told her. *I think he's special*. Holding the cool limp hand in hers, searching the face, the eyes, for a spark of understanding. *His name's Aidan, he owns a gallery. He's selling my heads. He's taken me out to dinner a few times*. And Gran had looked at her without seeing her, and said nothing at all in response.

Her mother gets to her feet. 'I think I'll make a start on the breakfast – we need to watch the time for Mass. Come and keep me company.'

'I'll be right there.' Poll lingers, watching two butterflies dance and dart around one another. Isn't it early for butterflies? The seasons are so out of sync these days.

What is it, what's nagging at her? What has snagged on something in her mind? What is scratching away inside her and demanding attention?

She retraces the conversation she's just had with Mum – the fuchsia, the unruly garden, Danny Cahill, Gerry being soft on Gran, the dressing gown – but nothing jumps out. Might be the caffeine, playing tricks with her head.

'Morning, beautiful.'

Aidan stands in the doorway. Fully dressed, with damp hair. The sight of him brings a wave of love and fear, in roughly equal measure. She gives him a bright, coffee-fuelled smile. 'Hi there. You were dead to the world when I got up.'

'Not any more,' he says. 'I'm the assistant cook. I'm on fried egg duty.'

'I'll help.' She tosses what's left of her coffee onto the grass and follows him into the house.

Lily

SHE STABS SAUSAGES CROSSLY WITH A FORK. WHAT on earth is wrong with her? She never cries, or hardly ever – and yet there she was on the verge of tears again with Poll, after almost breaking down in front of Thomas last evening. They'll think she's losing it, like Mam.

'Will I put them all on, Lily?' Aidan, looking into the bowl of large brown eggs from Karina's contented hens.

'How many are left?' she asks.

'Four.'

'Might as well do them all so.'

She gets the heavy frying pan from the scullery and lights the gas ring under it. She's tired, that's all: last term is always murder – and there are still five weeks of it to go. She pours in a splash of oil.

And there's the wedding, there's the stress of all that, even if they push it back a bit. She adds the sausages.

And she's worried about Poll, and to a lesser extent Thomas. She shakes the pan.

And she's trying to be all gracious and accepting about Chloë being here.

No wonder she's a bit thrown about.

Pull yourself together. Talk to Aidan. Say something.

'Poll tells me you like the house.'

'It's great. Must have been something, growing up here.'

'It was.'

It *was* something. It was several somethings. It was happy before her father died, and then for a long time it was lonely and confusing and sad. When the B&B opened it was disconcerting for a while, encountering new faces on the stairs, seeing strangers emerging from the bathroom, listening to unfamiliar snores at night, smelling a different perfume on the landing. Until she got used to it, Land's End didn't feel like it belonged to them any more.

In due course people assemble at the table. Sausages are dished up, and black pudding and fried eggs, and a mound of toast. They marvel at the change in the weather. The ones who went to Sully's tell Lily of the darts game, and Aidan's crushing defeat. Aidan declares himself a far better chess player, and Thomas promptly challenges him to a game after Mass. Compared to last night's dinner, the atmosphere is positively jolly.

By a quarter past ten, when the plates have all been cleared, there's still no sign of Chloë.

'She slept badly,' Charlie tells them. 'She was up at dawn.'

Thomas overturns his coffee: there's a fuss while it's cleaned up. Lily spots Charlie slipping from the room with a cup. 'Tell her to help herself to food when she gets up,' she calls after him: if he hears he doesn't let on.

Joe and Aidan opt to join them for Mass. The six of them walk the twenty minutes or so to the church, the day continuing pleasant. One of those warm days of late spring that come out of nowhere and vanish just as quickly. Pet days – isn't that what they're called?

Cars slow down on the road. A few windows lower, offering lifts. Lily waves them on, relishing the sunshine. With her fair skin she has to watch it – unlike Charlie who tans in ten minutes – but half an hour so early in the year will hardly do damage.

The church doesn't change. For as long as she can remember it's felt the same, smelt the same. Dolly Brady sits at the organ like she's done since Lily was in secondary school, playing softly as everyone assembles. The whispered shuffle into the pews is the same, the clutch of men that congregates at the back is still there.

After Mass, people make their way to her seat to shake her hand and tell her they're sorry for her loss. Friends and neighbours of Mam's, people Lily would have been familiar with growing up. Some she recalls easily, the ones who never left, the ones she'd encounter during the family summers at Land's End. Others are trickier, those who moved away around the time she did and settled somewhere new, who only appear now on occasional weekends. Those names she has to reach further for.

She's aware of the glances at Joe, the bemusement on some of the faces when they see Charlie there too. Everyone knows about the separation: impossible to keep something like that secret in a place like this, with her mother still living among them, and still of sound mind, when it happened.

Not that Mam would have been spreading it around – she was never a gossip – but she would have told the truth if people asked after Lily. Even if she hadn't, it would have been noted that Lily and Charlie had taken to visiting Land's End separately. Two and two would have been put together. And Joe has been to Sully's a few times over the last couple of years; they've had a few lunches there. That news wouldn't have taken long to do the rounds either.

As they emerge from the church, Karina Clery waylays her at the door: by the time they've finished talking, Lily has lost sight of the others. As she makes her way down the drive she spots Charlie in conversation with Dinny Reilly, one of the local fishermen.

'Lily.'

A voice from behind her. She turns.

'Timmy Scanlon,' she says. 'Long time no see.' She takes the outstretched hand, feels the calluses his job has given him.

'I'm just home for the weekend,' he says. 'I spotted you there in the church. And your poor mother is gone.'

'She is, a few weeks ago.'

Timmy Scanlon. Her age, in the same class all through primary school. Her first boyfriend; they must have been about thirteen. Walking her home every afternoon, stopping sometimes for a shared bag of chips on the way. Claiming a kiss at the gate to Land's End, the vinegar still on his lips. The innocence of it. Did they last six weeks, before one or other of them lost interest? She has no recollection of the break-up, the trauma or otherwise of it.

'How's your dad doing?' she asks. Malachy Scanlon, a fisherman all his working life, his days at sea behind him now. He must be well into his eighties, but the last she heard, still lifting a glass the odd evening in Queally's pub.

'He's grand. He doesn't come to Mass any more, he gets it on the radio. He doesn't stir from the bed these days till lunchtime.'

'Is he still living on his own?'

'He is. I've said he can come to us when he wants, but he's staying put as long as he can. The neighbours are very good to him.'

'I'm sure they are.'

Timmy was never a scholar. From very early on, it was obvious to everyone that he and studying had nothing in common. In trouble regularly for unfinished homework, untidy copies, lost books. School was the sentence he had to serve before he could leave and follow his heart to sea, join his father on the trawler the minute he was released.

But then, to everyone's surprise, he started woodwork classes in secondary and found a new passion. Moved to Galway after leaving school – passed his Leaving Cert, another surprise – did his apprenticeship in carpentry, eventually married a Galway girl. They had a child who didn't last beyond a week, another who must be a teenager or older by now.

Mam had kept her informed, whenever Lily and Charlie were at Land's End. Mam had known all there was to know about the local families and their various scattered members. It was Mam who told her about Timmy's mother's car going off the pier several years ago, the biggest tragedy the village had seen in years. Teresita Scanlon, whose nerves were at her, depression not a word that was bandied about much then. An accident, it was called – but who knew?

'I heard,' Timmy says now, in a lower voice, 'you and Charlie … I heard you went your separate ways, Lily. I'm sorry to hear it.'

She's taken aback, lost for a response. Nobody here has ever mentioned the break-up to her face.

'I hope I'm not speaking out of turn.'

'No, that's … We're still friends,' she says. 'He's with us, he came down for the weekend too.' She sees him off to her right, still chatting with the fisherman. 'He's over there.'

Timmy doesn't turn. 'I know he's here – I saw him inside. Shame all the same that it had to finish.'

'We lasted over twenty-five years,' she says. He hardly has a right to be talking about her marriage breakdown, the two of them all but strangers these days. Bit personal, bit cheeky.

He wasn't always a stranger though. There was a time when she must have woken up in the mornings looking forward to meeting him. The thought of him must have given her butterflies, once upon a time. 'We just came to the end of the road,' she says, 'that's all. No big drama.'

He nods. 'Myself and Jenny nearly went our separate ways too,' he says. 'Couple of years ago.'

It's the last thing she expected to hear. 'Did you?' She's never met his wife, didn't know her name until this minute.

'We went through a stage.' His shoulders lift. He dips his gaze to explore the ground between them. 'I suppose we felt there wasn't much mileage left in us, you know? And then …' he pauses, purses his mouth '… I don't know, we kind of decided maybe we should … have another go at it, I suppose.' He looks back at her then and smiles, the same bashful smile that must have won her over all those years ago. 'When it came down to it, Lily, the truth of it was, I didn't really fancy going on without her.'

I didn't really fancy going on without her. The phrase, homespun as it is, touches her. 'In that case, I'm glad it worked out for you,' she says lightly.

She makes no mention of Joe. There he is, standing by the church gate, waiting patiently for her. Timmy may not be aware of his existence, not living in the area any more. She could bring him to the gate, she could introduce them – but she feels it might be best to leave Joe out of it. Might only complicate things.

'Well,' Timmy says, 'I should get going, or Dad will be sending for the guards.'

She puts out a hand and he clasps it briefly again between

his rough palms. 'Good to see you,' she says. 'Give my best to Malachy.'

'Will do. Look after yourself, Lily.'

She watches him stride away in his Sunday suit, back to the life she knows nothing about. Back to the wife he nearly left, and then didn't. Back to the marriage they hadn't given up on. When it came down to it.

Maybe she should have protested a bit more when Charlie wanted out. Maybe she should have swallowed her pride, fought a bit harder to hang on to what they had.

He catches up with her as she makes her way to the gate. 'I'm heading out with Dinny for the afternoon,' he says. 'He's picking me up at the pier at two.'

She sees the glee in his face. Should have guessed why he was chatting up the fisherman: any excuse to get into a boat. 'What about Chloë?' she asks.

She sees the tiny alteration in his expression, the minuscule stiffening of his smile that nobody but herself would catch. 'I'll ask her if she wants to come,' he says, but she can hear the doubt. Chloë, she guesses, would prefer to pull out her eyelashes one by one than get into a working fisherman's boat.

'Charlie, you can't just desert her. You can't just disappear like that.'

'I'm not disappearing. I've said I'll give her the choice.'

And Chloë will say no, and he'll skedaddle, and they'll be left with her for the afternoon. One more day, she tells herself. You can do it.

They walk on. They reach the gate. 'Sorry,' she says to Joe. 'I got caught with a few.'

'No bother. The others have gone on ahead. They said they'd get the papers.'

They walk past the chemist, the supermarket, the first of the village's three pubs. Lily feels the sun on the back of her neck and turns up her jacket collar. 'I was talking to Timmy Scanlon just now,' she says.

Charlie frowns. 'Timmy Scanlon. Do I know him?'

'You wouldn't have met him much. He's lived in Galway for years. He was my first boyfriend.'

His eyebrows lift. 'Was he now? Is he sorry he lost you?'

'Not a bit – he married a Galway girl.'

'I'd say you were in demand,' Joe puts in, and she laughs and says not exactly. She doesn't add that Charlie Cunningham was her first proper boyfriend, her first real relationship after several flings that went nowhere. The first man she slept with, the only one before Joe.

'Thomas was swimming,' Charlie says then. 'This morning, very early. Before the sun came up.'

Lily stares at him. 'Swimming? He never said.'

'Chloë was on the beach. She saw him.'

'*Chloë*, on the beach?'

'She couldn't sleep.'

She digests this second round of astonishing information before returning to the more important one. 'I don't like the thought of him swimming on his own.'

'Me neither. We should have a word with him.'

'Charlie, Thomas will be thirty in November. I think the days of having a word with him are long past.'

'Thirty,' he says, and no more.

A man and woman walk towards them, the man holding a little girl by the hand. The child licks solemnly at an ice-cream cone, giving it her full attention. Lily is reminded of Poll at that age, her wild hair tamed into a plait each day by Mam after breakfast. The little trotting steps she had to take to keep up with Thomas when they'd set off for Gerry's farm in the mornings. The chubby little hands that Lily wanted to eat, so adorable they were.

'Fancy a cone?' Joe asks. 'Anyone?'

Lily looks at Charlie. 'I will if you will.' It's years, decades, since she had a cone.

'Go for it,' Charlie tells Joe, so they wait on the path until he emerges from Fox's with his hands full.

The whipped ice-cream is soft and cold and delicious. She'd forgotten how delicious. She's seven years old again. She's a girl with brown hair in pigtails, wearing a blue dress with pockets, and white socks that won't stay up. She has a mother who's stern but fair, and a father who adores her.

They reach the outskirts of the village. They pass the eighty-kilometre speed-limit sign. A car doing what looks like considerably more than that zooms past them, music blaring, and Lily is reminded of the youth who ordered Thomas from his car at knifepoint.

'What about dinner?' Charlie asks. 'Am I taking everyone to Sully's?'

'You are – unless you fancy cheese on toast.'

The pub's menu is limited – burgers, chicken wings, catch of the day fried in batter – but if they want to go out their only alternative is the hotel, which is old-fashioned and overpriced.

When they get home they find Poll on the veranda, seated on one of the rattan chairs they retrieved from the shed and dusted down after breakfast. She lowers her newspaper at their approach.

'Thomas and Aidan are playing chess,' she tells them. No sign of Chloë, no mention of her.

'Ready for that swim?' Charlie asks.

'Ready.' She closes the newspaper and lets it fall onto the neighbouring chair.

They're going swimming, the arrangement apparently made earlier. Lily offers a silent prayer of thanks to whoever might be listening.

'Your family are mad,' Joe remarks.

She smiles, tucking an arm through his. 'Come on – we're on lunch duty.'

In the kitchen she finds a half-full bottle of Sancerre in the fridge and gets two glasses – why not? Joe fiddles with the old radio until he hits on a jazz station. The two swimmers reappear, wrapped in towels.

'If Chloë shows up,' Charlie says, 'tell her I'll see her at lunch,' and Lily wonders where the child can have gone. Off to do her yoga in a field, maybe. Away to meditate among the cows. Hopefully she won't make the acquaintance of Terence Mulcahy's bull.

They slice and butter bread, and assemble sandwiches with cheese and tomato and ham. From the sitting room comes a shout of – what? Triumph? Dismay?

'I've been thinking,' Joe says, slathering mayonnaise.

'What about?'

'About this place.' He arranges slices of cheese carefully, lining them up end to end on the bread. 'It came to me yesterday, when I was out walking with Poll. I haven't had a chance to say it to you since.'

She lifts her glass, takes a sip. There's something very brazen, and very delicious, about drinking wine when the sun is shining. It reminds her of being abroad on holidays, sitting in the sunshine at noon, nothing to do but sip her wine and eat her salad and enjoy the day. 'Say what to me?'

'It's just an idea I have, about what to do with this place.'

She pauses in the act of cutting a sandwich in two. One of her eyebrows gives a small dip of its own accord. 'What to do with it? What do you mean?'

'Well, it's just lying idle, isn't it? We've been down … what? About half a dozen times in the last year?'

She feels a small hard something take root inside her. She brings the knife down slowly and eases the sandwich halves apart. She places them carefully on the serving plate. 'This place, as you call it, is my home. It's where I was born, where I lived till I was eighteen. It's lying idle because my mother got Alzheimer's and had to move out.'

He glances up. 'Sorry, love – that came out wrong. I think it's a wonderful place – house – honest I do. I just think more use could be made of it. It's a shame to leave it lying empty, that's all I'm saying.'

The hard thing grows and tightens. She feels the clench of it. 'So what's your idea?' Fingering the stem of her glass but not lifting it.

He places tomato slices on top of the cheese. 'Well, this might sound a bit daft' – throwing her a quick grin – 'and I know it's coming out of the blue a bit, but I thought I could run my practice from here.' Laying the second slice of bread on top, seeming impervious – how can he be impervious? – to her growing incredulity. 'It would be more animal husbandry, of course, but that's OK – I'd get used to it in no time.'

Run his practice from here. Move his business to Land's End.

It's a joke. Any minute now he's going to say, *Fooled you!* Or else she's dreaming. She went for a nap before lunch, and she's about to wake up.

'I also thought it would make an ideal animal sanctuary, which would tie in nicely with the practice. I mean, look at all the space you have out the back – you'd fit half a dozen donkeys there, no bother.'

A donkey sanctuary.

Half a dozen of them out the back, trampling the lawn. Eating the grass where her father died.

She feels anger beginning to bloom. It unfurls, it opens out like a peony rose. 'And me? Where do I fit in with your plan?'

He hears the steel in her voice now. He looks up again, a new wariness to his expression. The certainty fading now from his words. 'Well ... I thought you could commute, if you wanted to keep working. Up to you, of course, but you could stay in the city from Monday to Friday, come down for weekends. It would only be for a few years – or you could take early retirement. You could do that, couldn't you? It's not as if we'd need the money, living down here. Especially not if we sold the other.'

She sets down her knife and lifts her wine glass again. She drinks it all, she gulps down every drop. She feels the cold liquid splash its way into her gut, lets it settle there. She reaches across to turn off the radio, to silence a trombone tune that has suddenly begun to irritate her beyond all understanding.

'You've been busy,' she says, the anger hot as a boiled kettle now inside her. 'Making your plans.'

'Lily, love, it's only an idea. If you don't fancy it—'

'Charlie and I were planning to retire here.' Her voice harsh, the words flung out. 'No commuting, no donkeys, no sick animals. Just us, *after* we both retired.'

It climbs into the space between them. It sits in the air. It leaves a silence that's deafening in its wake.

'Well,' Joe says eventually, quietly, 'that's me told.'

She glares at him, not finished. Not nearly finished. 'This house belongs to *me*. It's not yours, it's *mine*. You don't get to decide what happens to it.'

'I'm sorry. It was just—'

'*My* house,' she repeats. 'I grew up here. It's *my* decision, not yours. And the house in town you're so glibly selling is mine too, mine and Charlie's. He owns half of it, in case you've forgotten. You moved in there, remember? You let your house and moved into *mine*.'

'OK.' He nods slowly. 'I'm sorry, Lily. I didn't think. I didn't mean to upset you.'

'Well, you *did* upset me.' To her dismay she feels tears threatening yet again. She swallows hard, clenches her jaw. Do not, she orders. Do not do that. Do not let him see that. She longs to be alone, but she has filled her house with people.

Her house. He wants to make a business out of it. He wants to fill the garden, *her* garden, with donkeys.

And then she remembers what anger made her forget.

'I'm selling it,' she says. 'I'm putting it on the market as soon as I get back to town.'

His mouth drops open. 'You're selling this place?'

'It's not a *place* – stop calling it a *place*. It's a *house*, it's a *home* – or it was a home.'

'Lily, love—'

'*No*.' She retreats from his attempted embrace, rubs her mouth hard to stop it trembling. 'I've decided to sell it. I was going to tell everyone last night, but then Thomas came in with his news and I couldn't. I'm going to do it tonight, so please say nothing.'

'I won't.'

She picks up her knife and cuts more slices, blinking hard. He takes them silently and butters them. The room feels too small for both of them.

'I'm sorry,' he says again. 'I'm an idiot.'

She doesn't contradict him.

She comes to the end of the bread. No more slices to cut. 'I want to put off the wedding,' she says, setting down her knife again.

'Put it off?'

'For a few months. It's happening too soon after the divorce, and after … Mam. I need more time.'

He regards her for what seems like an age. She picks a scrap of ham from the table and puts it into her mouth, although it's the last thing she wants.

'OK,' he says. Just that. He places ham on buttered bread.

'We could leave it till Christmas,' she says, watching his hands. 'Another few months isn't going to make a difference.'

'Fine. Whatever you say.'

They finish with no other word between them. When the plates are full, Joe places his knife on the draining board, as carefully as if it was an unexploded bomb. 'I'm going to grab a shower before lunch.'

She nods, not meeting his eye. Left alone, she tips what's left in the wine bottle into her glass and drinks it without pleasure. Now it's just a glass of wine too early in the day.

She slumps against the table and draws her hands wearily through her hair. She shouldn't have said that about Land's End being hers: it sounded petty – particularly when it's not going to belong to either of them soon.

If she wasn't selling up, the donkey idea mightn't have been a bad one. She's always liked donkeys, such placid, gentle creatures. A couple of them, not six, might have been nice out the back.

She shouldn't have brought up about postponing the wedding either – he'll think it's because of his grand plan. She'll explain later, when she's had time to cool down.

As she's drying the knives Thomas appears. 'Aidan is

winning,' he says, and she remembers the chess game. He takes a tumbler from the draining board and holds it under the tap. 'Alright?' he asks.

'Fine,' she says brightly. In dire need of a six-month sabbatical alone on a desert island, no luggage apart from a stack of books – maybe – but otherwise fine.

She thinks of something. 'Thomas, Dad tells me you were swimming on your own this morning.'

The colour rises in his face. 'I woke early,' he says. 'I couldn't sleep.'

'But you shouldn't go out alone, love, not without telling anyone. If anything happened to you—'

Already he's at the door. Making his escape, it feels like. 'I know. I won't do it again.'

'You could go now – Poll and Dad are gone down. You can play chess anytime.'

'I think I'll pass,' he says. 'Bit cold for me really, this time of year.'

The door closes behind him, leaving her alone again. She covers the plates of sandwiches with cling film and makes a pot of tea. She pours a cup and brings it out to the back, remembering her earlier conversation there with Poll.

She walks slowly around the garden, assessing the state of it. She'll need to get someone to tidy it up for prospective buyers. Keith Chambers from the village kept it in shape after Mam went beyond looking after it: she could see if he'd be willing to come back. No sign of him at Mass – she hopes he hasn't moved away. Without her mother to keep her up to date she's lost track of the comings and goings.

She reaches the end wall and stops. There is the tree her swing hung from, there the corner where she spread a blanket in the summer and had tea parties with her dolls. Such a practice frowned upon now, probably. Discriminating against little boys, or some such rubbish.

There have been changes to the garden since her childhood. The patio in front of the kitchen window was laid when Mam had made enough from the B&B to afford it. A tree had had to be cut down after a storm one winter pulled it half out of the earth. The small wooden shed has been replaced by the bigger galvanised one.

She thinks of the half-painted kitchen chair, the one her father was working on when he died. It was banished to the old shed, she remembers, its presence too sad a reminder of him. Was it eventually chopped up and burnt, the pieces thrown onto the fire along with a shovel full of coal?

The place where he died, the exact spot where he fell, is somewhere off to her right. It happened while she was at school. A few minutes after lunch she was called out of class by the secretary and brought to the principal's office, where she found Mam's friend Myra Dillon waiting for her, bad news written all over her red-cheeked face.

Lily was told gently, she was held and petted and crooned over while she wept. She was driven home, her bicycle in the boot of Myra's car, as her world came to a bewildering end. It wasn't until some time later, after the unreality of the funeral, everyone looking pityingly at her, school friends in their Sunday clothes struck dumb in the church at the sight of her – it wasn't until all that was over that she wandered disconsolately into the garden, a few mornings after he was buried, and spotted something on the grass that made her drop to her hunkers – and there it was.

Thick smears of blue paint on the green blades, evidence of his loaded brush falling to the lawn as he tumbled into sudden death. The brush had been removed, along with the pot of paint and the half-finished chair, but the grass still presented evidence to her of his loss. *Here it is,* it said. *Here is where he left you.*

She'd pressed a hand to the spot and looked at her fingers, but the paint had dried and didn't come away. She'd pulled up a handful of blue blades and slipped them into her pocket. She'd kept them for weeks, hidden between the pages of an old copybook. When had she finally let them go, those last tenuous connections to him? She has no memory of it now.

She completes her circuit and sits on the seat, and returns to the problems of the present. How could Joe have thought she'd want to spend the next several years commuting? Trekking to and fro every weekend, on her own all week: what would be the point of getting married? And when she eventually retired, was his plan to continue working? Would she have had to live in a house that doubled as a vet's surgery?

How could he have got it so completely wrong?

She sits there, heedless of time. Eventually the kitchen window is pushed upwards.

'Mum – we're about to eat. Are you coming in?'

Poll, her hair caught up in a damp bunch. Her face flushed, from heat and from swimming. She looks pretty – but then she always looks pretty to her mother.

'I'll be right in,' Lily says.

Chloë

THE BUNDLE OF CLOTHES ON THE BEACH, AND NO sign of him.

For most of the night she'd drifted in and out of sleep, missing the warmth of her grandmother's quilt, which they'd surrendered to Thomas. Hearing every so often the unearthly screech of some night creature, seeing shapes she couldn't identify in the corners of the room. Feeling unnerved, as she had since the moment she'd stepped over the threshold.

She was being stupid. It was just a shabby old house, full of draughts and other people's memories. It was her own preoccupation with what lay ahead that had her rattled, not her surroundings.

But old houses occasionally picked up ghosts along the way, didn't they? Old houses had secrets hidden within their walls. Old houses had seen it all. And this particular old house now belonged to the woman whose husband she'd stolen, the woman whose face had fallen ever so slightly when Chloë had got out of Charlie's car on their arrival. Maybe next Thursday was only partly to blame for the sleeplessness that was plaguing her now.

Coming here had been a mistake. It wasn't the distraction she'd hoped it would be: far from it. Lily at least was making an effort to hide the fact that she didn't want Chloë there, but Poll was openly hostile. *You didn't come to the funeral* – as if Chloë had been under some kind of obligation to attend the burial of a complete stranger.

And when Chloë had tried to be nice to her at dinner, offering her the salad bowl, attempting conversation, Poll had been barely civil. It was tiresome, her insistence on making Chloë public enemy number one. True, Chloë was the one who'd instigated the affair with Charlie, she'd been instrumental in splitting up Poll's parents, but that marriage had been dead in the water, or Charlie would never have agreed to end it so easily.

And *he* wasn't helping, more concerned with getting back into his precious daughter's good books than with anything else. Rushing off to swim with her practically the minute they arrived, vanishing to the pub with her and the others as soon as dinner was over. Not that Chloë was gagging for his attention right now, not at all – but here she was, surrounded by his family, in the house where the four of them had spent so much time. You'd think he'd be more supportive, more concerned that she was comfortable.

The hours dragged, and still sleep, real sleep, eluded her. It didn't help that Charlie was dead to the world beside her, filling the room with his beery exhalations. Finally she couldn't take it any longer. She had no way of checking the time, but she fancied the sky was growing lighter. It must be near morning – it had to be.

She fumbled into the clothes she'd worn the night before. She added a couple of wraps that she'd spread for warmth on top of the duvet. She slipped downstairs in the gloom, the banister cold as marble beneath her hand, a creaking stair making her heart jump. This house gave her the creeps, pure and simple.

She crossed the hall and put her hand to the front door to open it – and was startled to find it ajar. Had it been like that all night? Had they forgotten to close it when they'd returned from the pub? Little wonder the place was so cold.

And what about security? A house this age, and this size, might be thought to contain expensive antiques – any number of criminals might be eyeing it up.

She'd say nothing. That was all they'd need, for her to offer criticism of any kind. She'd mention it to Charlie: she'd get him to check that everything was locked up tonight.

One more night, that was all she had to endure.

She peered out. Ahead of her, beyond the gate, tiny lights popped and glittered on the dark oily surface of the sea. The sky was washing from black to grey, still dotted with stars, still showing a faint thin crescent moon. The cold air – she sniffed – had a fresh tang to it that wasn't unpleasant.

She loved beaches. On her travels with her mother she'd visited some spectacular ones: the Cayman Islands, Florida, Jamaica, Mexico, all featuring mile-long expanses of white sand and palm trees and lots of sunshine. This one didn't sound in the least like those. Still, she supposed she should check it out when it was so near.

She stepped out and pulled the door almost closed. She scurried across the gravel drive, her various layers clutched about her. Steps down to the beach, Charlie had said – and yes, there was an opening in the low wall, practically across the road from the gate. The house could hardly have been placed closer to the sea.

She stood, shoulders hunched, on the top stone step, taking in what she could in the thin dawn light. The beach curved off to her right in a wide arc, its pebbles grey and gleaming. Ahead of her, maybe twenty feet away, the water lapped to the shore. No waves to speak of, no great surge, just a small regular tumble and retreat. There was a quiet charm to it maybe.

Something caught her eye, down by the water's edge. A little darker heap – was it seaweed? She made her way down, the stones sliding away under her feet, and saw the clothes.

Jumper, pants, thrown down anyhow. A pair of shoes poking out beneath.

She bent and picked up the jumper. It was cold to the touch but dry. Red or maroon: in the half-light she couldn't be certain.

Thomas had been wearing a red jumper last evening, borrowed from Aidan after his own got drenched.

Thomas.

She searched the expanse of water, alert for the sound of a cry. He might just have gone for a swim – but at this hour? And if it wasn't a swim, what then? Why else would he shed his clothes and go into the water?

Why else?

He wouldn't. Thomas wouldn't.

But he might have gone swimming and got into difficulties, mightn't he? He might have got a cramp, or been dragged out to sea by a current. Mightn't he?

Her mind raced. How long had the clothes lain there? She had no way of knowing. Was the tide coming in or going out? Again, impossible to know. Should she go back to the house and wake Charlie? Should she raise the alarm? But with no sign of Thomas, and no sound of him, was it already too late?

She must do something, she must act – but as she turned from the sea she heard a splash, and another. She looked back and saw something, someone, moving through the water, a dark shape gliding through it, heading this way.

It must be him. Relief swept through her. She dropped the jumper and returned quickly to the house, and by the time he got back, bedraggled and cold, she'd made tea and was thawing.

Poor old Thomas. Poor skinny, lanky, blushing Thomas. As unlike his father as it was possible to be. Tongue-tied as ever, hopelessly devoted as ever. As if someone like her would look at someone like him in a million years. Still, you couldn't blame him for falling for her, could you? Good job Charlie had never cottoned on: imagine the ructions *that* would cause.

She'd slept almost as soon as she returned to bed. She'd slept until the sun was high in the sky. She woke to find Charlie gone and a note on her pillow to say he'd see her after Mass. She showered – the water pressure rubbish, the bathroom smelling unpleasantly of damp towels, a curly hair on the edge of the bath. She dressed and went downstairs.

The house was still and silent. All gone to church, by the sound of it. All praying for the repose of the soul of dear departed Granny. She made toast – no brown bread, only white – and drank tea, marvelling at the sunlight that splashed onto the kitchen tiles. Lit up like this, the place looked almost decent, and felt tolerably warm. Still could do with a major facelift.

After breakfast she wandered through the downstairs rooms, running a hand along dusty dado rails, peering at framed photos on a sideboard, pulling books from shelves to press her face to their yellowed pages.

She opened a photo album and there was a young dark-haired Charlie in a garden – this garden, maybe – holding a small girl in his arms, two or three. Had to be Poll, with that mop of hair and those freckles. He was barefoot in the grass, jeans rolled up a couple of inches, the sleeves of his check shirt pushed to his elbows. Father and daughter were face to face, almost nose to nose, both grinning.

She would have been Poll's age then. If Charlie had encountered her with her parents he might have chucked her under her chin, remarked on what a beautiful little girl she was. He might have lifted her into his arms to grin at her like this.

She could be carrying a girl now, his second daughter. He told her he didn't want more children, but what if he knew of her pregnancy? Would that change his mind?

He couldn't know. She couldn't tell him, couldn't take that risk.

She turned a page and he was there again, sitting now on a metal garden seat between a younger Lily and an older woman. Same clothes, probably same day. His arms spread across the back of the seat behind his companions, his pose confident, even cocky.

She studied the older woman, looking for resemblances to Lily. The dead mother-in-law it must be, the woman Charlie had had so much time for, even after she'd gone gaga. The woman he'd been ashamed to tell about Chloë.

Noon came. Noon passed. She stood on the veranda and listened to the sea, so different from a few hours ago, green and turquoise and white-capped now under an azure sky. All the cars were still out the front: they must have gone on foot.

She went back upstairs and got her book. She put on another layer and left the house and set off along the beach, smiling at a man with two toddlers who had to be twins, although one wore a tiny swimsuit and the other was fully dressed. *Nice warm day*, he said, and she agreed. She walked on, feeling his gaze on her.

She kept going until the pebbles ended, the sun warm on her back, and found a wooden stile that led up to a narrow earthen track. She followed the track past fields on one side and sea on the other until it turned away from the sea and brought her eventually to a little copse of trees through which a stream rushed on its way to the bigger water.

And here she is, away from them all. Here she is, far from the house that doesn't want her.

She sits in the dappled shade and leans against a tree trunk and opens her book.

She reads. The hours pass.

Poll

ON HIS THIRD ATTEMPT HE MANAGES FOUR HOPS. HE gives a loud whoop of delight, leaping into the air with a raised arm and a triumphantly clenched fist, causing a nearby party of four women on fold-up chairs, who seem to be eating their way through a tin of biscuits, to turn towards him in mild alarm.

'Calm down – you're scaring the tourists,' Poll tells him, throwing an apologetic smile in their direction. 'Anyway, five is the record, so I'm still unbeaten.'

Aidan rummages through the pebbles. 'Not for long.' He selects a new one. He takes careful aim and shoots it slantwise into the water. It bounces just twice before disappearing. 'Damn!'

Poll laughs. 'You're pathetic. I'm the champ.'

They are both barefoot, trousers rolled to their knees. Her hair, full of salt, is more impossible than usual. Her forearms are pink from the sun and the small breeze that blows in from the sea. She watches him as he ducks to scrabble through the pebbles again. She puts a hand absently on his hair, runs her fingers through it.

'Hey,' he says, not looking up, still searching, 'what if I took you out to dinner tonight?'

'Took me out?'

'Yeah. There must be somewhere we could go around here.'

'Are you sick of my family after one night?'

He glances up, grinning. 'Your family are lovely. I just want you all to myself.' Grabbing her suddenly around the calves, forcing her to clutch at his head – 'Hey!' – to keep from toppling. Out of the corner of her eye she can see the party of four keeping tabs on them.

'Well?' he asks, maintaining his hold. 'Is there a café, or a restaurant or something?'

'There's a hotel in the village. It's a bit stuffy, but the food's OK.'

He considers. 'Stuffy with OK food – I'll take it. Do I need to book?'

'Shouldn't think so, not at the end of April.'

'Good.' He hangs on. He rests his chin on her knees to gaze up at her. 'Poll Cunningham,' he says.

'What?'

'Nothing. Just Poll Cunningham.'

She's suddenly self-conscious. The sunshine has brought more people than the group of women to the beach today. Off to her right an older man and a girl of ten or twelve sit side by side on a dark red blanket, surrounded by bags and towels and bundled clothing. The girl is hunched over her bent knees, twirling long black hair around a finger as she reads a comic. The man, shirtsleeves pushed up, ginger hair beginning to grey, leans back on his hands and gazes out to sea.

Some distance beyond them two little children, pale as ghosts, paddle and splash at the water's edge; a woman wearing a comically large sunhat stands guard nearby. Two, no, three heads bob further out in the sea.

'Get up,' she says. 'Unhand me.'

He releases her, offers his hands. She grabs them and pulls him to his feet. 'We're being observed,' she murmurs, conscious of the women's continuing glances.

He doesn't even look in their direction. 'Let's give them something to see then.' He places his hands on her shoulders and kisses her loudly, theatrically, first on one cheek, then the other. She pushes him away, giggling.

They are so good together. They are perfect together. Why can't it be enough for her? Why must she distrust it? Why must she ruin it with her fears? Because the fears are still there, still simmering below the happy exterior. Maybe there's only so much Gran can do from the other side of the grave. Maybe working miracles is beyond her.

Or maybe she's not here at all.

'Come on,' she says, 'we need to pick up Gerry's lawnmower.' Despite Mum's order not to put Aidan to work, Poll has taken matters into her own hands. *I know you offered, but would you mind if I took Thomas to Galway? Mum will give me her car. I just fancy a bit of time on my own with him. We shouldn't be too long.*

Sure. I'll find something to amuse me.

You could cut the grass if you wanted – Mum was saying she must get someone to do it. Don't feel obliged.

Wouldn't mind. Is there a mower?

No, but we could borrow one from Gerry. Mum might be a bit annoyed, but it won't last.

As they pass the four women, one of them says, 'Excuse me, miss.'

The accent American, or maybe Canadian. Poll stops. The

speaker wears a pale blue raincoat over navy trousers. Biscuit crumbs caught in the raincoat's folds. Greying hair tightly permed, gold hoop earrings the size of saucers. In her sixties, Poll guesses. Is she going to complain that Poll and Aidan have been disturbing the peace of the beach?

'Might I enquire if you live around here?' No trace of annoyance. Light brown eyes fixed on Poll.

'No – we're just down for the weekend,' Poll tells her, 'but I know the area quite well.'

'Oh, in that case, would you happen to know if the lady from the bed and breakfast is still living there? The large blue house just up the way?' Pointing back along the beach with a maroon-tipped finger.

The large blue house. Poll grips Aidan's hand more tightly. 'You mean … Kitty Murphy?'

The woman beams suddenly, showing an array of perfect white teeth, and an expanse of improbably pink gum above. 'Why, yes, dear,' she says eagerly, 'Kitty is who I mean. You know her?'

'Yes – well, that is—'

'Is she still there? I know the bed and breakfast is closed up, because we tried, didn't we?' Turning here to her companions, who nod as one. 'We tried to make a booking but it was no longer listed, so we had to go elsewhere, a place in the village that isn't nearly – but anyway, I wanted to come and see if Kitty was still here. I stayed there, you see, and I wanted to say hello and introduce her to my friends, but we saw cars outside and didn't want to intrude.'

Poll looks from one woman to another. All four are regarding her expectantly. All four are waiting to hear what she is about to tell them.

'Actually,' she says, 'Kitty is – Kitty was my gran – my

grandmother. She … hadn't been well. She … died, just a few weeks ago, actually. I'm sorry.'

A lump rising in her throat, which she tries to swallow. Heat behind her eyes. Blink, blink, here we go again.

'Oh!' The woman's smile disappears abruptly as she claps a hand to her chest. 'Oh, my Lord, I am so sorry, my dear. I am so very sorry to hear that. Oh, my Lord.' Her eyes are filling too, as the others regard Poll in silent sympathy.

'When did you stay there?' Poll asks, conscious still of threatening tears but wanting to speak of Gran. Hanging on tightly to Aidan, who holds on to her just as tightly.

'Oh, such a long time ago, my dear. Oh, poor Kitty, I'm so sorry I never got to see her again. Such a lovely woman. Such a lovely *kind* woman.'

'Are you OK, Cecily?' one friend enquires. 'You want a Kleenex? You want some juice?' Reaching for the large red bag at her feet.

'No, no …' Cecily waves a hand without taking her eyes from Poll. 'We came on honeymoon here,' she says, 'Bob and I.' Pulling a tissue from somewhere, dabbing at the inner corners of her eyes with it. 'Forty years next month, it would be. We stayed at Land's End for two weeks – we were your grandma's very first visitors, if you can believe it, and we had, oh, the best time in the world. The weather wasn't very nice, but Kitty was so—' She breaks off, presses lips together briefly, dabs again with the tissue. 'Oh, my Lord, what news. What news.'

'Cecily,' another friend murmurs.

'I'm OK, Patsy, thank you.' Turning to Poll again. 'My condolences, dear. Kitty and I corresponded for several years afterwards. We always planned to come back, you see. We dearly wanted to come here again, but then the children started arriving, and Bob was so busy with his work and … well, it just never happened. And the letters ...' here she gives a tiny lift of her shoulders '... well, eventually they stopped, you know how it is – but I never forgot that dear woman. She gave me a recipe, you know, for her soda bread, which I still make – don't I?' Looking again to her friends.

Nods. Smiles. 'She does.'

'Oh, yes.'

'It's delicious.'

'I'll tell Mum I met you. She's Kitty's daughter.'

Cecily's face lights up. 'Her daughter – yes! I recall ... Lily, wasn't it?'

'That's right.' Poll pauses, wondering how her mother would feel about an unannounced invasion of visitors. Decides to chance it. 'She's here – a few of us are staying for the weekend. Would you like to come up and meet her? I'm sure she'd—'

'Oh, no, no—' Cecily almost overbalances, so vehement is her response, so quickly do her hands fly up in protest. 'We wouldn't intrude at this sad time, dear, no, not for the world. Do tell her I said hi, but chances are she won't even remember me – she was just a child. No, we're happy to sit here and enjoy the sunshine.'

'And ... your husband?'

'Oh.' She stops, gives a small quick shake of her head. 'He's no longer with me, dear.'

'Oh, I'm sorry—'

'He's not dead,' she adds hastily, 'no, no, we got divorced, coming up on fifteen years ago. It was a good move all round. He wasn't – well, let's just say it was best for everyone, and leave it at that.' Her smile returning, somewhat diminished. 'That's just life, isn't it, dear?'

That's just life. Poll's parents deciding to separate, both finding new partners. Poll, needing very little encouragement to fall in love, but unable, for whatever reason, to see that love through. Thomas, honest and generous, but lacking the courage to surrender his heart to anyone. That's just life, just unfathomable life.

'Well ...'

'Thank you for the invitation, dear. I sincerely appreciate it. And please pass our condolences to your dear mother, and your family.' Cecily gestures then towards the biscuit tin, sitting in Patsy's lap. 'Would you two care for a cookie?'

Poll smiles. 'Not for me, thanks.'

Aidan shakes his head. 'I'll pass too,' he says. He's not a biscuit man.

Poll extends a hand. 'Lovely to meet you. Thanks for your kind words about Gran.'

Cecily grasps it. 'Well deserved, dear – and I'm so happy I met Kitty's granddaughter.' Looking beyond her to stare sternly at Aidan: 'You take care of this young woman, sir.'

'I'll do my best,' he promises solemnly.

Poll waves to the others. 'Enjoy the rest of your holiday.'

They continue along the beach, the collected goodbyes of the women following them.

'That was interesting,' Aidan says.

'Mm.' What were the chances of encountering one of Gran's very first paying guests? Honeymooners Cecily and Bob, who had eventually parted ways. Coming up on fifteen years, Cecily said, and they were here forty years ago, which meant they'd lasted ... twenty-five years.

Same as Mum and Dad, who almost made it to twenty-six.

Hang on.

'What's today's date?' she asks.

'Last day of April, isn't it? Tomorrow's the May bank holiday.'

The first of May.

'It's their anniversary,' she says. 'Tomorrow.'

'Whose anniversary?'

'Mum and Dad's – I mean, it would have been. First of May.'

'Really? How many years?'

She calculates. It's not hard. Thomas will be thirty in November.

Nothing was ever said. She was thirteen or thereabouts when she realised that Mum must have been pregnant with Thomas when she and Dad got married. Thomas must have copped it too, somewhere along the way, although he's never mentioned it to Poll. No big deal, she supposes, not when Mum and Dad had stayed together afterwards.

She remembers, when they split up, wondering if maybe the entire marriage had been a mistake, if they'd only married to avoid a scandal, then stayed together because now they had a baby, and it was easier to stay than to part.

But then there was another baby, and another twenty-four years after that. Would you really stay with the wrong person for that length of time? There must have been love between them, to last that long. There must have been love on both sides, mustn't there?

'Thirty years,' she says. 'It would have been their thirtieth.'

'Pearl.'

She looks at him.

'Thirtieth is pearl.'

'How do you know that?'

He smiles. 'I sell jewellery, remember?'

Their thirtieth anniversary tomorrow, or what would have been their thirtieth. Has anyone else remembered? Probably not. The date is just a date now, its significance scrubbed out.

'I threw a surprise party for their silver anniversary,' she says.

'Did you?'

She'd contacted all of their friends, sworn them to secrecy. She'd asked musician colleagues of Dad's to play; she'd arranged for another couple to invite them for cocktails in a local bar while the guests assembled in the house. She and three of her friends had prepared all the food between them, mini quiches and sausage rolls and pizzas and chicken wings. She'd ordered a big cake with a wedding-photo image printed on the icing. She'd painted a banner with *Happy Silver Anniversary* on it.

Mum and Dad had seemed delighted. They'd chatted and danced all night. They'd thanked Poll for doing such a splendid job.

And less than a year later they split up.

They reach the steps, and climb them.

Charlie

THREE MACKEREL, BARELY A FISH AN HOUR. HE couldn't care less. It's never about the catch.

Dinny's boat is pretty much a replica of every other small fishing craft bobbing by the pier. A cramped, cluttered cabin, a wet and slippery deck piled with nets and plastic crates and coils of rope and a blue tarpaulin folded into a stiff rectangle. A luxury yacht it most definitely is not, but its lack of creature comforts doesn't bother him in the least.

He and Dinny sit for the afternoon on upturned crates, their rods dangling, the sun hot on their arms, the sea placid on this glorious day, its water reflecting the deep blue of the sky. Conversation, by mutual assent, is minimal – but every now and again Dinny throws a piece of local news into the silence. A fruitless search for a winning Lotto ticket in one unfortunate household; the outcry after the village's post office closed some months ago; the wedding that was called off on its eve by an uncertain bride, only to be rescheduled for the following week, causing organisational mayhem; a house fire that was discovered before it had a chance to take hold, thanks to the furious barking of the dog within.

At length they make their way back to the pier, where Charlie donates his paltry catch to Dinny, and offers, as is their long-established custom, a pint at Queally's as a thank-you. 'Why not?' Dinny replies, as he always does, so they walk the short distance to the pub and push open the glass-panelled door.

A few familiar faces sit on high stools at the counter: they acknowledge his and Dinny's entrance with nods. Lily would know all their names, but Charlie can't recall a single one. After he's placed his order with George Queally, one of the drinkers enquires about the dents in his car, which has been parked outside the pub for the afternoon. They miss nothing. Charlie tells them of the attack in broad daylight, and heads are shaken.

'Wouldn't live in the city if you paid me,' one remarks. 'No offence.' Charlie assures him that none is taken, and that, given the choice, he'd live here too.

A tactful silence follows this. They're thinking, of course, of his split with Lily, and the consequent impossibility of his ever coming to live at Land's End. When the drinks have been poured he and Dinny take them out to the somewhat rough and ready beer garden – scattered benches, mismatched tables – at the rear of the premises, so Dinny can smoke his pipe.

And there, seated alone on a wooden bench with a pint of something golden, is Joe.

'I felt like a walk,' he tells Charlie.

He was quiet all through lunch, and now he's drinking alone. How did Lily put it yesterday – trouble in Paradise? Maybe he and Chloë aren't the only couple to have had a falling-out this weekend.

'What was everyone else up to?' Charlie asks.

'Poll went to Galway with Thomas. Aidan was about to cut the lawn when I left.'

No mention of Lily. 'Any sign of Chloë?'

'No, not before I came away.'

She wasn't to be found when they got back from Mass. She hadn't reappeared when Charlie was heading to the pier. Keeping her distance, doing her own thing. Let her off: he's tired of humouring her.

'How did the fishing go?' Joe asks. Charlie tells of his three mackerel, and Joe, who has never fished, says he must give it a try one of the days.

One of the days when he's living here. One of the days when he half owns Land's End, and can fish any damn time he wants.

The three of them sit in the sun, Dinny puffing on his pipe until he drains his glass and refuses another. 'Better get off – the missus wants me to take her to Galway for a film.' He shakes hands with them and moves away. Charlie looks at the fisherman's retreating back and wonders if they'll ever meet again, if he'll ever again sit on an upturned crate on the deck of Dinny's boat.

He considers Joe's empty glass, and his own almost empty one. They really should get going. It's past six, and he's been gone since before two. If Chloë is back from her walkabout she'll be stuck with the others – and vice versa.

But one tasted like more, and one more won't hurt. And Chloë's a big girl, and this is his last weekend here.

'Will we go again?'

Joe leaps to his feet. 'I'll get it.' Glad, it would appear, to be putting off his return to Land's End. Charlie stretches his legs and wonders without much interest what he and Lily fell out about.

He doesn't have long to wait.

'I'm in the black books with Lily,' Joe says, setting down the two fresh drinks.

He and Joe don't get personal, or they haven't up to now.

They haven't met often enough to get beyond the superficial. But if Joe wants to share, it can't be too private. 'What did you do?'

Joe takes the top off his drink, wipes a hand across his mouth. 'I had this notion,' he says, 'of moving my practice here after we get married.'

In the act of lifting his glass, Charlie's hand stills. 'What - you mean open a vet's surgery in the village?'

'No. I thought at Land's End.'

Charlie stares at him.

'Well, with it lying empty, it seemed like a good idea - and Sully happened to mention, last time we were down, that the nearest vet—'

'But you're getting married in September - how could you move here then? Lily will still be working in the city.'

'I thought she might commute, come down at weekends, or maybe take early retirement.' Joe lifts a shoulder. 'It was just a notion. Lily wasn't too keen though, when I put it to her. She hit the roof, to be honest.'

He has it all figured out, before he's even married her. Latched on to some comment of Sully's, began to make his plans. Can't wait to get his hands on the place, get his feet under Kitty's table. It isn't enough that he's moved into the house in the city, the house that Lily and Charlie saved and scrimped to be able to afford. The house that still half belongs to Charlie.

He takes a drink, trying to marshal his thoughts. Letting the implication of what he's just heard fester in him. A vet's surgery. People and sick creatures traipsing through Land's End, the place stinking of animals and anaesthetic. He can just picture Lily's reaction. He wishes he'd been there to hear her tear strips off this dope, this person who hasn't a clue how to make her happy.

How can she be thinking of marrying him? How can she throw herself away on him? How can it be that this boring idiot – this *moron* – will soon lay claim to the house that Charlie has coveted for as long as he's known it?

He sets his glass down, taking his time to position it just so in front of him. He turns his attention to Joe, careful to keep his face casual, his voice neutral. 'Lily was born at Land's End,' he says. 'Did you know that, Joe?'

'What – in the actual house?'

'In the actual house. You didn't know that, did you?'

'No.'

'No,' Charlie repeats. 'Kitty was born there too. Remember Kitty?'

Joe gives a small uncertain laugh. 'Of course I remember her. She only died a few weeks ago.'

'Kitty was born there, and all of her siblings. She had five siblings, Joe, four sisters and a brother. All born in the bed you slept in last night.' He's guessing the last bit. It's worth it to see the slow fading of the smile, the small but definite pressing-together of the lips.

'And here's another thing you mightn't know, Joe. Lily and I would have been thirty years married tomorrow.'

The realisation had hit him earlier, when they were on the way home from Mass, and Lily made the remark about Thomas turning thirty in November.

Thirty years tomorrow since he walked her down the aisle. The first of May, the first day of summer, always an easy date to remember. If it fell on a weekday he'd arrange for a delivery of flowers to the school – a mix that always included the lilies she was named for – and take her out to dinner that night. She'd get him a new shirt, or maybe a book. Something small: they didn't go in for a fuss.

He keeps his eyes on her fiancé's face. 'Did she tell you that, Joe, about tomorrow being our anniversary?'

'No. She didn't mention it.'

A small clipped quality to the words now. A tiny, interesting note of peevishness evident. Bet he's glad he got those drinks in.

'That's partly why she chose this weekend to come here, for old times' sake. Maybe I'm not supposed to say anything about that.'

He knows it's not true – but Joe doesn't. It's not a triumph, it's only a cheap stab, but it makes him feel slightly less enraged. He runs a hand across the pocket of his jeans, feels the small hard bump of the object Dinny offered him on the boat, when Charlie admired it. That helps too, knowing it's there.

'I'm just telling you this, Joe, to make the point that Lily and I have a long history, and I know her a lot better than you do. I know, for instance, that she doesn't take kindly to assumptions being made about her future.'

'Jesus, I was only—'

'And I know that the last thing she'd want, the very last thing, Joe, is to have someone talking about turning her childhood home into a business when her mother is barely cold in the grave.'

'It was just a notion.' Stiffly. 'It was only a thought I had.'

'I know. I know it was, Joe. But if you want your marriage to last even three years, if you want to have any hope of that at all, Joe, you'll need to learn to do a lot more thinking before you open your mouth. That's all I'm saying.'

In response Joe lifts his drink, and Charlie listens to the small repeated gulps. When he lowers the glass, it's half empty. He turns then to look directly at Charlie, foam clinging to his moustache. 'I think it's a bit rich,' he says evenly, 'you giving me advice about marriage.'

Evidence of a backbone: unexpected. The lager making him brave. 'The point, Joe—'

'And what's more' – louder, cutting off Charlie – 'I don't think you have any right to speak for Lily, given that you walked out on her.' His fingers white around his glass. Big hands, he has. Big strong vet's hands.

'My point—'

'You made your point, Charlie. I don't need to hear it again.'

Charlie feels the sudden hot scald of anger. 'You haven't a clue,' he snaps. 'You'll never be good enough for her.'

'Like you were, you mean?' Joe flings back. 'Running out on her when a girl young enough to be your daughter batted her eyelashes at you?'

'Don't talk about her like that!'

'Like what? What am I saying that's not true? You ran out on Lily for a girl – and you have the gall to preach at me, you smug bastard!'

Suddenly it's escalated. Suddenly they're glaring at one another, at the back of Queally's pub, at the end of a sunny Sunday afternoon. There's nobody around, nobody to see Joe leap to his feet and pull Charlie to his, nobody to catch the badly aimed blow that glances across Charlie's cheek rather than straight into it, nobody to witness the answering swing that Joe ducks to avoid, his elbow sending the two glasses flying in the process.

Joe throws a second punch: this time Charlie feels the hard whack of it against his jaw, feels the hot sting it leaves behind. Even as he staggers backwards he's raising his hands in surrender – he's no fighter, and Joe is clearly in better shape.

'OK,' he says, 'OK, enough' – and thankfully, Joe seems as ready to stop as he is. They gather up the broken glass in silence, not looking at one another. Charlie prods his throbbing chin cautiously, opens and closes his mouth a few times. Everything seems intact.

His own fault, he asked for it. Wouldn't have thought Joe had it in him though. Shows what a few well-aimed words can do.

They leave the shards on the table and walk back through the pub. The gathered drinkers swivel on their stools to stare at them: must have heard the commotion. Charlie keeps going, praying George Queally will say nothing – and for once his prayers are answered.

Outside he gestures towards the car. 'Might as well sit in,' he says, 'even if you did try to break my jaw.' Idiot or not, the man is marrying Lily – best to let this go, put it behind them.

Joe eyes the car doubtfully. Charlie presses the key fob and the doors unlock. 'Up to you,' he says, getting in – and as he puts the key in the ignition Joe opens the passenger door and climbs in.

The mile or so to Land's End has never seemed so long.

Thomas

POLL DRIVES A LITTLE TOO FAST. HE MAKES NO comment. He's too busy trying not to dwell on what awaits him in Galway.

Poll asked for driving lessons when she was nineteen or twenty. It took her three attempts at the test before she passed. She's never owned a car, and never looked for one, but she'll sit behind the wheel of anyone else's without a thought.

She tells him of the women she met on the beach. She tells him of Cecily, whose honeymoon was spent at Land's End.

'Did you say it to Mum?'

'I did – she remembers them because they were the first people to stay there. And Cecily still bakes Gran's bread – isn't that lovely?'

'Wow. Gran sure could bake. Remember her rock buns?'

'And her almond slices. They were my favourite. Well, those and her lemon meringue pie.'

The sun slides behind a cloud, putting a filter on the surrounding countryside. A tractor emerges from a field and turns onto the road ahead of them: Poll swerves across the road to overtake it, forcing Thomas to grab onto the dashboard. 'Hey, steady on.'

'Sorry.' She slows a fraction. 'I think I have the soul of a racing driver.'

They pass a small white cross stuck into the ditch, a bouquet of plastic flowers tethered to it with a tatty ribbon. Memorial to a dead road user, marking the spot where he or she was killed. It always strikes Thomas as a macabre tradition. Why mark a spot where you lost someone? Wouldn't it make more sense to remember them in happy times, to put a marker, if you had to, somewhere they loved, somewhere you both loved?

'Will you show me where it happened?' Poll asks. 'Where that guy took the car, I mean.'

'If you want.'

He'd rather ignore it, let her speed past it, but he points it out when they get there. She pulls into the side of the road and looks across. 'I can't imagine what it must have been like for you.'

'It was pretty frightening.' He remembers the clutch of dread as the youth calmly reached inside his tracksuit top and pulled out the knife, the unpleasant lurch in the pit of his stomach as he was ordered out of his own car. 'I was bullied at school,' he adds. 'It felt a bit like that.'

Poll turns to stare at him. 'You were bullied? You never said.'

'Well, you don't, do you? Because you know it won't make it go away.'

'But it might have. Dad might have—'

He shakes his head. 'No. That would have made it worse.'

How was he so sure, as a young boy, that grown-up intervention would solve nothing? What subconscious voice dictated that he suffer the persecution alone, that he endure it until his bullies got bored and moved on?

'How long did it last?'

He shrugs. 'A few years. I'm not sure.'

'A few *years*! Was it boys in your class?'

'Yeah. Nobody you know.'

Not true. She was friendly with Richie O'Toole's sister: she'd have gone to their house lots of times. But why name names now, so long after the fact?

'Did they … hit you?'

'No – I was taller than them. I think that helped. They just followed me home, called me names. Spat on my copies, threw stuff at me. Things like that.'

'Oh God. Poor Thomas.' Reaching over to rub his arm. 'I wish I'd known.'

'It's fine. I got over it. I ran into one of them again actually. A few years ago, when I was still working in the hospital. His son was in for an X-ray.'

Long time no see, Richie said. Black tracksuit bottoms with a white stripe up each leg. Hair cut to the bone, probably to disguise the receding hairline that Thomas rejoiced silently to see. Losing his hair in his twenties.

Personal trainer, he said, married to a physiotherapist. *So you work here now*. Taking in Thomas's porter's uniform, all nods and smiles. No sign of remorse, not a hint of embarrassment on encountering his one-time classmate. Maybe he genuinely didn't remember how he and the others used to be.

The two of them stood at the entrance to the X-ray department while Richie's son was seen to. *Two boys. Little terrors, keep us on our toes.* Not a sign of guilt for the sleepless nights and the years of torment he had caused. *You married yourself, or …?* Or hooked up with a man, he meant. Gayboy had been one of their names for him. Thomas told him no, not married, and left it at that. Let him keep guessing. Let him keep getting it wrong.

'Did he apologise?' Poll asks.

'No. I'd say he'd forgotten all about it.'

'God. Some people.'

She pulls out again and drives to the roundabout and takes the Galway exit. More cars now, and a truck that passes them out, going too fast surely for its size and the speed limit. *How's my driving?* a sticker on its rear asks, above a phone number that nobody will bother calling.

'By the way,' Poll says, 'we won't be joining you for dinner this evening. Aidan is taking me to Donaghy's.'

'Is he now? Very posh.'

'Mm.'

She doesn't sound all that pleased about it. He remembers the four of them going to dinner in the village hotel at the end of each summer holiday, taking Gran out to thank her for putting them up. As a child it was like a palace to him, all that red velvet seating and flock wallpaper, and Eugene Donaghy in his grey suit coming out from behind the reception desk to welcome them when they arrived.

It looks precisely the same on the outside now as it did then. He wonders if anything has changed within, if desserts are still wheeled around on a trolley, if diners can still order the mound of profiteroles, stuffed with cream and drizzled with chocolate sauce, that was his choice every time. Might be a bit old-fashioned now; maybe that's why she's not making much of it.

She darts a glance at him. 'Thomas, can I tell you something?'

'Sure.'

He waits, but no more comes. She keeps her eyes on the road; what he can see of her face tells him nothing.

'What is it?'

She nibbles at her bottom lip, a habit of hers he's often observed. 'I think,' she says, and stops again, and again he waits.

'There's something wrong with me.' It leaps out of her,

bringing a flush to her cheeks. She shoots him another glance; he sees the shine of unshed tears in her eyes.

He feels a pinch of alarm. 'What do you mean? Are you sick?' She doesn't look sick, but that mightn't signify anything.

She shakes her head. 'Not sick. It's hard to explain. I seem to … have this compulsion, this need, to *finish* with people. With boys. Men.'

She's making little sense. 'Poll, I don't—'

'I can't *stay* with anyone. I have to *leave* them. Something makes me leave them.'

Still he struggles to understand. 'You mean – you break up with boyfriends?'

'Yes.' So low he hardly hears it. 'I'm always the one. Even if … I still like them. I can't stop myself. I can't let myself believe that … it'll last, so I get in first and put an end to it.'

He's at a loss. She's never confided like this. Maybe it was his talk of bullies, maybe it encouraged her to open up.

'I know,' she says. 'I know how daft it sounds.'

'Poll, it's not … I'm hardly one to advise on relationships.'

She makes a noise that sounds halfway between a laugh and a sob. 'No, I don't suppose you are.'

'But look – doesn't everyone go through a few people before they find the one they're meant to be with? I mean, isn't that how it generally works?'

'Yes. That's how it generally works.' She doesn't sound in the least reassured. Nibbling away at the bottom lip, face tense.

'And you and Aidan – well, you seem … I mean, as far as I can see, you seem right for one another. You seem very good together.'

She flashes him a ghost of a smile. 'Thanks,' she says. 'You're right, we *are* good together. I'm being stupid.'

She's not being stupid, she's being Poll. She's being his little sister, full of insecurities for as long as he can remember. Not shy around others like he is, well able to cope with most social occasions, just unable to see her own worth, unable to believe that anyone could love her.

He thinks of the clay heads she makes. The round, jolly cartoonish faces that she paints in cheery colours, the outlandish hair made from whatever takes her fancy. Maybe a little pair of wire spectacles perched on a snub nose, maybe a daft hat on top, all jaunty feathers and mismatched buttons and sequins and net.

Each head is attached to its ceramic base by a brass spring, so the slightest touch sets it nodding and bobbing and dancing. You can't look at them without smiling, without something unwinding in you and dancing along with them.

It seems to him sometimes that she puts all her happiness into them, leaving precious little for herself. He wants to lift her chin and say, *Look, Poll. Look at all you've got. See it, and be happy.* Her anxiety cracks his heart.

They reach the outskirts of the city. 'Poll,' he says, 'I wish … I wish you could see yourself the way we see you. You're great, you're talented and generous—'

'Thomas, you don't have to—'

'Poll, it's all true. I'm not making it up to be nice. I'm just saying you need to believe in yourself. And Aidan is mad about you, I know he is. We can all see it.'

'Good.' He gets a bigger smile this time - but it's one he's seen before. It's a smile that says, *Look how happy I am. Look at the happy face I'm making.* 'We'll need to ask someone where the garda station is,' she says - and just like that, the topic is dropped.

They get directions from a man walking his dog. As they negotiate the streets, silent now, Thomas feels yesterday's unpleasantness rushing back to meet him. He dreads having to relive the sequence of events, but there's no avoiding it. The boy's face looms suddenly in his mind's eye, the mouth twisted into a snarl.

Don't make me cut you. I will, I swear it.

At the end of a street they see the distinctive blue and white sign of the garda station. As they turn into the cramped parking area Thomas unclips his seatbelt, willing it to be over quickly.

The lobby of the station is long and narrow, and overheated on this warm day. A bench runs the length of it, facing a counter. Two uniformed guards sit at desks in a glass-walled room behind, tapping on computer keyboards; others mill about, some in uniform, some not. Thomas sees an overcrowded noticeboard, a bank of tall filing cabinets, leaflets and forms sticking from pigeonholes.

A wide-hipped woman wearing a long, brightly patterned dress and some kind of hat in the same fabric stands at the public side of the counter. Her skin is the rich deep colour of treacle. She leans across, talking intently in a deep, low voice to a fair-haired guard who scribbles in a large book as he listens.

Two men sit a few feet apart on the bench, the older staring morosely at the floor, a walking stick propped next to him.

'Fine day,' the younger one says as Poll and Thomas take their seats beside him. Dad's age, Thomas guesses. Small mouth, jutting chin. His grey suit has seen better days; his face has the colour and creases of one exposed regularly to the elements. 'My father was broken into,' he goes on, head tilting in the direction of the gloomy man. 'Eighty-eight years of age, three hundred euro gone. What's the world coming to?'

They look past the son at the victim, who gives no sign that he's aware of being discussed.

'Was he hurt?' Poll asks. There are no visible marks of injury on the old man.

'Not hurt, no, but only because he told them where the money was. Two of them – small little butty fellas, he says. I wasn't there, I was gone to Mass. Foreign, he says.' The last in an undertone, shooting a look at the brightly dressed woman, who continues her low monologue.

'Were they armed?' Poll again.

'Were they what – two big hurleys they had. Imagine the damage they could have done to him.'

'It was *not* two hurleys,' the old man pronounces peevishly, eyes never leaving the floor. 'It was *one* hurley and a stick. I *told* you that.'

'Ah, now, Dad.'

'And it was two hundred and eighty-five euro they took, *not* three hundred.'

'Ah, now.' The son turns back to Thomas and Poll. 'He's very upset,' he mutters.

'Of *course* I'm upset. Why wouldn't I be upset? And you're no help, getting it all *wrong*.'

'Ah, now, calm yourself, Dad.'

'My brother's car was stolen yesterday,' Poll puts in. 'He's here to make a statement.'

The son regards Thomas with renewed interest. 'Was it now? And where had you it?'

'I was in it. I gave him a lift.'

'*Did* you now? And what—'

'Who's next?'

They look up. The turbaned woman has disappeared. The son leaps to his feet, his question to Thomas forgotten, and puts out a hand to help his father, who waves him away pettishly and snatches up his stick.

Thomas and Poll sit through the fifteen minutes it takes for the pair to agree on the course of events, and for the guard behind the counter to record it in his book. During that time, three others enter the station separately, two older women, one younger man, and take up their positions on the bench, making eye contact with nobody.

When Thomas's turn arrives he and Poll approach the counter. Thomas gives his name. 'Stolen car,' he says. 'I phoned it in yesterday. I'm here to make a statement.'

'Yesterday.' The guard flicks the pages of his book. 'Time?'

'About five.'

He selects a page, runs a finger down a column, stops. Reads. 'Thomas Cunningham,' he says. 'Yes.' He lifts a flap of the counter. 'Come this way.'

'Should I stay here?' Poll asks him.

'Up to you' – so she goes with them. The guard leads the way down a corridor and shows them into a small tiled room with a table and four chairs, and nothing else. 'Hang on there,' he orders, and leaves them.

They sit side by side. The single window has two metal bars running across on the outside. A CCTV camera positioned in a corner of the ceiling is aimed directly at the table.

'Must be an interview room,' Poll murmurs. 'No mirror though.'

Thomas points to the camera. 'Big Brother is watching.'

The door opens. A burly fair-haired guard enters, late thirties or early forties, uniformed. A large book is tucked under his arm, a companion to his colleague's one. 'Thomas,' he says, hand outstretched. 'We spoke on the phone yesterday. Philip is my name.'

Poll is introduced. The guard sits across from them, stretches his long legs out under the table.

'The good news,' he says, 'is that we have your car.' He produces a set of keys from his pocket, places them on the table. 'I'd say you recognise those.'

They're undeniably Thomas's, Freda's *Titanic* keyring still attached. 'Where was it?'

'Just past the prom in Salthill, on the Barna road. Off-duty man heading home, car caught his attention.'

'How?'

'Driving was all over the place.'

'It was still being *driven*?'

'That's right. Off-duty man gave chase, forced the car off the road. Driver stopped suddenly, hit his head on the windscreen, got out and ran across a field. Our man caught him, no bother. You're lucky he didn't have a crash, state he was in.'

'What kind of state?'

'You had some alcohol in the car, I think.'

'No, I—' Thomas breaks off, remembering. 'Yes, I had some beer, two six-packs.'

'Right. He drank those, and he had some cocaine in his system too.'

Thomas thinks of the hundred euro or so that was in his wallet. The money used, maybe, to buy the cocaine the lad couldn't wait to take until he'd ditched the car. Too befuddled by the beer at that stage to think straight.

'Where is he now?'

'He's here. Super extended his period of detention - fellows from Limerick and Cork wanted to question him so we hung on to him. He's well-known to us. Small-time, in and out of trouble.'

Thomas conjures up the boy's thin, pinched face, the recently stitched cut on his forehead, the ill-fitting clothes, the unwashed odour that clung to him. He sees the flash of the knife, the grinning wave the boy gave as he drove away in a car that wasn't his.

'Here,' the guard goes on, opening his book, taking a loose sheet from it. 'Just so we're clear that he's the one who took your car, I have to ask you to identify him.'

He slides the sheet across to Thomas, who looks at the half-dozen unsmiling young males and easily picks out his attacker. 'That's him.'

The guard nods. 'He's our man alright. Been on our system for years.'

'How old is he?'

'Seventeen.'

Not yet eighteen, and on the system for years. Well-known to the guards.

'Started robbing cars at thirteen,' the guard tells them. 'Got in with an older crowd as soon as he hit secondary school. Father not exactly a shining example, in and out of jail himself.'

'What'll happen to him now?'

'He'll be let out of here shortly, if he's not gone already. He'll be told to report for his hearing in the District Court, Tuesday or Wednesday, and he'll be charged with unauthorised taking of a vehicle and dangerous driving, and a few other counts.'

'What if he doesn't show up?'

'He'll show up. We know where he lives.'

'So he's from here.'

'Oh yes, he's one of ours. Galway born and bred.'

A criminal for a father, odds against him from the start. Robbing cars at thirteen, egged along by others, or maybe all his own idea. Somewhere along the line, someone – his father? – offered him drugs, or money to deliver drugs, and he didn't refuse it.

He swiped at Thomas with the knife when Thomas tried

to grab the car keys, but he didn't touch him. Would he have made good on his threat to stab him, if Thomas had refused to budge? Maybe he would, maybe not.

'Will I have to go to court?' Thomas asks.

The guard shakes his head. 'Only if he doesn't put in a guilty plea – but since he was caught in your car, and we'll have your statement to back up our case, he'd be very foolish to try to make out he's innocent.'

'And what will happen to him after that?'

The guard slips the sheet back into his book. 'Well, he's had a few tellings-off from the juvenile liaison officer, and he's been referred to the HSE drugs services here, but he seems bent on staying on the wrong side of the law, so in all likelihood he's looking at a stint in Oberstown, the young offenders' place in Dublin.'

Thomas thinks again of his persecutors from school, Richie O'Toole and his cronies. They never threatened him with a knife, but they wielded what power they could over him. Even as schoolboys they managed to make him feel every bit as intimidated as he felt yesterday, when he was surrendering his car.

It's different now though. The bully is caught. The bully is about to get his comeuppance.

'Can I drive my car away today? It's not damaged?'

The guard shakes his head. 'A crack in the windscreen where his head said hello to it, that's all. You can have it back as soon as I've taken your statement.'

'Great.' Thomas turns to Poll. 'No need for you to hang around so.'

'I'll head off then.' She pushes back her chair. 'They'll be delighted when I tell them you got the car back.' She gives

Thomas a quick hug, and their earlier conversation comes back to him.

He reaches for her hand and squeezes it. 'Thanks for bringing me in. Enjoy your dinner, if I don't see you beforehand.' Holding her gaze, trying to say more than his words. *Don't worry, things will be fine,* when he hasn't a clue how fine they'll be.

When she's gone Thomas recounts his tale as Philip the guard writes it all down by hand. He wonders why they don't use computers but says nothing, anxious to have it over and done with. Twenty minutes later he's at the rear of the station, standing by the car.

He walks around it, checking outside and in. His case still sits on the back seat, looking undisturbed, his jacket beside it. The beer is gone, of course: the only evidence of its ever having been in the car are the torn remnants of two cardboard cases and a single empty bottle lying on the passenger seat. He must have thrown the rest out the window one by one as he finished them.

There are no slashed seat covers, no apparent damage to the car apart from a spidery crack in the front windscreen: how much force would it have taken to cause that? Thomas imagines the carjacker's head slamming into it, imagines the dull thump on impact, the pain he must have felt – and still he wrenched the door open and fled across a field to avoid capture.

His own fault, all of it. He could have killed you.

And still he feels a pang of sympathy for the boy. He could have killed Thomas, or injured him, but he hadn't.

He looks into the boot and sees the bundle of his bedding – and what's that in the corner? As he reaches for the shoebox he remembers the bread-and-butter pudding. Again, everything looks untouched.

He slams the boot shut and opens the driver's door and gets in. A strong smell of alcohol hits him, along with echoes of the unwashed stench that he remembers. He'll give it a good scrub when he gets home, or maybe get it valeted. He winds down the two front windows and checks the various mirrors and adjusts the driver's seat.

He turns the key – according to the fuel gauge, his tank is still over half full – and manoeuvres the car around the side of the building. As he approaches the area where Poll parked, he sees a figure emerge through the front door and walk ahead of him towards the gate.

It's him.

It's the boy who took his car.

His grubby clothes are unchanged. Even from the rear, it's unmistakably him. He slouches across the yard, hands thrust into the pockets of his dirty jeans.

No knife now. Nothing to threaten anyone with. A head and a half shorter than Thomas. Without thinking about it, without planning it, Thomas pulls the car into the parking space Poll used. He turns off the engine and winds up the windows. He gets out and slams the door.

'Hey!' he calls, crossing the space between them.

No reaction.

'Hey!' Louder.

The other glances back, sees Thomas, walks on.

'I want to talk to you!'

Does he? What's he doing?

The boy halts then. He turns and waits, no sign of wariness in his slouched pose. Thomas approaches, already regretting his impulse, fear beginning to prick at his skin. *You're outside a garda station. Nothing can happen.*

Still though.

He stops, six feet from the boy. They regard one another.

'Do you remember me?' Thomas asks. Trying to keep his voice calm, feeling his heart beating in his throat.

No response. The youth stares at him, narrow-eyed.

'You took my car yesterday.' Thomas feels heat come into his face. 'That car.' Pointing.

The boy turns his head slowly, takes in the car. Looks at Thomas again. 'You got it back, didn't you?' The words clipped, the voice hard. Aggression not far from the surface.

'You stole my car. You pointed a knife at me.' His mouth feels dry. 'My name is Thomas.'

The lad blinks. His ears are as small as a girl's. His pale scalp shows through the close-cropped hair. Is it darker in one spot, bruised from his contact with the windscreen? Impossible to be sure.

'Why did you do it?' Thomas asks. 'I gave you a lift. I did you a good turn.'

The boy gives an exaggerated sigh. 'What do you want, man? I got caught, didn't I?'

Thomas is wary as a cat, alert for a sudden lunge. It's not out of the question. 'Look, I'm not angry. I was, but I'm not any more. I just hope—'

What does he hope? Any possible ending to that sentence – you get the help you need; you don't do it again; things work out for you – sounds patronising.

The boy's eyes are light green, or maybe blue. The black stitches of the wound on his temple stand out starkly against the paleness of his skin. A blob of white spittle lodges at one corner of his mouth.

'You hope what?' he says, his voice as cold and dead as his eyes.

Thomas opens his mouth but nothing comes out. He feels

trapped, defeated, unable to look away. The boy's smell trails across to him, thick and fetid: he resists the urge to fan it away. 'I don't know,' he admits finally. 'I don't know why I stopped you.'

The boy takes his hands from his pockets. Every muscle tenses in Thomas – is he going to strike now? – but he simply folds his arms, shifts weight from one hip to the other.

'So you could act the big man,' he says.

'No—'

'So you could have a good laugh at me.'

'That's not—'

'So you could laugh at the fuckin' eejit who got caught.'

'*No.*'

'You know what I hope?' he says then, a new note entering his voice now. A cold deliberateness to the words now.

Thomas waits, fright clambering like ants inside him.

'I hope you crash your car and get brain damage, so you have to shit in a nappy every day of your life.'

No hint of emotion in the pale eyes.

'I hope your mother gets raped and glassed. I hope your children get cancer and die screaming.'

Reciting it like a litany, like something he has learnt off. Pinning Thomas with his stare, venom spewing like vomit out of him. Why is he saying this? What has Thomas done to merit this hate?

And then, unbelievably, he smiles. Teeth yellowed, one missing below.

'I'm just messin' with you, man. Your face though.' He extends a hand. 'Just havin' a laugh, alright?'

Thomas looks at the hand, scarred and grimy.

The youth's face is still full of amusement. 'Will you not shake my hand, man? I was just havin' a laugh, yeah?'

Thomas turns and walks back towards the car, his insides churning.

'Hope you didn't get too wet yesterday, man.' A raucous, phlegmy guffaw follows him. 'Your car is a heap of shit, by the way.'

Thomas opens his driver's door.

'My name is Thomas!' Mocking, falsetto. 'I did you a good turn!'

In an instant, Thomas's fear is banished and replaced with a white-hot anger. His hands form of their own accord into fists. He fights an almost overpowering urge to turn around and march back and punch the brute in the face.

While he's still trying to resist it, the door of the station opens. Thomas turns to watch two uniformed guards emerge and walk towards a squad car. At the sight of them, the boy vanishes through the gates.

Thomas gets into his car, the blood still racing in him. He sits there, looking out at the red-brick wall of the station, waiting till he feels calm enough to drive. *I hope you crash your car and get brain damage*. What kind of warped mind would think that was funny? Was that what drugs did, took away your humanity, left you devoid of any sense of what was right, what was decent?

I hope your mother— He cuts it off, pushes it from his head. He shoves the key into the ignition again.

He fingers the miniature *Titanic* that dangles from the keyring. Freda, with her many kindnesses, seems like a different species. Freda, if she was here now, would tell him he'd done the right thing in offering the lift. Freda would give the boy a second chance, and a third.

The minutes tick past. Others enter and leave the station: he pays them no heed. Eventually he winds down his windows again and starts the engine and leaves the station car park.

He drives carefully out of the city – *I hope you crash your car* – with the radio tuned to a classic hits station, his equilibrium slowly returning. A few miles on he catches himself humming along to someone – Randy Newman? A few miles further on he approaches the roundabout whose left turn will take him to Land's End.

He could keep going straight. He could drive home now, leave the rest of them to it, cut short this ill-fated trip. He'd be home around seven, pick up a takeaway somewhere. He and Rasputin could watch telly for the evening; he could eat the entire bread-and-butter pudding if he felt like it, with or without custard.

It's tempting.

He can't do it. He can't contact anyone without a mobile signal, and he can't disappear without telling them, without letting Mum or Poll know.

There's something wrong with me, Poll said.

He takes the left turn.

It's heading for five by the time he arrives at the house. He pulls into the driveway and switches off the engine – and as he's about to get out, he spots something in the cubby under the steering wheel that brings the smallest of smiles to his face. He reaches in and pulls out six Lotto cards.

Untouched. Unscratched.

Lily

'YOU'RE BACK,' SHE SAYS. 'POLL GAVE ME THE GOOD news. Is it alright?'

He tells her about the crack in the windscreen, and Lily says Poll mentioned it, and she feels the same satisfaction that she felt earlier at the thought of the boy's head smacking into it. Serves him right: shame he didn't go through it altogether.

Thomas shows her the Lotto cards. 'I bought these yesterday and left them in the car. He never found them.'

It feels like a good omen to her. They could do with a bit of luck. 'Hand them over,' she says.

He grins. 'You're not going to scratch them all?'

'There's no one else around. Your father is off fishing, Poll and Aidan have gone for a cycle, Chloë's in her room and Joe disappeared after lunch. Come on, let's live dangerously. We can take it in turns.'

The final card, scratched by Lily, yields fifty euro. The win pleases her more than it probably should.

'Would we forget about Sully's?' she asks, gathering up the used cards. 'I'm really not in the mood for it.'

'Don't mind. What's the alternative?'

She looks at the kitchen clock. 'The supermarket doesn't close till six on a Sunday' – so Thomas gets back into the car and returns to the village to cash in the winning card and to pick up two chickens and a bag of frozen chips, giving her plenty of time to go on wondering where Joe has gone.

'I need a shower,' Thomas says when he returns. 'My car's a bit smelly.'

Left alone again, Lily rubs butter under the chicken skins and sprinkles them with salt and black pepper. She's sliding them into the oven as Charlie and Joe walk in.

Something's up: she senses it immediately from them. Joe doesn't meet her eye as he heads straight to the sink and fills a glass with water. Afraid she's still mad at him – or maybe still mad at her for snapping at him.

'How come you're together?' she asks no one in particular, and Charlie says they met in the village, which doesn't tell her much. One side of his chin looks a bit pink – he must have caught the sun on the boat. Strange, he normally never burns.

She tells them about Thomas's car, conscious of Joe's silent presence.

'Will he be needed in court?' Charlie asks.

'No – they have enough evidence. Thomas picked the fellow out from a page.'

'I hope they lock him up.'

'They'd better. We've decided against Sully's, by the way. We're eating here instead. Do you mind?'

'Not in the least … Any sign of Chloë?' Looking around the kitchen, as if he expects her to pop out of a press.

'She's upstairs,' Lily tells him, and off he goes.

She turns to Joe. 'Where did you disappear to?' she asks.

'Felt like a walk.'

'And you met Charlie.'

'Ran into him in the pub.'

The pub. She'd driven him to drink.

She slides her arms around his waist. 'Sorry I was mad. I'm a bit sensitive where this house is concerned.'

He doesn't return her embrace. 'I shouldn't have said anything. It was only a notion.'

He smells of beer. 'So are we friends again?'

'We are.' But still he's wary. He draws away, pushes up his sleeves. 'What can I do to help?'

'You could open a bottle of wine and set the table. Only five of us tonight – Poll and Aidan are eating out.'

He finds the corkscrew in silence. Maybe it's more about postponing the wedding, maybe that's what still has him so stiff. She'll say nothing further about that now: no point in putting a dampener on their last night here.

Their last night. She thinks about the news she has yet to break to them, the news that will have to wait now until after dinner, when Poll and Aidan get back. She's running out of time.

'Any harm to ask,' Joe says, taking glasses down from a shelf, 'why you chose this particular weekend to come here?'

She looks at him. Strange question. He's definitely in a funny mood. 'Because of the bank holiday. Why?'

He doesn't answer immediately. He places glasses by tablemats, straightens a fork.

'Joe?'

'No reason,' he replies then. 'Just a comment Charlie made in the pub.'

'What comment?'

Before he can respond Thomas reappears, carrying something wrapped in tinfoil. 'Dessert,' he says, placing it in the fridge.

'What is it?' Lily asks.

'You'll find out later. How long till dinner?'

'A good hour.'

'I've time for a swim so.'

'A swim? I thought you said the water was too cold.'

'It was cold earlier.' Already making for the door. 'Should be OK now with all the sun.'

'I'll see you on the beach,' Joe says. 'Might chance a paddle.'

Lily stares at him. 'You? You said my family were mad to go swimming.'

'I still think that. Paddling isn't the same thing at all. See you later.'

And he's gone too, leaving her alone once again. She wonders what Charlie said to him about the weekend. Must remember to ask him later.

She fills her glass with Charlie's wine. She's had more wine this weekend than she'd drink in a month at home. Back on the straight and narrow tomorrow, with school looming on Tuesday.

She sits at the table. She looks around the familiar room. All the meals she ate at this table, all the growing up she did within these walls.

The few days have tipped her off-balance, no doubt about it. Inevitable, she supposes, that Mam's death and its aftermath would have some effect. Joe was great around the time of the funeral, doing everything he could to make it easier, but she was still the bereaved one, nothing he could do to make that go away.

Ah well. Sunday night and they've survived, more or less. Tomorrow they'll pack up and return to the city, and real life will kick in again.

She raises her glass. 'Cheers,' she says, to nobody at all.

Charlie

HE GIVES A LIGHT TAP ON THE DOOR. HE OPENS IT without waiting for a response.

She sits as he's seen her so often, cross-legged on the floor with her back to the wall, upturned hands resting on her thighs, thumbs and forefingers forming twin circles.

Eyes closed. Fully dressed.

'Chloë,' he whispers.

She opens her eyes. Blinks at him, unsmiling.

He crosses the floor to hunker down beside her. He covers her hands with his. 'Where were you?'

'Reading.' She makes a face. 'You've been drinking.'

'I had a pint ... But where did you go?'

'Not far, a mile or so. I walked along a track, up from the beach. I stopped by some trees.'

'Darling, nobody knew where you were. You went off without telling anyone.'

'No one was here when I got up. Everyone was gone to Mass. And *you* were gone when I got back here.'

You could have left a note, like I did for you. Best unsaid. 'A fisherman invited me out on his boat for the afternoon. I would have brought you along.'

A shudder. 'No, thanks.'

No. Dinny's boat with its lack of creature comforts wouldn't interest her. He runs his hands along her thighs; beneath the cotton of her trousers her skin is warm. 'Have you eaten?'

'I have a lot on my mind,' she says, ignoring his question. 'What happened your chin?'

He'd forgotten it. The throbbing has eased, but there must be a mark. He gives a small laugh. 'Would you believe I had a row with Joe? He gave me a thump.'

She frowns. 'Joe *hit* you?'

'It was nothing, the heat of the moment.'

'But why? Why did he hit you?'

'It doesn't matter,' he says. 'We were arguing – it was something silly.' *A girl young enough to be your daughter batted her eyelashes at you* – or was it Joe's cock-eyed plans for this house that had made him so incensed? He can't be sure now. Bit of both, probably.

Just as well to be going home tomorrow. Mightn't have been one of Lily's better ideas, to throw them all together here.

Ironic, though, that it was Joe who'd thumped him, rather than the thug who'd attacked the car. Bit more to Joe than he'd thought.

His calf muscles begin to ache. He shifts to kneeling and turns his mind to the more immediate matter. 'Sweetheart, I'm concerned about you. What is it? What's bothering you? Tell me. Are you still thinking about what happened on Friday night?'

'Don't,' she says quickly.

'Are you still mad at me?'

'... No.'

'Well, what is it then?'

She shrugs.

'Chloë. Look at me.' He takes her face in his hands, trying to ignore the hard floor digging painfully into his knees. 'Look at me,' he insists, and she does. 'What's wrong? You haven't been yourself since we arrived.'

She grimaces. 'This house. It's spooky. It doesn't want me here.'

He laughs, he can't help it. 'The *house* doesn't want you?'

She pulls away crossly, gets to her feet in one fluid movement. 'I should have known you wouldn't understand.' She stands by the window, her back to him.

It takes him somewhat longer to rise, a clumsy palms-braced heave from knees to feet, a gradual straightening. 'Sorry – I didn't mean to laugh. It's just the idea of this house being spooky, I suppose. I know it so well—'

'That's just it,' she throws back, turning to him accusingly. 'It's *your* house, *your* family—'

'Chloë, it's not my house.'

She gives an impatient toss of her head. 'You know what I mean. You've been coming here forever, you and Lily and the others. You know this place inside out: it might as well belong to you.'

True, all true. He needs to tread carefully here. He suspects something bigger is going on, something more than just resentment of Land's End – but if she won't tell him, what can he do to fix it? He follows her to the window but makes no fresh attempt to touch her.

'Darling, maybe I shouldn't have brought you here. Maybe I should have come on my own, like we originally planned.'

'Yes, you'd have liked that.' Bitterly, arms coming up to fold across her chest. Keeping him out. 'You and your precious family, all together again.'

The unfairness of it stings. 'Aidan and Joe are here,' he points out, a little stiffly. 'They're not family.'

Silence. Nothing but a continuing resentful glare. He *should* have come alone: she's a square peg in a round hole at Land's End. Maybe she's right: maybe the house doesn't want her. Kitty never knew of her existence: maybe it was disrespectful to bring her here, now that Kitty can no longer object.

'We'll be off tomorrow. We can head away right after breakfast.'

Still she doesn't move, still she doesn't speak. Suddenly he's weary of it. 'I'll go down and give a hand with dinner. I'll come and get you when it's ready, OK?'

A silent nod as she folds her body down in a fluid movement to resume her position on the floor. Closes her eyes, tunes him out.

He leaves the room.

Poll

THE DINING ROOM IS HALF FULL. THEY ARE GIVEN A table near the window with a view of the rear garden, which featured last year in some glossy magazine. They look out onto precisely manicured shrubs, and a thriving rockery that borders a little pond, and stepping stones that wend their way across the perfect lawn to a pair of dainty pergolas and a cluster of weeping willows. The garden is probably the best part of the hotel.

The owner, who hasn't met Poll for years, remembers her. He approaches their table soon after their arrival and declares himself delighted to welcome her back. He sympathises with her about Gran's death – *a lovely lady, a sad loss to us* – and enquires after Poll's parents, and offers them a drink on the house.

She's forgotten his first name. She introduces him to Aidan as Mr Donaghy, and he says, smiling, 'Eugene, please,' which clears that up.

A russet-haired female singer and a saxophonist deliver jazz standards at the top of the room, loud enough to be heard, soft enough not to make conversation a challenge.

Poll orders the roast lamb, which arrives pink and tender,

and sitting in a pool of rosemary and red wine gravy. It's accompanied by buttery asparagus spears and parsnip chunks with a Parmesan crust.

It looks delicious. It smells delicious. She cuts into the meat. She chews and swallows.

'How is it?' Aidan asks.

'Delicious,' she tells him. 'Have some.'

'… Very nice. Take some trout.'

'… Mm, I like that.'

She's trying. She's trying so hard.

She hadn't planned on telling Thomas about the demons. She can't say why she did. She knew he couldn't help – but out it came. And Thomas, in fairness, did his best. *You're great,* he said. *You're talented and generous,* he said. *Aidan is mad about you,* he said, and his words did buoy her up. Maybe it wasn't what he said, maybe it was the relief of finally admitting it to someone – but for whatever reason, she did feel a bit heartened.

Driving back from Galway, further cheered by the return of Thomas's car, she vowed to make changes. She would start by accepting Chloë: she was there, and it looked like she was there to stay. If Mum could put up with her, so could Poll.

And when the voices came back, as they undoubtedly would, she would ignore them. When the demons told her she was useless and worthless, when they insisted that Aidan deserved better, that it was only a matter of time before he realised this, she would refuse to be cowed by them. She would stand firm, and she would prevail.

And now she's standing firm, despite the whispers within her. She's standing firm, despite the battle that rages quietly in her head.

You're pathetic.

No. Keep quiet.

He'll soon see how pathetic you are.

No. Go away.

Finish it before he does. Have some pride.

No. Shut up.

Do it now. Do it tonight.

NO. NO. NO.

After the main course they order the cheeseboard between them, and she smears goat's cheese onto a sesame cracker and tops it with mango sauce and offers it to Aidan. Smiling, all the while smiling.

Coffees are ordered and delivered. Aidan pulls his spoon through the froth of his cappuccino. 'Poll,' he says.

She looks up from her Americano.

'I have something to say.'

How pale he is. How did she not notice? 'Are you OK?'

He'll find you out, any day now.

No.

'I'm fine.' He sets his spoon on his saucer. He places his napkin on the table and falls from his chair.

No – not a fall, a slide. A deliberate movement that brings him onto one knee.

At the next table, a woman gives an audible gasp.

Aidan draws something from his pocket.

Poll looks from his face to his hand.

And back to his face.

And back to his hand.

He's holding a dark blue velvet box.

Suddenly she's shaking. Suddenly she finds it hard to breathe. Her hands fly to her cheeks. She swallows, or tries to. Everything inside her begins pattering madly about. *Madly*.

What is this? What can this be?

He opens the box and holds it out to her. 'Poll Cunningham,

my sweet, funny, generous, kind girl, my best pal, will you please do me the very great honour of marrying me?'

She sees nothing but a blur. She blinks and the blur clears and there it is.

An amethyst encircled by diamonds, and set into a band of silver. It is quite possibly the most wondrous thing she's ever seen. She looks from the ring back to his face. His smiling, hopeful, nervous, pale, beautiful face. His face that she loves more than any face in the world.

He wants to marry her.

The woman at the next table dabs her eyes with her napkin. Her companion starts to say something; she shushes him.

'Poll,' Aidan says. 'You might think about putting me out of my misery here.'

She seems to have lost the power of speech.

He wants to marry her.

She's hugely flawed. Every day of her life she struggles with happiness. All she's good at is creating ridiculous caricature heads out of clay. All she's good at is inventing lives for people who don't exist.

But he wants to marry her. He's not getting tired of her. She doesn't bore him.

He wants to marry her.

She doesn't deserve him. She's worthless. He's making a huge mistake.

He's asking her to marry him.

She thinks of Mum and Dad, and Cecily and her husband, whose name she has forgotten. Both couples going their separate ways, parting after a quarter of a century together. *That's life,* Cecily said. That's life, which comes with no guarantees, no promises, no peeks into tomorrow. This is life. This is Aidan asking if they can live it together.

She takes a deep shuddering breath. She takes a great leap into the terrifying unknown. 'Yes,' she says. 'Yes, I do. Yes, I will. Yes please.'

'Oh boy,' he says. He takes the wondrous ring from its box and reaches for her hand, which is still trembling violently. 'Ssh,' he says, sliding it on. 'I've got you,' he says, taking both her hands in his. 'You're safe with me,' he says, pressing her hands to his chest, to his heart. 'You'll always be safe with me.'

Before he can rise to his feet she drops to her knees beside him. He enfolds her in his arms and kisses her. She kisses him back.

He wants to marry her. He asked her and she said yes.

They're getting married.

She hears applause. She breaks off the kiss to see the woman at the next table clapping. The sound makes heads turn at other tables. The word flies around: *Proposal! She said yes!* In less than a minute, less than half a minute, every single solitary person in the room is standing and applauding.

A song starts up, something about wedding bells.

Poll kneels beside Aidan, wrapped in his arms. Safe. Gran might be gone but Aidan is still here. Aidan will save her from herself, from the demons she has cloned from every insecure thought she ever had.

She kisses him and kisses him and kisses him.

Lily

DINNER IS INTERESTING.

Joe is quiet, eating little, saying less. Definitely out of sorts. Chloë is quiet too, picking at the single slice of chicken breast she requested, saying yes to a glass of wine and leaving it untouched. Thomas, as usual, eats heartily – she could never keep that skinny little boy fed – but makes little or no attempt at conversation.

Which leaves Lily and Charlie.

She tells him about the women Poll encountered on the beach. 'One of them stayed here for her honeymoon – imagine.'

'What – here at Land's End?'

'Yes.'

At the end of the table Chloë makes a noise that's somewhere between a snort and a cough. Lily shoots a glance at her, but the girl's face is impassive.

'Do you remember her?' Charlie asks.

The mark on his chin is still there. It isn't sunburn, Lily thinks now. Why would he burn in just that one spot? 'Not really – I mean, I remember Mam being all excited because they were her first booking, and she and Mam did write to one another for a good while after. She'd send photos of her babies when they were born – they're probably here in an album somewhere. Shame she didn't come to the house though. I was going to go down and find her, but ...'

She trails off. She should have gone to the beach: four women together would have been easy to find. She should have invited Cecily and her friends up for a cup of tea. She could have hunted through the photo albums and found the pictures Cecily had sent to Mam.

She didn't, though. She didn't because Cecily was part of the house's history. Cecily had known Land's End when Mam was still a vigorous woman, bowed by widowhood but not defeated by it. Cecily would have reminded Lily of all that, and Lily was afraid it might just tip her over the edge. She was afraid she might make a fool of herself, like she's been threatening to do all weekend.

They finish dinner. Despite Thomas's best efforts there's two-thirds of a chicken left. Lily will stop at the supermarket on her way home tomorrow and give it to Sheila behind the counter, whose husband Gavin owns a pig farm.

Chloë gets to her feet. 'Thank you for dinner,' she murmurs to Lily.

'There's dessert,' Lily tells her.

'No, thank you. I'm going to bed.'

She's eaten practically nothing. It's half past eight and she's going to bed. Presumably she's got a bit more life in her when she and Charlie are in town. Presumably she eats regular meals there, or she'd have died of starvation long before this.

The others wish her goodnight, all except Charlie, who just looks wordlessly after her. The kitchen door closes, and immediately Lily senses a small lessening of tension.

'Right,' Thomas says, getting to his feet, taking a stack of bowls from the press. He'd slipped his tinfoil-wrapped dish into the oven without comment as soon as the chickens were removed from it. Now he lifts it out with his grandmother's quilted oven gloves and places it carefully on the hob.

It smells of cinnamon. The scent tugs at Lily's memory.

'What have you got there?' Charlie enquires.

'It's just something I remembered from here.' Tearing at the tinfoil, peeling it off. 'I was supposed to make custard to go with it, but I forgot.'

'There's a bit of whipped cream left,' Lily says. She finds it in the fridge and places it on the table. Thomas spoons his dessert into the waiting bowls and passes them silently around the table.

Lily looks into her bowl. She sees what she hasn't seen in many years. 'Bread-and-butter pudding,' she says.

Slices of bread scattered with plump raisins and soaked in an eggy, milky mixture. The spicy steam wafts up to her – and out of nowhere comes a startlingly vivid memory of her mother in a flowery housecoat, lifting an enamel dish of bread-and-butter pudding from the oven, placing it between Lily and her father with a satisfied '*Now* so!' Cutting thick slices for them, pouring her silky custard over.

Every Sunday they had it, after the lamb or the chicken or the beef. The main course changed, but the dessert remained a constant, right through all the Sundays of Lily's childhood. Using up the week's leftover bread, nothing wasted in those days. And when it was their turn for the Land's End bread-and-butter pudding, Thomas and Poll loved it too.

Lily had never made it, not once. Why did she never make it?

'Mum.'

She looks up to find Thomas's eyes on her.

'Aren't you going to try some?'

'Did you do this?' she asks.

He shakes his head. 'Freda did really. I just baked it. Taste it.'

She picks up her spoon. She pushes it through the sugary crust and through the spongy layers. She lifts it, loaded, to her mouth. She chews and swallows.

Now so!

Thomas is waiting. Thomas is watching her, and smiling, and waiting.

'It's delicious,' she says, aware that something is happening inside her. Something is climbing up inside her, interfering with her breathing, bringing what feels like a stone to her throat. Something that will soon, she knows, demand to be released, that will not be denied. Something that's going to burst out of her, very shortly now.

She sets down her spoon. She pushes back her chair. 'Excuse me, everyone,' she says. 'I'll just be a minute.'

She walks out to the hall, aware of eyes following her. She climbs the stairs slowly, pulling herself up with the help of the banister, praying she doesn't meet Chloë.

She turns at the top of the stairs and crosses the landing and pushes open her bedroom door. She closes it gently behind her and sits on the side of the bed. She lets it out then, lets it rush, thunder, pour out of her in a torrent, a gush, a flood of salty tears, and heaving, shuddering sobs that she tries to smother behind her hands.

If anyone saw her. If anyone heard her. Lily Murphy, the capable school principal, the great organiser, the fixer of every kind of broken thing, the rescuer of situations, the problem solver. Lily Murphy, fifty-two years old, strong, fearless and independent, soon to be divorced and remarried.

Lily Murphy, falling apart. Lily Murphy, crying for her mother like a little girl.

It's being back here, it's loosened something in her. No, more than that – it's ripped away her outer layer and left her pale and exposed and vulnerable. It's being back here when her mother is gone, when her mother is dead.

Her mother is dead. Her bossy, supportive, loving, irritating, stubborn, protective, generous, proud, hardworking, faithful mother is dead. How can she be *dead*?

She shouldn't have come. It was a mistake coming here. It was too soon. She should have waited until summer at least, but here she is, falling to pieces in her mother's old room.

And of course it's not just Mam, and the long goodbye that preceded her death. It's Dad too, and his much more sudden departure. The man she loved, waving goodbye that chilly March morning as she cycled off to school, giving her no inkling that she was never to see him alive again. The man she adored, gone from her in an instant.

And it's not just them, it's the other love that was snatched away from her four years ago. It's that, it's all of that. It's everything that's been lost to her over the years. It's every bit of her sadness pouring out, all the bottled-up pain, all the bad stuff she never acknowledges aloud, all of it washing out in a giant wave.

In her great grief she hardly hears the tap on the door. She doesn't see the man who enters, who crosses swiftly to the bed and pulls her gently to her feet, and into his arms.

'Lil, it's OK, ssh. It's alright, Lil. You're OK, you'll be OK. I've got you.'

She fits into him, she nestles against him, spilling her tears onto his shirt, feeling the familiar warmth of him, inhaling the familiar smell of him as she cries, as he holds her, as she continues to disgrace herself. 'Let it out,' he murmurs, 'let it all out.'

Time passes, minutes pass as they rock together, as he cradles her head and rubs her back, as her sobbing diminishes, as her tears gradually abate. Still they stand, still entwined.

'*Charlie!*'

The word, so sharply spoken, coming out of nowhere as it does, startles her. She attempts to step away, but his arms tighten around her.

'Now, Chloë,' he says, a warning note in his tone that Lily recognises but Chloë evidently doesn't.

'Very cosy,' she says, voice brittle as cinders. 'Reunited – how charming.'

Lily closes her eyes. A row, a hissy fit: all she needs. She pushes more forcefully away from him, and this time he releases her. They stand apart, Lily careful to keep her head turned away. No need for the little madam to see her in this state.

'Chloë, for Christ's sake, Lily's upset – I was comforting her, that's all.'

A laugh that's not a laugh. 'Is that what you call it?'

'Oh, grow up!' he snaps.

'Grow up? That's not what you said all the times you were *comforting* me in your office! You didn't want your little girl to grow up then, did you? You *loved* that I was so much younger – you couldn't believe your luck!'

'*Jesus*, Chloë!'

Comforting me in your office.

Lily looks at him. She sees the truth in the way he won't meet her eyes.

She should have known.

Maybe she did know.

She turns to the angry young woman, no longer caring about her tear-stained face. 'You're welcome to him,' she says, her cheeks burning, her voice thick and cloggy with the mucus aftermath of her weeping.

She watches Chloë open her mouth and shut it again. She watches Charlie stalk across and steer her away, back to the bedroom at the rear of the house. When their door closes behind them – when Charlie slams it – Lily goes to the bathroom, where she does what she can to look decent again.

She feels emptied of everything, limp as a convalescent. Better, though. Lighter, with all of it cried out of her. 'That's it now,' she tells her mirror self, her blotchy face, her swollen eyelids. 'That's that done. No more of that.'

She descends the stairs. In the kitchen she finds Joe and Thomas still sitting at the table, the remains of the bread-and-butter pudding in a dish between them.

Joe didn't come looking for her. It must have become apparent that something was wrong when she didn't reappear, but he stayed sitting at the table. He left it to her ex to find her and comfort her.

She can't think about that. She can't deal with it now.

She gives a bleak smile. 'Sorry,' she says, to no one in particular.

'Are you OK, Mum?'

'I'm fine, love.' She picks up her spoon and finishes her dessert.

Even cold, it tastes wonderful.

Chloë

SHE SHOULDN'T HAVE SAID IT. AS SOON AS IT WAS out, she knew she'd made a mistake. It was just that they fitted so well together – they looked so *right* together. She couldn't take it.

'What the hell is wrong with you?' Charlie hisses. 'What the *hell* is up with you?'

She's never seen him so angry. His face is dark with it. He looks like he wants to hit her.

'I didn't—'

'The woman was *upset* – I was doing what anyone would have done! I can't *believe* you thought anything else was going on!'

'It just—'

'Now she knows I was seeing you behind her back – Jesus *Christ*, Chloë!'

Enraged. He is enraged. His face, the way he's looking at her, as if he hates her. The tight, grim, brutal line of his mouth, the steel of his eyes. She's never seen him like this. She's afraid she might throw up. She wants to be anywhere but here, in the house that doesn't want her.

Suddenly it's too much, on top of the dread that has been steadily building in her over the past few days, on top of the foreboding that this house seems bent on feeding. Suddenly it's all too much.

'I'm sorry!' she snaps. 'I'm very sorry I upset your precious ex – but so what if she knows now? What difference can it make?'

He stares at her, eyes narrowing. 'What *difference* can it make? Are you seriously asking me that?'

'Yes – I *am* seriously asking! You've been split up for years, you're getting a divorce – the fact that we had an affair can't *possibly* matter now!'

He shakes his head, his face full of disbelief. 'You have no idea,' he says tightly. 'You don't have the slightest idea what this could do to my family.'

'Your family! I'm sick to *death* of your bloody family! I'm *sick* of your messed-up daughter who can't abide me! I'm *sick* of your loser son who moons around me like a lovesick girl! I'm *sick* of the lot of them!'

'Don't you dare! Don't you *dare* talk about my children like that!'

'Why not?' she shoots back. 'It's true, isn't it? Poll *is* messed up. She's had four years to get over me being with her darling daddy, and she just can't do it – and Thomas nearly wets himself with excitement when he sees me!'

'Shut up! Shut up!'

He raises a hand and she flinches, waiting for the blow – but it doesn't come. Instead he draws back and whips away from her. He stalks across the floor to the furthermost point of the room, putting as much distance as he can between them. From there he turns and glowers at her, arms crossed. 'You bitch,' he says quietly.

The anger gone, the anger replaced by something far more

frightening. In the silence that follows she can feel her heart pounding, her scalp tight, her eyes prickling with incipient tears. She can hardly believe it. They've had rows before but never like this, nothing like this. Where has it come from, this rage that has erupted between them?

She crosses to the bed. She sits on the edge. She grabs handfuls of the duvet and squeezes them. She keeps her eyes on the leaf pattern of the duvet cover, the greens and yellows and oranges that seemed so fresh, so vibrant, when she bought it a few weeks ago. It doesn't matter now. Nothing matters now. They're finished, she can feel it. They're done and dusted.

She squeezes the coloured leaves until her fingers ache. She opens her mouth.

'I'm pregnant,' she says, because she has nothing, nothing to lose.

'What?'

She looks at him, and sees all they have built together crumble into dust.

Charlie

'I'M PREGNANT,' SHE SAYS, IN A VOICE SO LOW HE CAN hardly hear it. But he does hear it.

No. He got it wrong. She couldn't have said that: it's not possible.

'*What?*'

She raises her head. She's white as a corpse, eyes brimming, chin trembling. She blinks: a single tear rolls down a cheek.

He disregards it. 'What did you say?'

'I'm pregnant.' She lowers her head again, presses the heels of her hands to her eyes.

No mistake. It doesn't make sense.

'You can't be.'

He approaches her, sees her shoulders tense. Afraid he's going to hit her – and wouldn't he almost be justified? Hasn't she just told Lily what he never wanted Lily to know? Hasn't she just dropped a second bombshell? Is she trying to destroy him?

'Look at me!' he snaps, and her head comes up again. Cheeks wet with tears, and pale as chalk. 'You *can't* be pregnant. How can you be?'

'I *am*!' she cries. 'I just *am*!'

Somewhere a door opens and closes. Someone climbs the stairs, or descends them. Joe's voice, or maybe Aidan's, calls something he doesn't catch.

She's pregnant.

His mind flies back thirty years. *I'm late*, Lily said. Her scared face. And then they had Thomas, after nearly not having him.

And now Chloë, against all his expectations, is pregnant.

'You told me you couldn't,' he says. 'You told me you'd had a botched abortion, and you could never have children after it.'

'I didn't,' she says, blotting with her sleeves the tears that keep falling.

'You didn't what? You didn't have an abortion?'

'No.'

'So what are you telling me – you had a child at fifteen?'

'No. I wasn't pregnant. I didn't get pregnant.'

His mind does another about-turn. He struggles to process what he's hearing. 'Hang on. Are you saying you made it all up, the whole thing? Are you saying it was all a lie, from start to finish?'

'… Yes.'

My boyfriend, she told him. *I was fifteen, he was a year older. I got pregnant, his brother knew someone who could … take care of it. I got sick afterwards, an infection, and I had to tell my mother. I was taken to hospital. I was told I'd never have children.*

All lies, every word of it a lie. He lets this bed in while she waits.

'Why did you make it up? What was the point of that?'

She makes a sound, halfway between a sigh and a sob. 'You said you didn't want more children—'

'So what? That doesn't explain your cock-and-bull story.'

'It's what you wanted to hear, wasn't it?' she shoots back,

some of her fire returning. 'You were happy when you thought I couldn't give you a child.'

'Jesus, Chloë—' He breaks off, shaking his head. He moves away, drags a hand through his hair. Tries to gather his muddled thoughts. 'Look,' he says, 'I still don't know why you had to invent that story—'

'Because I don't want children either. I'll *never* want them!'

His bewilderment, his bafflement increases. 'You told me you wanted children. More than anything, you said.'

'Well, I *don't*.'

'So that was another lie.'

Silence. He's at a loss, doesn't know what to believe. She's pregnant with his child, after telling him she couldn't conceive. She's not happy about it, after declaring that she wanted children, that she was devastated by the botched abortion. The imaginary botched abortion.

'So why couldn't you just have told me you didn't want children?'

She dashes fresh tears away. 'I thought – I was afraid you'd – think less of me.'

He frowns. 'Why on earth would I think less of you?'

'Because women are supposed to want babies. It's *natural* for them to want babies.'

He shakes his head. 'Not every woman wants a baby, Chloë.'

She's twenty-seven, intelligent and capable. She's not some innocent, ignorant teen. By her own admission she's been sexually active since the age of fourteen – unless that's another lie. But he doesn't think so – it's clear she's had plenty of experience – so how on earth could she be so naïve as to think she had to lie about not wanting children? Why did she feel compelled to concoct such a fantasy?

'I was afraid,' she says, reading his face. 'I was afraid you wouldn't want me, and I couldn't bear that.'

She was afraid he wouldn't want her, so she'd made up a story for him, thinking it would cast her in a better light. Not having the smallest idea how much he had longed for her, how grateful and disbelieving he'd been when she'd made it plain that she wanted him too.

Take me, she said. *You can have me*. And he'd thought all his Christmases had come at once.

He can feel the rage oozing out of him. He sits on the bed next to her.

'So what do you want to do?' he asks.

Her tears are subsiding too. 'I want to get rid of it. I *am* getting rid of it.'

No.

Thirty years ago, it was different. He and Lily hadn't been together long; he was her first serious boyfriend. They weren't ready for a child; they didn't know if they were ready for a life together. Everything was different then, and travelling to England seemed the only feasible course of action, even if both of them were quietly unsure about it – and in the end, they'd turned away from that path.

Thomas wouldn't exist if they'd gone ahead: he recalls the thought crossing his mind as he cradled his infant son. As soon as Thomas was handed to him for the first time, he became unable to countenance a world without him.

He can't do it now. Despite not anticipating the advent of another child, despite not wanting, at his age, to start all that again, he can't end this nascent life, can't allow her to put an end to what will one day be his child. Contraception is one thing: he has no problem with that. This is very different.

'You won't have to be involved,' she says. 'Abby is coming with me.'

'Who's Abby?'

She lifts a hand an inch, lets it drop. 'Someone I know. You haven't met her.'

'She's going where with you?'

'A clinic. London. I have an appointment on Thursday.'

'Thursday,' he says, remembering the gig in Donegal that Gloria with her viola wasn't aware of. Gloria knew nothing about it, because it doesn't exist. 'Were you even going to tell me? Were you ever going to tell me about this?'

'Why would I?' Playing with the duvet, pleating and folding it.

'So why are you telling me now?'

She shrugs, remains silent. He studies her profile, this young woman he'd thought he knew. 'Were you on birth control?' he asks.

'Yes.'

'The Pill?'

'Yes.'

'You've been on it all the time we've been together.'

A nod. She's been deceiving him for years. She concocted a fairytale, and he believed it without question.

'So how did you become pregnant?'

She turns to face him. 'How do you think? I was caught. It's not foolproof.'

'When did you find out?'

'On Thursday. I did a test.'

He knew nothing, nothing. While he was planning his trip to Land's End, while he was looking forward to seeing the place again, she was peeing onto a plastic stick.

He remembers his horror at her tale of the abortion that

went wrong and its terrible consequence. He remembers the sympathy he felt for her. He'd believed her without question.

I would have loved a child, she told him, *lots of children, more than anything. But it will never happen now.* The tragic smile she'd given him, when all the time she was taking a small white pill every day to make sure they didn't start a baby.

He takes her hand. It lies limply in his. 'We need to talk about this,' he says.

She looks at him. The skin around her eyes is puffy. 'You're not going to leave me?'

He lets a beat pass. 'Right now, I honestly don't know what I'm going to do.'

'... You were so mad.'

'Of course I was mad. I had a right to be mad.'

Silence.

'Didn't I?'

A small nod. Her fingers tighten around his.

'But we do have to talk about this, Chloë.'

'What's to talk about?'

'I don't want you to have an abortion.'

She bows her head.

'Chloë,' he says, 'you're pregnant, and it's mine' – *is it?* – 'and we need to discuss it. We need to decide together. I don't want to make you do anything you don't want to, only please let's at least talk about it. Let's sleep on it tonight, and wait until we get home, and take it from there.'

Another child, twenty-six years after Poll. A new turn in his life, one he wasn't expecting. If he can persuade her to keep it, he'll be turned fifty-nine when his son or daughter is born.

He thought the next newborn he'd hold in his arms would be a grandchild. But changes happen. Marriages end, new bonds form, and the world doesn't stop turning.

'Can we?' he asks. 'Can we talk about it?'

A defeated nod. He'll take it. He gets to his feet. 'I'm going for a walk.' He'll go to Sully's: he'll try to get his head around this over a couple of whiskeys. 'I'll see you later.'

'Can we leave in the morning? Can we leave first thing?'

'Yes.' He doesn't imagine anyone will object.

He opens the bedroom door – and there, neatly folded on the floor, is Chloë's grandmother's quilt that they lent to Thomas the night before.

Thomas was here. Thomas was outside the door, maybe at the very time she was yelling about him mooning over her. Thomas, who never turned down a dinner invitation to the apartment. Thomas, who was hardly able to look at her, hardly able to string a sentence together in her company. And Charlie had assumed his discomfiture was born of disapproval.

Lord. How blind he is. How stupidly blind he is.

Let him not have overheard. Please let Thomas not have heard what she said about him, or how she said it.

He picks up the quilt and deposits it without comment on the bed, and leaves the room.

MONDAY,
1 MAY

Lily

AFTER THEY'VE HAD BREAKFAST AND WASHED UP, after she's swept the kitchen floor and Joe has mopped it, after Aidan and Poll have left to break their news and show the ring to Karina Clery, after Thomas has headed out on a cycle, the day remaining dry despite the leaden sky, Joe suggests, laying aside the mop, that they go for a walk on the beach.

And there, with the water for his backdrop, with the music of the sea for his soundtrack, he puts an end to things.

'We're not right for one another,' he says.

'I wouldn't make you happy,' he says. 'You wouldn't make me happy.'

'It's better that it happens now,' he says.

'I'm sorry,' he says, 'but one of us had to do this.'

She should have seen it coming, but she didn't. She feels terrible. She feels regretful and guilty. She also feels relieved, which makes her feel worse.

He's right, of course. Everything he says is true.

He wouldn't make her happy because she doesn't love him. She wouldn't make him happy because she doesn't love him. She's tried, she's made every effort, but she doesn't love him.

He's a kind, decent man, and he deserves more than he's got from her, more than she's capable of giving him. She recalls her devastation when Charlie left, and wishes with everything in her that she didn't have to be the cause of the same sadness in Joe, but she is. The cruelty, the brutality of love that's unrequited.

She didn't introduce him to Timmy Scanlon outside the church because she didn't want to acknowledge him. She was mad at his plans for Land's End because she didn't want him having any plans for anywhere that involved her. Her tears last night were for her parents and for the ending of her marriage, and also – this only becoming apparent now – for the fact that she doesn't love him.

He cries a little. Silently, his hands pressed to his face, his shoulders lifting and falling. She stands off to the side and waits for him to finish.

'Are you still in love with Charlie?' he asks then, and she looks at him and says no, and she can see that he doesn't believe her, but it's true.

They were gone this morning when she got up. Their bedroom door was wide open, the bed stripped, everything packed up and taken away. She was glad not to have to face them. Last night, when he reappeared downstairs, she couldn't look at him.

They'd had an affair while Chloë was still his student. They met in his office. He had sex with Chloë and then came home to her. He introduced her to Chloë at the end-of-year concert when Chloë was in second year: for all Lily knows they might have been involved then.

He didn't break up with Lily because the marriage had become stale: he broke up because of Chloë, possibly at Chloë's request. Probably at Chloë's request.

She doesn't love him any more. Last night's revelation, from the angry mouth of a twenty-seven-year-old, killed whatever feeling there was left in her for him.

'I couldn't believe it,' Joe says, 'when we met, and you were interested in me. I never thought I'd be lucky a second time.'

It was nice at the start, with Joe. It was rather lovely to be so patently appreciated, to have someone devoted to making her feel special again, after Charlie's rejection of her. Someone spoiling her, saying things she yearned to hear again.

It was the comfort, the security of having a partner, of being one of a pair. It was being able to hold up her head once more among the friends who'd pitied her when Charlie had left, who hadn't believed her when she'd told them it was a mutual decision.

Being loved by someone again was gratifying, but it wasn't enough. It was nowhere near enough.

She wonders if she'd have gone through with the wedding, and thought probably not, when it came down to it. But maybe.

Imagine if she'd married him though. Fooling herself all the way to the registry office, making the same promises she'd made to Charlie. Pretending she meant them.

'I knew I didn't deserve you,' he says.

'Joe, it's not a question of … You deserve every happiness.'

'But not with you.'

There is nothing she can say to that.

He kicks at a pebble. She offers him the ring he gave her: he waves it away. 'Keep it,' he says. 'I'd like you to have it.'

Such a waste. It will sit in a drawer, gathering dust.

'I'll be off,' he says. 'I'll be in touch over the next few days to get my things.'

She wonders where he'll live, now that his house is let on a long lease to a Lithuanian family.

He makes no attempt to kiss or embrace her. 'If your feelings change I'll have you back,' he says. 'No questions asked.'

She hopes he finds someone new. She hopes it doesn't take too long.

'Goodbye,' she says. 'I'm sorry,' she says, but he has already moved off, and his footsteps clattering across the pebbles bury her words.

Left alone, she walks slowly along the beach, turning over the implications of what's just happened. She's back where she was when her marriage came to an end. She thinks about being single again, the surplus guest at dinner parties, the one who turns a sociable six into an awkward seven. She thinks about the worse prospect of being obliged to sit for the evening beside a hastily found man whose only reason for being invited is that nobody wants him either.

And even with all the well-meant matchmaking attempts in the world, she might never find anyone else. She might spend the rest of her life alone – and what of it? Plenty of others do. Better alone than with the wrong one.

She gives him forty minutes to pack up and leave. She walks up the steps and stands by the gates of Land's End, and looks at the big blue house that she is not, after all, going to sell.

It was Poll who made up her mind, Poll who burst into the sitting room last night, radiant with happiness. Dying to tell them all that she had been proposed to, and that she had said yes.

And when the flurry of congratulations had subsided, when the hugging and the handshakes were over, when the ring had been admired, when the engagement had been toasted, Poll said, *I'm so glad it happened here, right here at Land's End* – and it came to Lily as she heard the words that parting with the house would break Poll's heart.

And maybe hers too. Maybe it's something else she wouldn't have done, when it came down to it.

She'll have to think again. She'll have to work something out.

She listens to the waves plash onto the shore as they had when she was a child. Is there a sound more soothing, more evocative, than the soft to and fro rush of the sea? Growing up she hardly noticed it, in the way that someone living by a railway track might come to pay no heed to the trains that rattle by every so often – but today the sound of the ocean is like the sweetest symphony she's ever heard.

As she crosses the driveway – Joe's Land Rover gone – something catches her eye, something cream and oblong, resting on the dashboard of her car. She opens the door – it's never locked here – and finds a folded page. As she unfolds it, something, some tiny white thing, tumbles from it onto the driver's seat. She picks it up. She places it on her palm and looks at it.

It's a pearl, the size of a garden pea, the colour of buttermilk. She puts it carefully between her teeth and bites down on it as hard as she dares, and it doesn't break.

She takes it from her mouth and turns her attention to the page, which has been ripped from a book.

Lily,

Today would have been our pearl. Thank you for this weekend. I hope Joe makes you happy. I hope he deserves you more than I did.

Charlie

She rereads it. She lets the sense of it sink in.

It's the first of May. It's the day she married him.

The date, each year since the split, was a difficult one to negotiate. She'd feel it looming as April drew to a close, forcing her to remember what she'd rather forget – but this year, with

Mam's death, and the funeral, and planning the weekend here, it had completely slipped her mind.

Thirty years ago today. The rain falling outside the church as she stood beside him at the altar in a hurriedly bought dress, as her mother and his parents looked on in badly disguised disapproval, as they slipped on rings and promised to love one another forever.

She tears the note into tiny pieces and drops them into the car's ashtray. She returns to the beach and stands on the shore and flings the pearl as far as she can into the ocean.

As she climbs the steps again she meets Thomas, coming back from his cycle. He dismounts and walks with her up the driveway.

'Where's Joe's car? He's not gone already, is he?'

She tells him yes. She tells him why.

He doesn't appear too surprised. Did he see what Lily had refused to see, until Joe forced her to look?

'So no wedding.'

'No wedding.'

'Are you OK?'

'I am. It's the right thing.' She is. It is.

He props the bike against the railings and follows her inside. 'What'll happen now? To Land's End, I mean.'

She shakes her head slowly. 'I don't know, Thomas. I have no idea.'

'I'd live here all year round, if I could get work nearby.'

She regards him in surprise. 'Would you? I didn't know you were that attached to the place.'

'I love it,' he says simply. 'I loved it as a kid, and I still love it. Sometimes I forget that in the city, but when I come back I remember. This weekend ... hasn't been the easiest, but I still love Land's End.'

And she'd been planning to sell it, without even consulting them. Without even asking them how they'd feel about it.

'You can use it anytime you want,' she says. 'Wait till the days get longer – maybe Sam and Matt would come with you for the next bank holiday.'

'They might … How about you though? Are you planning to spend time here over the summer?'

She thinks of the long days of June and July and August, the darkness not given much of a chance to take hold. People on the beach when the weather is kind. Radios and picnics, the smell of sunscreen, the squeals of children. Cars parked on the lane.

'I'd say I will,' she says. 'Yes, more than likely I will.'

Shortly afterwards, Poll and Aidan reappear. Poll enquires as to Joe's whereabouts, and again Lily relates the circumstances of his departure.

'Oh, Mum. I'm sorry. Are you very sad?'

'I'll miss him – but it's for the best. It's the right decision.'

'Poor Joe. I liked him.'

Already he's sliding away from them, already being spoken of in the past tense. Poor Joe indeed.

The morning passes. The four of them spread a blanket on the back lawn and sprawl there for a while. The sunshine of yesterday is gone but the day is mild. At one they cobble a lunch together from what's left – cheese, fruit, bread – and after the clean-up, Lily announces that she's going to get moving.

'There's school stuff I need to get done before tomorrow,' she says, which is only half true. There's plenty she could be doing for school – when is there not? – but nothing that can't wait. No, she wants to be alone now to collect her thoughts, to think some more about what's happened and to plan her next move.

Upstairs she strips her bed and bundles towels and sheets

into the black plastic bag they arrived in three days earlier, freshly laundered and ironed. She packs up shoes and dresses and toiletries, and Joe's book, forgotten on his bedside locker. She closes the window and leaves her mother's lilac dressing gown hanging in the wardrobe.

She'll be glad of it next time she comes.

She drops her things at the top of the stairs and walks into the room Charlie and Chloë used, telling herself she's checking for anything they might have left behind. She gazes at the mattress of the stripped bed. She remembers the joy of waking up next to him in the early days and months and years of their marriage. No, in *all* the days of their marriage, even the last ones, even if the joy had become a little diluted, even if she was hardly aware of it any more. It was there, it was always there.

A single long hair, looping around itself, clings to the edge of the windowsill. She opens the window and puts it out.

Aidan brings her luggage to the car. 'I'm so glad for you,' she tells him. 'Thank you for making Poll so happy.'

'Works both ways,' he says, smiling. 'We're going to organise a little party when we get back. We'll keep you posted.'

'I look forward to it.'

Poll hugs her tightly. 'Thanks for organising this weekend. Drive safe. I'll phone you when we land this evening.'

'Don't swim out of your depth.'

'I won't.'

'Promise.'

'I promise.'

Poll and Aidan will use Land's End, for sure. In the fullness of time they might repeat history, make it their family holiday place. Fill mugs with hot chocolate for the next generation, swim together in the same sea, watch the same sun go down in the evenings.

'Will you come out to dinner with me next week?' Thomas asks. 'My treat.'

She's touched. She can't remember the last time they spent an evening together, just the two of them. 'I'd love that.'

She'll have to tell Charlie about Joe. She won't have him hear of it from someone else. He doesn't deserve such consideration, but he'll get it.

She shuts her car door and drives off. Poll and Aidan and Thomas stand side by side in her rear-view mirror, waving, until she rounds the bend.

Poll

THEY HAVEN'T GONE AWAY.

Last night, she thought they were gone. Last night, her happiness stifled them, deadened them, refused them a voice. Last night, lying side by side, she and Aidan talked and talked.

I'd planned to take you to Edinburgh this weekend, he told her. *I wanted to propose somewhere different. I had everything booked, flights, hotel, the lot – and then you asked me to come to Land's End. In case I sounded less than enthusiastic, that was why.*

She apologised for ruining his plans, and told him she was free to go to Edinburgh any other bank holiday weekend. He forgave her, and said he'd see what he could do.

They talked about visiting his parents to give them the news in person once they were back in the city. They talked about flying to France as soon as they could arrange it to tell his daughter Loulou and her mother Éloïse.

And after Aidan fell asleep, Poll didn't. Her head was too full of excitement to shut down. No room in it for the demons last night, with so much to think about.

Children, for sure. She'd like three, or maybe four. Kitty for the first girl. Maybe Robert for a boy, for the grandfather she never knew. After that, she didn't mind.

They'd need a house with a garden when the children came along. A swing, a trampoline - no, not a trampoline: she saw broken ankles, broken necks. A swing and a sandpit then - and a goldfish, or maybe a rabbit. Or both. Anything that didn't make her sneeze.

Poll Cunningham. Poll Grimes. Poll Grimes-Cunningham. Poll Cunningham-Grimes. Decisions, decisions.

She'd stop working when the children started to arrive. No, she'd cut down on her hours. She'd convert a room in their house into a studio. She'd allow the children to play with the clay - she'd encourage them to be very messy indeed. She'd give a prize for the biggest mess.

Lying there in the dark with Aidan's arms around her, her happiness made her generous. She'd get Dad to teach the children to swim: he'd like that. She might make him and Chloë godparents - but here she called a halt. A little too generous.

Five minutes' sleep she must have got, at the very most - and the second she woke up there they were, clamouring in her head as loudly as ever.

He didn't mean it. He made a mistake.

All through breakfast she tried to ignore them.

Who in his right mind would want to marry you?

All the way to Karina's, sitting beside Aidan in the car, she tried to ignore them.

He'll realise it soon. He'll call off the wedding. He'll tell you he's sorry.

While Karina was exclaiming and admiring the ring and making tea she tried to ignore them.

It's only a matter of time, you know that. It can't last.

All through lunch she tried to ignore them.

Put an end to it before he does. Why wait, why prolong it?

But there's no stopping them, there's no ignoring them. Why did she ever imagine she could? What made her think she could defeat them, get rid of them, when they're her, when they're inside her?

And still she tries, still she struggles. She focuses on all the good stuff.

He asked her to marry him. She said yes. They're engaged.

He didn't mean it.

He commissioned a designer to make the ring.

He made a mistake.

He chose an amethyst because it's her birthstone, encircled it with diamonds to make it more special.

Tomorrow, or next week, or next month, he'll realise.

The curved band is platinum, not silver as she'd thought: it must have cost him a fortune. It fits her finger perfectly.

You're a fool for thinking he'll go ahead with it.

The thing is, they're right. The thing is, they're always right. And sooner or later, she'll have to give up the struggle and let them win.

Sooner or later she'll call it off. She'll hand him back the beautiful ring and tell him she's sorry. She'll move out of his apartment and go back to Mum while she finds another place to live.

Sooner or later, it will happen. But for now, she's going to go on pretending everything is alright because she can't face the other just yet. Not yet.

She left Aidan at the house, helping Thomas to return the wicker furniture to the shed. She's on her way to Gerry's with the galvanised bucket that she found in the scullery, the one he filled with potatoes for them. When she gets back they'll pack up and go, they'll leave Land's End and Aidan will never see it again.

She can't think about that. She can't go there. So she walks to Gerry's farm and she pretends to be happy, like she's always done. Like she will always do.

She rings his doorbell and gets no response. He'll be out the back somewhere. She walks around to the yard, calling his name. It must be twenty years since she last set foot on the farm. She opens the doors of the outbuildings one by one, but there's no sign of him.

She makes her way to the barn.

As she approaches the big wooden door, something happens.

Bad girl.

She hears it as clearly as if someone said it aloud.

What?

She stops, disconcerted. She looks around and sees nobody.

Wicked girl.

What?

Bad, evil girl.

What? What?

She stands before the door, her skin tingling. It's just the barn, where she and Thomas searched for eggs, where they played hide and seek. It's Gerry's barn, where his hens pecked and rambled, where his dog dozed on rainy days. It's her mind playing tricks, it's the demons having fun with her.

'Gerry?' she calls. 'Are you there? It's Poll. Poll Cunningham.'

No sound. She pulls the door open and peers inside. 'Gerry?'

Silence. The space is gloomy, shadowy, musty-smelling. He's not there.

Still she stays put, letting her eyes adjust. Something holds her there, even as fear creeps down her spine, nestles behind her knees.

And then, as she stands there, she begins to remember. As she hovers in the doorway it comes back to her, piece by piece. Minute by minute.

She's come to hide from Thomas, who is counting to a hundred. She's tiptoed into the barn to find a place – but there's a man there. The unexpectedness of him makes her heart jump, makes her stop dead. He's not Gerry, he's someone else. She can't see his face, his back is to her, but she knows who he is.

He's crouched over, his head bent. He's making an odd noise – it sounds like he can't breathe right. She thinks he might be crying. The sound increases her fright. She wants to turn and run away, but her legs won't move.

His trousers are all the way down, bunched at his ankles. His legs are thick and white in the gloom of the barn. His bottom is big and round, shining like the moon.

She's frozen to the spot, trying not to breathe. Trying not to make a sound – but a sneeze catches her unawares. She feels it coming and clamps her hands over her nose, but it bursts out of her.

The man who isn't Gerry whips around and spies her. She stands stock still, too terrified to move. He snatches at his trousers and pulls them up. His face is very red, and very angry. He makes a sudden lunge for her, grabs her arm before she can run.

'Bad girl!' he says. He whispers it, but it feels like he's shouting. 'Wicked girl, sneaking around like that! Bad, evil girl!' His mouth inches from her face, bits of his spit flying out from it, hitting her cheeks.

She is petrified. His hand is squeezing her arm, hurting it. She wants to scream for Thomas but her voice won't work. She feels her pee coming: it runs down her legs, warm and wet and stinging. It soaks her favourite red tights with the black spots.

'You are a wicked, wicked girl!' he hisses, shaking her arm. 'If you tell anyone about this, I will tell them how wicked you are, and they will lock you up for ever and ever!'

She begins to wail then, loud, terrified crying. He pushes her away from him, stalks to the door and disappears, still fumbling with his trousers. She huddles into a corner and waits for Thomas to find her, and when he does she tells him she has a pain in her tummy and wants to go home.

Standing there at the barn door, she remembers it all.

Gerry's cousin, home from somewhere for his aunt's funeral, for Gerry's mother's funeral. She'd met him the day before in Gerry's house. They'd all gone up for the wake and she'd been in the kitchen, helping Gran to wash cups, when he'd come in looking for a glass. *This is Spencer,* Gran said. *He's Gerry's cousin. Say hello, Poll.* He tousled her hair and told her she had beautiful Irish freckles. His breath smelt like Daddy's when he came home from Sully's.

Gerry's cousin, who was doing what he'd felt an urge to do in the barn, thinking himself to be unobserved. Calling her wicked and evil, because at five years old she'd wandered in and had seen him doing something she didn't understand. Making her believe she was bad, and undeserving of anyone's love.

If you tell anyone about this, I will tell them how wicked you are – so she'd told no one. She'd pushed down the fright and the shock, she'd buried it deep where nobody could find it, and from then on she'd stayed away from Gerry's barn, and Gerry's farm, and anywhere she might encounter Gerry's cousin again.

Here was where it had begun. Here was where she'd learnt to despise her wicked self. Here was where the demons were born.

Didn't Mam mention him this morning? Poll asked her who would inherit Gerry's farm, and Mam said probably a cousin. Something about his unusual name, and his awful sideburns – and Poll felt someone walking over her grave, and didn't know why.

She closes the barn door slowly and leans against it. Her right hand moves of its own accord to her left. It finds the engagement ring and holds on.

Bad girl, wicked girl, evil girl – but she was none of those. For over twenty years she'd believed him. For over twenty years he'd controlled her, told her how to think, even though she'd never laid eyes on him again.

And the inexplicable thing, the baffling reality is that, despite this awful thing happening here, she still grew up loving Land's End, loving the big blue house with Gran in it.

It's Gran, she thinks suddenly. It's Gran who led her to the barn, knowing the memories the sight of it would unlock. It's Gran, who has returned after all to her beloved home, Gran who knew exactly what to do for Poll.

She looks at the sky, feels a drizzling shower begin. She'd better get going. She leaves the bucket outside Gerry's back door and turns her collar up.

Now I know, she thinks. *Now I understand.*

It feels like the start of something. It feels like a new beginning. She hurries back to Land's End. She hurries back to her future, filled with tremulous hope.

Thomas

I'M SICK OF YOUR LOSER SON WHO MOONS AROUND ME like a lovesick girl.

Thomas nearly wets himself with excitement when he sees me.

His own fault. He shouldn't have eavesdropped. As soon as he realised a row was in progress – and it was immediately apparent – he should have dropped the quilt and gone, instead of remaining at the door listening to the raised voices on the other side. Serves him right.

Your loser son.

Like a lovesick girl.

Nearly wets himself with excitement.

But it's good that he heard. It's a good thing that she wounded him like that, because her words had an immediate effect on him. They showed her in a new light, they killed what feelings he had for her. They allowed him to unlatch himself, and now he can move on.

As he approaches the village his phone gives a series of beeps, telling him of missed calls or texts while he was out of coverage. Nothing, he's sure, that can't wait until he lands.

He'll make changes. From now on he'll keep his distance

from them. He'll meet Dad on his own, but he'll turn down future invitations to the apartment. Of course, maybe he won't be invited there any more, now that Dad has been put in the picture.

But maybe Dad didn't believe her. Maybe he thinks she just said it to annoy him. Maybe if Thomas says nothing, the subject will never come up between them.

No: enough secrets. He'll phone Dad. He'll phone him at work so Chloë can't answer. He'll tell him the truth, that he had feelings for her but that they're gone now. He'll see how Dad takes it.

He thinks it will be OK. He thinks everything will be OK now.

He passes the spot where his car was stolen. At the roundabout he turns for the city. He left Land's End before Poll got back from Gerry's. He'll phone her this evening: they haven't had time alone since her and Aidan's announcement last night. He wants to congratulate her again, give her the opportunity to talk about it, to revel in it. Surely this will finally put her mind at rest, quell her anxiety.

And he'll ask her to make him a head for Freda. It came to him this morning on his cycle. He thinks Freda would like a bouncy head: he thinks she'd enjoy the fun of it. He'll let Poll decide what to make.

He has something else for Freda. It's a perfectly intact queen scallop shell, its creamy white ridges interrupted with stripes of tan and rusty orange and pale coffee and darker brown.

He found it on the beach, when he went for a last swim after Mum left. It reminded him of the shells he'd collected as a boy. He'll present it to her tomorrow, a souvenir of his trip, like the souvenirs she always brings him back. It'll do until he can give her the head Poll will make.

He'll come back to Land's End soon. He'll ask Sam and Matt if they want to join him, like Mum suggested. He wants to wipe the memory of this weekend, and the best way to do that, he thinks, will be to have another, better one.

He wonders what it would be like to live there all the time. Of course it'll never happen: he'd never find a job that suits him as well as the one he has. But he thinks it might be something to call Land's End his permanent home. It might really be something.

Traffic is heavy as he approaches the city. Cars whoosh by him – drivers eager, it would seem, to return to the place they were so keen to escape from only a few days before. He was one of them then too, little imagining the unpleasantness he was about to face.

It's heading for five when he reaches his own neighbourhood. On an impulse he doesn't question, he changes course to pass the café. He turns onto the street where it's located and slows to take it in as he passes. A notice of some kind has been posted on its shutters: he double-parks and gets out to investigate.

Closed until further notice.

Hand-written in blue biro, but the writing isn't Freda's. Attached to the shutters with brown parcel tape.

What? That can't be right. Yes, closed today, but open as usual tomorrow, or it should be. He finds no other clue, no possible explanation. He returns to the car and takes his phone from the pocket of his jacket, remembering the beeps he heard as he drove, as he regained mobile coverage: *8 missed calls,* he reads, all from the same number, one he doesn't recognise. No message, not a single voicemail.

Eight calls.

He charged his phone with Dad's charger on his arrival at the house on Saturday. Not because he needed to, just out of habit. It sat in his room after that, useless for calls or texts without a signal. He didn't touch it again until he was packing up today, didn't bother taking it with him when Poll drove him to Galway.

He's filled with foreboding. Who on earth needs to talk to him so urgently? Surely it's connected with this sign on the café. He tries calling Freda and gets an out-of-service message, and his fear grows. He dials the unknown number and listens to the rings. When he's about to hang up he hears a click, followed by a long fumble.

'Hello?' A female voice, older. A chesty catch in the breath.

Thomas gives his name. 'I've been missing your calls, I'm afraid. I was—'

'I tried ringing you, *lots* of times!' Snapped out at him.

'Sorry, I was—'

'You *never* answered!'

'I was—'

'About *ten* times, I must have tried you!'

He changes tack. 'Have you some connection with Freda O'Donnell? I've just seen—'

'I'm her *mother*!'

Her mother. For as long as Thomas has been working in the café, the woman hasn't set foot inside it. He's aware of her existence but precious little else - Freda, who chatters all day long, rarely gives her a mention. Could be a number of reasons for this: right now he's not interested in any of them.

'Is Freda alright?'

'She is *not* alright! She's *far* from alright! Why would I be ringing you if she was alright?'

He feels a clutch of real alarm. 'What happened? What's wrong?'

'She had a fall, didn't she? Closing up on Saturday. Climbed a chair to pull down the shutters, lost her balance, off she tumbled. You were gone away early. She was all on her own.'

Accusatory. She might as well have said *your fault*.

'Is she – was she hurt?'

'Well, of *course* she was hurt! Wasn't her leg broken in three places? Carted off in an ambulance. First I heard of it was a phone call from the hospital – well, you can imagine the *fright* I got!'

'Oh God.' He feels sick. Poor Freda. He should have been there, should have insisted on staying till closing time. 'Is she still in hospital?'

'Well, of *course* she is, and she only being operated on yesterday. A *pin*, they had to put in.'

A fresh realisation hits him. 'Saturday was her birthday.'

'Oh, *birthday* – who cares about that? What does *birthday* matter when she's lying in that hospital, and her leg held together with a *pin*? It wasn't as if she had anything *planned*.'

Nothing planned, no. He thought of the concert tickets she'd won, useless to her because she had nobody to share them with. 'Which hospital?'

She gives the name. 'They're keeping her in till tomorrow. First thing she said when I went in was ring you, told me to keep trying. Wasn't *my* idea.'

'Are you with her now? Can I talk to her?'

'I am *not* with her. I'm at home. I'd have to get *two* buses, with my hip. Bad enough that I had to go in on Saturday with her toothbrush and whatnot. I had to take a taxi – the *price* of it!'

'I've tried calling her,' he says. 'I can't get through.'

'Well, of *course* you can't get through – wasn't her phone in her pocket, wasn't it smashed up when she fell? Isn't that why *I* had to do all the ringing?'

He remembers teasing Freda about her ancient Nokia, so outdated it could barely manage calls and texts. *At least nobody will ever steal it,* she told him – and she was right. It hadn't been stolen, just broken like her leg when she fell.

He thanks her and hangs up, and drives home with a stone in his heart. What a thing to happen. He should have stayed till closing time – he should have insisted.

He pulls up outside the house. He'll unload the car and unpack his case. He'll have the shower he skipped this morning and afterwards he'll phone the hospital and find out when visiting hours are.

Bugger that.

He starts the car again. He drives across the city through heavy traffic. He negotiates the pitifully small and tightly packed hospital car park for ten minutes before grabbing a newly vacated space just ahead of a similarly cruising woman who glares at him.

For the first time in his life, he glares back. He's amazed by how satisfying it is.

As he gets out he remembers the white shell he plucked from the pebble beach. He locates it in his case and slips it into his pocket. It's nothing, but it's all he has to offer her.

'Freda O'Donnell,' he says at Reception, and is directed to the third floor, where he meets a nurse who tells him sternly that visiting hours don't start till seven.

'I'm her only brother,' he says. 'I've just arrived from Australia.' The lies flowing effortlessly out of him. 'I've driven here straight from the airport. I haven't slept in over a day, but I had to see her.'

She relents. He steps through the door of Freda's ward, which contains four beds – and there she is, in the one by the window, asleep.

He crosses the room, ignoring the other patients, and stands at the foot of her bed. He folds his arms.

Her hair, which he's never seen untied, pours across the white pillow. Her face is pale but unmarked, apart from a small yellowish-purple bruise that sits high on her right cheek. She wears what looks like a pale blue nightdress; her freckled arms emerge from the short sleeves. A drip sends something colourless into the back of her left hand. The bottom of the bed is elevated slightly: beneath the covers he sees the bulge of her plastered leg.

He's aware of a lump in his throat. He thinks of her in her bottle-green apron, singing along with the CDs as she cooks, using the wooden spoon as her microphone. Laughing every time at his awful knock-knock jokes, even though she's heard them a thousand times. Coming out from behind the counter to tickle babies under their chins. Bringing him back a present every time she goes anywhere.

Never judging anyone. Ridiculously trusting. The kindest person he knows.

I'm sick of your loser son who moons around me like a lovesick girl.

Thomas nearly wets himself with excitement when he sees me.

He's a fool. He's a prize idiot.

He fingers the shell in his pocket. He wills her eyes to open.

Charlie

EVERYTHING HAS CHANGED.

She lied to him. She concocted a series of lies and fed them to him. How can he ever trust her again?

He recognises the hypocrisy, of course. For at least a year he lied to Lily, who has just found out, and who will probably never trust *him* again. When it comes down to it, he's no better than Chloë.

Does he still love her though?

Does he?

He left his marriage for her. He put his relationship with his children into question for her. Since they've been together she has brought him immense happiness. But now?

All he knows for sure is that he doesn't want her to abort their child. And as it turns out, neither does she.

'I'm dreading it,' she admits, when the new day comes and they leave behind the anger of the day before. 'I'm sick at the thought.'

'Then don't go through with it. Cancel the appointment.'

'But I don't want a baby – and you don't want one either.'

'I didn't want one.'

'But now you do.'

Now he does. Now that events have overtaken them, now that fate, or whatever, has presented them with this scenario, he finds himself unaccountably drawn to the notion of being a father again. He finds the idea of bringing up a new child more and more appealing.

He'll be older: so what? He'll shape up and reclaim his lost vitality – it will be his mission for the next seven months or so. He'll be hands-on with this child; he'll play his part. Thomas and Poll were products of a different generation, one in which mothers, whether working outside the home or not, handled most of the child-rearing, and fathers were happy to let them. Second time round, he'll do it differently.

He'll make time for this son or daughter. He'll take advantage of his seniority in the college to adjust his schedule and organise his working day to suit his new status as a born-again father. He'll make himself available for the school runs, the dental appointments, the play dates. Everything Lily handled in the past.

He'll be there for the teething and the colic. He'll walk the floor at night. He'll slip money under the pillow when teeth begin to fall out. He'll introduce music: maybe this one, with such a musically talented mother, will take to it. He'll teach it to swim, like he taught the others – only it won't be at the Land's End beach.

He'll be there for all of it. The first haircut, the first pair of shoes, the first bicycle with just two wheels.

He knows it won't be plain sailing. Who can tell how Chloë will be, after the birth? And what of the possible upheaval in his first family?

What will Lily think? What will she say when he breaks the news to her? Will she even listen, after the revelation of last night?

Following Poll's difficult birth, and the tough time she went through afterwards, they'd made the decision not to try for more. How will she feel upon hearing that Charlie is to be a father again, when the possibility of her having another child is well and truly behind her?

Last evening he escaped to Sully's without encountering her. He slipped from the house without meeting anyone. When he got back, it was to find Poll and Aidan the centre of attention with their news, and in the general good cheer nobody noticed that Lily didn't even glance at him.

He wonders what she thought of the pearl.

He'd spotted it among the clutter on Dinny's boat, and when he remarked on it Dinny told him he'd found it in the belly of a bass caught some months earlier. *Take it*, Dinny said. *I've no use for it* – and so Charlie took it with no real plan, but with their anniversary, or what would have been their anniversary, still fresh in his head.

Leaving it in Lily's car this morning, along with a hastily scribbled note, had been an act of impulse, but it seemed fitting. Maybe she'd soften, seeing it. Maybe she'd forgive his infidelity, given the passage of time, given that she was now with Joe.

Had she always known? Had last night simply put it into words for her, given her the proof she didn't really need?

He wonders how Thomas and Poll will take to a much younger half-sibling. It occurs to him that if Poll and Aidan start a family soon, their children will be contemporaries of this new one. How messed up will that be for everyone?

But now it's started – and despite the tricky road ahead, he wants very much to make it work.

'We can handle it,' he says. 'It's not what either of us planned, but we'll cope. I'll be with you all the way.'

Seven months, give or take.

From where he stands, it feels like an eternity.

ONE YEAR LATER

Lily

MARCH WAS CRUEL, WITH UNPRECEDENTED blizzards in the first week, the snow building and drifting as it fell, grinding most of the country to a halt. Night after night on the news there were reports of snowbound households, businesses desperate for custom, farmers struggling to reach animals stranded on higher ground, dreadful crashes on icy roads.

The longed-for thaw, when it finally arrived, brought some relief but also new hardships in the form of burst pipes and flooding. It wasn't until well into the month that more normal weather conditions began to prevail, and while the cold still reddened noses, and the showers were often more hail than water, hearts lifted at the sight of a clump of wild primroses on a grassy verge, and the chirruping of nesting birds on blue-sky mornings.

Now with the approach of May it's just about mild enough to sit on a veranda, say, for an hour in the middle of the day. Wrapped up well, no summer clothes yet, but the worst of the bite has gone out of the breeze and the rain is mostly soft and gentle. It's mild enough now, in the lengthening days, to sit outside with a mug of coffee and to watch the sea doing what it has always done, what it will always do.

Today is April twenty-eighth, a Saturday. The May bank holiday is still a week away, later this year than last, and five weeks after that, secondary schools will close their doors for the summer holidays, and exams will begin for the unfortunates whose turn it is to sit them.

Lily Murphy, fifty-three since February – two days before her daughter Poll turned twenty-seven – stands at the front door of the house where she grew up, admiring the metal sign that Patsy Kinnehy has erected by the gate for her. *Land's End Bed and Breakfast*, it reads, navy blue lettering on a cream background, the same font and colour scheme as the new website Aidan set up for her in January.

Mam never had a sign, or a website. When she opened the B&B in the late seventies she asked her sister Cora in America to put a weekly ad in a few newspapers there. Cora placed ads in all the national papers and told everyone she knew – and by then she knew a lot of people – to tell everyone *they* knew.

Lily was in her fourteenth year when guests began to arrive. Cecily and Bob, followed by lots more. Once she'd adapted to the new way of things she enjoyed helping out after school and at weekends, and throughout the months of the summer holidays.

Even after she left for college she came home each summer to lend a hand. It wasn't until she became pregnant that things changed, but when the family holidays to Land's End commenced just a couple of years later she resumed her role as Mam's assistant when they were there.

She can't say for sure when the idea first occurred to her. It wasn't an epiphany, more a quiet unfolding in the sometimes lonely weeks after she and Joe separated. It began with a certain evening in early June, as she worked her way through paperwork she hadn't managed to deal with during the day. She remembers thinking, some way into the process, that bidding a premature farewell to her job might not be altogether unappealing.

It was a throwaway thought, born of tiredness and general frustration, and maybe from the unsettlement caused by the news of Chloë's pregnancy, in a phone call from Charlie just days after their bank holiday weekend – but before it floated away she grabbed it and took a closer look.

Why not retire? She was tired of struggling to steer the unwieldy ship that was the school, tired of disciplining the three hundred and twenty-seven teenagers in her care, tired of humouring awkward parents and managing uncooperative teachers. She was tired of the interminable courses and board meetings and endless circulars she was expected to deal with. She was sick of it all, so why not walk away?

It wasn't as if she'd miss the salary. Between the lump sum that would be due to her on retirement – a smaller one, of course, than if she'd worked a full forty years, but still quite generous – and the quite respectable pension that would drop into her bank account every other Thursday after that, she'd be comfortable enough.

Worth considering, she decided – and over the weeks and months that followed, she considered it from every conceivable angle.

In July and August she divided her time between the city – where she played golf and met friends for lunch and read the books she didn't have time for during the year – and Land's End, where she walked the beach and pottered in the garden and read some more, and where she was joined intermittently by Thomas, on a quest of his own, and by Poll and Aidan the odd Saturday night, and one full week towards the end of August.

She found that staying alone there between the others' visits didn't bother her in the least. She was surrounded by ghosts, or fancied herself to be – her grandparents, her parents – but their presences, if indeed they *were* present, served to reassure and comfort rather than unnerve her.

All summer she continued to ponder the possibility of retirement. On into the autumn she considered it, when school began for another year. Weighing the merits and the pitfalls of giving up her job for good, anticipating the obstacles she might encounter.

What most concerned her was how she would occupy her days. She'd have to find something to do if she didn't want to go quietly mad. Golf was all very well twice or even three times a week, but she didn't intend to live out her retirement on the course. So she began thinking of other ways to keep busy.

Volunteering was an option, but not one that appealed greatly. She couldn't see herself behind the counter of a charity shop, or distributing dinners to pensioners, or reading to patients in nursing homes: she simply wasn't noble enough for any of that. Starting a business might be interesting – but what was she qualified to do other than teach? What skills did she have apart from that?

Well, that and running a B&B. With all the years she'd helped out at Land's End, she could do that in her sleep.

A B&B.

Strangers in the house. Different accents, different languages. Sheets on the line, sausages in the morning. Nothing she couldn't cope with.

Not in the city, though – the house didn't lend itself to it.

Anyway, the house was half Charlie's: that would complicate things, when she was trying to simplify.

But Land's End wasn't half anyone's. Land's End was all hers. And Land's End had already done service as a B&B.

Could she walk in her mother's shoes?

Around the end of October she decided she could.

I'm thinking of taking early retirement next summer, she told Poll and Thomas. *I'm thinking of moving to Land's End and reopening it as a B&B.*

To her relief, her plan was enthusiastically received by both of them. '*Oh Mum!*' Poll cried, and burst into the right kind of tears, which was probably par for the course. When she was able to speak again she vowed to give what help she could, between work and wedding preparations, and Thomas offered his and Freda's support too.

His and Freda's. Lily wasn't the only one with a plan.

She decided she had to talk to Charlie, to tell him she was leaving the house they owned together. She rang him and asked to meet, and he sounded pleased to hear from her. In the café of a local hotel, she told him of her plans.

Sounds like a good idea, he said.

They hadn't met in the six months since the May bank holiday trip to Land's End. Her only contact had been his phone call telling her of Chloë's pregnancy, the call that she'd used to let him know of her separation from Joe. *I'm sorry,* he said, and seemed to mean it.

Now, on meeting him again, she was aware of a new guardedness between them. They weren't as easy with one another as they'd been before. But regardless of what he'd done, regardless of how cruelly he'd behaved, he was the father of her children and always would be, and she would remain civil to him.

What about the house? she asked. *Will you and Chloë move in when I go?* It seemed the obvious course of action, with him about to start a new family.

There was a long pause, during which he studied the table between them. *I'm not sure,* he said eventually, so she left it at that. Now that she'd made the decision to relocate, her interest in the city house was waning. Let what happened to it happen.

How's Chloë? she asked then, a little belatedly, and he said fine, everything was fine. Four weeks or so until he became a father again. She wondered how he felt about it, and if he'd wanted it, but of course she didn't ask.

Towards the end of November she made the journey west and met Larry Traynor, a local builder whose grandfather had worked with hers on the construction of Land's End. She asked him to put en-suite bathrooms into four of the bedrooms, and enquired how long it would take.

Few months, he told her – and anytime she visited after that she found him there, working away. He finished up by the end of March which gave her plenty of time for a summer opening.

In the intervening weeks she'd had the entire house painted, inside and out. For the bedrooms she'd chosen a primrose shade that lit them up on gloomy days. For the rest of the house – apart from white in the kitchen – she'd opted for a pale turquoise that put her in mind of the sea at its most serene.

The outside, of course, remained blue.

She had the wooden floors sanded and varnished. She threw down new rugs here and there but kept Cora's two for the small back bedroom where Thomas had slept during the bank holiday, the only one now without an en-suite. The one that would become hers when she filled the others with paying guests.

Last week she'd rooted out the yellowed clipping of the first ad to appear in the *Chicago Tribune*, mailed from America by Cora to show Kitty how it looked. It was folded and kept in an envelope: Lily pressed out the fold and put the clipping in a little silver frame and hung it in the hall at Land's End, next to Gabriel Murphy in his matching frame.

> Planning a holiday to Ireland? A warm welcome awaits you at Land's End, Kitty Murphy's bed and breakfast, overlooking a pebble beach on the west coast. Home cooking, simple country comforts, reasonable rates. Ideal base for exploring Ireland's beautiful coastline. We look forward to your call.

Lily hasn't placed an ad in any American newspaper. Instead she's listed the B&B on three different holiday-accommodation websites, and already she has two definite bookings for July and one for August, and several other enquiries.

The city house has been on the market for the past three weeks. Not, after all, wanted by Charlie, so they'd decided to sell. Several people have already viewed it, and so far, there are two offers on it.

She closes the front door and returns to the kitchen. She bastes the leg of lamb and gives a shake to the potatoes in the roasting dish and puts four dinner plates into the top oven to warm. She sticks three candles into the cake she made that morning, and hides it in the scullery.

Freda and Thomas don't have far to travel, ten minutes at the most. Freda thinks it's just a regular dinner. *It's her birthday on Sunday,* Thomas told Lily during the week. *I'm taking her to lunch at the hotel – we'll get George to fill in for us for a couple of hours.*

What about bringing her to Land's End for dinner on Saturday night instead? Lily asked. *I was ringing to tell you I'm heading there for the weekend – the Sunday Mass in the village is for Gran's anniversary.*

Mum, Gran's anniversary was last month. You had a Mass in the city for her.

I know, but I wanted one here too. She won't mind that the date isn't right. I've invited your dad and Mel along. We can have a surprise party for Freda – so that is what's happening.

She can't figure them out, Thomas and Freda. They're business partners certainly – they took the lease on Queally's, the smallest of the village's three pubs, when it came up last August. Within a fortnight they were installed in the upstairs living accommodation that came with the place, along with Freda's mother, a cantankerous character who'd decided before a month was up that country living wasn't for her. She'd packed her bags and taken herself back to the city – much, Lily suspects, to everyone's relief.

She was bemused when Thomas told her of their plans to take over Queally's. She knew he'd been hunting about for work in the village, but he'd said nothing about Freda being part of the equation. And neither of them had a clue about running a pub – how on earth would they manage?

So far, they've managed fine. George Queally was generous with his advice, and they caught on fast. Freda offers homemade soup, and sandwiches made with her fresh-baked bread – already she has a following – and both of them man the bar. Eight months later they're still there, and the door of Queally's remains open.

Lily is glad for them. Freda needed something good to happen after her accident, losing her little café because of it, several weeks of physio before her leg was right again forcing her to give up the property. Thomas's job had gone, of course, along with the café, four months of dole for both of them until they made the surprising move on Queally's.

Business partners – and who knows what else? Anyone with

half an eye can see how Freda feels about Thomas, but with him being such a closed book it's harder to tell if her feelings are returned. Lily doesn't ask, and so far they haven't enlightened her. She'll wait, and hope.

Freda would make a wonderful daughter-in-law. Lily would be treated like a queen when she got older.

She'll give them something when she gets her lump sum. They could do with a few days off. They can hand over to George, who takes back the reins of his old business whenever Freda asks him to. Nobody seems able to say no to Freda.

Shame Poll and Aidan won't be around this weekend too: honeymoons tend to get in the way of social occasions. Poll texted a snap last evening of the two of them standing in front of Edinburgh Castle, and the smile on her daughter's face, the real, genuine smile, was wonderful to see.

Poll began seeing a man called Billy last year, shortly after she and Aidan got engaged. *Things I have to sort out*, she told her mother, and Lily tried not to be hurt that she'd turned to a counsellor instead of to her mother. Never mind: maybe she needed him to be a stranger – and he does seem to have helped. Of course, preparing to marry Aidan might have had some bearing on her new-found peace of mind too.

Both her children happy: what more could a mother ask for?

She bumps into Joe from time to time, inevitable with so many mutual acquaintances. At first it was awkward – well, he was awkward, she was guilty – but they've got over that now.

For the past few months he's been seeing Norma Wall, whose husband died a few years ago in a boating accident. She hopes it lasts.

She climbs the stairs to close windows and check the radiators in the two front bedrooms. In the green room – despite the new colour scheme, the name has stuck – she turns down a corner of the duvet and plumps the pillows and straightens the mat by the bed.

He always liked this room.

She hears a car on the gravel outside and crosses to the window. She watches as he climbs out. Short hair suits him so much better, takes years off him. He's lost a bit of weight too, no harm.

She sees him go around to the passenger door and lift out the baby carrier. Mel's face is hidden from view by the hood of the little yellow puffy jacket she wears, but Lily knows it by heart. The elfin shape of it, the startling deep blue of the eyes, the tiny pointed nose, the darling pink mouth. The soft, soft, soft feel of the plump cheeks.

She has fallen in love with her ex-husband's daughter.

Mel, Melanie. Born in the last days of November, abandoned by her mother less than a week later. Left in the care of her father, who turned to Lily for help. *She's gone*, he said, standing on her doorstep with his tiny bundle. *She's left us. I don't know what to do*. So Lily brought them in because she had to, and made him coffee and held his daughter while he drank it, while he told her more.

She kept saying she didn't want children, all through the pregnancy she kept insisting. I was convinced she'd change her mind once Mel was born, but …

He'd come home from work to find her bags piled in the hall. She'd handed him Mel and called a taxi and left without telling him where she was going.

Lily promised to help. She has helped. She found a woman to care for the baby while Charlie was at work. She took Mel herself on Tuesday and Thursday nights, settling her to sleep in the old wooden cot that had once held Thomas and Poll. She fed and burped and changed her, the know-how coming back effortlessly. It didn't take long at all to fall in love with ten tiny toes, and a small round belly that smelt of baby, and a head of downy white hair.

How could Chloë have done it? How could she have turned her back on this little piece of perfection? How could she walk out on Charlie and their daughter, cut them out of her life without a thought?

In the days that followed her departure, Charlie's calls to her mobile went unanswered. He sought information from her mother, who told him that Chloë had gone to Sweden. Moved to another country, just like that – and in the intervening five months he's heard nothing from her, despite sending letters, and photos of her daughter, via her mother.

To give Nadia her due, she has pitched in too. She wheels Mel to the park most Sunday afternoons. She buys her toys and little dresses. But there is a lack of warmth to the woman: when their paths cross, Lily can see no evidence of her having bonded with her tiny granddaughter.

Maybe Chloë's behaviour wasn't so inexplicable after all.

She watches Charlie crossing the driveway to the steps that lead to the beach. She sees him raise the carrier, his free arm extending to the sea. He's showing her around Land's End, her first time to see it.

Not her last, if Lily has anything to do with it.

She'll tell him they'll be welcome here, once she's in fulltime residence. She'll say to come anytime, and she thinks he will; she thinks he'll be glad to. She'll free up the green room for them when she hears they're coming. *Spend the summer here,* she'll say, *if you want*. History repeating itself, or a version of history.

She knows it won't be like before. She'll never love him like she used to: too much has gone on, and he's hurt her too deeply for that ever to happen again. But they might find their way to another kind of feeling, a more settled, less dangerous kind of feeling. Good friends rather than lovers. You never know.

They might yet end their days here together.

The doorbell rings. She goes downstairs to let them in.

Acknowledgements

Big thanks as always to Ciara Doorley, Joanna Smyth and all at Hachette Books Ireland for their unstinting support and encouragement.

Sincere thanks to my agent Sallyanne Sweeney for always being there when I need her, and for her constant efforts on my behalf.

Thanks as ever to copy-editor Hazel and proofreader Aonghus for getting *The Anniversary* safely over the final few hurdles.

Thanks so much to Philip Gleeson and Nicky Quinn, who gave generously of their time and expertise when I came calling.

Thanks a million to everyone who gets in touch to tell me they enjoyed one of the books – it helps more than you know when I'm deep in the mire.

Special thanks to you for choosing this book: I'd be nothing without my readers.

www.roisinmeaney.com

@roisinmeaney

ALSO BY ROISIN MEANEY